LIFE AS IT IS

LIFE AS IT IS

NELSON RODRIGUES

TRANSLATED FROM THE PORTUGUESE BY
ALEX LADD

HOST PUBLICATIONS

AUSTIN, TX

Host Publications, Inc. 277 Broadway, Suite 210, New York, NY 10007

Editor: Alex Ladd
Layout and Design: Joe Bratcher & Anand Ramaswamy
Cover Art: Alexander "Olo" Sroczynski
Jacket Design: Anand Ramaswamy

First Edition

Library of Congress Cataloging-in-Publication Data

Rodrigues, Nelson.
[Vida como ela é-- English]
Life as it is / Nelson Rodrigues ; translated from the Portuguese by Alex Ladd. -- 1st ed.
    p. cm.
Summary: "English volume of selected short stories from Brazilian writer Nelson Rodrigues"--Provided by publisher.
ISBN-13: 978-0-924047-60-2 (hardcover : alk. paper)
ISBN-10: 0-924047-60-7 (hardcover : alk. paper)
ISBN-13: 978-0-924047-61-9 (pbk. : alk. paper)
ISBN-10: 0-924047-61-5 (pbk. : alk. paper)
I. Ladd, Alex. II. Title.
PQ9697.R6613 2008
869.3'42--dc22
                                        2008036552

TABLE OF CONTENTS

INTRODUCTION

For ten years, between 1951 and 1961, Cariocas (as residents of Rio de Janeiro are called) opened their copies of the evening newspaper *Ultima Hora* as they commuted home from work on crowded buses and trolleys and, right below the funnies and the crossword puzzle, read the tales of adultery, murder and suicide contained in this volume.

The column was *A Vida Como Ela É* (*Life As It Is*), and the author, Nelson Rodrigues, was already well known to readers when he began writing it at age thirty-nine. Ten years earlier, Rodrigues had become an overnight sensation in Brazilian theater with *The Wedding Dress,* a play that utilized time-tripping, three planes of reality and a stylized dialogue that was electrifying and new. After that initial brush with almost universal praise, he proceeded on a brilliant, but increasingly darker and more experimental path that alienated critics and audiences alike and forever changed Brazilian theater. It was not until a generation later that those plays were reexamined and the "reactionary in suspenders" was recognized as Brazil's greatest dramatist.

Rodrigues's assignment at *Ultima Hora* in 1951 was to write fictional accounts based on the day's crime headline of his choice. This mix of journalism and fiction has a long tradition in Brazil in the *crônicas*, a form that originated in France and has taken particularly deep roots in Brazil, where it has attracted some of its greatest writers, from Machado de Assis to Clarice Lispector. Its definition depends on who one asks, but generally speaking, *crônicas* are short, entertaining sketches that run in newspapers and magazines and that explore topical issues of interest to the author. Ever the rebel, Rodrigues proceeded to ignore the journalism part and focus on the fiction. In his masterful biography of Rodrigues, *O Anjo Pornográfico* (Companhia das Letras, 1992), Ruy Castro wrote: "Rodrigues obeyed the first two days. By the third he was making it up. It took [the publisher] one week to notice; by then it was too late. 'Life As It Is' was all the rage."

Although the stories in *Life As It Is* are now generally classified as *contos,* or short stories, they still preserve characteristics of the *crônicas*. After all, Rodrigues had a newspaper deadline hanging over his head when he wrote them, and so by necessity the stories were snapshots, with lightly drawn characters. According to Castro, Rodrigues typically clocked in at two hours

– or twelve cigarettes – from start to finish, with the requisite breaks for coffee and discussions of soccer and politics. Rodrigues was no stranger to newsrooms – at thirteen he began covering the police beat for his father's newspaper, and by fourteen he had his own column. He had written everything from political essays to opera reviews, and he even did a stint as the lonely-hearts columnist.

With an estimated two thousand of these stories to his name (the column ran six days a week), it is little wonder that Rodrigues repeated himself, often using the same tropes and even story lines. What is astonishing is the creativity and resourcefulness he displays in exploring his constant theme of human mendacity. Some stories seem to unfold almost identically, like "The Great Widower" and "The Mausoleum," but Rodrigues adds ingenious twists at the very end, suddenly shedding new light on a plot we thought we knew. And like *crônicas,* the stories are written in an easy, conversational tone, giving the impression that the events, as outlandish as they appear, might actually have happened to a neighbor.

Which brings us to the almost unendurably morbid themes (Reader, beware: You might not want to read them all in one sitting). Is that morbidity a characteristic of *crônicas,* too? No, that was Nelson Rodrigues. And everyone seemed to take issue with it; readers and colleagues alike complained (although they continued to read). Rodrigues defended himself with typical fervor: "Some say *Life As It Is* insists on being sad and abject. Maybe, but so what? Man is sad, and he's sad from the cradle to the grave, from the first tear to the last. Nothing rings falser to me than happiness. To laugh in a miserable world like ours is like walking up to a coffin at a wake and lighting one's cigarette from one of the candles that surround it."

But the stories *are* funny, at times hysterically so. Of course, a lot of the best tragedy is – a fact that Rodrigues was keenly aware of in his theater. If we are uncomfortable, we become even more so when we find ourselves laughing, and for Rodrigues making us uncomfortable was tantamount to a life mission. He had this to say about his plays: "To save the audience we must fill the stage with murderers, adulterers, madmen; in short, we must fire a salvo of monsters at them. They are our monsters which we will temporarily free ourselves from only to face another day."

In reading, it helps to know a little about the geography of Rio de Janeiro, which plays such a prominent role in the stories. Just as New York is not only Manhattan, Rio is not only the Zona Sul (home to Ipanema, Copacabana and Leblon). There is a Zona Norte, too, just as there are the outer boroughs, and Rodrigues was one of the first to depict this vital but less glamorous part of Rio in fiction. It was where he grew up, surrounded by huddled immigrants and nosy housewives, and where tuberculosis threatened at every turn. And then there was the Centro, or downtown. Writer Carlos Heitor Cony sums up the geography as follows: "The characters live in the Zona Norte and sin in the Zona Sul. They work in the office buildings of the Centro. Like early Chaplin movies, the sets never change."

It is hard to explain Nelson Rodrigues's stature in his country to non-Brazilians. He always seemed to be in the public eye, even if the literary elite typically ignored him and the public did not always know what to make of him. *The Wedding Dress* was a milestone, and Brazilian theater is typically divided into what came before and what came after the play. Zbigniew Ziembinski, a highly regarded Polish director, who was passing through Rio on his way to conquering New York, is said to have changed his plans after reading the play in 1941. "I am unaware of anything in world theater today that resembles this," he is reported to have said, before signing on to direct the first triumphant production (he never did make it to New York). Rodrigues's next play, *Family Album,* depicts a family history so rife with incest and murder that it rivaled anything the ancient Greeks ever wrote. The play was considered so scandalous it was banned for twenty-one years, and Rodrigues became a bête noire of sorts; the joke is that to the Right he was a degenerate and to the Left a reactionary. And just when people were about to write him off, he would come out with another shocking and brilliant play – seventeen in all.

He began writing the stories in this book during one of the several lulls in his career. They made him more famous, or infamous, than ever. In the 1960s he reinvented himself yet again as a TV commentator. His penchant for aphorisms, both on the air and in his many columns, was such that he has become one of the most quoted of all Brazilians, with books dedicated to his sayings. He famously defended the military coup of 1964 and subsequent dictatorship, and he seemed to relish the commotion and ostracism that resulted from his stance. In fact, he became a thorn in the side of the Left, taking every opportunity to criticize its blindness concerning Cuba and the Soviet Union. His position was tempered when his son, a leading figure of the underground, was captured and tortured by the military.

Movie directors discovered Rodrigues in the 1960s and 1970s, and several of his better-known plays were adapted for the screen, with mixed results. After his death in 1980, his work began to be reassessed, with the staging of several seminal productions of his plays and the publication of Ruy Castro's biography, which revealed just how little had been known about this seemingly very public figure. The book detailed a life that in many ways rivaled his plays for twists and turns and tragedies.

It is unclear whether Rodrigues wrote the stories in *Life As It Is* for posterity. Slowly, though, they made their way beyond the pages of the newspapers and infiltrated Brazilian popular culture. They were first collected in a two-volume set edited by Rodrigues in 1961, with several subsequent editions released in the following decades. In the 1970s *A Dama do Lotação,* based on the last story in this volume ("The Lady on the Bus"), became one of the top-grossing Brazilian films of all time. The germ for the play *All Nudity Shall Be Punished,* which was made into a film by the same title (winner of the Silver Bear in Berlin, 1973), can be found in "The Mausoleum." In the 1990s several of these stories were adapted for the stage in an award-winning production; and one of the finest hours of Brazilian television was the adaptation of these stories into vignettes by TV Globo, also in the 1990s. All this is to say: they have endured. As in his plays, Rodrigues in these stories constantly takes us places that we would like to pretend do not exist. He is here to remind us that they do, and that we ignore them at our peril.

TRANSLATOR'S NOTE

Really? Can Nelson be translated? He is too Brazilian!

This is a common reaction when one informs a Brazilian that Nelson Rodrigues is being translated into English. They are, of course, right, in the same way a Russian might insist it is impossible to fully appreciate Chekhov in translation. In Rodrigues there are many idiosyncrasies: the mixture of high-brow and low-brow language, the machine-gun dialogue, and the profanity never actually uttered (he prided himself on never using obscenities; they are all to be found between the lines). And then there are the outlandish plots, the obsession with betrayal, the rarely mentioned but pervasive Catholicism. It is little wonder that the *New York Times* quoted one of the foremost Brazilian theater directors as saying that translating Rodrigues's plays into English would be like translating Mamet into Portuguese.

Fortunately these stories are Rodrigues at his most accessible. After all, the editor of the daily *Ultima Hora,* shortly after its launch, enlisted Rodrigues to help build readership. The progenitor of the "theater of the unpleasant" did not disappoint. He wrote these stories in an easy and elegant style, with a predilection for adultery, murder and suicide, and they were an immediate success.

The stories should not seem wholly foreign in English. For one thing, there is the prevalence of American references. Rodrigues was famously guarded about his influences (Eugene O'Neill and Fyodor Dostoyevsky were two notable exceptions), yet everything points to his having been a keen observer of American pop culture. Names like Barbara Stanwyck, Kay Francis and Victor Mature pepper his writing. The occurrence of such names in this volume does not represent an attempt to transpose a pantheon of Brazilian actors into American equivalents. Likewise, references to Buffalo Bill, Jack the Ripper and *Gone with the Wind* are pure Rodrigues.

Another element of these stories surprisingly well suited to English is the extreme concision of Rodrigues's style, which allows him to tell tales of operatic complexity in four pages. Anyone who has ever translated from a Romance language knows that the original usually shrinks 10 to 15 percent when rendered in English. That is rarely the case with Rodrigues, whose writing skills were forged in the newsrooms of Rio from the time he was fourteen.

On the other hand, Rodrigues's use of slang presents a challenge with no easy solutions. The language is a quirky mix typical of Rio in the 1950s, along with expressions from his youth thirty years earlier. Further complicating the issue is that Rodrigues's choices were almost always informed by the musicality of words. Trying to replicate the slang in these stories by using American equivalents is always perilous and never fully satisfactory. Hipster lingo of the 1950s gives the reader a false analogy that distracts from the storytelling. Rodrigues's rule against vulgarities further limits the choices. Unless an expression as inspired as the original screamed out in English, I tried not to force the issue; after all, his style always seems so effortless. Consequently, the solutions in English are often not as colorful as the original Portuguese. The translator has to learn to pick his battles.

No translator works alone, and the peculiarities of Rodrigues's text led me to avail myself of plenty of help from colleagues and friends, both Brazilian and American. I would especially like to thank Carmen Nigro, who patiently sifted through the text for errors. Reginaldo Alcantara helped clarify several expressions that hark back to his youth in Brazil in the 1950s. On the English side, Michael Christofferson's assistance was fundamental in purging the text of dreaded *translatese*, as were Selma Marks, Josh Gilinsky, Peter Jarvis and Joan Reyna. Margaret Ritchie's intervention in the later stages of revision was essential. Of course, they could not be expected to catch every misstep, and I am solely responsible for any that have remained.

Americans ask whom Rodrigues can be compared to. Many writers come to mind: In his short stories, I think of the dark and colorful tales of Damon Runyon or the economy and hard-boiled wit of Ben Hecht. As a playwright he has been likened to Eugene O'Neill; both men dragged their country's theater into the modern era. Others see Tennessee Williams in his larger-than-life characters. His use of dramatic dialogue has been compared to that of Pinter. Yet a play like *Doroteia* seems like pure Ionesco. To make matters more complicated, for a while he wrote pulp fiction under the pseudonym Suzana Flag, and he is considered one of Brazil's greatest sportswriters!

If comparisons seem hard to come by – or maddeningly abundant – it is only because Rodrigues was such an original. It is my sincere wish that his originality is conveyed by this English edition.

LIFE AS IT IS

The Pediatrician

He hung up and announced to the whole office, "She said yes! She said yes!"

Three or four colleagues surrounded him. Meireles nudged him.

"For real?"

Menezes unbuttoned his collar.

"For real!"

Someone else asked, "Is she worth it? Is she worth the trouble?"

He would have none of it.

"Is she worth it? What do you mean! She's the finest woman in Rio de Janeiro! She's married, and what's more, she's as pure as they come!"

Someone couldn't resist.

"She's so pure, and she cheats on her husband?"

On hearing this, Menezes rallied to her defense.

"Listen here. She loves me, you understand? Really loves me. And her husband is a brute! A real jerk!"

Meireles looked at him in awe and sneered.

"You really have a way with women. I've never seen anything like it! The heavens seem to smile upon you," he said, dripping with envy.

The Immortal Beloved

Menezes had been talking up his latest immortal beloved for three or four weeks now. His colleagues would listen, open-mouthed.

"She's the wife of a pediatrician. A real goddess."

They all wanted to know, "Will she or won't she?"

He rubbed his hands, elated.

"I'm on top of it," he said, salivating. "Any day now."

Every morning, when Menezes stepped into the office, his colleagues greeted him with the question: "So, did she say yes?"

All smiles, he would take off his jacket and answer, "Almost. Yesterday we talked on the phone for nearly four hours!"

His colleagues marveled at such extravagance and could not comprehend such persistence.

"This is no longer a simple pursuit, it's turned into… *Gone With the Wind*." Meireles lived by the rule that neither Ava Gardner nor Cleopatra were worth four hours on the telephone.

Menezes protested.

"This one's worth it! Yes sir! No doubt about it! And what's more, she's never done this before! She's morbidly faithful. You understand? Unnaturally so!"

Menezes, who had fathered children in many neighborhoods throughout Rio de Janeiro, abandoned all other affairs and showered all of his attention on the pediatrician's wife. He laid his heart bare at the office.

"I always had a thing for virtuous women. I'm only attracted to virtuous women!"

Finally, after forty-five days of passionate phone calls, the woman capitulated. The whole office celebrated. And Menezes, wiping his brow with a handkerchief, admitted, "It wasn't easy. Never has a woman held out on me this long." Suddenly, Menezes smacked himself on the head.

"Damn. I forgot one thing! The apartment!"

He grabbed Meireles by the arm.

"Lend me yours!

Meireles broke loose in a panic.

"Give me a break! I live with my mom!"

But Menezes would not take no for an answer. He insisted.

"Listen, listen! Let me speak. She's a good girl. A very good girl. I've never met a better girl. And I can't just take her to any fleabag motel. Listen carefully, it has to be in a respectable residential building. I'm asking you as a brother."

Meireles wasn't buying it.

"How about my mother? What am I gonna do with her, come on!"

Menezes worked him over for two whole hours.

"Just this once. Send your mother out for a little while. Two hours, tops!"

He insisted so much that finally his friend caved in.

"All right! But listen, this will be the first and last time!"

He shook his friend's hand.

"You're a doll!"

The Decision

Shortly afterwards, Menezes called the object of his affection.

"I found a wonderful apartment."

On the other end, the woman wanted to know the details.

"What's it like, tell me?"

Exuding desire, he explained: "It's a residential building on Voluntarios Street. As a matter of fact, the mother of a friend of mine lives there. You can hear children playing outside."

Her name was Ieda, and she sighed.

"I'm scared! Scared!"

The arrangements for the following day were made; they were to meet at four in the afternoon. At the office his colleagues asked, "What about the pediatrician?"

Menezes was taken aback. He was so consumed with desire for this woman that he had forgotten all about her husband. There was something poignant, even touching, in the betrayed man's profession. If he had been an ear, nose and throat doctor or a general practitioner or an allergist, that would have been one thing – but a pediatrician! Even Menezes couldn't help but think, "While the poor guy's at his office treating kids, I'm with his wife." And for a brief moment he even felt guilty about cuckolding the pediatrician. But the following morning, with the collusion of the entire office, he did not show up for work. His coworkers made only one demand: that he describe everything, every last detail. Menezes wanted to concentrate on his afternoon session of lovemaking. He took, as he would later recount, word by word, what could only be described as a bath worthy of Cleopatra. His mother, a saint of a woman, lent him some cologne. At about noon, all dressed in white, smelling like a baby, he called Meireles.

"How about it? Did you work everything out with your old lady?"

"Yes. Mother's going to spend the afternoon in Realengo."

Menezes ate lunch.

"I have to eat a hearty meal," he thought to himself. He threw in an egg yolk for good measure. Before leaving he called Ieda.

"Honey, listen. I'm on my way."

"So soon?" she asked

"I have to get there before you," he explained. "And listen, I'm going to leave the door ajar. When you arrive just push it open. You don't even have to knock. Just push."

She shuddered.

"I'm very nervous."

Barely able to restrain himself, he said, "A nice wet kiss on that cute little mouth of yours."

"You too."

Panic

By three-thirty he was in the apartment smoking anxiously. By four he was by the door waiting. Ieda arrived at four thirty. She put her purse on the table.

"Sorry I'm late, my husband took forever to arrive."

Menezes didn't understand.

"Your husband?"

"He agreed to bring me, and he got tied up. Honey, let's go because I only have half an hour. My husband's waiting for me downstairs."

In disbelief, he grabbed her.

"Listen here. What do you mean your husband? Downstairs! Does your husband know?"

"Help me with this button, will you?" she said. "Sure my husband knows. Of course. Help me with this button."

Dumbfounded, he held his head in his hands.

"This can't be happening. It can't be. Is this some kind of joke?"

Losing her patience, Ieda led him to the window. He looked down and saw him standing there, bald and obese, the pediatrician. In despair, Menezes stammered, "You mean to tell me that... look, I think we better end this right now. It's for the best, you understand? It's just not right. Not like this."

And then, that beautiful, voluptuous woman held out her hand.

"Two thousand cruzeiros. That's what my husband charges. He sets the price. Two thousand cruzeiros."

Menezes broke down and cried.

A Lost Case

Right from the start the family did not approve.

"He's a good-for-nothing!"

"A bum!"

"A wise guy!"

Maybe he was all that and much more. For starters he didn't have a job and had no time for work. Furthermore, he drank, gambled, and associated with people of ill repute of both sexes. Some pointed to a woman of shady background, who, so the story went, supported him. Edgardina's relatives tried to dissuade her from this star-crossed and scandalous love affair.

"There's no shortage of men. Pick another one, one who's worth your while."

"I love Humberto," she responded. "I couldn't care less about the others."

She had loved him since she was a little girl; and as time went by, she had eyes for no one else. They could say whatever they wanted about the young man, but she would have none of it.

"It just goes in one ear and out the other."

She only paid heed once, just one single time. It was when they said the young man was supported by the aforementioned lady.

Edgardina leapt up.

"Lies! Slander!"

But, in spite of her vehement reaction, a seed had been planted. She questioned her beloved point-blank.

"What's this I'm hearing?"

"What?"

She continued without taking her eyes off him, "That you take money from women."

The Confession

Confronted by his girlfriend who, in truth, was his first great love, Humberto had two choices. Deny vehemently or... he would deny everything, he decided in a panic. But when he opened his mouth something came over him, a sudden, almost frenzied heroism. Bug-eyed, lips trembling, he went even further than his girlfriend with the following revelation: "It's true, yes! I take money from women! I always have!"

A mortal pallor came over the girl's face, like in an old-time novel. She gasped for breath.

"Humberto!"

It was a magnificent and frightening scene. His courage grew, and he went all out, revealing everything and omitting nothing. He confessed that, jobless and penniless, he had in fact, on occasion, received money from women. He beat his chest and stomped his feet. He called himself "a scoundrel," "a good for nothing," "a lost case." And he ended with a frantic challenge.

"Now you know everything. Now spit in my face. Spit! Go ahead! Spit!"

He offered her his face. When Edgardina, petrified, did not utter a single word or make one gesture, he broke down in tears. Then the girl, a real angel, exhibited a momentous change of heart, a spontaneous show of mercy. If she had loved him before, she loved him even more now. In her eyes, her beloved's confession had completely redeemed him. And she did not stop there.

"I don't care what you did, Humberto. I love you, plain and simple. End of story."

"You're an angel," he said. "If it weren't for you, I would put a bullet through my head, now, this very moment!"

So, when things calmed down, they settled everything: the date of the wedding, etc., etc. When all was said and done, Edgardina imposed only one condition.

"You've got to promise me one thing."

"What?"

"That you'll never accept money from women again. It's beneath you!"

"I swear! You have my word!"

The Wedding

And, in fact, after his confession, Humberto was a new man. He stopped drinking and gambling. When he entered a café and saw a waiter, he would raise his head defiantly, as if flouting the power of alcohol, and say, "Mineral water!"

He went further, returning the following items to the lady who had supported him: a watch, a ring engraved with his initials, a belt with a silver buckle, and a very expensive key ring. He broke off all previous relationships in no uncertain terms. His friends tried to entice him.

"Get out! Have some fun!"

Though very tempted, he reacted vehemently.

"I'm through with that life. I have a fiancée, I'm engaged, end of story!"

It was such a heartfelt transformation that even the future father-in-law, who never had anything positive to say about anyone, became a believer.

"It looks like my son-in-law has finally seen the light."

The rest of the family chimed in, "Let's hope so! Let's hope so!"

Two days before the wedding, Humberto, on his way home, ran into the lady who had previously supported him. His heart sank. In a panic, he looked every which way.

"Imagine what would happen if they saw us!"

He dragged her to a discreet corner, and there they argued in whispers. To his shock the woman implored him.

"Just this one time! Just this one time!"

"Are you crazy! No! I'm getting married tomorrow!"

She clutched him tightly.

"For old times' sake, Humberto!"

Digging her nails into the young man's hand, she insisted, "One last time!"

In truth, what tempted her just then was that he was another woman's man, someone else's fiancé, *her* fiancé, and that it was the day before the wedding. And Humberto, who was weak when confronted by women in general – even the homely ones – nearly succumbed to that nighttime assault. He thought of Edgardina though, and making a super-human effort, he desperately freed himself and dashed into the house.

Disheveled, gasping for breath, he locked the door behind him. Outside, the lady screamed, "I gave you a lot of money, you bastard! Look here, you can't trade me in for that tramp!"

Horrified faces appeared at nearby windows. The following day, Humberto told his fiancée everything. He had learned that it was best to tell the truth and, in some cases, to even exaggerate the truth. His fiancée marveled at his sincerity and kissed him on the forehead.

Destiny

The young man did not have a job. But his future father-in-law showed tremendous magnanimity. He asked to speak to him.

"It's like this: As far as I'm concerned, I couldn't care less if my son-in-law has a job or not. As long as he treats my daughter well."

And it was thus. They tied the knot, and from that moment on they were never in need. Every morning Edgardina, in the most delicate and subtle way possible, placed a bill in her husband's pocket, sometimes a twenty, sometimes a fifty, sometimes a hundred.

To his credit, Humberto accepted the situation with splendid equanimity. Out in the world, on the street corners, in the cafés, in the neighbors' homes, they would say all sorts of things about the young man. They called him "clown," "shameless," "disgusting."

Edgardina got wind of this and took her husband's side.

"Don't pay them any mind, baby. They're just jealous."

Happy and satisfied, she confided in her friends, "Humberto is of the opinion that between a man and a woman nothing is deviant. Everything is fair game."

By then Edgardina was seven months pregnant. She wouldn't let her husband do anything. She paid the bills and managed all of the household affairs. You could say she was the man of the house. Humberto couldn't care less. He wouldn't take on any responsibility and showed no initiative whatsoever. He had a habit of saying, "You can take that up with my wife. I have nothing to do with that."

He wanted peace and quiet. So when the father-in-law threw his weight around as the bill payer in the house and demanded a grandson, Humberto was hesitant. He was afraid of childbirth, of children. He confided in his wife, "Children act up. They're a handful."

The father-in-law put his foot down; he wanted a grandson, come what may. Incapable of putting up any type of resistance for very long, Humberto at last acquiesced. When the old man found out that Edgardina was going to have a baby, he dug his hand in his pocket, pulled out five hundred cruzeiros, and told his daughter to give it to his son-in-law.

But the truth of the matter is that the possibility of having a son made the young man uneasy. He constantly worried when thinking of all the diseases the child might catch.

"What if he comes down with a raging case of whooping cough?"

Time went by. At last, the big day arrived. Humberto heard his wife wailing in pain.

"Ah!"

The father-in-law screamed: "Get the midwife! Now!"

Humberto shot down the stairs and ran towards the midwife's house, two blocks away. And he never came back, ever.

Years Later

The baby was delivered just the same. A neighbor filled in as midwife when the other one, the real one, never showed up. An absolutely perfect baby was born. And then they began looking for the father.

They went to the police, the hospital, the morgue. Nothing. The thought that he might have fled or committed suicide seemed absurd. After all, Humberto lived the life of a pasha in that house. One month later all doubts were erased. He had to be dead. The only thing left was to find the body, but it was perfectly clear he was dead. And thus the widow, all in black, began insisting on a corpse. She ranted and raved.

"I want the body! I want the body!"

There was a nearby river. It was assumed that Humberto had drowned and that the current had dragged the body to a faraway land. Edgardina resigned herself to her fate; but in the depths of her soul she resented her state as a widow denied the right to mourn over her dead husband's body. Immersed in a deep stupor, she would say, "I never buried my husband."

And, without her noticing, the years went by. Edgardina, always in black, found happiness and pride in the fact that the pain in her heart never subsided. Twelve years later, to everyone's surprise, she consented to attend, for the first time, a circus that was passing through town.

The two went off to the circus; she, all in black, and her twelve-year-old son in a sailor's suit. They were watching the show when, suddenly, a drumroll began, evoking danger and an abyss. It was a world-class tightrope act. The performer appeared on the cable with an open parasol. Edgardina sat up. It's not possible… it can't be. Finally, she whispered in her son's ear, "Your father… it's your father."

The child's scream echoed through the circus.

"Daddy! Daddy!"

The tightrope walker froze; he looked down, terrified. He let his umbrella go, let everything go, and tumbled from up above. Later, in the hospital, there was a scene of great joy. Humberto lay in bed, his leg suspended in a cast. He wanted to know whether his son had had whooping cough. When he was informed he had, he sobbed, "Great… great…"

They made up splendidly.

But no one ever knew why he had disappeared that night, twelve years ago.

Delicate

Their first seven children were daughters. The father, Macario, scratched his head and let out a single exclamation in dismay.

"Drats!"

He was a saintly and stubborn man. When still single he considered the ideal family size to be two children, one of each sex. Then his first daughter was born, then the second, then a third and a fourth. By then any other man would have given up, especially considering the cost of living. But stubbornness was one of Macario's principle traits. When his fifth daughter was born, sensible people counseled him, "Throw in the towel; quit while you can!"

Macario took a deep breath.

"No, never! Never! I won't rest until I have a son!"

Luckily he had in Dona Flavia a wife who was above all a mother. Her pregnancies invariably went smoothly, without even the slightest tinge of nausea or cravings. On the contrary, while she was with child she was the picture of calm, a calm verging on bliss. As for labor, it was the strangest of things. She brought babies into the world without letting out a single groan or even a grimace. One could say her husband suffered more. I say "suffered more" because he would come down with a toothache to end all toothaches, emotional in origin. It made one wonder, considering that he had dentures, both uppers and lowers. When his seventh daughter was born, Macario sighed deeply and announced, "Sweetheart, we're going to try one last time!"

A New Birth

Macario's nerves were in shreds just before Dona Flavia gave birth to her eighth child. The midwife, a squat, solid woman who weighed in at two-hundred-and-eighty pounds, was called. She took one look at Dona Flavia and with one-thousand-seven-hundred births behind her, pronounced:

"It won't be any time soon."

To which, as fast as can be, Macario responded, "Ahhhh, my teeth!"

In fact, the best gauge of when Dona Flavia was due to give birth was Macario's dentures. The midwife was skeptical, but sure enough, five minutes later she had to be called in again. And then a last-minute crisis – the seasoned professional couldn't find her gloves. There was mayhem as everyone searched the house. Finally, Macario let her have a piece of his mind.

"What do you need your gloves for? The hell with your stupid gloves!"

Little Eusebio

Thus, little Eusebio was born in the most painless of births imaginable. A spinster aunt asked, astonished, "Did she need stitches?" She was scolded, "Hold your tongue."

The truth was that Macario had finally attained his goal as a father. A son had been born, his dentures stopped aching, and he let out a sigh.

"I have a son! I can die in peace!" And sure enough, forty-eight hours later, while eating lunch, Macario's head fell into his plate. He suffered a massive stroke just before dessert. For Dona Flavia it was a shocking blow. She wept and banged her head against the wall until she had to be restrained.

13

The truth of the matter is that she only found consolation when it came time to breast-feed. She would blow her nose and say to whoever was nearest, "Bring me little Eusebio; it's time to feed him!"

A Flower Of A Child

Little Eusebio was raised clutching the skirts of his sisters, aunts, neighbors, and, of course, his mother. From the time he was little he only liked the company of women. Men terrified him. What's more, his mother and sisters instructed him to keep away from other boys.

"You should only play with little girls, you understand? Boys say dirty words!"

And so, in a house that was a bastion of womanhood, he turned sixteen without saying one dirty word or even smoking one cigarette. When it came to his temperament, thoughts or sentiments, a sweeter, more sensitive child could not be found. Everyone in that house adored little Eusebio, even the maids. His sisters refrained from getting married because to do so would mean time away from the boy. Everything would have continued like this, the best of all possible worlds, if not for one unexpected occurrence. An uncle came to visit.

"Do you have a girlfriend?" he asked Eusebio.

"No."

"Have you ever had one?"

"No."

He'd heard enough. The house nearly shook as he unleashed his fury. He frightened those women with dire predictions.

"What are you trying to do to the poor boy?" He turned to Dona Flavia, "This is a crime. You hear? What you are doing to this child is a crime. Come here, Eusebio! Come here!"

He mercilessly turned the boy into an exhibit. He pointed at him.

"Is this any way for a man to stand? Tell me! This boy has got to get married. Right away!"

Marriage Problems

By the time the uncle left, the household was in a panic. The mother and her daughters looked at one another.

"He's right. He's right! We've been very selfish! We haven't thought about little Eusebio!"

As for the boy, he was cowering in the corner, still resenting his uncle's brutal honesty. He snorted, "Things are fine the way they are!"

The truth is that the very thought of any changes to such a blissful existence terrified him. But his mother replied, "No, son, your uncle is right. You have to get married."

Horrified, Eusebio looked around the room, seeking any sign of support. But he found none. Finally, trembling, he asked, "Why? Why do I have to get married? How about you?" he asked his sisters accusingly. "Why don't you get married?"

The answer was vague and unsatisfactory: "Women are another matter. They're different."

The Girlfriend

Thus began a female conspiracy of almost international proportions. Sisters, aunts, neighbors, the mother – all searched far and wide for a wife for Eusebio. Of all the young girls to choose from, they ended up deciding on one. Sadly, the main interested party was never consulted until one fine day he was introduced to Iracema.

She was only seventeen, but she already had the hips of a married woman. With her voluptuous, thick lips and resplendent air, she initially provoked terror in the young boy. She nearly crushed him with her impetuous ways.

Then began the strangest courtship in recent memory. Their dates took place in the family's spacious living room in Tijuca. But under no circumstance were the two ever left alone. At any given moment there were between ten and fifteen women in that room eager to nudge the romance along. Eusebio, frozen with mortal fear, was completely incapable of holding Iracema's hand. And she, for her part, felt just as uneasy. The one who remedied the situation, once again, was the intrusive and disruptive uncle. When he saw all of those women hovering around the couple during their dates, he exploded, "Do you think you're watching a soccer match? Leave the two of them alone, for crying out loud!"

Alone at last, the following incident occurred: Iracema landed a kiss on her boyfriend's neck. The poor boy cringed in horror.

"Please don't do that, it tickles."

The Wedding Dress

Preparations for the wedding began. One day Iracema entered in a frenzy of excitement, leafing through a magazine. She had discovered something spectacular and almost rubbed Eusebio's face in the photograph to show him.

"Isn't this dress gorgeous?"

The young man's reaction was surprising. If Iracema liked the dress, Eusebio liked it even more. He seemed mesmerized.

"How beautiful! My God! It's gorgeous."

Indeed, there was total unanimity about the dress. All approved of the pattern that had enthralled Iracema. So the boy's mother and sisters decided to give the young girl the dress as a gift. What's more, they decided to make it themselves. Yards and yards of fabric were purchased. With boundless energy they set out to make the dress. Each one focused on her chores as if it were her own wedding dress. No one, however, seemed more fascinated by what was going on than Eusebio. He would sit by his mother and sisters and marvel, "It's so beautiful! It's so beautiful!" He was so absorbed that one of the neighbors casually commented in jest, "You'd think the dress were for Eusebio!"

The Thief

Four days before the wedding the dress was ready. Eusebio sighed dreamily, "A bride is the most beautiful thing in the world!" All fine and well. One more day went by. Suddenly, there was some alarming news in the house: "The wedding dress is missing!"

Women ran left and right. They turned the house upside down – nothing. There could only be one conclusion: someone had stolen the dress! Since the wedding was only a few days away, they suggested to the desperate Iracema, "You'll just have to get married without a wedding dress!"

"Why?" she asked, offended. "Get married without a wedding dress, never! Who ever heard of such a thing?"

They even called the police. The mystery was infuriating: Who could be interested in a wedding dress? The investigations were fruitless and led nowhere. They only found the thief when, two days later, Dona Flavia woke up in the morning and ran into a white shape, dangling in the hallway. Dressed as a bride, wearing a veil and a wreath of flowers, Eusebio had hanged himself and left the following note: "Bury me like this."

Thy Neighbor's Wife

He walked into the pool hall asking, "Has anyone seen that dirtbag Gouveia?"

A guy with bad teeth who was chalking his cue answered, "It's been three hundred years since I've seen Gouveia!"

Another guy who was just arriving asked, "Isn't today Friday? Fridays are when he has his date with the clerk's wife."

Arlindo, who was a clerk too, muttered under his breath, "That's right, that's right!" Indeed, Gouveia could never be found on Fridays. He would disappear without a trace. But his friends, his close friends, all knew he was somewhere around town with a thirty-something woman who he claimed was his most recent immortal beloved. This one weekly rendezvous was sacred for Gouveia. He would drop business meetings, appointments, other women, everything, in order to rush to an apartment in Copacabana that a friend lent him or, better said, rented to him at two hundred cruzeiros a pop. But since it was a deluxe apartment with refrigerator, record player, hot and

18

cold running water and an ocean view, Gouveia recognized it was well worth the price.

"It's worth two hundred smackers, even more!"

Arlindo left the pool hall furious.

"Geez Louise!" He did the math. Gouveia's affair with the clerk's wife began on Fridays at four in the afternoon. From seven in the evening on, Gouveia would not answer the telephone, with the excuse that love required his undivided attention. Bottom line – he would only show his face again to the outside world at eleven p.m. or midnight. Surrounded by friends, he would say, "Mark my words, they'll have to drag me out of that apartment in a body bag."

That Friday Arlindo needed to speak with Gouveia urgently, and to underscore the matter he added, "It's a matter of life and death!" But he had to wait his chance. It was eleven at night when he walked into the pool hall.

Ten or fifteen minutes later Gouveia showed up. Arlindo rushed to him.

"Finally! Let's go for a walk. Let's have a chat!"

Gouveia, tired, yawning, practically falling asleep, just wanted to sit down and shoot the breeze over a beer. Arlindo, walking down the sidewalk next to his friend, began, "Do you trust me? Huh?"

He was taken aback.

"Why?"

"Do you?"

"Of course."

They stopped at the corner. Arlindo took out a cigarette and lit it. He tossed the match and continued.

"Well, if you trust me, I want you to tell me something: Who's the clerk's wife? What's her name? Do I know her? Speak! You never hide a thing from me! I want to know, or I should say, I need to know."

Silence. Finally Gouveia shook his head.

"Give me a break, my lips are sealed. This is serious stuff; it can end in gunshots, death, who knows what else. I'm sorry, but names are strictly out of the question."

Arlindo took a deep breath.

"You mean to say you're not going to tell me?"

Gouveia answered firmly, "No."

Arlindo placed his hand on Gouveia's shoulder.

"Since you're not going to tell me, then I'm going to tell you. It's no use trying to hide it. I know. I know who this dame is."

"You do?"

"Yes. Absolutely. I know."

Another pause. Gouveia decided to call his bluff.

"Who is she then?"

And Arlindo, very softly and unthreateningly said, "My wife. Yes sir, my wife, that's right."

Gouveia stepped back aghast.

"No, no!"

By now Arlindo had him by the collar. In a contained rage he went on, "Last night she said a man's name in her sleep. Your name. She kissed me thinking I was you. That's when I figured out my wife was the clerk's wife. And that I was the clerk."

Pale as a ghost, Gouveia denied everything.

"I swear! I swear!"

He tried to break loose in a violent spasm. But Arlindo was much stronger and subdued him with frightening ease. Gouveia began crying. He begged, "Don't kill me! Don't kill me!" Arlindo let him go.

"Look here, you son of a bitch, no one's going to get killed. Not you, not her. I can't kill her because I love her too much. And I love her so much that I won't kill you just so she won't suffer. But I want you to know one thing…"

He paused, then asked, "Are you listening?"

Sobbing, Gouveia answered, "Yes."

"This will be my revenge: from now on, whenever I run into you, no matter where we are, I spit in your face, starting now!"

It was late at night, and the streets were deserted. Like a hypnotized man, Gouveia didn't flinch. He even unconsciously lifted his face, as if to offer a better target. He saw Arlindo walk away calmly and confidently as he stood on the corner with a gob of another man's saliva hanging grotesquely from his face. Finally, he took out the expensive perfumed handkerchief that he used on Fridays for his meeting with Arlindo's wife and cleaned up. He left in a daze. He asked himself, "Now what do I do, now what?" He knew in the core of his being that Arlindo would track him down and spit on him, over and over, till their dying days.

That night he couldn't sleep. In the morning, his eyes bloodshot, his lip quivering, he appealed to mutual friends. He told them about the episode and asked for advice. One particularly hotheaded fellow was unequivocal.

"If a guy spit in my face I'd shoot him in the mouth."

Gouveia replied, "But I slept with his wife! You understand? I slept with his wife!"

"So?" the friend asked. "You won't be the first or the last to covet his neighbor's wife! No one's perfect, geez, no one's perfect!"

Of all the pieces of advice, the one that made the most sense came from one of his uncles: "Leave the country. Move to Mongolia, Outer Mongolia! If you don't have the balls to react, to break his face, the only solution is for you to leave the country."

Not that he didn't want to. But it was as if he were paralyzed, hypnotized. Whenever he saw his enemy approach, he would freeze, and the instinct to flee would vanish. Arlindo would approach and, for all to see, would spit in his face without Gouveia even flinching or trying to avoid what was coming. He even began walking around with a special handkerchief that he tucked in his breast pocket for just such occasions. The last straw came at the wake of a mutual friend. Arlindo showed up and, without the slightest respect for his surroundings, marched straight to Gouveia, who managed to stammer, "Not here! Not here!"

But Arlindo, unmoved, spit on him once again. This was more than Gouveia could bear. Desperate, he ran out. When he arrived home later that day, he put a bullet through his brain.

Justice Will Be Done

She was only fifteen. A gorgeous dark-skinned girl with a beautiful face and a figure to match. Prettier than the boss's daughters, she enjoyed all of the same privileges they did. The head of the family, a sober man who rarely drank anything harder than water, was fond of saying, "She's like family. As good as family."

One day Isaurinha froze while going down the stairs. She felt dizzy and came very, very close to fainting and falling all the way to the bottom. She was carried from there pale and covered in sweat. A short time later the family doctor, an old, kindhearted but ineffectual man appeared. He took her blood pressure, examined her throat, and placed a stethoscope to her chest over a thin towel. He paused and shook his head.

"It's serious!" Then he asked all of those present to leave and locked the bedroom door. The clock showed he was in there for forty-five agonizing minutes. Outside in the hallway the family waited anxiously, fearing cancer, tuberculosis, or even worse. Finally, the old man appeared and called for the lady of the house, Dona Dinora. He cleaned his glasses with a handkerchief and asked, "Does she have a boyfriend?"

"No. Why?"

He put his glasses on and announced, "Beyond a shadow of a doubt, Isaurinha is pregnant. She is going to have a baby."

Dona Dinora nearly fell over backwards.

Calamity

Dona Dinora, who was incapable of uttering a single word without first consulting her husband, sobbed on the telephone as she spoke to him.

"Come home right this minute. Hurry!"

He jumped into a cab and made it home in record time. He was the main, or more precisely, the only authority in that household. Everyone knew who was in charge – his wife, his daughters, married and single, his sons and his sons-in-law. His word was law, and there was no right of appeal. But it should be noted that his authority was based on the bedrock of his superhuman virtue. For Clementino did not drink, smoke or gamble; he was even sober and restrained at the dinner table. He ate little, in fact only enough to keep from dying of hunger. On the day of his silver wedding anniversary he surprised his guests by announcing in his deep voice, "I've known only one woman in my life: My wife! I've never cheated!"

Clementino arrived. As soon as he was made aware of the catastrophe at hand, he called a family meeting. Daughters, sons, daughters-in-law and sons-in-law all gathered in the living room. The only one absent was Isaurinha, who was lying in the bedroom next to a bucket, suffering the inevitable nausea typical of her condition. Downstairs the enraged old man began the meeting by slamming his fist on the table.

"This puts every man in this house under suspicion! Bar none!"

With his lips quivering, he went on.

"That means I expect explanations from son and son-in-law alike!"

The Suspects

No one said a word. There were many suspects. Three of his sons-in-law and three of his sons lived in that immense house with their respective wives.

One male child, the eighteen-year-old Juca, was still single. He was the youngest and as such was treated with kid gloves by everyone. As a matter of fact, even the father was less harsh with him. Clementino frothed at the mouth, full of indignant righteousness as he paced from side to side in that immense living room. Suddenly he stopped and lifted his arms to the heavens. He filled the room with his baritone voice: "Forgive me, God! But I have one vice in this life. The desire to be just!"

He paused and stared at his astonished sons and sons-in-law and went on, "And justice will be done, even if it means going against my sons-in-law, my sons, even my own mother! God willing!"

Looking over the suspects, he posed an indiscriminate question: "I want to know which one of you dogs did this! I want to know who was the lowlife who took advantage of that young girl, a girl who should be sacred to all of us. Who? Who?"

Silence. The men sat there, pale and cowering; the women began to cry. In desperation, Dona Dinora ventured a theory.

"Maybe it was someone from outside."

The old man leapt up violently.

"What do you mean from outside? No, ma'am! No! Impossible!"

In spite of his rage, he did make a lot of sense.

"These things require time, intimacy, familiarity, access. Isaurinha never goes out by herself. She's always accompanied by one of you. No! The lowlife is in this room! He's one of you! He's a son or a son-in-law of mine! But whoever he is, he's going to pay. Speak!"

No one dared open his mouth.

"Cowards! Clowns," he lashed out.

Finally, gasping for air, he announced, "Since you won't confess, since you don't have the guts to confess, I am going to use a method that never fails."

With a terrible laugh, he announced, "The victim herself is going to identify the guilty party."

Isaurinha

He marched out. No one moved. As soon as he was gone, whispering was heard between husbands and wives. The latter asked amid tears, "Was it you? Do you swear?" The poor devils answered, "I swear." The old man spent half an hour locked in the bedroom with his foster child. Finally he appeared, fiery-eyed, holding Isaurinha by the arm. He shook her.

"Go ahead! Who was it! Speak!"

She fell to her knees before Clementino. She covered her face with her hands and sobbed, "I can't! I can't!"

He forced her to her feet. With that booming voice of his he demanded, "Speak! Or I'll strike you right here and now!"

Dona Dinora wanted to intervene, but he rebuffed her.

"Go to the devil!"

That saintly woman sat back down gasping for breath, experiencing a sudden onset of palpitations. Drenched in sweat, Clementino continued his grilling.

"Is he single? Married? Speak!"

"Single," she sobbed.

The old man opened his eyes wide in a sign of satisfaction. "Ah, he's single, is he?" He let go of the girl. He flashed a cruel sneer and walked around the table slowly. He stopped in front of Juca, his youngest son. He lowered his voice.

"My only single son, the only one who's not married." Suddenly, he grabbed his son by the collar with both hands, lifted him up, and let out a triumphant howl.

"So, it was you, huh? Lowlife!"

His youngest son began crying.

"No! I swear! It wasn't me!"

His father lifted his hand and struck him down. For over twenty minutes, almost half an hour, he showered his son with insults and blows, showing a frightening tenacity.

"Confess! Confess!"

Those in the room sat there mesmerized, unwilling to intervene. At about midnight, beside himself, his lips bloodied, the young man cried out, "It was me! Me!" He repeated hysterically, "Me, me!"

The old man let go of his son. Exhausted and triumphant, he took his place at the head of the table again.

"Fortunately, this lowlife is still single. He can make amends by marrying her. Miserable wretch!"

The Just

The next day, Clementino began making the marriage arrangements. He didn't let up on his son. When asked whether this would be a marriage with wedding dress and all, he answered, "Yes, sir! Wedding dress and all! Or do you think marriage is a game? That you knock her up, tie the knot, and no one will be the wiser?"

In the family's eyes Clementino had undergone a virtual apotheosis. Sensing that he was the object of unanimous admiration, fear and respect, he assumed the air of a living statue wherever he went – at home, on the bus, at the office. Juca, on the other hand, was a broken man, a pitiful sight to behold. He wouldn't utter a single word but instead remained buried in a dull and brutal silence. Every night his harsh father insisted that he and Isaurinha sit in the living room side by side in "courtship." There was, however, an eerie silence between the two. They had nothing in common; they did not exchange one phrase, word, smile or look. Thanks to the urgent arrangements made by the father, however, the marriage papers were prepared in record time. The night before the wedding, the bride and the groom crossed paths in the hallway. Isaurinha blocked Juca's way and begged him, "Forgive me! Forgive me!"

He didn't say one word or make one gesture. He went on his way, clenching his lips.

The Wedding

They wed. The last guest said goodbye around midnight. The family retired, and the newlyweds entered the bedroom that had been chosen especially for them in the rear of the house. Juca turned the key while Isaurinha sat in front of the mirror removing her tiara. The young man approached and asked, "Who was it? Who was it?" She turned, startled. He went on, "Bitch! Bitch!" The young woman was standing by now. Suddenly, Juca grabbed her by her arms and with surprising force yelled, "If you don't tell me, I'll kill you!" He repeated those last terrifying words with poisonous glee.

The Punishment

The next morning he waited for his father to leave his bedroom on the way to the bathroom.

"I want to talk to you, now! Let's go!"

They locked the door to the study. The father, suddenly grown old, waited for his son to begin.

"I know everything. I'm going to tell everything. I am going to tell Mother, my brothers, my brothers-in-law, the neighbors."

Clementino latched onto his son pathetically.

"The dead are forgiven! The dead are forgiven!"

At first his son did not understand. Or he only understood when the old man took out a gun. Clementino put the barrel to his temple and pulled the trigger. It was a tremendous blast that startled the household, the neighbors, the entire street. He died before an ambulance could arrive. Much later, at the wake, Juca cried more than the others, more even than the widow. But as the procession was about to leave, he stood at the window and screamed, "Lowlife! Lowlife!"

The Scorpion

They fought like cats and dogs — epic battles on a daily basis. One row was particularly memorable. Belchior walloped Elvira with a fist to the forehead. She tumbled over some chairs and then stood up, still seeing double from the force of the fall and the impact. But she did not hesitate for one moment; she picked up the radio and hurled it at Belchior. He ducked and the projectile struck the china cabinet with a thunderous crash. It was then that the neighbors invaded the house en masse. A patrol car even pulled up. The couple's legs were still flailing when the two were finally subdued. Belchior's body heaved in violent spasms.

"I'll tear you to pieces! I'll break your face!"

And, like a force of nature, Elvira answered in kind.

"Moron! Idiot!"

For the neighbors these reciprocal daily beatings were a cause of both fascination and disgust. They had been living like this for five years now, and no one could understand how they could still be together.

"You're not compatible. Why not separate?"

They both readily agreed.

"I can't wait!"

"I can't wait!"

But they delayed their separation for weeks, then months, then years. It could be said that in spite of their incompatibility there was some mysterious and fatal tie that bound them together. Until finally, the relatives of both Belchior and Elvira began to grumble.

"This has gone far enough! It's unseemly! It really is!"

Marina

Then one day, Belchior met Marina. With a name straight out of a Dorival Caymmi song, she was a delightful girl: tiny and beautiful with a sweet disposition, refined, and in every other respect well-mannered. After the ornery, foul-mouthed and violent Elvira, Belchior was smitten by Marina's gentleness. At their second or third meeting, the girl inquired, "Are you married?"

He hesitated. But he worked up his courage and said, "Look here honey, I want to be on the up and up with you. I am not married, I live with someone who is like this and like that, who is separated from her husband. Do you understand?"

"I understand."

"But I want you to know she is a poisonous snake, a viper, a scorpion. She hates me, and I hate her. Before I met you, I'd already decided to give her the boot. And now that I've met you, of course my mind is made up."

Marina seemed satisfied with the explanation. The following day Elvira was leaving the house after lunch. When she returned in the evening, she saw the following message scrawled on the wall, in her husband's handwriting: "GO TO HELL, STINKING BITCH! GOOD RIDDANCE!"

Elvira, who despised Belchior, should have relished the news. Instead, she rolled on the floor in fits and heaves. When the neighbors entered to see what the commotion was all about, she pointed to the wall, "Look what that dog wrote!"

The neighbors read it and reread it, aghast. Elvira sobbed:

"He'll be back!"
And she repeated it with an eerie fanaticism.
"He'll be back!"

Happiness

When the separation was finalized, Belchior's joy was overwhelming. The first thing he did was to give Marina a call, "I'm free! Free!"

On the other end, Marina sobbed, "God bless you!"

That night, Belchior, still radiant, gathered his friends at a bar. He drank all night. At the top of his lungs he made the most compromising of admissions. At a certain point, his eyes bloodshot, his mouth contorted, he yelled out, as if reciting a lecture, "There's no such thing as conscience! The only conscience I know of is fear of the police!"

He unbuttoned his collar, loosened his tie and let out a howl:

"It was fear of the police that kept me from killing Elvira!"

He had to be carried home, vomiting on his friends.

The Angel

As a teenager he had read a dime-store novel called *The Redeeming Angel*. And now, staring at Marina in all of her tender meekness, he tried his hand at literary eloquence, "You are my Redeeming Angel."

She lowered her eyes and, with goose bumps all over, said, "I do the best I can!"

He introduced the young lady to his parents. Afterwards, he anxiously wanted to know their opinion.

"She's a sweetheart!"

And the father added in a grave tone...

"This one I like!"

Two weeks later Belchior asked for her hand in marriage. The afternoon they became engaged, he took the girl out on the porch and, after a dramatic pause, he proceeded, "When I met you I had two options, murder or suicide. You saved my life."

Idyllic

It seemed as if they were made for one another. Every fifteen minutes Belchior would discover some new affinity they had. Amazingly, they seemed compatible in all respects. They liked the same movies, the same songs, the same landscapes, the same desserts. He, who had been so miserable in love before – to the point of busting his lover's head with a transistor radio – now seemed to see only blue skies ahead. There were no more feuds or squabbles, but instead a calm that bordered on tedium. Little by little, though, without Belchior even noticing, a certain melancholy crept into his soul. His fiancée couldn't help but notice.

"You seem, I don't know, sad."

"Me?"

"You. You seem strange. What's the matter?"

He protested cheerfully, "Why strange? On the contrary, I've never felt so good."

He cleared his throat uncomfortably and exaggerated, "I'm the happiest man in the world. I have you, which is to say, I have everything."

The Other

And in fact, Belchior was, or should have been, the happiest man in the world. He loved and was loved; he had rid himself of the hysterical and unstable woman who had ruined his life, his soul and his liver. In spite of this, or perhaps precisely because of this, he began to appear depressed, dissatisfied. He tried to explain it away, "It must be stress." Close to the wedding date he ran into an old friend, Peçanha, who pulled him to the side.

"Elvira swears you're going to come back to her. She says she'll be damned if you don't!"

He jumped up furiously.

"The bitch! I wouldn't look at her if she were the last woman on earth. Leave me alone!"

Could she be right? Could she be wrong? No one really knew. There were, however, some who saw in the case of Belchior and Elvira one of those somber, inexplicable mysteries of the sexes.

The Wedding Night

Finally, the wedding day came. When Marina walked down the aisle, there was a general gasp of delight. In her intense and fragile grace, she painted an unforgettable picture. Once the ceremony was over, the two returned to Marina's parents' house where they would be living from now on. At eleven the last guest said goodbye; after blessing the newlyweds the elderly couple called it a night.

Marina, transfigured, whispered:

"Wait a minute. I'll call you when I'm ready. Wait."

Just then the phone rang and Belchior, surprised and anxious, answered. It was Elvira.

"Listen! I'll wait up for you. I'll place the key under the mat. Come right away!"

He hung up. Belchior leaned against the door, his head spinning and his legs weak. He felt a sudden violent pang of nostalgia for the woman who was the source of both his hatred and desire. Just then, Marina opened the door.

"You can come in now, honey!"

But he was no longer thinking about his wife. He had become a man possessed. Disoriented, he glided down the stairs, hugging the wall for support. Half an hour later a taxi pulled up to the door of his old address. He felt under the mat with his hand and found the key. He walked in. There, standing in the middle of the stairs, wearing a pink robe, a nightgown and ermine sandals, stood Elvira, waiting for him. Not one word was uttered. Exhibiting a mixture of hatred and desire, Belchior grabbed Elvira and kissed her over and over again. And then she threw her head back and laughed.

"Mine!"

It was this bit of pride that sealed her fate. Belchior slowly clasped his hands around her smooth neck. Then he squeezed without realizing he was choking her, without realizing he was killing her. Afterwards, clutching the corpse, he screamed out:

"I'll never bury you! I'll always be by your side!"

And he laid his head over her no-longer-beating heart.

workaholic

He was a father of the highest moral standards. So when he found out that his daughter was seeing someone, he didn't waste any time: He wanted to know everything about the young man. For four or five whole days he left no stone unturned. It so happened that those questioned about the boyfriend's attributes, without exception, said the same thing: "A very hard worker!"

Before long the old man was convinced that nothing characterized the young man so much as his phenomenal capacity for work. He felt satisfied. He called his wife and daughter. Pacing back and forth, he said, "Well. I've been asking around."

He paused for effect. The daughter held her breath, anxiously awaiting the verdict. Finally she asked, "And?"

Juventino stopped in his tracks.

"He seems to be a good boy, hardworking and so forth," he said.

Laurinha, who was seated, stood, her eyes gleaming.

"So you give your consent, Dad?"

He took a deep breath.

"I do."

The Worker

Juventino felt contempt for sloth and the slothful. The possibility of having a hard worker as a son-in-law delighted him.

"He's one of mine!" he said, rubbing his hands, profoundly satisfied.

Laurinha, radiant, ran to her boyfriend to tell him the news.

"Daddy is a fan of yours! He admires you!"

Raimundo, a solemn look on his face, cleared his throat.

"Good! Good!" he said.

The engagement lasted a year and a half, give or take a few months. During that time Raimundo visited his girlfriend three times a week. He would arrive after dinner, would spend half an hour with the girl, and then would leave hastily to get to his other job. He had three jobs and was looking for a fourth. He would go to bed at three in the morning and get up at six. It should have been enough to crush the boy. Indeed, his exhaustion was overwhelming: He slept on the trolley, on the bus, in the jitney, seated or standing. Above all, he slept when on dates with his girlfriend. Raimundo seemed innately and perpetually tired. Taken aback by his fatigue, Laurinha ventured a hypothesis.

"Don't you think you might be working a little too hard, sweetie?" she asked.

The answer was obvious. However, Raimundo, who just then happened to be dozing off on Laurinha's shoulder, came to, almost indignant.

"Laurinha, let me explain something," he said. "There is no such thing as too much work. OK? You can never work too much!"

Hero

The entire family, with Juventino leading the way, applauded Raimundo's fearsome drive. Not to mention Laurinha, of course. The most she could complain about was that with so many jobs and responsibilities, there was hardly enough time and energy left for their relationship. Weeks and months would pass without even a show of tenderness, a kiss, a compliment. But

Laurinha had enough perspective to understand and accept the situation. Besides, her father, her mother, everyone was fond of saying, "You're in luck! Raimundo is quite a catch!" If, in the middle of a date, overcome by fatigue, he should fall asleep, Juventino or his wife would rush to turn the radio off. They would add, "Don't make any noise; Raimundo is sleeping!"

Matrimony

The truth of the matter was that the young man's immense and overwhelming fatigue became a source of pride, of vanity for the family. When the two became engaged it was actually moving. Juventino, sobbing, hugged his future son-in-law.

"My son! My son!" he cried. He blew his nose and declared for all to hear, "I'm certain, absolutely certain, that a young man like you will bring my daughter happiness."

Raimundo, wiped out as always, stammered, "Great! Great!"

Three months later they were married.

Romantic

Laurinha was, to use her own words, "very romantic." Two things in marriage attracted her irresistibly: first, the wedding ceremony with the fabulous dress and all the nuptial pomp; and second, what she herself, shuddering, called "the first night." She had a married girlfriend who was sassy and wise to the ways of the world. According to her, "The future of the entire marriage depends on 'the first night!'"

Laurinha, tremulous, asked, "Is it everything they say it is, is it?" Her friend sighed. "Wait and see!"

Prompted by her worldly friend's insinuations, Laurinha daydreamed.

"If I must die, let it be after the first night, not before."

Well. They were married, and after the religious ceremony, in grand style, with music, outdoor illumination, etc., she left with her husband for the apartment in Grajaú where they were to reside from now on. They arrived and entered. It should be pointed out, by way of illustration, that in the limousine Raimundo went so far as taking a nap. Laurinha, distressed in her veil and tiara, shook him.

"Honey, it's unbecoming! Wake up!" Now in the apartment, Laurinha opened a crack in the bedroom door and announced, "You can come in, sweetie."

She moved to the middle of the room and waited. She was wearing the latest fashion in nightgowns – transparent, with just the right amount of cleavage. She had never felt so naked. On her feet she wore little white slippers. In her imagination, she visualized her loved one's delight in seeing her. The minutes passed and nothing. She said to herself, startled, "Huh?" She went to take a peek and saw the following: her bridegroom, in an armchair, his head hanging, sound asleep. She was so stunned that she went out to him, forgetting to cover herself. She shook him.

"Honey, you're sleeping!"

The poor devil jumped up startled. He squinted, recognized his bride, and scratched his head.

"Is that you?" He let out one of those frightful yawns.

Laurinha, aghast, did not know what to do.

Raimundo hugged her.

"Shall we, honey?" he asked.

First Night

They made it to the bedroom. The accumulated fatigue of the man who worked a lot, too much, gave a slow rhythm to everything he did, thought or said. Nonetheless, Laurinha was once again in the mood. She offered him her fresh, beautiful lips.

"Kiss me, kiss me!"

It was not to be. Her bridegroom smacked himself in the head.

"Where's the alarm clock?"

"Why?" she asked.

Raimundo roamed around the room, frantically searching.

"Where's the damned alarm clock?" He looked everywhere.

"What do you need an alarm clock for?" Laurinha asked.

He came to a halt in the middle of the living room, irritated.

"I have to get up early! Please! I have to go to work!"

Laurinha stepped back in disbelief.

"You're going to work tomorrow? Are you? Tomorrow?"

He exploded, "Of course! Yes! I have an urgent matter to take care of. I scheduled a meeting with the boss at 7 a.m.!"

The girl sat on the edge of the bed. She had trouble registering what she'd just heard.

"It can't be!"

He finally found the alarm clock behind a little flower vase. He rejoiced and pressed the clock to his chest. "Now I can sleep in peace!" he said to his wife, euphorically. He placed the alarm clock on the nightstand. Laurinha, her arms crossed, did not utter a single word and merely followed her husband with her eyes. He squatted in front of the chest of drawers, grabbed his pajamas and went into the bathroom to change. He returned in his pajamas, barefoot and yawning up a storm. He faced his wife, scratching his chest, and said, "Will you do me a favor? A huge favor? I'm really pooped. Let's do the following: Let me sleep for half an hour and then wake me up, OK?"

"OK."

Delirium

It was interesting what happened next. Once he had obtained her permission he collapsed on the bed and passed out. Laurinha contemplated that man with a certain amazement and disgust. She stood and changed the alarm from six to twelve. Next she turned off the light and walked to the window and gazed out at the street and into the night. And she stood there in a tormented vigil. She thought to herself, "There goes my first night!"

Three or four hours later, there she was, still at the window. Suddenly, she heard a noise down below: It was the milkman making his first delivery to his new clients. Something came over her, a sudden fury, a dull and overwhelming rage. Not knowing exactly where she was going, she threw on a robe over her transparent nightgown, dashed out of the bedroom, and rushed down two flights of stairs. She opened the front door and ran out into the yard. She caught up to the milkman just as he was about to leave, pushing his little cart. He turned, in shock. Laurinha stood on the tip of her toes and kissed him, passionately.

White Powder

When she got married it was assumed she couldn't have children. Thirty days later, however, she said to her husband, "Armindo, I'm feeling strange."

Her husband, who was reading a newspaper, turned to her and scratched his head.

"Must be the flu," he said.

He was one of those men for whom any symptom meant the flu. His wife had to explain that, no, it wasn't the flu, that it was a mysterious, very strange feeling of nausea. The husband put the newspaper down.

"Nausea?"

"Yes. And I'm always on edge. I don't know what it is. Something, I don't know what."

"Tomorrow you're going straight to the doctor," Armindo said. "Before it gets any worse."

Sure enough, the next day she was at the doctor's office. The doctor examined her and, when he was done, asked her, amused, "What disease might a woman who just got married one month ago have? Huh? Tell me?"

Astonished, she stammered, "Could it be I'm…?"

"Of course you are!"

That night the husband, delighted by the news, rubbed his hands.

"We're two dummies! How come we didn't figure it out right away? It was so obvious!"

The Daughter

The daughter was born on schedule. She was a tiny little thing, incredibly fragile, just big enough to fit in a shoebox. The father intercepted the doctor in the hallway.

"Is there something wrong with her?"

"Why?"

"She's so tiny!"

The doctor cordially patted the father on the back.

"Not at all! It's normal. No need to worry."

But it wasn't normal. She was a flickering flame that could be extinguished at any moment. The first month was heart wrenching. No one could sleep for fear that she would die. It was only with constant care, love and attention that she was able, little by little, to pull through. Even then, she was still sickly and tremendously fragile. She'd cry and cry for hours on end. The mother would pick her up from her cradle and pace back and forth with the child in her arms. She tried breast-feeding, but Eliete (her name was Eliete) would refuse; she tried the pacifier, with the same results. Finally, she lost her patience.

The aunts, at their wits end, suggested, "When a child starts crying like that it can only mean one thing – a stomachache. You can bet that's what it is!"

And then all of the advice would begin: "Give her some of this." "Some of that." A third would suggest, "How about some chamomile tea?"

The mother, in tears, would hand Eliete off to someone and scream angrily, "God, what did I do to deserve this?"

Love Lost

Nighttime was hell. Eliete's mysterious malady seemed to manifest itself like clockwork. At midnight the baby girl would start wailing. And that was that: All the holding, caressing, and singing in the world couldn't stop the crying. Armindo despaired. Any child's suffering tore at his heart, but much more so his own daughter's. He told his wife, "Massage her tummy, will you?"

At first, she tried to hold it together, until she couldn't any longer. She turned to her husband.

"Here, take your daughter, take her. I can't stand it anymore. I just can't!"

Armindo didn't say a word; he grabbed his daughter and from then on spent nights on end with her in his arms. But one thing astonished him and seemed like a crime: While Eliete cried for hours on end, the mother slept peacefully, like an angel. With his daughter in his arms, he would exclaim, "How could she! How could she!" He endured this situation for a little while longer until, finally, he exploded.

"It's like you don't care!"

She stood up to him.

"Look here! I'm the mother, you're the father!"

"You don't give a damn!"

From that moment on, there was constant friction between the father and mother over their daughter. The wife's impatience grew and grew. She abandoned all pretense.

"God, that girl loves to whine!"

During the day, while Armindo was out, she'd leave Eliete in her cradle and wouldn't allow anyone to pick her up. She began defending certain theories that alarmed her husband.

"Crying is good for the lungs, it's the best thing in the world!"

One time, when Armindo criticized her lack of sensitivity, she became furious.

"She ruined our marriage!"

So the husband, fed up with all of the arguing, began to care for his daughter whenever he was home. The wife would go to the movies, the theater, out with her girlfriends or to visit neighbors, while he, wholly resigned to the situation, would say, "Go ahead, I'll stay. I'll take care of Elietinha."

It was Armindo who changed her little diapers. One afternoon, his wife said something that really infuriated him: "Damn it! Wash your hands after you change her diapers, will you!"

The Other

Neither husband nor wife was under any illusions by now; their love was dead and buried. Until one day, suddenly, Eliete stopped crying. Nights on end, she'd sleep like an angel, without waking even one single time. Once, so astonished at the peace and quiet, Armindo woke up frightened and went to take a look. He put his hand on the baby's chest and only went back to bed when he'd felt her heart beat.

In the morning, while he brushed his teeth, he said, "Eliete doesn't cry at night anymore."

His wife, who was in bed, answered, "Or during the day."

He seemed intrigued.

"Strange, don't you think?"

That was when his wife, after hesitating for a second, revealed, "I found this great medicine. I put it in her bottle, and it works miracles."

"What medicine?"

"You never heard of it."

It was around this time that Armindo began noticing something strange about his wife. It was a change he couldn't put his finger on. It was physical too. At times he would perceive a new gleam in her eyes, and she'd walk around as if in a complete daze. Whatever the case might be, one thing was certain: she wasn't herself. Until one day, feeling sick, he returned home from work much earlier than usual. His wife was preparing their daughter's bottle. With her back to him, she didn't see her husband come in. He could have said something or made some noise. But he chose not to. His wife was mixing a powder into her daughter's milk. She set aside some for herself, which she then sniffed. She screwed on the top of the bottle, turned, and was startled to see her husband. Instinctively, she tried to hide the bottle. That gesture of fear, of having been caught in the act, explained everything.

Pale, Armindo stammered, "Cocaine!"

White Powder

It was, in fact, cocaine that the mother was sniffing and mixing into her daughter's milk. Beside himself, he lunged and grabbed her by the wrist. With unsuspected strength she broke free. She was faster and made it out the door and dashed towards the bedroom. Only later did Armindo understand why she had not run for the front door. They arrived at the bedroom almost at the same time. She desperately tried to close the door behind her but was unsuccessful. Armindo, who was prepared to commit all sorts of atrocities, froze in his tracks. Inside the bedroom sat a man on the bed, in a trance-like state. He didn't seem at all fazed; it could be said that he was in his own world. His wife placed herself between her husband and the man. She lifted her head as if to challenge her husband.

"Don't you lay a finger on him! Don't you lay a finger on him!"

But Armindo, blind with rage, threw her aside. He grabbed the stranger by the collar, lifted him up, and, with his teeth clenched, said, "It's your fault, you dog!"

The man, defenseless in the face of Armindo's rage, did not make one move. His wife, however, ran and lifted her daughter from the cradle and held her in her arms. By now Armindo's hands were starting to close around the stranger's neck. He was going to kill the man who had given cocaine to his daughter. The man was turning blue, and… just then his wife screamed, "I'll kill your daughter! I'll kill her! I'll kill her!"

Armindo turned, frightened. He let go of the man, and repeated over and over again, almost in tears, "No! No! No!"

From then on she was in charge, in control of her husband's every action. She said, "You're going to stay here, and I'm going to leave. I'm going to leave the baby with the neighbors. If you make one move, you know what will happen."

The stranger seemed dumbstruck. He put on his jacket. Armindo did not make one gesture, did not say one word as the two walked out.

A Cadillac For A Kiss

He went around town for days asking, "Has anyone seen Percival?"
"Which one?"
Mendes had to describe him.
"You know! Dark, handsome, strong, looks like Cesar Romero."
The resemblance to Cesar Romero was usually enough. They would say,
"Oh, yeah! Sure! But I haven't seen him in ages." Mendes would say thank you
and resume his search. Wherever he went, though, the answer was always the
same: no one had seen Percival. He would scratch his head: "I'll be!" He left
anguished notes in every dive, in every pool hall. He was about to give up
when one day he ran into Meireles in Cinêlandia. He asked him, "Have you
seen that dope Percival?"

Meireles lifted his arms as high as the clouds.

"Percival? What a coincidence! I just dropped Percival off! Not even a minute ago!"

"You serious?"

"Damn right! He's working at some furniture store over in Lapa. He's on his way there right now."

"OK, bye-bye," Mendes said, and hurried off.

Ex-Promoter

Back in 1930, '32, '34, Mendes had been a boxing promoter. Money, cars, women, the works. But boxing went into a decline, the public lost interest, and ticket sales took a nosedive. The inevitable occurred, and his career as a promoter crashed and burned spectacularly. He would wander around town without a nickel to his name, unshaven, in a grease-stained suit, trying to dodge creditors. He never again signed any deals worth mentioning; he lived off odd jobs or hitting up friends and acquaintances. Now old, broke, and missing several teeth, he was going from bad to worse when he remembered Percival. He thought to himself, "That dummy might just be my salvation." He started the search that led him to the furniture store in Lapa.

He waited for Percival to get off and then sidled up to him on the sidewalk. He began by asking, "What do you make doing that stuff?"

The good-looking Percival, taken aback, said, "Eighteen-hundred cruzeiros." Standing on the curb, Mendes screamed at him, "Aren't you ashamed? Answer me! A guy like you, sitting on a gold mine? Aren't you ashamed of that salary?" He stabbed his finger at Percival's chest, "Or don't you know you're sitting on a gold mine?"

"Me? What gold mine?"

Mendes winked and lowered his voice.

"Your physique! OK? Your physique is a gold mine. You just have to learn how to use it. It's a cinch!"

Intrigued, but still clueless, Percival asked, "How? Explain this to me!"

The Plan

They walked into a café to talk about the plan that Mendes himself touted as "sensational" and "brilliant." The impresario tried to be as clear as possible.

"A guy like you, a hunk, should be living on easy street; you can pull yourself out of this gutter. You know how? Easy as pie: renting out your affections. Let's say some woman sees you and likes what she sees. OK? She pays you for your company, pays to spend some time with you, pays you for your kisses. You catch my drift?"

Aghast, Percival stood up in slow motion.

"Is this a joke? Do I look like someone who takes money from women? Anyway, how about the police? This will draw the cops!"

Mendes objected emphatically.

"Screw the cops! Listen you moron, it might or it might not draw the cops. It depends on the lady, OK? If she's some hard-luck story, yes. But if she's serious, classy, respectable, then nothing will happen."

Percival was having none of it.

"Never! Who do you take me for? I'd rather live a quiet life, do my own thing, and earn my salary. I don't want any trouble."

Persistence

It could be said that it was a closed case. But Mendes was shrewd and stubborn. He wouldn't leave Percival's side. At times he would resort to reason, at other times, sheer insults: "Don't be an idiot, kid! Get it while you can." And he would add, "I already have the lady. Loaded. Gaga over you. She'll give you a Cadillac just like that."

"Does she know me?" he asked.

"Of course she does," Mendes replied. "She's seen you a bunch of times. No father, no mother, no sisters. Completely alone in the world, no one to meddle in her affairs!"

Percival, pale, but still fascinated in spite of everything, resisted.

"No, no, and no!" Until one afternoon he expressed curiosity, his Achilles' heel. "Cute?"

Mendes, caught by surprise, cleared his throat.

"Well. She's OK. But look here, you don't mention money to her; I'll take care of that. After we get paid, I'll give you your share, and I'll take mine."

Little by little, after several more conversations, Percival learned the details. She owned buildings, avenues, the works. Since she had never had a boyfriend, she lived with an unquenchable hunger for love. Percival wanted to know, "How old is she?"

Mendes scratched his head.

"She looks thirty-something."

The Meeting

Where and when had this lonely, sad, rich lady met Mendes? No one knew for sure. What was certain, however, was that it was impossible for Percival to hold out forever... shortly afterwards, he fought with his boss and left his job. Mendes immediately jumped into action; he dragged him by the arm.

"I don't want to hear any more excuses. Today we're going over there. I'll introduce you and that's that!" This time Percival, terrified at having no job, capitulated.

That evening, both stood in front of the lady's door, two nervous wrecks. On the way over, Mendes had warned Percival: "She's not much to look at, physically speaking. So don't get your hopes up."

Her name was Olivia. She lived in mysterious solitude. Where were her relatives? Mendes had asked himself this question and had found no answers. When Percival was introduced to her he was dumbstruck. There are ugly women, and then there are ugly women. Dona Olivia's ugliness defied description, with her little possum face, bent nose, buckteeth and crossed eyes. When she walked down the street, they'd whisper, "There goes old cross-eyes!" Mendes put her age at thirty-something. Truth be told, being generous, Dona Olivia was closer to fifty and change.

There came a moment when she asked Percival to excuse her and went to an adjacent room with Mendes. Percival was left alone in the living room. He stood and walked to the window. He might have been short on intelligence, as Mendes was wont to say. He was, however, good-hearted, kind, compassionate.

Dona Olivia provoked two reactions in him: first repulsion and horror; then pity, a pity that made him feel like crying, screaming, flailing his legs.

The Deal

In the other room, Dona Olivia broke out in tears while the ex-boxing promoter watched uneasily. She twisted and untwisted her hands in heart-wrenching despair.

"I've never been kissed. No one's ever kissed me." She paused and then continued in fits and starts, "No man's ever been interested in me. I know I'm not pretty… but there's only one thing I want…" Barely able to see Mendes, she extended her hands.

"I would give anything for a kiss. Just one kiss from your friend. Oh, God!"

Mendes went brutally to the point.

"For a Cadillac?"

"Yes," she said.

Mendes dashed into the other room. Ecstatic, he grabbed Percival. He told him about the spinster's dream, how she had never been kissed. The impresario gnashed his teeth.

"It's the deal of the century! A steal! A kiss for a Cadillac! How about it?"

Percival seemed to hesitate: At last, feeling the pressure, he made up his mind. He walked over to Dona Olivia, who was on her knees, blinder than ever. She stood upon seeing him. Percival, without uttering a word, grabbed the woman and kissed her on the mouth for what seemed like forever, like in the movies. Finally, needing to breathe, he let go. Dona Olivia began sobbing in a frightful outpouring of emotion. She pulled herself together and said, "You deserve anything you want! Anything!"

She opened a drawer, pulled out a checkbook and filled out a check. She handed it to the handsome Percival. He held it, read an amount sufficient for a Cadillac, and methodically tore up the fabulous check. He bowed.

"You don't owe me a thing, ma'am. Not one penny. Good night."

Percival left, followed by Mendes, who was begging to know what had gone wrong. The spinster walked to the window as if drawn by a magnet. It was nighttime, and up high a star shone a little brighter.

The Bridal Shower

Twenty-four hours before the wedding, Detinha sighed.

"Sweetie, can I ask you a question?"

Peçanha, Antonio Peçanha, who was cleaning his nails with a matchstick, yawned.

"Shoot."

"How many baths did you take today?"

"Why?" he asked, taken aback.

"Answer me. How many baths do you take a day?"

"One, OK!"

"That's it?"

Peçanha was stupefied.

"You think that's not enough?"

"I do."

The Bath

Peçanha turned, mildly surprised and amused.

"Are you serious?"

"Why wouldn't I be?" she asked.

Peçanha stood.

"If this is a joke, it's not funny!"

Detinha continued: "I know that as a general rule everyone only takes one bath. But I don't care what anyone thinks. I take two. At least two. If it's hot out I take three. Sometimes four. I can't stand the smell of sweat, not on me or on others. I mean it!"

"Four baths?" her fiancé huffed.

"Yes sir, four. In a climate like ours one bath is not enough. It just won't do."

Peçanha exploded, "Come on, Detinha! Give it a rest! Or do you think I can spend the whole day, twenty-four hours a day, under a shower? Do you think I have nothing better to do than take showers? Come on!"

Detinha was about to reply when she was called into the kitchen. She went inside to see to matters and left her boyfriend on the porch. Peçanha, still amazed, cursed under his breath, "Damn!"

The Engagement

The house was full of women. Even an aunt from the poor side of town, whom the family had thought dead and buried, reappeared in spectacular fashion. A spinster, rather cross-eyed, she wanted to glimpse in her niece the happiness she herself had been denied. Very well.

Soon after Detinha had gone inside, she came back out.

"Peçanha, leave, leave because I have things to do, OK?"

He kissed her lightly on her cheek and yelled out a collective farewell to those inside.

"Bye-bye!"

"Bye-bye!" came the answer from a chorus of women.

Peçanha left with a sensation, a vague and uncomfortable sensation, of having been banished.

Obsession

On the way to the bus stop, Peçanha thought of what he himself called Detinha's "half-baked hint." He thought that he had perceived in his fiancée's words an extremely nasty inference.

He asked himself, "Do I smell?"

He sighed, "Naaahh!"

Hours later in his bedroom, extremely agitated, he could not fall asleep. Only at four in the morning did he finally close his eyes. All of his insecurities subsided into a deep slumber. He woke up at seven and joyfully exclaimed, "Today's the day! Today's the day!"

He walked into the bathroom and took a painstaking and exhaustive wedding day shower. He brushed his teeth vigorously, almost desperately, and only stopped when he felt his gums begin to bleed. Then he put on cologne, talcum powder, the works. He went downstairs relishing his own cleanliness. He asked, "Does my breath smell, Mom? Does it?"

He blew in her face.

The mother, who was extremely emotional and sentimental, said on the verge of tears, "Excellent. God bless you, sweetheart, God bless you!"

A few minutes later he was drinking a fortifying concoction of egg yolks and sugar. The emotions surrounding the wedding, instead of diminishing his appetite, only increased it. Before calling his fiancée on the telephone, he asked his mother: "Answer me honestly. Did you ever notice I smell? Tell me the truth, Mother!"

She was unequivocal.

"Never!"

Feeling better now, he called Detinha. After the reciprocal "good mornings," Detinha wanted to know, "Did you take a bath yet?"

"Jesus! Is this an obsession, or what? You're really something!"

"Are you offended?" she asked. "It's the most natural question in the world!"

They left it at that. Only at noon was the civil marriage finalized. At last they were, for all intents and purposes, husband and wife.

Then they left, accompanied by the two families and their closest friends, and when the first opportunity presented itself, Detinha whispered in his ear, softly, her lips almost immobile, "Hurry home and take a bath, OK? I want you nice and clean; don't miss a spot."

"Hold your horses!"

In Love

Peçanha rushed home in a cab in order to get ready for the church ceremony. He couldn't help but feel a nagging annoyance. It was very likely the idea of another bath would have occurred to him spontaneously, but it hurt that his fiancée wanted to dictate hygiene norms to him. He was so dejected that out of spite he nixed the proposed bath. He limited himself to rubbing some alcohol under his armpits and putting on a new coat of talcum powder. Still, when hours later he drove to the church, an inopportune thought occurred to him: "Do I smell like sweat?"

Fortunately, the trip to the church did not take long. And then everything subsided in the splendor of the ceremony. The bride in her magnificent gown painted a sweet and unforgettable picture. The ceremony defied description. The next thing he noticed, Peçanha was in a fairy-tale automobile next to his bride. Anguished, he lowered his voice.

"Angel, let's hurry up, OK?" And then, oozing a mixture of affection and carnal impatience, "Let's wrap this up early!"

Detinha did not respond, as if she were in a state of hypnosis. On the way to her parents' house, she only opened her mouth once, one single time, to ask, "Did you take two baths today?"

Peçanha was taken aback.

"What do you think I am? Come on!"

First Night

At the in-laws, Peçanha discreetly urged the bride, "Speed it up! Speed it up!"

His impatience was palpable by now and was inspiring playful comments. In order to avoid the lengthy goodbyes they left through the back. Detinha experienced a delicious feeling of elopement, of abduction. The automobile that delivered them to the mountain chalet made the entire journey at a smooth, imperceptible pace. They arrived in no time at all and rushed to their room reserved well in advance, clutching one another. They entered and Peçanha, with a glimmer in his eye, turned the key. He tried to grab her, but she broke free with unexpected agility.

"What's going on?" he asked.

"First I'm going to take a bath. I insist."

He asked, begged, implored but she was unequivocal. She got the last word in.

"Don't you see a woman has to be one hundred percent at a moment like this?"

He was forced to capitulate. He left the room in frustration. He remained just outside in the hallway, chain-smoking. Meanwhile, his wife took a prolonged bath – a bath worthy of Cleopatra. After approximately forty-five minutes he peeked in.

"Honey?"

He was at his wit's end, but once again she held him off.

"Hold on! Hold on!"

He retreated, dumfounded.

"Why do I have to hold on?"

She answered him sweetly but firmly, "I took my bath. Now it's your turn."

He wanted to react.

"Come on, Detinha! What bath? You're being childish. Come here, come on, come here!"

He tried to grab her. Once again she broke free. The sweetness in her face vanished. She clenched her teeth.

"You have two choices. Either you take a bath, or you don't lay a finger on me!"

Peçanha opened his arms wide.

"What are you saying, that I didn't take a bath? Do I disgust you? Speak! Do I?"

There was a small table between the two, which served to protect her. Peçanha insisted, his eyes welling up: "I could take a bath, sure. But don't you see it's humiliating? How will it look if I take a bath? Like I'm dirty, filthy, stinky. You hear me, sweetie?"

He lowered his voice: "There are certain things a husband shouldn't be subjected to!"

He paused, "Now kiss me!"

She pulled back, "No! First take a bath! A bath or nothing doing!"

Facing his wife, who made the little table between them into a barricade, he implored again. No reaction from Detinha. For a brief moment the poor devil looked at the bathroom as if he were going to cave in. Suddenly, one of those terrible rages came over him. He chased her into the bathroom and managed to grab her. But she broke free once again, opened the door and fled down the hallway screaming. Guests and hotel employees came to see what the commotion was about. Then, sobbing, she pointed at her husband.

"He's a pig! I married a pig! Get that pig away from me!"

Young Little Thing

He was the most insufferable husband imaginable. He would pick fights with his wife, the maid, the whole world. God forbid a button should be missing from one of his shirts, one lousy button. The whole house would tremble. His wife would come running, gasping for breath.

"What's going on? Why the commotion!"

Ubirajara grabbed the shirt and nearly rubbed her face in it.

"Where's the button? For crying out loud! How's a man supposed to live like this!"

"Calm down, sweetie!" Gloria said, bewildered. "Where there's a will there's a way!"

While the wife fastened the button with heart-wrenching poise, Ubirajara paced from side to side screaming.

"Fire the washing lady! Throw her out on the street! One thing's certain: I can iron better than she can!"

Sickness

With his peeves and his nasty temperament, the truth of the matter was that no maid, cook or washing lady ever lasted very long. Poor Gloria, who had the patience of a songbird, was forced to take over the duties of the stove, the sink, the washbasin. In that household, husband and wife were as different as water and wine. While her husband was a born neurasthenic, Gloria had the sweetest of temperaments. As far as she was concerned, everything was fine and wonderful, and if she could have paid to avoid arguments she would have. What tormented her was not her husband, who was the real root of her problems. No. She overlooked that. The problem was the maids who left one by one, in a constant procession. Scratching her head with a hairpin, Gloria would sigh, "This is serious! Very serious!" One day, however, Ubirajara went to the doctor, and just like that the truth was revealed: Ubirajara had been sick all along without anyone, even himself, suspecting. The insidious, tenacious, and stealthy disease that was eating away at him had a name. The doctor called it *sympathetic dystonia* and if that wasn't it, it must be something of the sort. It explained everything: his irritability towards his wife and the maids, his tantrums when a button was missing from his shirt and a series of other symptoms. Yawning, the doctor warned Gloria, "Don't contradict your husband, OK?"

Pathetic

If Gloria had been barely capable of contradicting her husband before, she was much less so now. Knowing he was ill, she would grin and bear all sorts of indignities. Any little thing set him off.

"How do you expect me to live like this?"

"But, sweetie…!"

"I'm treated like a dog in my own home. Yes, like a dog!"

Protected and excused by sympathetic dystonia, Ubirajara now knew no bounds. He found out that the maid had spoken badly of him to the neighbor. This time, even he was frightened by his reaction. He screamed any number of atrocities, among them, "If you were a man I'd break your face!"

"Animal!" she shot back.

The neighbors who witnessed the scene from their windows would not soon forget what they saw. Several days without help, Gloria was forced to take on every household chore. The result of this drudgery from sunrise to sunset was that she had no time to wash her face, bathe or observe the usual niceties, such as perfuming her arms, hands, neck, etc, etc. Her clothes were drenched in sweat. The husband, in his striped pajamas, reading his newspaper, sniffed with a look of disgust on his face.

"You smell like a goat! Take care of that, will you!"

Politely and with a selfless smile, Gloria explained, "Sweetheart, a housewife without a maid doesn't have time to smell good."

The New Maid

Fortunately, through the help of a distant relative, Gloria found a maid. On the phone she asked her, "Do you do everything?"

"Everything!"

She did. Every service for five hundred cruzeiros. Gloria thanked God. Before she arrived, Gloria made a heartfelt appeal to her husband.

"Sweetie, this time try not to…"

Ubirajara exploded, "No way! You know how it is with me: You screw up, you pay!"

The maid arrived the next day. What was immediately apparent was that she was young, a mere child.

"How old are you?" Gloria asked.

"Fifteen."

Gloria could see what was coming. Suffering from his nervous condition, her husband was going to make a ruckus because of the girl's age. Indeed, when Ubirajara got home that evening, Debora (that was her name) was asleep, but when he found out that the new maid was fifteen he flipped.

"Nice!"

"What?"

"Imagine! My house has turned into a kindergarten!" He asked his wife, "What do you have in that little head of yours? Huh?"

Gloria, shattered, felt like fighting back. She explained that the maid, in spite of her tender age, knew what she was doing. Ubirajara, who had been

56

losing a lot of money at the races, took advantage of the occasion to float an idea he had been contemplating for some time.

"What do we need a maid for anyway? You're not a cripple, you're not an invalid; you can do the work. Isn't that what a healthy marriage is all about? The husband works out in the world, and the wife stays at home?"

This time Gloria came very, very close to losing her temper. But she had the courage of a sparrow. She remembered, furthermore, that her husband was sick.

She sighed.

"We'll send her away, and that will be the end of that."

Little Devil

The following day, the tank for the upstairs bathroom was low on water. Ubirajara had to go downstairs and shower in the maid's bathroom. He got a brief glimpse of Debora. When he returned from his shower he called his wife. Rather disjointedly, he said, "Well. Let's do this: Let her stay another two weeks, then I'll decide. OK?"

Gloria was so overjoyed she almost made the sign of the cross. Fortunately, Debora agreed one hundred percent. After two weeks, Ubirajara himself, in spite of his disease and all, sang her praises to his friends and all the neighbors.

"We found a maid who's a real keeper!" One thing bothered him, though: the possibility that she might find a boyfriend, fiancé or husband. At night, before falling asleep, he turned over.

"The trick is for us to figure out a way for her never to leave us!"

Without anyone noticing, much less Ubirajara himself, his condition seemed to improve; at least those outbursts of his that caused the walls to shake ceased. On the other hand, he almost never left the house anymore, not even to go to the movies or the theater. He became a homebody like never before. All of the sudden, he was of the opinion that Debora was working too hard; he implied that Gloria should give the poor little girl a hand. He even resorted to demagoguery: "Let's at least try to be a little more human, damn it!"

When Debora appeared with earrings and bracelets, Gloria ran to her husband immediately, imagining the girl had found a boyfriend. Ubirajara chided her.

"Are you the only one entitled to have jewelry? That's a good one!"

The rest happened very quickly. One morning, Gloria called the police alleging that her most expensive piece of jewelry had disappeared. Her husband stood next to her, pale, saying nothing. The first thing Gloria did when the detective arrived was to take him straight to Debora's room. She led the way.

"This way, please!" In the bedroom, she even gave him a tip.

"Look underneath the pillow!"

And indeed, there it was. The detective grabbed Debora by the arm. She resisted desperately until the detective lost his patience and slapped her with the back of his hand.

Then, Debora, her lip bleeding, fell to her knees and began screaming.

"I know why she's doing this: Because she saw her husband kiss me!"

She stood face to face with the lady of the house and continued.

"Well, he did kiss me! And it wasn't just one time! It was a whole bunch of times!"

That evening, accompanied by his wife, who nudged him every now and then, Ubirajara gave his statement at the police station. He called Debora a thief and worse.

The Mausoleum

He stood for one whole hour in stunned contemplation. There lay his
wife, surrounded by the flames of four large candles, her heels touching, her
fingers interlaced. Relatives and friends kept saying, "Sit down! Sit down!"
But, wanting to remain true to his pain, he ignored their appeals. When they
insisted he exploded, "Leave me alone, will you!" He just stood there, stiffly.
Deep down, he felt that to not stand during his wife's wake would be to show
a lack of respect for the deceased. Until, one hour later, he began to exhibit
signs of tiring and, in the end, it was that physical and prosaic fact that finally
caused him to yield. He sat between two friends. A fat lady, a neighbor,
sweating, leaned over and said, "That's why I don't get on airplanes!"

That was enough: The widower's pain, which had temporarily subsided,
came back in full force. He stood up, a man possessed. And it was quite an
ordeal to restrain him. He held his head in his hands and moaned.

"Do you know what really gets to me? Huh? Do you?" he asked. "It's
that no one ever dies on the Rio-São Paulo shuttle. There's never a crash!

Ever! It's a cinch, everyone takes that flight, you can take that flight standing on your head. Am I right?"

"Yes."

He buried his face in his hands and began sobbing uncontrollably.

"So why did Arlete have to die on that stupid flight? Why?"

Several people rushed to console him.

"Take it easy, Moacir, take it easy!"

He screamed, "I want to die too, oh God!"

Love Story

They'd been married for one year. Now, in the middle of the wake, Moacir, disheveled, was revealing intimate details of their marriage in public.

"Our life was like one long honeymoon!" He gnashed his teeth as he described their epic kiss at the airport, right before the plane took off. His wife was going to São Paulo to visit a sick aunt, and Moacir, detained in Rio by a series of business meetings, could not accompany her. Now he was overcome with regret. He screamed, "Oh, if I had only known! If I had only guessed!" He defended the position that it would have been preferable, infinitely preferable, to have been on that same plane, hugging his wife, as it went down. He repeated, "How could this have happened? How could this have happened?"

At ten in the morning the procession was ready to leave for the cemetery. A Herculean effort was required to restrain Moacir in all of his wounded rage. He hurled himself at the walls and fell to the floor every chance he got. It was enough for the deceased's parents and her sisters to interrupt their crying. They didn't want him to go to the cemetery; he had to promise, "I'll be quiet! I swear I'll be as quiet as a mouse!" As it turned out, he behaved relatively well. As they were leaving the cemetery, he turned to the gravedigger, and in a heart-wrenching moment implored, "Take good care of her grave and I'll give you a tip, you hear me?" He dug his hand in his pocket, pulled out a one hundred cruzeiro bill, and handed it to the man.

"Buy yourself a beer! But don't forget what I said! All right?"

The Pain

He locked himself in his house and braced himself for a life of pain. He was prepared to suffer the rest of his life. He filled the house with portraits of his wife. According to the mean-spirited gossip in the neighborhood, there were portraits even in the kitchen. The friends and relatives began commenting among themselves, "This is crazy!" For his part, he strictly adhered to wearing black. He felt offended when his business partner suggested, in a good-natured way, "Wear a black band. Just a band. It's more modern, and it's more discreet." Moacir recoiled, and went into a rage.

"What's this talk about modernity... don't waste your breath!"

His partner tried to reason with him.

"Hold on a minute, Moacir, I'm your friend, damn it! Dressing in black is morbid, sick, unpleasant!"

"So be it! Great!" he yelled defiantly. "I like being morbid. I insist on being morbid!"

The partner was stunned. He went to tell their mutual acquaintances, "I'll be damned if Moacir hasn't gone off the deep end!" He predicted, "At this rate he'll be in the loony bin in no time."

The Partner

The partner's name was Escobar. He might not have been on the greatest terms with Moacir, but between the two of them, there were stronger ties than those of friendship: They had business interests in common. And, indeed, Moacir's absence from the firm was deeply felt. He was the administrative genius while Escobar provided the ideas. Immersed in mourning, crying constantly for his dead wife, Moacir was in no mental state to concern himself with practical matters. With good reason, Escobar grew alarmed.

"Things can't go on like this. Either Moacir returns or we're done for." He therefore dedicated his energies to wresting his partner away from his crushing pain. Every day he'd pay him a visit.

"The company is going downhill fast!"

Moacir, with a full beard, fire in his eyes, disheveled, mildly resembling the Count of Monte Cristo, sneered, "I don't give a damn!"

Escobar, horrified, insisted, "How can you say that? You have interests, duties, responsibilities."

This time Moacir simply didn't answer. He was immersed in a fiery and morbid meditation. It was obvious that his thoughts were elsewhere, in a faraway and unreachable place. Suddenly, without rhyme or reason, he began to extol his wife. He was categorical.

"You have no idea, you can't even begin to imagine! She was the best wife in the world! No wife came even close to her! Could hold a candle to her!" Putting his hand on Escobar's arm, he added, "Never again, you hear, never again will I look at another woman. I swear! You have my word!"

Escobar stood, aghast.

"Take it easy, Moacir! You can't go on like this! It's not normal! It's not natural!"

Trembling, Moacir replied, "To hell with what's normal, what's natural!" His only consolation now was the angel-themed mausoleum he had ordered in honor of his dead wife.

The Idea

Two more months went by, and Moacir was still a mess. Escobar racked his brain.

"I have to discover a way, some method, of saving this idiot!" Since he was prone to fantastical schemes and prided himself on coming up with good ideas, he soon came upon a solution. He convened a meeting with his partner's relatives, and laid it all out.

"This is where things stand," he said. "Either Moacir comes back to work or this firm will have to close its doors. Do you trust me or don't you?"

The answer was comforting and unanimous: "We do."

Escobar cleared his throat.

"I have an idea that is just what the doctor ordered. It's sure-fire. I need to know whether you authorize me, whether you give me the go ahead to use this idea. Do you?"

Silence. The relatives looked at one another. A spokesperson asked, "Can we at least know what this idea is?"

"No," Escobar said. "Secrecy is of the utmost importance. I don't want to spoil it. Suffice it to say that it's a lie. A necessary lie that will save the day. Do you authorize me? Yes or no?"

More silence. Finally, the spokesperson said, "Yes."

Escobar rubbed his hands gleefully.

"Then I'm going to dive in head first."

The Lie

He barged into his friend's house and sat next to him. As he himself would later say, his approach was to take no prisoners.

"Look here, Moacir," he began. "Your problem is women, you understand? You must find a woman or several women as soon as possible. Either that or you're done for."

Moacir, who had been seated, stood, trembling.

"Are you crazy? Have you gone mad?"

Escobar plowed ahead with impressive boldness.

"Are you up for some fun tonight?" he asked. "I know a place where the merchandise is top shelf. I'm telling you! The women are out of this world!"

Moacir's answer came in the way of a howl-like sound: "Never! Never!"

The great moment had arrived. Escobar put out his cigarette. He stared straight into Moacir's eyes and said, "You know we're bosom buddies, right?"

"Sort of."

"Very well. There's something you need to know and the sooner the better. I'm going to tell you because I don't like to see a friend of mine playing the fool."

"What?"

Escobar placed his hand on his partner's shoulder.

"Why did your wife go to São Paulo? Because of an aunt?" Escobar, triumphantly, answered his own question: "No! She went to see her lover! Yes, her lover!"

It was a frightening scene. Moacir came very close to choking his friend. But Escobar did not flinch. He made his lie persuasive, rich in details, undeniable.

"I saw them with my own two eyes, in Copacabana…" Escobar had taken the trouble to memorize the name of a randomly chosen passenger who had been on board the same flight, and he repeated the name now.

"Look at the flight list… go ahead, see if his name isn't on it. Go ahead! She made up the story about her aunt just so she could be on that flight with him."

An hour later, Moacir fell back into his chair, shattered. He sneered, "Tramp! Tramp!"

Escobar stood, victorious.

"Now are you up for some fun? Are you?"

Moacir stood with a wild look in his eyes.

"Yes."

Cherubs

All the fight having seeped out of him, he went with his friend to the aforementioned house belonging to a certain Madam Geni. He practically had to be carried out, drunk, at dawn. That same morning, without saying a word to anyone, he headed straight for the cemetery. For about fifteen minutes he stood and watched as the workers toiled away on Arlete's mausoleum. It was an outrageously priced, extremely intricate piece that depicted cherubs crowning the deceased. Suddenly, he lost it. He grabbed the closest pickax he could find, and in a rage, he charged. He smashed marble cherubs wherever he could find them. When they finally managed to subdue him, the ground was strewn with mutilated angels. They had to drag him away.

He could be heard screaming, "I'm not paying one more damn penny for this piece of crap! Not one more penny!" His voice broke as he screamed, "My wife was a bitch!"

The Divine Comedy

After seven years of marriage the only thing keeping the couple together was her husband's blackheads. Marlene loved to squeeze them. Except for this profound and all-important task, they had nothing in common. Under the same roof, surrounded by the same walls, they felt like utter strangers with nothing to talk about, no shared interests, no shared dreams. The tedium that engulfed them was exacerbated by the fact that they had no children. Until one day Godofredo decided to take a stand and tackle the issue of conjugal boredom head on.

"You know what our best bet is?" he asked. "The best bet? The great solution?"

"What?"

"Separation. What do you think? Let's separate."

Godofredo's head was on his wife's lap. Marlene was engrossed in her task, squeezing and collecting her husband's blackheads with utter delight.

"So? How about it? What do you think?" Godofredo asked.

Marlene was in a state of near ecstasy. She had just made a discovery of the greatest significance. Her mouth watering, she announced, "I found an amazing one! It's gigantic!"

She wouldn't rest until she had extracted the monumental blackhead. Then, satisfied, nearly euphoric, she turned to her husband.

"What did you say?"

"Let's separate."

At first she didn't understand.

"Separate?"

"That's right," Godofredo said.

She didn't make a scene or appear shocked; she merely seemed mildly surprised.

"Why?" she asked. "What do we get out of it? Honestly, I don't see why we should."

"There are lots of reasons. Come on, you know there are! Do you want one? Our life is mind-numbingly boring. I guarantee you this: There is not a duller, more meaningless existence than ours. Is there? Come on, be honest."

Marlene was preparing to survey her husband's face a second time.

"Give me three days to think about it, OK?" she said distractedly.

Godofredo thought about it.

"Three days? OK."

The Neighbor

In their marital history they could not remember a major squabble, a serious rift, a long-held grudge. They shared a miserable existence together; that was all. As far as Godofredo was concerned, monotony was more than enough reason to separate. As for Marlene, for whom the opinion of relatives and neighbors carried the weight of the Last Judgment, she had her doubts. Be that as it may, since she was a martyr, a Joan of Arc of tedium, it is likely that she would have agreed sooner or later. But an interesting thing happened: The following day she met Osvaldina, her new neighbor. They were chatting about this and that, and then the neighbor began praising her own husband to the skies.

LIFE AS IT IS

"Maybe there's a wife happier than me in this world, but I doubt it very much!"

That was just for starters. Several women had assembled by now. Osvaldina continued as if addressing a rally.

"I've been married for five years now. OK. Do you think my honeymoon is over? Think again!" There was a silent gasp from the neighbors and very likely a few spiteful thoughts. A frolicsome and perpetual honeymoon was unheard of on that street where the dreariness of married life typically set in after a week of wedlock. But the neighbor wasn't through.

"Today Jeremias kissed me as if it were our first night, etc, etc, etc."

That evening, when Godofredo arrived home, he found Marlene seething. She exploded when she told him about the new neighbor.

"She's a big phony! Who does she think she is? Does she think she's better? Please!"

"Just forget about it!" Godofredo growled.

Her anger was so sincere and profound that she just couldn't let go.

"Have you seen her husband? Have you? Huh? He's a mouse, a pipsqueak! I'll tell you something else: He's not half the man you are; he's no match for you!"

Godofredo was crouching by the radio searching for a station. Suddenly, his wife turned to him. What she said next was cryptic.

"Wait and see. I'll show her. When I put my mind to it I can be downright Machiavellian!"

The Change

The following morning, as her husband readied himself for work, she announced, "I'll walk you to the gate." He was putting on his jacket and froze suddenly.

"Is this some kind of a joke?" His reaction should not have come as a surprise, considering that since their ten-day honeymoon she had never paid him such an honor. Feeling defensive, she raised her voice.

"Why does it have to be a joke? Gee whiz! Aren't you my husband? Should I treat my husband like a bum?"

He couldn't make heads or tails of the situation.

"Unbelievable!" he snarled.

And he walked out the front door. Marlene gave him her arm and said, "Pay attention. When we get to the gate, I'm going to kiss you, OK?"

What happened at the front gate Godofredo would later describe as an all-out show. Hanging from her husband's arm, Marlene gave him a kiss on the mouth worthy of a movie. As the stunned Godofredo walked away, Marlene leaned over the gate and was all smiles as she fluttered her fingers bye-bye.

What had transpired was so unusual that Godofredo called her from his job downtown, smoldering. He didn't mince words.

"Have you been drinking? Have you gone nuts? What was that all about?"

She was at a loss for words.

He went on, "It's been two hundred years since you kissed me on the mouth. Why the spectacle?"

The Explanation

When he arrived home that evening, he sat his wife down and she told him everything. The one who had started with the amorous scenes at the front gate for the neighbors and occasional passersby to see was the new neighbor. Indeed, Osvaldina had given an unbelievably suggestive show. Marlene had witnessed this and become livid. "I'll show her," she vowed right then and there. Now, to her husband, she said, "That stuck-up diva wants to rub my face in her happiness. Maybe she thinks she's the only wife whose husband loves her. No other woman is loved by her husband; she's the only one. But she's messing with the wrong woman!"

Duly informed, Godofredo raised his voice too.

"You decided to give a show, and I'm the one who has to suffer the consequences? Me?"

All worked up now, pacing back and forth, Marlene came to a full stop.

"What do I have a husband for, huh?"

"But think about it!" he answered. "Stop and think for one minute. Weren't we just talking about splitting? Separating?"

It's a wonder Marlene didn't hit him.

"Do you think I'm going to give that phony the satisfaction? If I separate she'll yell it from the mountaintop; she'll spread it around town that I failed as a wife. No, never! Didn't you marry me? Besides, let me break the news to you: There's no divorce in Brazil. Now you're going to have to stick it out!"

Livid, he threw up his arms.

"This beats everything! This really beats everything."

Rivalry

So every morning the two couples put on a show of utter marital bliss. At the front gate Osvaldina would grab her husband and plunge into the most salacious demonstrations imaginable. She would kiss him as if the poor devil were being shipped off to Korea or some such destination. For her part, Marlene refused to be shown up. Since both husbands left for work at about the same time, both spectacles often occurred simultaneously. At first Godofredo was embarrassed by this charade and was reluctant to participate. Marlene, however, was unbending. She laid out the situation in precise terms.

"It's like this," she said. "Here, inside, you can kick me in the teeth. But not outside. Outside we have to be lovey-dovey no matter what, OK? I never asked anything of you. That's all I ask of you."

Godofredo scratched his head, unsure what to make of the situation. But he was good-natured, agreeable and weak at heart. He understood that for Marlene this early-morning farce was a question of life and death. He sighed, defeated, "OK! OK!"

True Love

Every day Marlene spurred him to new heights.

"Now we're going to really show them. Tell me you're madly in love with me and I'll do the same." Little by little Godofredo's competitive spirit, his sense of rivalry, began to take hold. In the evenings, after dinner, the two would step out and engage in groping sessions worthy of teenagers. People on the street began talking, "Those two are unfit for minors!" At the movies they simulated make out sessions in such a spirited fashion that it made the other patrons uncomfortable. Back home behind closed doors they would take off their masks and behave with their usual detachment. They pretended so much, however, that one night in the privacy of their bedroom Godofredo turned to his wife and said, "Come over here and give me a little kiss." It was as if he were savoring a new and magical flavor for the very first time.

He stood and moved in to give her another ardent kiss. Coming up for air, he stammered, "I like that."

And that was that. From then on they began a new and illicit honeymoon.

The Silent Husband

Twenty-four hours before the wedding, Dona Eunice noticed a sadness in her daughter's eyes and asked, "What's the matter?"

Maria Lucia tried to brush off the question.

"Nothing. Nothing, Mother, why?"

Dona Eunice insisted.

"It's just that you seem rather, well, strange, that's all. Did something happen between the two of you?"

Maria Lucia laughed nervously.

"Oh, Mother. Don't be silly! Why would we fight the day before our wedding?" She clasped her hands. "God forbid!"

Not wanting to prod her daughter, Dona Eunice sighed, "Great! Just as well." But she wasn't convinced. She sensed something insincere, even fake in her daughter's smile. Half an hour later she surprised her with the question, "Are you happy?"

"Me?"

"Yes."

Maria Lucia hesitated for a split second.

"Yes, I am. Why shouldn't I be?" She paused. "I have an almost perfect husband."

Dona Eunice was taken aback. "Almost?"

Something seemed to be bothering Maria Lucia. Finally she spoke.

"He doesn't talk much. He almost never talks. He's like a statue!"

Discreet

It didn't seem so bad. Dona Eunice, who had been seated until now, stood.

"If that's his only fault, then thank God!"

They left it at that. Dona Eunice, an optimist by nature, gave the matter no more thought. In theory, the union of Maria Lucia and Abelardo was what you would call a perfect match. Both were healthy, good-looking and very similar in education, temperament and wealth. In fact, Dona Eunice had on more than one occasion told her daughter, "Maria Lucia, you should be jumping for joy. Finding a man like Abelardo nowadays is hard, very hard."

"I know, Mother."

But Maria Lucia had a point when she described the young man as uncommunicative and taciturn. In truth, Abelardo spoke little, very little. He measured his every word and seemed to be always immersed in a cloud of silence that could be very disconcerting. At times, with sudden irritation, Maria Lucia would plead, "Speak, say something, darling!" but he would simply smile and not answer. Mind you, the young woman loved him; she loved him dearly. She would sigh, "I am marrying him for better or for worse, so be it." And in fact, they exchanged their wedding vows the following day. Maria Lucia quickly became caught up in the festivities, forgot her worries, and reveled in being a bride. When she arrived home from church she changed her clothes. Forty minutes later, no longer wearing her veil, her wedding dress, or the wreath of flowers in her hair, she departed with Abelardo to the mountains where they would spend their honeymoon.

The Silent One

The automobile sped along the Rio-Petropolis Road at a smooth, almost imperceptible pace. On the open road, Maria Lucia, with a tone of sadness in her voice, said, "Honey, ever since we left the house you haven't said one word!"

No reply. Abelardo simply squeezed her hand. Ten more minutes passed. It pained the young woman that her husband was as quiet as the driver. But she wouldn't leave it at that. She tugged at his arm and pleaded in an anguished tone, "Speak, honey. Say something!"

Maria Lucia waited for him to speak. Nothing. He simply smiled faintly. She insisted.

"Abelardo! You have nothing to say to me on your wedding day? How could you?"

Instead of answering, Abelardo gave her a quick, short kiss. Then he passed his hand through her hair without uttering a word. With heavy heart, Maria Lucia sighed, "If you'd only speak you'd be the perfect man. I'd give the world to hear you say something!"

The Honeymoon

According to most accounts a honeymoon should last one month. On the twelfth day, however, to the surprise and astonishment of the whole family, the newlyweds were back in town. Dona Eunice inquired upon seeing them, "What's this all about? What are you doing here?"

Abelardo, standing, answered laconically, "Ask her."

Dona Eunice, extremely worked up, turned to her son-in-law.

"Sit down, Abelardo."

The young man obeyed, picked up a newspaper and yawned. The mother then grabbed her daughter and escorted her out of the room. In her mother's bedroom, Maria Lucia began to cry. She covered her face with her hands and sobbed.

"I can't take it anymore, Mother! I can't. I want to, but I can't!"

Dona Eunice was taken aback and didn't know what to say or do. She sat next to her daughter and held her hand.

"Tell me what happened."

Maria Lucia stood, walked from side to side and stopped suddenly.

"He doesn't talk, Mother! He doesn't say a word! Do you know what it's like to spend hours, entire days, next to a man who doesn't utter a word?"

She held her head in her hands.

"I'll end up going crazy. I swear I will!"

Dona Eunice simply listened in silence as if trying to understand. Finally she spoke.

"Is that it?"

Maria Lucia erupted in anger.

"And you think it's nothing? Oh, Mother!"

"Don't 'oh' me! I can't believe you're making such a fuss over something so silly. Calm down."

Shaken, Maria Lucia replied, "It might seem silly to you, but know this: I'm going to ask for a separation. Take your pick, either we separate or you won't have a daughter for much longer."

Panic

There was panic in the family. What caused the commotion was that there didn't seem to be any real, legitimate motive for a separation. The father was furious.

"What do you mean? Are you crazy!"

Shattered, his daughter yelled, "God, I can't take it anymore!"

Aunts, sisters, cousins exchanged glances as if they suspected there was something wrong with her mental state. As a matter of fact, insanity was the only possible explanation for her behavior. There was a pilgrimage of relatives. Their words varied but their argument, or arguments, were essentially the same: "Gosh, that's not a flaw! No one leaves a husband because he talks too little!"

The father went even further.

"I can see you getting separated, divorced, whatever the hell you want, but there has to be a good reason. That's not a reason. Not here, not in China, not anywhere! Your mother has a heart condition. Do you really want her to have to go through all of this?"

In tears, Maria Lucia said, "When I see my husband sitting in silence, for hours on end, without saying a single word, I feel like he's plotting a crime!"

The father was really worked up by now.

"This is ridiculous! It makes me want to laugh!"

But the young woman, under all of this pressure, seemed unbending.

"You want me to go back to him, don't you? But I'm not going back!" She screamed, straining her voice, "I'm not going back, I'm not going back, I'm not going back!"

The Solution

She went back. She had spent seven days away from her husband. He had let her leave without uttering a single word and now in welcoming her back he was more silent than ever. In fact, one would have thought that nothing had transpired, nothing at all. With an inhuman serenity he opened the door for Maria Lucia and kissed her on the forehead. And that was it. The father, who had accompanied his daughter, rubbed his hands together and tried to make the best of things.

"Everything is OK then. Let bygones be bygones. Got to leave. Au revoir."

It was nighttime and dinner was served. Husband and wife ate in the most desperate of silences imaginable. Maria Lucia thought to herself in anguish, "I can't take it. God, I can't take it anymore."

After drinking their after-dinner coffee, they moved to the porch. He perfunctorily grabbed a cigarette and lit it. Beside herself, his wife tugged at his arm and implored, "Speak! Say something! One word." She raised her voice in desperation. "Just one word. Say something. Say it!"

He sat there mute, and put his cigarette out in the ashtray. She could take it no longer. She stood up and ran inside. Abelardo simply sat there for two hours, buried in a deep and empty meditation. Late at night, sleepy now, he decided to go upstairs. On arriving at the top of the stairs he stopped. At the end of the hallway he saw a shape suspended in the air. Desperate, no longer able to stand her husband who spoke so little, so very little, Maria Lucia had hanged herself. Her skirt fluttered in the air.

Unscrupulous

On their fourth or fifth date he picked up her right hand.

"What's this?" he asked.

"An engagement ring."

"You're engaged?"

"Huh! You didn't know?"

"I swear I didn't."

"Well, I am," she said. "Engaged. The wedding is in May."

"You're serious?"

"Cross my heart!"

Geraldo huffed, "I'm stunned! I'm bowled over!"

He had met her outside of a movie theater, just as the show was letting out. Sensing she was staring at him, he felt emboldened. She might not be a knockout, but she did have a cute face and body, he reasoned. Geraldo hesitated, then decided to give it a try.

"Are you busy, or can we kill some time together?"

Ten minutes later they were chatting on a park bench. Jandira confessed, "There was something I liked about you right away." She wasn't lying. Very spontaneous and intuitive, she was a woman for whom first impressions meant everything. They made a date for the following day. Geraldo was all smiles when they parted. Rather shy, he found carefree women to be the sweetest thing in the world. Jandira fit the bill perfectly. True, she had a ring on her right hand. But he made up his mind, "It's probably just a ring." And he forgot about it. On the fifth date, however, he asked her straight out. She broke the news to him. If he still had any doubts, Jandira calmly opened her purse, took out a page torn out of a magazine with a beautiful picture of a bride, and showed it to him. Geraldo's eyes grew wide.

"You see this?" she asked.

"Yeah."

"That's the pattern for my wedding dress. Isn't it beautiful?"

He scratched his head, bewildered.

"Yeah."

She folded the page and put it back in her purse. She looked at him, very serenely, almost sweetly. For a moment Geraldo didn't know what to say. Finally, he sighed.

"Can I ask you a question?"

"Sure."

He cleared his throat.

"Don't you feel guilty doing this to your boyfriend?"

"Why?"

"Answer me."

"My fiancé is stuffy! Way too stuffy!"

The Fiancé

That same night Geraldo needed to vent his frustrations. He thought of several friends and finally hit upon Antunes. He told him what had happened and asked for advice.

"You know me," Geraldo said. "I think infidelity is revolting. I don't understand how a woman can cheat on a man!"

Antunes listened in silence.

"Are you done?" he asked.

"Yes."

Antunes leaned forward and planted both elbows firmly on the table.

"Don't be a moron! Do you think she's the first woman who ever cheated on a man? Go for it!"

Not convinced, Geraldo shuddered.

"But it feels dirty!"

His friend exploded.

"So what! It's a piece of cake; it's a cinch! No one gives a damn! Dive in!"

The Love Affair

Putting his scruples aside, Geraldo went ahead with the affair. But against his wishes and without realizing it, he became increasingly obsessed with the girl's fiancé. On his dates with Jandira he would dwell almost exclusively on him.

"What's he like?"

Jandira would oblige with details.

"Can you believe he hasn't kissed me on the mouth yet?"

"Why?"

"How should I know!"

"That's weird."

"You know what his big thing is? You can't do anything until after the wedding. Even kiss."

"That's strange!"

"Isn't it?"

Since they were talking about kissing, she rested her head on his shoulder.

"I like the way you kiss me. Come on! Kiss me!"

In a kind of guilty rage, he obliged. And thus their love story continued. Until one day a coincidence occurred. He saw them together for the first time, her and her fiancé, at a movie theater. She seemed perfectly affectionate and happy next to him. Geraldo managed to resist for about fifteen, twenty minutes, until he could take it no longer. He stood up, indignant, and marched out in the middle of the movie. He couldn't sleep that night. Between 11 p.m. and 7 a.m. he smoked two packs of cigarettes. Then, in one of those sudden flashes, he understood that deep down he loved Jandira about as much as any man can love a woman. Holding his head in both hands, he had the following insight: "I'm being cheated on too! She's cheating on me with her fiancé!"

Dilemma

When they met that afternoon, he was seething.

"It's either me or him!" His lips trembling, he asked her, "Or do you think I'll share you with another man? No way!"

Taken aback and rather amused, she asked him a question.

"Who's the fiancé?"

"He is."

"That's right. As the fiancé he has all of the rights, whereas you have none. It's as clear as day, honey. As clear as day!"

Beside himself, he grabbed her by the arms.

"Let's put an end to this once and for all. He's the fiancé and gets to marry you. And I'm the chump. No ma'am! I'm not interested!" When they were about ready to say goodbye, Geraldo proposed a solution.

"Let's do the following: Call off the wedding."

"Then what?"

"Well. Then you marry me. OK?"

She took a while to answer.

"OK."

Doubt

Everything seemed settled. However, she showed up for their following date distraught.

"Why should I break up with my fiancé? Aren't things fine just the way they are?" She tried to convince him, "I'll still be with you, silly!"

He asked her an anguished question: "Even after the wedding?"

"Of course!" she said.

For a brief moment he was speechless. Suddenly, he became furious.

"No, I'm not interested! Not that way I'm not!"

"Why?"

He was almost in tears by now.

"Because the fiancé has all of the advantages. The husband lives the life of a pasha. He has it made! Meanwhile, the lover is a poor slob, a loser, a clown. I don't want to be the lover, OK?"

She sighed.

"If you say so!"

Drama

From that day on whenever they met, he'd ask her anxiously, "Did you break up with him yet?" She'd answer, "No, not yet. Tomorrow, for sure." But "tomorrow" would never arrive. Until one afternoon he lost it and yelled at her. A steely look of resolve came over her.

"It's not going to work out. We should split up."

He looked at her bug-eyed.

"Why won't it work out?"

"Because I love both of you," she said softly.

He stepped back, aghast.

"Both of us?"

She looked him dead in the eye and responded affirmatively.

"Are you OK with that?" she asked.

All bent out of shape, Geraldo said, "You know what you deserve? With all your ways? Do you? A shot in the mouth! You tramp!"

Then, perfectly in charge of her faculties, she calmly lifted her purse off the grass and stood.

"Too bad!"

Stunned, he watched her walk away. He couldn't resist. He chased after her down the empty tree-lined park lane, sobbing, "I'm OK with it! I'm OK with it!"

Then, almost out of breath, he said, "I want to be the husband, though! I don't want to be the lover!"

They were married one year later. In both the civil and religious ceremonies, Geraldo saw, standing there among the guests, wearing a sharp navy blue suit appropriate to the occasion, the ex-fiancé.

The Grandson

He nearly checked out at fifty-four. One day it looked like he would make it, the next like he wouldn't. He ended up surviving and was taken off the respirator. Sensing he was at death's doorstep, though, he called in his wife and only daughter.

"My days are numbered!" he began, overcome with emotion.

The wife did what one would expect and protested.

"Don't be silly!" she said. "Why numbered? Oh, please!"

For her part, their daughter, exceedingly cute, knocked on the nearest piece of wood.

"You're obsessing, Dad."

"I know what I'm talking about," he insisted. "I have one foot in the grave. Any day now I'll keel over."

He was trying to be strong, but his eyes welled up. He cleared his throat and said, "Before I die I want two things. First, I want to see my daughter married. Second, I want to get to know my grandson."

The daughter, who was prone to crying, had just blown her nose in a little handkerchief.

"Of course, Dad! You'll be at my wedding. Don't even think of not attending. And you'll baptize my son. God willing!"

The mother, standing by her side, corroborated what her daughter said.

"Of course you will!"

The Problem

Jurema had been dating Clementino for about one year with her parents' knowledge and blessing. It was an uneventful relationship, without great passion, but stable. They should have been engaged, but since Clementino earned little and both were set in their ways, they kept postponing it. Jurema would confide to her girlfriends, "Things are fine the way they are!" One of her friends was astounded by her infinite patience.

"Now I understand everything!" she exclaimed.

"What do you understand?"

Her friend lowered her voice and gave her verdict.

"You're a cold fish!"

And life went on. The father's illness – he had had a heart attack – changed everything, though. Jurema was sentimental and, what's more, an excellent daughter. She figured, "Daddy might die after all, and then..." Twenty minutes later, with her mother's encouragement, she called Clementino at work.

"Come home early, sweetie. Great news." That evening, when he arrived, the three of them huddled together to discuss an early wedding. Clementino, a bank clerk and methodical by nature, grew alarmed.

"But I don't earn enough!"

To which both women responded, "Too bad! We'll just have to make do! No one dies of hunger in Brazil!"

Jurema was all worked up now. She put her foot down.

"I want to do this for my father. I just have to!"

Clementino was dazed. He scratched his head.

"Damn it! Damn it!" It wasn't so much the wedding, but the necessity to produce a child that terrified him. He resisted at all cost.

"Everything is so expensive! A pacifier used to cost fifty cents. Now it's a fortune!"

No argument could make him come round. Until, finally, the mother had the last word.

"You'll live with us. If we can feed two of you, we can feed four of you!"

Jurema escorted him to the door. She was in high spirits, which was unusual for her.

"Honey, God willing, Daddy will have his grandson. I can't wait!"

The Wedding

Clementino had no choice but to agree. The next day, however, very early, before going to work, he paid a friend a visit. It so happened that the friend was in his fourth year of medical school. The young man, rudely awakened in bed with a shake, barked back, "Leave me alone!" Finally, he sat up, sleepily. Clementino was there to pose a question.

"Let's say a guy has such-and-such a condition. Can he have a child?"

The friend was categorical.

"Absolutely not!"

Clementino insisted.

"Are you certain, or are you just guessing?

"Get off my case! Of course I'm certain, you idiot!"

Since Genival was only a fourth-year medical student, Clementino consulted two or three real doctors. There was total unanimity: A man who had this certain condition was incapable, completely incapable of fathering a child. Since one of the doctors knew Jurema, Clementino insisted, "Not a word! In due time she'll know everything. Not now. Now is not the time."

For the next two months, everyone was consumed with the wedding preparations to the exclusion of everything else. Much to the dismay of the groom, however, no one could stop talking about the future grandson. Others spoke of this remote, hypothetical child as if he were about to be born any day. The neighborhood women had already picked out a name, the sex of the child and everything else. An aunt, who considered herself an expert on the subject, piped up, "Her waist size is perfect for children!" Jurema leaned in closer and asked the assembled mothers, "Does it really hurt as much as everyone says?" Then there was the old man. Ever since his heart attack, he'd start crying over any little thing. His wife or daughter would have to calm him down: "Don't get yourself all worked up! Be careful!" Clementino would listen to all of this and would remind everyone, "Children are a complicated matter. Sometimes it takes a while. It doesn't happen just like that."

Protests rained down upon him.

"Yes it does! It happens when you least expect it! What are you talking about?"

They got married in city hall and in church. At 11:30 pm, after the last guest had left, the newlyweds retired also. Then after a kiss, not as intense as the situation warranted, Clementino sighed, "Sweetie, I have some bad news." Later he would regret his timing. At that very moment, though, he was swept up in a sudden bout of sincerity.

"I can't have children," he said, slowly and solemnly. "The doctor told me I won't be able to have children, ever. Do you understand? Ever…"

Jurema looked at him aghast.

"What do you mean can't? How about my dad? How will I ever be able to show my face again to my dad and everyone else?" Walking back and forth, the poor devil kept repeating, "Damn! Damn!" Suddenly, she flew into a rage. She grabbed him.

"Why are you telling me this now? Why didn't you tell me this before, huh?"

The young man tried to grab her and kiss her. She managed to shake herself loose.

"Don't touch me!" she said in no uncertain terms.

The Little Grandson

Jurema spent her entire wedding night wide-awake. In the morning, miserable from the lack of sleep, she unloaded.

"I feel like never leaving this room again!" Thus, day after day, their lives became a living hell. The parents couldn't talk about anything other than the remote grandson. The old man did the math.

"We should book an appointment at the doctor in a month's time…"

His wife objected, "One month is not enough time. She won't even be showing a tummy by then." In two weeks time the poor heart patient was already looking at his daughter a little more carefully for some sign of physical transformation. In one month's time, Jurema, in despair, went to the doctor. When she came back, the father, trembling, asked, "So, how did it go?"

She put her purse on the table; she sat down, and her eyes welled up. "Nothing."

The father's reaction was childish and frightening.

"Oh, come on!"

That night Jurema and her husband had a talk. He tried his best to sound reasonable.

"It's like this: We have to fool your dad. Forget about telling him the truth."

Then, beside herself, Jurema latched on to one last, frantic hope.

"What if the doctors are wrong? Who knows?"

Clementino, unnerved, admitted, "Maybe…" Jurema, in her desperation, made all sorts of vows. She fell to her knees, and in her husband's presence, she lifted her arms to heaven and sobbed.

"I want a child! I want a child! Who knows, it might be a question of positioning. What if I put a pillow underneath?"

The Grandfather

Two, three, four months went by. Every month it was the same thing. Finally, Jurema told the doctor everything. Old and kindhearted, he had no qualms about deceiving the family; he was vague.

"Sometimes it takes a while."

As for the disappointed grandfather, he was constantly on edge. Occasionally, he would grumble, "A marriage without children is almost immoral." At other times he would cross-examine his son-in-law with sarcastic comments.

"So, how about it, young man? What's the matter with you? Is my grandson on the way or not?"

Or he would turn to his daughter, somberly: "Amazing that my daughter would deny me this favor!"

Three more months went by. At Jurema's birthday party, in the presence of all the guests, the father raised the question, "So, after all, whose fault is it? My daughter's or my son-in-law's?"

The awkwardness in the room was palpable. The girl's mother, who was a know-it-all, was categorical.

"It can only be his fault. Because in my family the women give birth like clockwork. My mother had fifteen children."

The Father

Clementino had lost a lot of weight and seemed always dejected. He had even been seen wandering around the streets talking to himself. One night he arrived home to find his wife face down on the bed sobbing. Suddenly, he was overcome by love and pity for her. He startled her by announcing, in an outburst, "You're going to have that child. Whatever it takes!"

It was shortly after that that he began to appear at home with a friend, a young, strong, handsome fellow brimming with vigor. His name was Richard, and he became a very close friend of the family. Jurema's parents would sigh, "Now, that's what I call a real man!" The three would go out on drives, picnics, daytrips to Barra da Tijuca together. Once, returning from one of those trips, Clementino made a cryptic comment to his wife: "Richard is very discreet. Completely trustworthy." Three months later she returned ecstatic from her doctor's visit.

"Finally! Finally!" The house was filled with joy. Neighbors appeared en masse to offer congratulations. The husband arrived home later that evening. He put on a forced smile and blamed the flu to explain his downcast appearance.

That night, in the bedroom, behind closed doors, husband and wife had a heart-to-heart. She stared crying, and he hugged her to his chest.

"You did nothing wrong." Crying too, he went further: "I'll love him as if he were my own."

The Mystery Woman

He asked his buddies point-blank, "Am I good-looking or what?"

One of them, who was drinking a soda pop from a bottle through a little straw, answered, "I don't think men are good-looking; if you ask me they're all butt-ugly."

They found this funny and laughed. Andrezinho, however, in his belted blazer and shirt a shade of gray that bordered on purple, insisted.

"I know I am. Women love me."

"All women?"

He shoved both hands in his pockets.

"All women."

Just then Peixoto, who was seated at a corner table sipping his coffee, stood. He came closer, still chewing on a piece of bread, butter running down his chin like drool. He sat next to Andrezinho and spoke with his mouth full.

"I'm going to prove that you're full of it," he said. "You wanna see, huh?"

Andrezinho leaned back in his chair.

"Fat chance!" he said.

"Fat chance? Listen up, you guys too: I know a girl who won't give you the time of day. I'll bet on it!"

Andrezinho winked at the others. He leaned in and said mischievously, "What if you're wrong?"

"If I'm wrong, you get to spit in my face."

Andrezinho stood and announced: "You're on!"

The Hunk

Wherever he went he liked to ask, "Am I good-looking or what?" At first it was a joke. But, little by little, through force of repetition, it became a habit, a vice.

Interestingly, it was not rare for him when introduced to someone for the first time, instead of saying "Pleased to meet you," to ask, "Am I good-looking or what?"

It became second nature. Since he happened to be really good-looking anyway, and furthermore, very congenial, everyone found it funny. It should be added that he was tremendously successful in love. At home, the telephone wouldn't stop ringing. Girls of all types and shapes hounded him. It was said that even married women much older than him adored him. The part-tender, part-childish, part-sensual way in which he extolled his own looks made him that much more attractive to them. Furthermore, for Andrezinho, a confessed Narcissus, the same vanity extended to the clothes he wore. He liked to show off socks of an extravagant yellow hue, multicolored ties, not to mention his shoes. He would ask acquaintances point-blank, "Not bad, huh? Classy, right?"

"Sort of."

To which he would simply laugh, "They can't get enough of me!"

The Mystery Woman

Until that day in the café when Peixoto, who disliked Andrezinho, said he knew this woman. Andrezinho leapt to his feet. With the instinct of a passionate, born seducer, he put his hand on Peixoto's shoulder.

"As far as I'm concerned, there is no such thing as a woman who can't be seduced."

Peixoto, whose one leg was shorter than the other, was a man of few words; he stuck to his guns.

"For your information, this one can't. Two hundred guys like you can't get her." Andrezinho rubbed his hands together, relishing the conquest that to him seemed near and inevitable.

"Just give me the name, address and phone number; I'll take care of the rest."

Peixoto simply flashed a sardonic half smile.

"Why? Why should I? It's no use."

"Are you afraid?"

Peixoto stood.

"Forget it, forget it. I don't want to see a friend of mine play the fool. See you later."

He limped towards the door with his one leg shorter than the other. Andrezinho followed at his heels.

"Tell me more about this dame! Is she pretty?"

Peixoto stopped.

"Is she pretty?" he said gnashing his teeth. "A sight to behold! Two hundred times finer than Hedy Lamarr! Puts Lana Turner to shame!"

Love

That night, Andrezinho had trouble falling asleep. He was used to beautiful women, to easy conquests, but the truth of the matter is that Peixoto had diabolically planted a seed. Who might she be? What was she like? He imagined a name and then a face; then he imagined several names and several faces for this mystery woman. In the morning, as he brushed his teeth, he was still fixating on her. He rode the bus with a friend. First he asked him, "Am I good-looking or what?" Then he made the following admission: "I've fallen for a girl I don't know from a bar of soap. Don't you find that funny?"

He called Peixoto from his office.

"Stop playing dirty. I want you to tell me right now, who's the dame?"

Peixoto cruelly relished the moment.

"I thought you had enough women. That you had to kick them out of bed."

"Single, married or widowed?" Andrezinho demanded.

Peixoto was unwavering.

"It's no use, because I'm not going to tell you. Or do you think my job is to find women for you?"

Andrezinho was taken aback.

"Look here, you son of a bitch: Wasn't this your idea? Wasn't it?"

He agreed it had been.

"Yes. But I've changed my mind. What do I get out of this, huh? What? Nothing!" Andrezinho hung up, stunned, and said to himself, "Well, I'll be damned!"

Imagination

That night they met at the bar. Andrezinho, whose imagination was running rampant, dragged Peixoto to a corner table. He monopolized his friend and gave him his undivided attention. He kept the beer flowing to try to get on his good side, and, in fact, the more Peixoto drank, the more he opened up. Licking the foam from his lips, he revealed that the woman knew Andrezinho.

Andrezinho was surprised.

"Oh, she knows me? And what does she think of me?"

Semi-drunk, Peixoto winked.

"She thinks you're a moron. A big stupid moron!"

This stung Andrezinho.

"You're lying!"

"Cross my heart!"

The conversation continued as the two drank prodigious amounts of beer. To make Andrezinho's mouth water, Peixoto exaggerated a little.

"She's fine, real fine. She melts the sidewalk when she walks down the street. She's scorching!" Finally, emboldened by the beer, he began cursing like a man possessed. "Look here you stupid oaf! Yeah, I'm a cripple, that's right! But you know what my revenge will be?" He paused to catch his breath. "That you will never meet this dame, you understand?" In his drunken rage, he tore into him viciously. "At least this one you're not going to have because I won't let you!"

Obsession

Three or four days later, Andrezinho admitted, in a panic, to his closest friends: "I'm in love, and I don't even know who she is. Can you believe it?" He sent envoys to Peixoto with desperate appeals.

But Peixoto would not budge; he made a gesture as if closing a zipper: "My lips are sealed."

And he added, "You think I give a damn if Andrezinho is handsome? It means nothing to me." The truth of the matter is that after his outburst at the bar, Peixoto changed when it came to Andrezinho. When his friend, or better said, ex-friend would approach him, he would fold his arms and stare at him blankly.

"Just tell me who she is," Andrezinho implored. "Just give me a name. I just want a name. That's all."

Peixoto smothered the cigarette ember out in the bottom of the ashtray. He appeared to hesitate then leaned in.

"The name I can't tell you. All you need to know is this: She's the finest woman in all of Rio de Janeiro. The finest, you hear?"

Andrezinho left in despair. His friends, concerned for his well-being, tried to talk some sense into him.

"What if Peixoto is just pulling your leg? I bet you that's it!"

Unable to listen to reason, he exploded, "I just want her name. The name is enough. Or at least a photo!" He stopped saying "Am I good-looking, or what?" and "Classy, huh?" He admitted, "I'll go crazy, if I haven't already." At work, he spent hours on end in a feverish and futile meditation. Until one day he received the news: Peixoto had died crossing the street, crushed between a bus and a trolley.

Andrezinho screamed, "Dead? That's not possible! It can't be!" About fifteen minutes later he entered the morgue. When he saw Peixoto there, on the table, silent forever, he knew he was doomed to love a woman he had never even met. He snapped. He threw himself at the body, he shook it, and screamed, "Tell me her name! I want the name! Tell me!"

They had to pull him away and subdue him. Then he fell to his knees on the tile floor. The sound he made as he cried bordered on a howl.

The Blind Cat

The boy was the darling of that family of women. The only two men were the father, a frustrated doctor, and Bebeto, an only son who was five at the time. Raised clutching the skirts of his mother, his aunts and the black nanny, Bebeto was subjected to an extreme and hysterical affection and turned out to be really something. In spite of his age he still used a pacifier, and in the absence of one he would put his five fingers in his gluttonous little mouth and suck ferociously. On his fifth birthday the aunts gathered around in a circle and placed Bebeto in the middle. Then one of them leaned in and asked, "What would you like to be when you grow up?"

Silence. Frightened, with his little finger in his nose, the boy seemed uncertain of his calling in life. One of the aunts, exhibiting a maladroitness typical of adults, offered up the following example of her wit: "President would be nice, don't you think?"

Laughter. Then the father approached, smoking the cheapest cigar imaginable. He looked over the assembled shoulders and announced, "He's going to be a doctor – end of story. A doctor like his dad!"

Medicine

That night in the conjugal bedroom, Dr. Sinval and Dona Detinha had a heart-to-heart. The wife, who had a bias against medicine, asked, "Why a doctor? So he can starve to death like you?"

Standing in the middle of the bedroom, unbuttoning his shirt, her husband took exception.

"Have you ever gone hungry, huh? Give me a break!"

The truth of the matter was that Dr. Sinval bore the weight of two failures in his life – one at the clinic and the other at home. He himself, with brutal bitterness, would complain, "I'm a bum in my own home!" All of his opinions in that house were considered, out of hand, as "dead wrong." Unappreciated by his wife and sisters-in-law, his one meager pleasure in life was his foul-smelling cigars. Accustomed to defeat, Dr. Sinval was already bracing himself for new frustrations by way of his son. Until, suddenly, an ominous event occurred that slightly tipped the balance in his favor. Bebeto was only eight when he was surprised by his mother with a pocket knife in his hand, shaving off the leg of a live bird. What more could you ask for? How could you argue with such overwhelming evidence? Dona Detinha picked up the little bird, still quivering, and hurried into the house, euphoric. She exhibited the legless creature as if it were a small, precious trophy.

"He's going to be a doctor! He's going to be a doctor!"

That evening, when her husband arrived, Dona Detinha announced, filled with emotion: "He's going to be a surgeon!"

Destiny

Time went by, and Bebeto, always treated with kid gloves, grew up, finished high school, etc., etc. When he was about to enter college, Dr. Sinval called him in for a talk.

"Come here son, come here!" He grabbed a cigar from his pocket, bit off the tip and asked, "So, what type of medicine do you want to practice?"

The young man did not hesitate; he looked up and dropped a bomb: "I want to be a veterinarian."

He was being sincere. The ex-slasher of birds' legs had taken a one-hundred-and-eighty degree turn. He now exhibited an overwhelming sympathy for animals. He was incapable of seeing a scab-ridden stray dog without rushing to pet him. The father, who dreamed of a flourishing practice for his son, was shattered. For the first time he lost his patience and composure.

"A veterinarian? You've got to be kidding!" He went to work mumbling to himself, "My son's grown up to be a blockhead!" He pondered the issue bitterly for a whole week, and then he called his son in for another conversation, this time behind closed doors. He did his best to dissuade him.

"Do you want to know where the action is in medicine, do you? Do you?" He lowered his voice. "Psychiatry!"

"Why psychiatry?" the young man asked.

Lighting one of his offending cigars, the old man elaborated, "Because psychiatry is a gold mine, a license to print money."

"Really?"

Dr. Sinval snapped back, "Really!" He laid out his case.

"I'm an obstetrician, where has that gotten me?" He answered his own question bitterly: "Debts, defaults. No one pays me. My clients stiff me, do you hear me? They leave me holding the bill, yes sir!"

The Drama

At the mere mention of psychiatry, Bebeto's mother and aunts made the sign of the cross.

"You want Bebeto to treat kooks?"

And then they would add: "God forbid!"

Deep down what they feared was that one of Bebeto's clients would strangle him in a homicidal rage. Dr. Sinval had to clarify: "Bebeto will be a psychoanalyst."

He explained that psychoanalysis represented no danger for the doctor or the patient. He threw in a joke to the effect that, of the two, the psychoanalyst was the more dangerous. Amazed, Dona Detinha asked him to elaborate. Dr. Sinval, chewing his cigar, added, "Do you want to know what psychoanalysis is in a nutshell? A chat."

"A chat?"

"The doctor sits down, and the patient lies down," he said authoritatively.

"They have a little talk, and that's it. That's psychoanalysis." His words left a deep impression on everyone, including Bebeto.

Dona Detinha swallowed and then said, "That's it?"

"That's it." He went on, "And there's more. The patient isn't sick. Not here, not in China. Most of the time they are as healthy as can be, and they go to a psychoanalyst because they have nothing better do to with their time, and they can afford two hundred smackers a session."

Nightclub

Months and years went by, and Dr. Sinval continued to defend his point of view stubbornly. And indeed the women were intrigued by the tremendous ease of this profession. Finally Bebeto found himself in his last year of medical school. Though he never talked about it, he carried in his innermost recesses the sadness of a frustrated veterinarian. He capitulated to the notion of being a psychiatrist because he had little willpower and because his mother and aunts had reached a consensus. He made it clear, though, right from the start, "I'm not treating crazy people." He completed his studies. His classmates swore in a somewhat cruel exaggeration that he was incapable of giving an injection or even prescribing an aspirin. The day he returned from his graduation ceremony, the family gathered again, and Dr. Sinval announced, "Now all you need is an office. Now listen carefully. It's essential that the office have the ambience of a fancy nightclub. The ambience of a nightclub is key."

And then, with his melancholy air, Bebeto sighed, "The thing is, I don't know the first thing about psychiatry!"

But his ever-vigilant father cut right to the chase.

"It doesn't matter, you don't have to! Besides, don't forget, you're treating people who are totally sane."

The son, who was weak of character and spoiled, mumbled faint-heartedly, "OK, OK!"

That night his mother, as she did every night, brought him a cup of hot tea. Bebeto sighed. He let out a moan from the innermost reaches of his soul.

"I wanted so much to be a veterinarian!"

The Opening

Over the years the women had saved a cruzeiro here, a cruzeiro there, and had been able to put aside a substantial amount. Thus Bebeto was one day able to open an office downtown that looked like something out of *Arabian Nights* and had the aura of a fancy nightclub. It was such a beautiful and singular sight that Dona Detinha demanded of her husband, "Look here, Sinval, you can't smoke your cigars here. Smoke wherever you want, just not here."

Right away he obliged. He went to the window and tossed out his smelly torpedo. Deep down he thought his wife was right. It seemed like smoking a cheap cigar in such an environment was sacrilege. The office, in all its quasi-Oriental splendor, opened on a Thursday. Dr. Sinval, with both hands in his pockets, looking all around and even up above, with the pride that comes from being the father of a business owner, exclaimed, "With an office like this you can charge two hundred smackers a session, easily!"

That evening the young analyst came home with a little kitten he had found meowing in a gutter with the most heart-tugging sincerity. In the kitchen he gave the tiny, defenseless creature a saucer of milk. Then he sat in a rocking chair with the kitten in his lap and petted him. He smothered him for hours on end with the most desperate tenderness imaginable.

The First Client

The first client who submitted herself to Bebeto's psychoanalysis was a gorgeous blond society lady who forked over the hefty fee without even flinching. She was there because two weeks earlier she had put out a lit cigarette in a cat's eye, blinding him. Smoking a cigarette, curious and slightly amused, she asked the young doctor, owner of such a fancy office: "What does it mean, doctor?"

For a long, almost interminable minute, he remained perfectly silent. Suddenly, he extended his hand.

"Give me your cigarette for a moment, please."

Not understanding, the rich lady obliged. He lunged. He was able to overpower her quickly. Then he put out the burning ember in one of her beautiful blue eyes. He let go of her as her screams filled the building. When they broke down the door and raided the office he was waiting there, perfectly calm, arms crossed, showing no signs of remorse. First they took him to the police station. Then to the asylum.

Twins

He was standing at the bar drinking an espresso when he saw the girl he went out with the night before. He dropped his cup and chased after her like a man possessed. He nearly knocked over a man then bumped into a woman before finally catching up to her. He walked alongside her smiling.

"Hello, beautiful."

The girl, who was drop-dead gorgeous, froze for a second. She looked at him from head to toe, surprised and startled, then turned and continued walking. Osmar, taken aback, quickened his pace and asked, "What's the matter? Don't you recognize me?" No answer. In a tone of irritation mixed with disbelief, Osmar asked, "What's with the face?" More silence. By now she was nearly running. Finally, Osmar lost his patience and grabbed her by the arm.

"Look here, Marilena…"

On hearing the name, she stopped in her tracks, smiled, and turned to him confidently.

"I get it!"

"What are you talking about?"

She looked relieved.

"I'm not Marilena. Marilena's my sister."

Stunned, he shouted, "God! It can't be."

The girl just smiled, relishing the confusion.

"I'm Iara."

Osmar's next question was totally unnecessary.

"Are you twins?"

He had only met Marilena the day before. It was one of those delicious flirtatious encounters between strangers on a bus. They traveled side by side, each one hanging from a strap. By the time they got out at the same stop, it was evident that the attraction was mutual and irresistible. Marilena gave him her phone number, address, the whole deal. If she hadn't mentioned her twin sister Iara it was because time did not permit.

When they met again, Osmar told her what had happened in disbelief.

"My jaw dropped to the floor! I couldn't believe it. It's scary how much you look alike. A dead ringer. I've never seen anything like it."

They sat on a park bench. Marilena explained to him that this wasn't the first time nor would it be the last time. Their close friends and even their relatives occasionally went through a similar ordeal. The only way to tell the two apart was a bracelet that Iara wore and her sister did not. Deeply impressed by what he'd heard, he said:

"Twin sisters are usually very close, right?"

Marilena hesitated for a moment.

"It depends," she said.

"Are you?" he insisted.

"You're asking too many questions. Let's change the subject."

The Drama

From the very first, Osmar knew that he had found in Marilena the woman destined to be his wife. One week later he was announcing at home, on the job, to anyone who would listen, "I'm going to get engaged! I'm going to marry her!" Two weeks after he met her, he was already frequenting her house, and two months later they were indeed engaged. His friends slapped him on the back.

"That was fast; you just met. It has to be a world record."

He joked, "I don't waste any time!"

Every free moment he spent at his girlfriend's. And in spite of seeing the two sisters daily, he still couldn't get over the resemblance.

"God, how is it possible? How can two people look so much alike!" And on occasions when he went out accompanied by Marilena and Iara, he would joke, "It's like I have two girlfriends!"

One day, however, Marilena, put her hand on his arm.

"I am going to ask you a favor. Don't joke like that. Please. Don't do it again. I'm asking you as a favor."

"Why?"

"If you only knew how much it irritates me that we look alike. I'm sick and tired of looking like her!" She paused then added with a muted pain, "I don't want to look like anyone. I don't want to look like another woman."

Another Request

A few days later, Marilena made another request.

"I don't want you getting too close to Iara, do you understand?"

Osmar, who abhorred family rifts, especially between siblings, was shocked. He cleared his throat and said, "But I thought you were the best of friends."

Marilena recoiled.

"Friends? Me and her? Never!" And for the first time she opened up and told him the truth.

"We never fight. We never argue. She actually treats me very well. But she hates me, do you understand? I know she does!"

Clutching her fiancé, Marilena spoke of those murky and persistent feelings that can't easily be put into words.

"Iara never said anything to me, nothing, but..."

Osmar cleared his throat, astonished.

"I think you're exaggerating!" Be that as it may, Osmar tried with the greatest tact and discretion possible to distance himself from his future sister-in-law. But he could not believe that Iara, who was so cordial with everyone and so kind towards Marilena, could hate anyone, much less her own sister. Around this time Iara came down with a very bad case of the flu, verging on pneumonia. She overcame the disease, it's true, but her convalescence presented a new problem. Miserable, battered by chronic melancholy, she spoke of nothing but death. The family doctor scratched his head.

"Anxiety. The trick is to send her away."

Marilena's wedding was scheduled to take place shortly. Her mother asked, "Aren't you going to attend the wedding?"

Iara answered: "Don't worry, Mother; I won't be missed. And if I stay, I don't know; I might do something I'll regret!"

The family had no choice but to send her to an uncle's farm in Mato Grosso. Very weak, Iara faintly said, "It's just as well that it's in Mato Grosso. The farther away the better."

The Wedding

When the airplane took off, Marilena turned to her fiancé.

"Thank God! Thank God!" Her joy seemed cruel, almost perverse to Osmar. It was evident, however, that her sister's absence filled Marilena with joy. "Finally," she said. "Now I can be certain that nothing will happen to me." And, sure enough, one month later they were married in civil and religious ceremonies. As a wedding gift they received a small house, idyllic and connubial, in Lins de Vasconcelos. At 10 p.m. they left Marilena's parents' home and headed to their new house. They were alone there like Adam and Eve. She announced, transfigured, "I'll call you soon!" She entered the bedroom, her wedding gown still on, and closed the door behind her. Outside, Osmar smoked impatiently. Fifteen minutes later he knocked on the door. From inside he heard, "Coming." Fifteen more minutes went by, and Marilena peeked through the door.

"Come in, honey." Hours later, at the crack of dawn, an enraptured Osmar passed his hand over her arm. He sat up suddenly. He stammered, terrified, "The bracelet!"

She answered, sweetly, "I'm not Marilena. I'm Iara."

Beside himself, he got up, looked under the bed, under the furniture, overturned a chair. He turned in circles in the middle of the room, not understanding. Finally Iara pointed.

"Over there."

Out of his mind, he ran to the armoire; letting out a scream, he opened the two doors. And he stepped back in horror. Inside, was Marilena's corpse, still in her wedding gown. Iara lay on the bed as she lit an American cigarette.

The Cripple

He was against marriage and made no bones about it. He would confess
to one and all that he had a certain vice. There were raised eyebrows.
"Vice?"
"That's right. Vice, yeah."
"What do you mean?"
"I only like married women," he would say, smiling nonchalantly.
"Honest?"
"Honest. I can't stand single women. I'm not interested."
This barroom cynicism left a deep impression, especially on women.
Single women would open their eyes wide, but deep down were charmed;
married women found something infinitely amusing in his brazenness.
Sandoval, flattered by the splash he made, insisted, "Cross my heart!"

The Mystery Woman

One day, as he was leaving the house, the phone rang. He went back inside to answer it.

It was a woman's voice.

"Sandoval?"

"Speaking."

"This is a fan of yours."

Sandoval had nothing better to do just then; he liked her voice and was willing to wile away ten to fifteen minutes. First the woman asked him a question.

"Is it true what you said?"

"What?"

"That you only like married women. Is that true?"

Sandoval smiled.

"More or less."

"What a shame!"

"Why?"

She sighed.

"Because I'm single. I don't even have a boyfriend, imagine!"

Amused by her sassiness, he joked, "Let's do the following: Get married, then come and see me?"

"Watch out or I will!"

Married Women

A strong and good-looking young man, Sandoval's love life proceeded swimmingly. No one, however, could remember any adventures with a single girl. It could be said that married women were his destiny. He would earnestly explain the innumerable advantages to being with someone else's wife, the first and foremost being that she was already married. He would conclude with great conviction, "It's a terrific deal! What's more it's extremely economical. The one who subsidizes everything, who incurs all of the costs, is the husband!"

Little by little, without realizing, he began to forget some elementary rules of secrecy, of modesty. His behavior bordered on the ostentatious. The vanity of being seen, pointed at, even cursed, took hold of him. He got caught up in two or three scandals. His behavior became so imprudent and notorious that finally a friend asked to speak to him. The friend gave him grave warnings, including the following admonition: "You might get shot!"

It so happened that at the time Sandoval was having an affair with this very friend's wife. Pensively and earnestly, staring him straight in the eyes, Sandoval said, "Thanks. But there's no danger. Why do you think I don't get married? Because husbands, the whole lot of them, are total morons."

"Damn it!" his friend insisted. "You have to be more discreet!"

On the way out, the friend even said, "You want to come over for dinner tomorrow? My wife always complains that you never come around."

The Woman

Time went by. Life, events, and people in general turned Sandoval into an increasingly cynical human being. It was said of him that he was scum. For him, one of the greatest pleasures in life was to become friends, close friends, with the cuckolded husbands. It was a cruel, not to mention unnecessary, touch that he relished greatly. For him it was sport. Then one day he heard a woman's voice on the telephone ask him, "Do you remember me?"

He didn't remember her straightaway and neither did her voice trigger any distant memories.

She gave him more details.

"I'm that cute girl, etc, etc…."

"OK! Now I remember! How the hell are you?"

"I followed your advice. I got married."

"Are you serious?"

"Very serious. It's been one month today."

"Excellent!"

Two days later they had their first date at a beachfront bar. He ordered an appetizer of some sort and she a drink with a little straw in it. Sandoval was as excited as a teenager in love; he liked everything about her, including the carefree way she'd interrupted her honeymoon to meet him for sin.

Sandoval wanted to know who her husband was and what he was like. He laughed and rubbed his hands.

"Introduce me to him. OK?"

"OK."

She went on to explain how she'd known Sandoval for a long time, ever since she was a little girl; how she'd stare at him in awe from her window as he walked by; how he was and continued to be her first and only love. Why did she get married? So she could be free to live it up. She gave no thought to her husband and was incapable of admitting that he could represent a threat, danger or even an obstacle. So much so that in her perversity she'd handpicked, among her many suitors, the young man who was most acquiescent and inoffensive.

Proud at her own deviousness, she whispered, "You want to know something? He's a cripple."

The Cripple

It was true: One of Domicio's legs was shorter than the other. Thus, his "complex," as Sonia called it. Things between Sonia and Sandoval transpired very simply, clearly and directly. Minimal effort was required on his part to conquer an already conquered woman. Occasionally, in spite of all his experience, Sandoval felt disconcerted by this young woman who was so sure of herself and had such a firm and unwavering predilection for sin.

"Strange creatures, women! They're really something!"

Without the slightest notion of good and evil, Sonia introduced the two; she brought Sandoval home.

Domicio walked Sandoval to the door at the end of the evening and, with heartbreaking sincerity, said, "Drop by whenever you feel like it. Our doors are always open."

The next day, alone with Sandoval, proud of her cunning ways, she boasted, "Nice scam! Was that amazing or what?"

Taken aback, Sandoval reclined and listened to her feminine reasoning. In short, Sonia felt that a crippled husband was "a gold mine"; he can't complain, he has to grin and bear it, or else...

Sandoval, with a certain melancholy air, sighed.

"Very unpleasant, your husband's deformity."

Evil

It could be said that both needed an element of humiliation. Little by little their prudence fell by the wayside; being seen together began to arouse them. They would go out to buy ice cream, to the beach, everywhere. Even at her home they became increasingly bold. As if irritated by Domicio's sweetness, Sandoval would turn the subject to infidelity. He would say things like, "A guy who gets married is a real idiot. No man can ever vouch for a wife!" It seemed like a needless and very vulgar provocation of the poor wretch who sat across the table from him finding everything so very funny.

"You're a piece of work, Sandoval! A real scream!"

During dinner, Sonia's and Sandoval's feet were hard at work beneath the table. If Domicio should look to the side, Sonia would pucker her lips for her lover. At other times, Sandoval would suggest, "Wear just a dress. Nothing underneath." Sonia would comply. And the two needed the poor wretch to be right there, as if his presence only added to their pleasure. Eventually, so much blindness came to irritate Sandoval.

"That husband of yours is a real moron!"

After dinner, Domicio would leave them alone, chatting, while he would sink into his armchair and snore with shocking abandon.

The Selfless One

Sandoval, however, was not born to be with one woman. Variety was for him a habit, a vice, a disease. His interest turned to another woman, also married, also with a good and naive husband.

Limping, Domicio went looking for him.

"Not another one, you bastard! I won't allow it! You hear me? I'll pump six bullets into you!"

That night, Sandoval appeared at their home. After dinner, while he chatted with Sonia, Domicio dozed off in his armchair.

Gastritis

He just sat there on a suitcase in the middle of the bedroom, crying like a baby.

"I swear, I never imagined this could happen! I never imagined anyone could suffer this much!"

He paused and then had another outburst.

"Being dumped is the worst pain of all. All other pains, physical or moral, are a breeze, a cinch!"

Eurialo, who was in the room with him, contemplated this savage despair in stunned silence. With a mixture of pity, embarrassment and loathing, he put his hand on Juca's shoulder.

"Take it easy!"

Juca jumped to his feet.

"Take it easy! Why should I? Take it easy because it's me and not you! The truth of the matter is I've died. I'm dead and buried, do you understand?"

Eurialo decided to take a gamble.

"OK, do you want me to sit down and talk to her? Have a chat with her?"

"You?" Juca stammered.

"Yes, me. You know she and I are buddies; she'll listen to me. Who knows? It can't hurt!"

Juca clutched his friend tightly in a moment of sudden euphoria.

"Good idea, good idea! She likes you; she really thinks the world of you. You'd be doing me a big favor. A huge favor! But don't waste any time; go right now. I'll wait for you right here. And listen. You're the tops!"

Eurialo sighed, "Amen."

Lover's Quarrel

Juca was Jandira's boyfriend; they were practically engaged. It was, for both, one of those love stories out of the soaps, the movies, the opera. Every now and then in between kisses, she would sigh, "When I love, it's for keeps."

"Me too, me too!" he would respond, enraptured.

Jandira, however, warned him soberly, "Sweetie, I can forgive anything, anything. There's only one thing I can't forgive, cheating!" Very well. That evening Juca arrived late for their date, blaming the traffic. They sat on a park bench. Suddenly, Jandira asked, "What's this red mark on your neck?" Well, it so happens that on his lunch break Juca had gone to the movies with a girl from the office. There, in the last row, they kissed and groped. When he heard Jandira mention a red mark, he panicked. Stunned, he tried to improvise.

"It must be a rash!"

"How can that be a rash?" Jandira asked. "That's no rash!" She took a closer look and concluded, "Lipstick! It's lipstick, I know it is!"

They got up almost simultaneously. Juca, his face white, stammered pathetically. Jandira, however, was categorical.

"If you were a thief, a pickpocket, a murderer, I'd forgive you. I just can't forgive creeps who chase after every skirt they see! Goodbye!"

She turned her back and went on her way. Beside himself, he chased after her. Jandira stopped in her tracks and shattered him with what she said next.

"Leave or I'll call the police!"

The Intermediary

He ran home in a daze. A little while later, Eurialo found him, face down, in bed, sobbing. Eurialo knew both of them. He volunteered to go to Jandira and to act as an intermediary. And, sure enough, about half an hour later he was standing before Jandira. She repeated what she had told Juca.

"It's over. I don't want to see Juca ever again. I don't care if he's the last man on earth."

Eurialo pulled out a cigarette and, without taking his eyes off of Jandira, began, "I'm only here because Juca asked me. But between you and me, I think you did the right thing. Juca is a womanizer, he doesn't know when to stop. It's like a disease."

She wouldn't budge.

"That's just the way I am. I demand exclusivity. Either he's mine, only mine, or I'm not interested."

Eurialo cleared his throat.

"I'm the same way." Silence, then he asked, "You mean to say there's no possibility you two will ever get together again?"

Jandira flashed a half-smile.

"You tell Juca the following: I would only make up with him if he had a fatal disease and only if there weren't the slightest possibility of a cure. If it were an incurable disease. Only then. Otherwise, I never want to see him again."

Exile

Eurialo went back to his friend. He told him of the conversation he'd had. Juca, in despair, opened his arms wide.

"You mean to say I have to die to be forgiven? No, please, no!"

"Yep, that about sizes it up!" Eurialo confirmed gloomily.

"I give up then!" Juca said at his wits' end. "I know what I'll do: I have a job offer in the Amazon. Well, I'm going to take it. That's what I'll do! That way I'll live out my life where no one knows me."

"You'll forget her. You'll find someone else!"

Juca buried his face in his hands and began sobbing.

"The hell I will! Damn all of them as far as I'm concerned! If I can't have her, I don't want anyone else!"

Everything pointed to the definitive end of that love story. About two weeks later Eurialo, as empathetic as ever, accompanied Juca to the airport. There, in line to board his plane, Juca hugged Eurialo.

"My only consolation is that I still have you as a friend. You've been a true friend, through thick and thin!"

Eurialo struggled to hide his emotions.

Nostalgia

In the Amazon, Juca lived tortured by an inconsolable nostalgia. He made acquaintances, even friends, but his life followed the following routine: from his home to his job and from his job to his home. His new friends wanted to take him out on the town. "The woman I loved dumped me," he told them. "As far as I'm concerned, there are no other women in the world!" One year later he received the news: Jandira was married. When he heard her husband's name he almost fell over backwards: Eurialo. If it had been anyone else, the impact would have been less. But his friend, his go-between...! He stopped going to work and spent three days at home in fervid and empty meditation. At the end of those three days he got up and looked himself in the mirror: He was a ruin of a man. Think of a tuberculosis patient on his deathbed or worse. Twenty-four hours later Juca dropped everything in the Amazon and boarded a plane for Rio. On his arrival he immediately went about discovering where Jandira was spending her honeymoon. He called her.

"It's me. You said, didn't you...? That you would forgive me if I had an incurable disease? Well, I do. I'm dying. I love you and I want you to forgive me."

From the other side came the question, "What disease?"

"Cancer. Please! Before I die, I need you...." He began sobbing, "You owe me this one last moment of happiness!"

By now, she was crying too.

"Yes! Yes!"

He had arranged for a friend to lend him his apartment. He gave Jandira the address. The following evening they met there. They kissed amid the tears. He stammered, "I love you! I love you!" Jandira, beside herself by now, tore off her dress. Then her petticoat. She stood there in her panties. When he kissed her neck he felt as if he had died and gone to heaven. Two hours later he whispered, "I lied. I don't have cancer. I have gastritis."

She seemed to wake from a deep slumber. She let out a sigh of relief. "Thank God for gastritis!"

The Burglar

He flew to São Paulo, where he was supposed to stay for about a week on business. He got off the airplane, attended meetings well into the night and at two in the morning picked up the telephone in his hotel room.

"Long distance."

"Where?"

"Rio."

He gave the operator the name and number. Euzebiozinho looked out the window on the twelfth floor and thought how much he missed his wife. They'd been married for three years now, and he was crazy about her. "I'd die if I were to lose her!" he liked to say. It was an exaggeration, of course, but no one could deny the passion he felt for her. It should be noted that physically his wife was deserving of such passion. At twenty-three, she was considered one of the prettiest girls in all of Rio de Janeiro. And at home, on the street, on the buses, wherever they might be, the two were seen groping like newlyweds, like lovers. Their friends, faced with such strong and compelling proof of conjugal bliss, would say, "The only happily married couple in the world!"

The Burglar

Finally, the call went through. Euzebiozinho, hardly able to contain himself, melted like butter when he heard her voice.

"How's the love of my life, huh?"

She answered something he could not make out. The connection was horrible. In his state of love he didn't want to miss a single word.

"What? What?" Suddenly, Euzebiozinho thought he heard the word "thief."

"What did you say, sweetie?" he asked. "Talk louder! Bring the receiver closer to your mouth! Repeat what you just said!"

She did, nearly spelling it out: "A thief broke into the house today!"

"A thief?"

"Yes."

Stunned, he yelled at the telephone.

"What did you just say? Louder! I can't hear a damn thing!"

His wife's voice faded altogether. He pressed the phone button frantically.

"Damn it! Operator! Operator!"

Exasperated, he finally hung up. In his hotel room he began thinking about the burglar who had broken into his house. The thought of material damage did not bother him. What horrified him was that Luciana was by herself, and thus defenseless in the house. Every scenario crossed his mind. Let's just say that the poor wretch, on imagining Luciana beautiful and alone in that state of immodesty which sleep brings, on imagining Luciana in one of her low-cut, diaphanous nightgowns, lost his mind. It was the hypothetical possibility of who knows which scenario that finally did it for him. He sped to the airport. There, after paying a king's ransom, he managed to charter a special flight. He told the pilot, "It's a matter of life and death."

The Assault

He lived on a peaceful and idyllic little street in Tijuca. All of the neighbors knew each other and got along as if they were one big, tight family. When Euzebiozinho stepped out of the cab, half the neighborhood was already in the house. Luciana, in a beautiful robe, threw herself into his arms.

"Thank God you're back! Thank God!"

He was deeply moved.

"I'll never leave you again. Never. What happened, honey pie? The burglar broke in, is that right?"

A look of fear swept across her face.

"Imagine the danger, sweetheart! You know who saw the thief? Dona Tereza!"

Euzebiozinho turned to the woman, who confirmed what his wife had just said. She proceeded to give a detailed account. Poor Luciana went to bed at 10 p.m., totally oblivious. Since sleep came very easily to her, before long she was deep in her dreams. Her husband listened on at his wife's side, chain-smoking, thinking about this stranger, this man who had entered their bedroom while Luciana slept. It occurred to him just then that on hot nights his wife had the habit of sleeping in the nude.

In his innermost recesses he felt jealous of the thief. The neighbor continued her story: At about midnight Dona Tereza, unable to sleep, wracked by insomnia, had walked over to her window. It was then, suddenly, that she saw a very suspicious shape exiting Euzebiozinho's house. Since the owner was in São Paulo, one thing was obvious, or as Dona Tereza said, "clear as day": That man she saw coming out of the house must be a thief. Those present were unanimous: "Of course!"

What was most striking was the thief's brazenness. He had left through the front door as if it were the most natural thing in the world, as if he were leaving his own house. The incident had frightened Dona Tereza so much that it was as if she'd lost her ability to speak. Thus it took a while before she announced far and wide what she had seen.

Instantly the entire street had been in a frenzy, and poor Luciana had awakened, startled by the commotion. In a moment of impotent rage, Euzebiozinho wanted to know, "What did he look like?"

"Well dressed, sharp, very handsome!" Dona Tereza answered.

The Gentleman Thief

It was one of those cases that captured the imagination by sounding like something out of a romance novel. The fact that he was a handsome burglar and not ugly and brutish only added to the story's allure. Furthermore, there was one extraordinary fact: Nothing was missing, absolutely nothing. For Euzebiozinho, who was even jealous of the furniture, the case took on an ever more worrisome aspect. He was willing to accept a tattered, pug-faced burglar. But the fact that he was a dashing thief really stuck in his throat. He asked a friend to loan him his gun.

"I'll shoot the son of a bitch, just watch!"

Luciana pondered the issue. "Why shoot him, honey?"

Euzebiozinho, who was beside himself, confirmed his bloodthirsty designs.

"I'll kill him!"

Indeed, ever since the lamentable incident he'd had trouble sleeping. Any little noise was enough to make him jump out of bed, gun in hand. One afternoon on returning home from work, he stopped in front of Dona Tereza's door and asked, "Would you recognize him if you saw him?"

"Of course!" she said. "Thank God I'm excellent with faces."

What dazzled the blessed lady were the obvious similarities between this burglar from Tijuca and the character of Raffles, the gentleman thief from the popular book series. Not in her wildest dreams did she ever expect that she would come across such a dashing thief. When alone she would fantasize, "At the very least he attends balls, wears a tailcoat, and God knows what else!"

Surprise

One night there was a very chic party in Gávea, and coincidentally Dona Tereza accompanied the couple. In the car Euzebiozinho talked to his neighbor.

"If there's one thing I can't stand it's thieves!" He went further, "They should round them all up in the middle of the street and beat them to death!"

Dona Tereza, who was amused by such talk, objected, "You can't complain. You found a very nice thief – he didn't steal a thing!"

At last they arrived at the party. Luciana looked stunning, and even Euzebiozinho, her own husband, stared at her bold and revealing cleavage with interest. He reflected with a touch of melancholy, "It's not easy having a beautiful wife!" Shortly thereafter the three moved into the ballroom. Euzebiozinho hesitated, but decided to pay the sweaty and obese Dona Tereza the conventional courtesy: He asked her for the first dance, which happened to be a foxtrot. A few steps into the dance, Dona Tereza froze. Wide-eyed, she stabbed her finger in the air: "The thief!"

"Where?"

"There."

Startled, Euzebiozinho looked in the direction indicated. It was him; it was the son of a bitch, almost handsome, wearing a flawless tuxedo, surrounded by women with bare shoulders. Euzebiozinho wanted to be certain.

"Are you sure?"

She was categorical.

"Absolutely!"

On hearing this, the young man did not waste any time. He went straight to the lady of the house.

"There's a thief at your party." When the woman saw the suspect she laughed.

"Him? But that's Dr. so-and-so; he's an engineer, a millionaire; he owns several Cadillacs…!"

Shaken, Euzebiozinho was forced to admit his mistake and to say it was a misunderstanding. It was two in the morning by the time the couple and Dona Tereza drove home. The neighbor had a worried look about her, like something was eating away at her and repeated that it was probably a mistake. Every now and then she would steal sideways glances at Luciana and sigh. Euzebiozinho did not utter a word; Luciana seemed to be in high spirits.

It might have been a mistake, a gaffe, God knows what. But the fact is that later in the bedroom, still wearing his tuxedo, he was overcome by a mortal certainty. His wife was seated in front of the mirror taking off her earrings. He grabbed the revolver he had borrowed and said very calmly, "I don't have the courage to kill you."

In the mirror, Luciana saw her husband lift the muzzle to his temple and pull the trigger.

The Love Check

He was a little rich boy and did as he pleased well into his twenties. He would get so plastered that they would find him rolling in the gutter. Friends and police would have to drag him home nearly comatose. Every now and then the father would lose his patience. He'd call the young man in and stare at him grimly.

"I'll throw you out on the street without a nickel to your name!"

Since the father would never follow through, Vadeco continued leading the same life. One night at a club, he outdid himself and provoked a horrific fight. It created a scandal. Next morning the father was in his son's bedroom, fuming.

"You're an embarrassment to the family!"

Vadeco did not open his mouth. For all of his defects, which were many and serious, he still respected his father. When all was said and done, the father had the last word.

"From now on you're going to have a job, you animal."

Sure enough, the next day Vadeco reported to his first job ever: as a manager in one of his father's companies. His first move was to name a friend from his nightly escapades, Aristides, as his administrative assistant. Their first day on the job the two did absolutely nothing except sit and stare at each other. Every now and then one would look at the other and exclaim, "What a drag!" When lunchtime came around, Aristides decided to take a stroll through the office. He came back a changed man. He rubbed his hands in glee and announced: "You've got to see the chicks around here!"

Don Juan

So, wasting no time and with Aristides' help, Vadeco took charge of the situation. Neither of the two knew how to do a damn thing, but on the other hand, they did manage to pack the office with female employees. And from then on it was virtually nonstop carousing during business hours. At certain moments in the day, Vadeco, his eyes bloodshot, would turn to his assistant and say, "Lock the door!"

Aristides would obey, and the other employees could only imagine the shocking scenes inside. One of the female employees took a liking to Aristides, but he was clear, loyal and emphatic.

"No, not with me! It's out of the question!"

She didn't understand, so he had to spell it out. He explained that in the office the boss had absolute priority.

"He comes first, then me," he insisted. The truth of the matter was that Vadeco did not have to lift a finger. Aristides, with admirable tact and efficiency, would persuade the women. He would resort to all sorts of arguments, including the most practical of all: "He'll increase your salary, silly!" Every now and then they encountered resistance. This was the case with the new switchboard operator, a blond who looked like she had just stepped out of a movie screen and had a habit of walking around in skin-tight dresses. As soon as he set eyes on her, Vadeco called in Aristides.

"Get to work!"

Aristides obeyed straightaway and began hanging around the switchboard. The operator's main argument went as follows: "What about my boyfriend?"

Aristides was categorical.

"Your boyfriend needn't know. He'll never know!"

Fearing the possible consequences, she replied, "I can't! I can't!"

She succumbed in the end. First they went to the movies, and after the movies they went on an exhilarating car ride. The next morning Aristides asked, "So, how was she?"

"All right," said Vadeco, yawning.

The Unconquerable

Until one day Vadeco ran into a new girl in the hallway. His entire love life was predicated on variety. He ran to Aristides.

"Who is that girl?"

His friend left to inquire and came back with answers.

"Tough to get!"

"Why?"

"Engaged. She's getting married next month. She's all business."

Vadeco was terse.

"Go to work on her," he said.

And that was Vadeco for you. He himself admitted, "I have one flaw in life: I only like women with principles." He liked the others too, but his passion lay with the hard to get, the nearly unconquerable ones. Aristides came back half an hour later. He let out a heavy sigh.

"Things aren't looking good. I warned you; she's all business. She came this close to slapping me."

But the rich little boy would not take no for an answer. He nearly rubbed his checkbook in his friend's face. He ranted, "I'm rich; I have money. That's what women want. Moola."

Aristides sighed.

"Not all of them. Not all of them."

Anguish

So Vadeco became obsessed with the woman. Aristides tried to distract him by dangling other options before him. .

"So-and-so is fine too. She'd be game."

Vadeco's answer was to the point.

"I'm not interested. I want *her*. Only her. Damn! How I'd kiss those perky little breasts!" He grabbed Aristides by the collar and shook him.

"Either you get me that girl, or you and me are going to have serious problems!"

Aristides went back to work on her. He found the same resistance, though, or better said, a more unbending resistance. The girl, whose name was Arlete, loved her fiancé; she was crazy about him. Aristides did his best to tempt her.

"This is a great deal, don't be a fool!"

Finally, the girl had heard enough.

"I'm not who you think I am. Who ever heard of such a thing!"

Aristides, who was afraid of trouble, of even the whiff of scandal, slipped away. That evening Vadeco went on a tirade.

"Moron!" He concluded by saying, "It looks like I'm going to have to take care of this myself!"

By now, though, he was no longer the same man. His happy-go-lucky demeanor and spontaneous ways had given way to an all-encompassing anguish that consumed his every waking hour. It could be said that for Vadeco only one woman mattered, and her name was Arlete. He waited another two days. Then, he appointed her his secretary.

"I'm going all out!" he told Aristides. Indeed, he didn't waste time. He began by asking an apparently inoffensive question: "Do you earn enough?" Arlete was rather taken aback.

"Two thousand cruzeiros."

"That's nothing! It's an outrage!"

He left it at that. But that night Vadeco couldn't sleep. Aristides, when he'd driven him home had reminded him, "I told you. You're wasting your time." Vadeco, consumed by anguish, retorted, "Money buys everything!"

The following day Vadeco entered the office with a bottle of whisky under his arm. He had a glass brought, and he started drinking. The alcohol made him cruel and cynical. Suddenly, he asked, "Are you faithful to your boyfriend?"

Arlete, who was looking for a document in the file cabinet, turned, startled. She hadn't heard him clearly.

"What?"

He repeated the question.

Without taking her eyes off him, she answered, "Yes."

He stood and approached.

"You're sure about that?"

"Absolutely."

For a few seconds they merely looked at each other. He returned to his desk and sat in his swivel chair. Arlete stopped what she was doing and kept her eyes on his every move. Then Vadeco, with a tortured voice, asked: "Do you want to earn one-hundred-thousand cruzeiros?" At first Arlete understood "one-hundred cruzeiros." He had to repeat: "One-hundred-thousand cruzeiros. One-hundred Gs! Do you?"

She leaned against the file cabinet for support. She still could not believe what she had heard.

"A hundred-thousand?" By now she was no longer so sure of herself. She wanted to know, "What for?" Vadeco stood next to her again.

"You just have to spend one hour with me in my apartment. Just one hour. One-hundred Gs for one hour!"

And right there in front of the astonished girl, he filled out the check and handed it to Arlete. In a brief moment of fascination, she read the check: "Pay to bearer…"

"But I'm engaged," she said desperately. "Can't you see I'm engaged? That I'm getting married next month?"

Shivering as if consumed by a fever, he told her he would wait for her the following morning at ten at his apartment. He wrote the address on a piece of paper and handed it to the girl.

"One-hundred-thousand for one hour. Just one hour and then never again. You'll leave with this check in your hands. One-hundred-thousand, you hear? One-hundred-thousand !" he said, as if possessed.

The Check

When Aristides found out he was shocked.

"One hundred G's? Are you nuts? Completely out of your mind?" Beside himself, Vadeco kept asking, "Do you think she'll come?" His friend joked,

"For one hundred G's I'll go!" The truth of the matter was that in his state of mind Vadeco would have doubled the amount. He wanted to see her naked, completely naked.

The following day, Arlete, who had not slept a wink, got out of bed, as if transfigured. Never before had a woman taken so much care and delight in getting dressed. She chose her most beautiful and transparent panties. In front of the mirror she felt exceedingly beautiful, almost immorally beautiful. Aristides had chosen the morning on purpose to avoid suspicions. And thus at the agreed upon hour she rang the doorbell to his apartment in Copacabana. Before Vadeco could touch her, she coldly made her mercenary demand.

"The check!"

The young man got the check out and handed it to her. Arlete read it and re-read it; she verified the amount, the signature, the date, etc. Then suddenly, in a rage, she tore it into a thousand little pieces. Vadeco managed to stammer, "What are you doing? Don't do that!" She silenced him by throwing the little pieces at his face like confetti. Petrified, he would have let her leave without lifting one finger or saying one word. But in her feminine rage she went further and slapped him. Then she grabbed the young man's face with both hands and kissed him furiously.

The Dead

Suffice it to say that it was a small town, barely a blip on the map, way out in the middle of nowhere. No radio, no telephone, not even a dentist. But what most made this town stand out was the absence of women. Half a dozen at most for about one-hundred-and-fifty rubber tappers. It should be added that they were all married and that their husbands were all able-bodied and exhibited a fierce and homicidal possessiveness.

They would warn, "If anyone tries anything, God help him. He gets shot like a dog!"

And indeed no one dared try anything with those miserable women who lived in their hovels under lock and key, devoid of joy. When they opened their mouths, it was to flash cavity-ridden smiles. They simply didn't take care of themselves and didn't make themselves pretty. Why should they? Just for their husbands? Barefoot and filthy, those women wouldn't have interested any men other than their own husbands and those wretched one hundred and fifty rubber tappers who lived in the middle of the wilderness and had all but forgotten their humanity. It was in this godforsaken town that Quincas arrived one day. He got there, looked around, and began to ask, one by one, "So what's the deal here?"

"It stinks."

It was a vague and unsatisfactory answer for someone who came from so far away and who knew nothing about the town, its inhabitants, its customs. At the only dive in town, sitting next to whoever fate had placed there, Quincas explained, "You know what brings me here?"

He lowered his voice.

"I killed a dame. I'm on the lam."

The Woman

With the tremendous vigor typical of a twenty-five-year-old, Quincas had only one thing on his mind.

"Any nice broads around here?"

"Yes and no."

Alarmed, he asked, "What do you mean?"

The other man clarified: "They're all married."

"All of them?"

"All of them."

Quincas, in the grip of his twenty-five-year-old hormones, insisted, "Isn't there a way around that? There's got to be a way."

The man he was sitting with turned his head, spit, and answered categorically: "There's no way."

There were no limits to Quincas' disappointment. He leapt up.

"That can't be!"

Then he nudged another man on the shoulder.

"What if I pay more? A lot more? Double?"

Tapping his pocket, he added, "See what you can do, OK?"

The Hunger

Dismayed, Quincas began wandering around town. Little by little his illusions all faded. Ten days later he was another man altogether. He had made about half a dozen friends and asked, "So how about it? Don't these women show their faces in public?"

"Are you stupid?"

"What?"

They laughed in his face.

"You think their husbands will let them? If a woman shows her face she's done for."

Quincas scratched his head and snarled, "This town is cursed!"

He missed the city, the coast. His thoughts turned to the girl he'd just killed. He told the others she'd cheated on him. But here out in the boondocks in the middle of the Acre Territory, his impressions of her started to change. You could say that the hatred in his heart slowly began to melt. He was forced to admit: "She wasn't all bad."

The friends, practically salivating, asked point-blank, tortured questions: "Nice body?"

With elbows glued to the table, with utter conviction, he answered, "What thighs!"

The others looked at one another, green with envy. One of them finally exploded, "Fool! You should never have killed her! What were you thinking!"

"It was a dumb move!" Quincas was forced to admit.

By now he would settle for the bare minimum, in other words with "seeing" one of these local women. It would be a visual satisfaction, a sad and pathetic consolation. He grilled the inhabitants of the town.

"How can you put up with this?"

"You get used to it," they answered.

He ran his hand through his mane of hair à la Buffalo Bill and pounded the table.

"Well, I won't get used to it! One of these days I'm going to lose it!"

The lack of women in that town pained him more than hunger or thirst. And then he asked himself, "What would happen if one of these sons of bitches keels over!"

The Idea

One day in the dive he floated an idea.

"You know what I don't get? What drives me nuts?"

"What?"

In a seething rage he went on, "That none of you losers ever thought of knocking off one of these jerks and taking his woman."

Silence. Every face seemed to register a look of fear. One guy who was picking lice from another one's head interrupted his duties. He looked on, open-mouthed, completely dumbfounded. He fell back into a chair marveling that the idea had never crossed his mind. Quincas, seeing the effect his words were having, plowed ahead. Was this right? Was it? That half a dozen should have women and one-hundred-and-fifty not? He pounded the table.

"We're no one's clowns!" And he grew bolder and shouted louder and louder in a crescendo of anger, "It's not right! It's not right, I tell you!"

And then, one by one, the mouths, the hands, the eyes of those men were transformed. You could say that Quincas's madness had become contagious. And the young man, openly appealing now for followers, screamed, "Why should a husband have more rights than we do?" He formulated the problem triumphantly.

"Answer me!" Beside himself now, he laid out the numerical argument. "A husband is only one man! We're one hundred and fifty!" In short, he wanted them to go from house to house and drag the women out. A collective scream was heard from the bar. Who knows what would have happened if at that moment a man, bearded and barefoot like all the others, had not burst into that bar and announced: "Baiano's wife is dying!"

The Face

From one moment to the next, fury merged with confusion. Quincas squeezed his head moaning, "This beats everything! This really beats everything!"

And without uttering another word, those tormented men headed in a unified mass to Baiano's house. What were they up to? Not even Quincas could say for sure. They walked with clenched fists, their throats dry and scorched. As they advanced through the wilderness, Quincas was overtaken by a blind rage against the mysterious forces of fate. He repeated over and over again through clenched teeth, "How is it possible? How is it possible?" It seemed to him to be too cruel a hardship that a woman should die in a place where there were so few. Finally, they stood in front of Baiano's house. Quincas stepped forward, but before he could knock, Baiano himself emerged and stood in front of the men pointing a rifle. Inside no tears were shed for the woman who had just died of consumption. The owner of the house, his eyes bloodshot and his mouth contorted, warned, "No one touches my wife! The first one who takes one step swallows a mouthful of lead!"

He was taciturn and mean and would likely carry out his threat. And then Quincas, who was younger than the rest and still had city women fresh on his mind, asked, begged, "We're not asking for much. We just want to take a look at your wife. Just a peek, that's all."

The husband agreed. And they lined up in awe and passed through the bedroom where the poor woman was lying, all bones covered with a thin, a very thin, layer of skin. They seemed possessed, on the verge of madness. But they respected death. Late at night the husband grabbed the rifle again and nudged the men along.

"Scat! All of you! And don't think I'm fool enough to bury my wife! I don't trust any of you, you filthy dogs!"

They all marched out, already missing the woman's face they had just seen minutes before. The husband locked everything and bolted the door. Alone with his wife's body, he poured kerosene on the corpse and on himself; he struck a match and lit a double pyre. Outside the men prowled around, furious.

Cowardice

For months on end he kept begging her on the telephone: "Come on, baby, come on!" Rosinha, high strung and quick to anger, was about to explode.

"Listen, Agenor! For the love of God! Haven't I told you already! Oh, God! Are you...? Listen! Are you capable of spiritual love?"

"Yes, but... they're not mutually exclusive. We're body and spirit. Aren't we body and spirit?"

Finally, she lost her temper.

"All you think about is sex!"

Agenor lost it too.

"Baby, I didn't invent sex. What's more... listen: Sex can be sublime. Do you understand? Sublime. Why are we in this world anyway?" Then came the triumphant conclusion: "Because of sex!"

Until one day Rosinha had the last word.

"I give up. Too bad. What you want, I can't give you. I'm married, and it's not right; it's just not right. My husband doesn't deserve this."

Feeling that he was losing her, he swallowed his pride.

"I swear. OK. Never again, you understand? I will never bring it up again."

Suddenly, Rosinha was overcome with pity for this man who loved her so. She smiled at the telephone as if Agenor could see her. She said, with sad tenderness, "Look, sometimes friendship can be better than sex."

Star-crossed Love

She might have cheated on any other husband. Marcondes, though, was one of those melancholy, humble souls — meek by birth, by heredity. His father (and likely his grandfather too) was a singular type — delicate, yet poignant, incapable of losing his temper or uttering a single vulgarity. Marcondes had not fallen far from the apple tree. He adored his wife. He had eyes for Rosinha and for no one else. She was keen on Agenor, a close friend who was always at their house and whom they couldn't get rid of. From the very first, however, she was very upfront, very true to her husband.

"I like you. I do. I don't deny it. But do you really think I can cheat on Marcondes? He wouldn't hurt a fly."

Agenor, in spite of his frustration at having been rejected, had to admit grudgingly that, objectively speaking, Marcondes was as inoffensive as a hummingbird. But since Agenor was a strong, healthy male brimming with energy, this unrequited love pained him greatly.

One would like to have thought Rosinha incapable of cheating on Marcondes. However, a fateful event occurred. These are the facts: One morning the delivery man came knocking about an unpaid bread bill. Marcondes had just left for work, and Rosinha answered the door.

"Come back tomorrow," she said.

"I don't think so! Are you going to give me my money or what?" said the delivery man, a burly and exceedingly gruff fellow.

She snapped, "Listen here! Since when do you think you can talk to me in that tone?" In all his brutishness the man with the thick, bovine neck threatened her, "I'm through giving breaks!"

She was beside herself now.

"You bum!" A neighbor from across the street appeared at the window.

"You're the bum!" the man shot back.

She was screaming at the top of her lungs by now.

"Thief! If my husband were here, he'd break your face!"

A huge grin crossed the man's face.

"I'll be back! I can't wait for your husband to break my face! I can't wait!"

He left, cool and disdainful, while she yelled after him.

At work Marcondes didn't even have time to take off his jacket. They handed him the phone.

"I was assaulted!" his wife screamed. "Drop everything and get over here!" When he walked in, his wife, surrounded by supportive neighbors, was sobbing. On seeing him, Rosinha rushed into his arms.

"Sweetheart! You can't imagine!" She told him everything in a frenzy. She finished by insisting hysterically, "I want you to promise me one thing. You're going to shoot that bastard!"

Marcondes freed himself violently from her clutches.

"Shoot him? Me? I hate guns! Guns never solved a thing! Don't even joke about this!"

A silence came over the room. Rosinha looked around, appalled. She turned to her husband.

"Are you scared?"

In a total panic he was going to say, "Scared is my middle name." But there were guests present. He resisted the urge, but he was visibly shaken. His cowardice was so obvious, so patently obvious, that Rosinha was left with a feeling of utter disgust.

She turned to her neighbors.

"Will you excuse us, please?"

They left one by one. When Marcondes learned that the man was coming back, he jumped like an Indian in a Western.

"I'm not in. When he comes back, tell him I'm not in. I don't care who it is!"

Rosinha looked at him in silence. That night when a knock was heard at the front door, she shot her husband an angry look.

"Go on! What are you waiting for?"

Marcondes was about to run to the bedroom and lock himself inside. Shame got the better of him though.

He managed to take three or four steps towards the front door. Suddenly, though, he froze and held his stomach. Then he made a run for it. He crossed paths with Rosinha as he dashed for the bathroom, nearly gagging. She opened the door: It was a beggar asking for change.

"God bless you," he said.

She closed the door and didn't think twice: She called Agenor. While her husband was in the bathroom retching, she was on the telephone, saying, "I changed my mind. I'll go. What's the address again? Let me get a pen."

Chance

Marcondes exited the bathroom wheezing.

"Was it him?" he stammered. When he learned that it hadn't been, he collapsed into the armchair. "I should learn jiu-jitsu," he said, woefully. The following day Rosinha skipped lunch. Instead she took a bath, dabbed perfume all over her body and sprinkled talcum powder on her feet. She peeked under her arms and lightly skimmed beneath them with a razor. Finally, she looked at herself in the mirror: She was beautiful and ready for sin. One hour later she got off the bus on the corner of Viveiros de Castro; she stopped briefly in front of the house to check the address. Then she heard a cheerful voice.

"Imagine running into you around here, Dona Rosinha?"

She turned, terrified. It was Dr. Eustaquio, a family friend who worked as an attorney at city hall. He bowed. He was forty-eight, well-dressed, perfectly coiffed, a true gentleman. Not sure what to do, Rosinha invented a lie.

"I'm waiting for a girlfriend. We made a date and...."

Dr. Eustaquio showed impeccable manners.

"I insist on waiting with you until your girlfriend arrives."

She looked at him in horror.

"You don't have to," she stammered.

He bowed enthusiastically.

"On the contrary. My pleasure!" And, lowering his voice with a twinkle in his eyes, he repeated, "My pleasure."

"Jerk!" she thought. She felt like crying.

And Dr. Eustaquio, who pulled in seventy-two grand from the city, was not finished.

"Has my friend read any Drummond lately?" he asked. "Carlos Drummond de Andrade? The poet! That's right, we learn something new every day, don't we? He was fervently against the building of Brasília. Did you know that? Lambasted the whole project. See if you can follow my logic: If Drummond rejects Brasília, then he is a false great poet. Wouldn't you agree? It's as if Camões were to reject the sea. It's as if Camões were to look at the sea and ask: 'Why so much water?' Well, you better believe it: By rejecting Brasília, Carlos Drummond is revealing himself to be a Camões of the swimming pool. Not even! A Camões of the washtub!"

At her wits end, Rosinha looked at her watch. Dr. Eustaquio asked another erudite question.

"Do you like poetry?"

Almost in tears, she answered, "Araujo Jorge. I like him." She hated that old man with his manicured nails, his cologne, his face that always seemed as if it had just been washed ten minutes ago. She tried to send him on his way.

"You really don't have to."

With a solemn and emphatic politeness, he answered, "I have plenty of time." With a mischievous twinkle, he added: "I didn't go in today. I took the day off." In fact, the man was of the opinion that the state existed precisely to subsidize its more intellectually enlightened employees while they "played hookey." They stood there for ten, twenty, thirty, forty minutes. Dr. Eustaquio wouldn't stop; by now he was saying, "We've had one Homer in Brazil. Jorge de Lima. He's dead now. He prophesized Brasília in *The Invention of Orpheus*."

Rosinha interrupted him.

"My girlfriend's not coming. I'm leaving."

She thought she could shake her obnoxious companion, get off at the next stop and walk back. But, ever the gentleman, he insisted, "I'll take you home! I won't take no for an answer!"

Rosinha realized that it was useless. "This clown won't leave me alone!" she thought. She rode from Copacabana all the way to Aldeia Campista with that man by her side. And he talked all the way.

"Over at the prosecutor's office we have a very talented writer; his name is Otto Lara Resende." She listened, numb. Dr. Eustaquio walked her to her door.

"Farewell! Farewell!" he said. Rosinha went inside.

On the bus, Dr. Eustaquio thought to himself, "Nice girl! Very nice!" Later that evening her husband arrived. She pounced on him.

"Do you love your pussy cat? Do you?" She offered her husband all of the frantic voluptuousness that she couldn't give her would-be lover.

Spite

The husband was the jealous type or, as he was wont to say, "the insanely jealous type." If Marlene should happen to laugh a little louder than usual, that was the end of that. All hell would break loose. He thought a woman's laughter was akin to an act of lewdness. Marlene mustered a feeble protest.

"What did I do, sweetheart? I didn't do anything!"

"Yes you did," he said, resentful, almost offended. "Only riff-raff laugh at that!"

She had to eliminate laughter from her daily life. When she was with Rafael she would feel terribly self-conscious about her every look, smile or word. Family and friends soon took notice.

"What's the matter? You used to be so happy."

She couldn't help but sound bitter.

"Rafael just won't let up on me!" she would whisper to her closest friends. "He doesn't give me a break. He doesn't let me out of his sight. He's even jealous of lampposts!"

"Don't be a fool. Fight back!" one girlfriend suggested.

How could she? What no one knew and what Marlene was not even willing to admit to herself was that she was afraid of her husband. Rafael had a temper out of *Cavalleria Rusticana*; he was a bottled-up barbarian. Once he made a concrete threat. He squeezed his wife's face between his hands, and, with his mouth almost touching hers, he said, "Cheat on me, and I'll kill you. I swear I'll kill you!"

Fidelity

When it came to her husband's jealousy, Marlene could safely say, "Rafael is barking up the wrong tree." This might sound clichéd, but it was the plain truth. Married for three and a half years, her conduct was above even the slightest suspicion. No life was more transparent, more of an open book. Her uprightness at times defied believability. She never let herself be alone with men other than her husband, her brothers-in-law, and her own brothers. She only danced with Rafael or, at most, Leocadio, the only friend deserving of her husband's total trust.

Rafael loved to say, "I trust Leocadio more than my brothers."

Marlene was so faithful and so loyal that she was astounded to discover that her girlfriends could, with utter frivolity and detachment, engage in affairs for mere sport. Her astonishment was sincere and heartfelt: "How do you have the courage?"

Several answered essentially: "Your day will come!" One was a little bolder than the rest.

"Do you still love your husband?" she asked Marlene.

"Of course!"

"I don't believe it. Please! I don't believe it."

"Why?"

"Because no woman can love a man for more than two years," she said. "And even that's pushing it!"

"That's horrible!"

"You better believe it, baby!"

The Trip

This conversation deeply disturbed her. For the first time she thought, "Could it be that...?" She shivered in fear and excitement and tried her best to think of something else. Then, just days later, her husband came home with the following news: He would have to accompany his boss to the capitals of Europe.

"What about me?" she asked.

Rafael sighed.

"You'll stay here. I won't be long. A month, maximum."

When the same girlfriend found out, she called.

"Congratulations! Congratulations! Don't be a fool; this is your big chance." And she added, "Chalk it up to experience. Just this one time."

Marlene protested vehemently, almost belligerently. But she felt the shiver once again. The truth is that inside her, in her innermost recesses, she carried her friend's words: "No woman can love a man for more than two years." She closed her eyes and did the math: She had been married to Rafael for three years. Did she still love him? Did she have the same feelings for him as before? Was it still the same? A little while later she was in front of the mirror applying powder and rouge. Looking at her reflection, she thought, "No. It's not the same."

Before his departure Rafael had a heart-to-heart with her. Already anticipating reasons to be jealous, he repeated, "If in my absence... I'll kill you, you hear?" Ten minutes later he confessed with heroic sincerity, "No, I'd never kill you. Not you. But I would kill the man who had the courage, the nerve...!"

The following morning, Marlene accompanied her husband to the airport. When she saw the four-engine airplane take off, she felt a feeling of utter freedom.

The Friend

She returned home almost giddy. Before boarding the plane, her husband warned, "I don't want to hear about you chatting with other men. Leocadio is the only man you can have a conversation with. The only one!" Back home she hummed a song and dragged her fingers across the piano keys. The sensation of total freedom was intoxicating. She took a long and delicious bath; she passed her hands over her naked body like a long-lost lover. She applied makeup, sprayed perfume on her hands, her arms, her neck; she put on her favorite negligee, stepped into her little ermine slippers. She had no concrete plan, really, no definite design, but she prepared with such delight and attention to detail that it was as if she were getting ready for someone. She sat next to the telephone and dialed. A man's voice answered. Marlene gave her name and spoke.

"I want to ask you a favor, Leocadio," she said.

"Of course, what is it?" he replied.

She lowered her voice.

"Would you like to come over? Now?"

Leocadio seemed taken aback.

"Is something the matter?"

She avoided answering him directly.

"I need to talk to you." The initiative to call, the conversation – both were unplanned, the result of some mysterious and inexplicable impulse. She was acting in a completely unpremeditated, carefree way, and she did not recognize herself. Finally, Leocadio arrived. He seemed glum and nervous. She explained the call.

"I was feeling a little lonely... I wanted you to keep me company..."

Leocadio, who had been seated until then, stood. He seemed uncomfortable.

"Well. Let's do the following: I have an appointment now. I'll be back in half an hour, forty minutes, OK?"

The Pursuit

He never returned. Marlene herself was not sure what her designs had been. She was confused and scared. She rushed to the mirror and looked at herself with new and critical eyes. You could say the image she saw was of a stranger. Freed from her husband's yoke, she desired who knows what new and delightful experiences. Her girlfriends spoke of caresses she had never known from Rafael. She waited forty minutes, one hour, two hours for

Leocadio to arrive. He was nowhere to be seen. She became irritated, and her irritation made her feelings clearer. Now she knew what she wanted. She called her frivolous friend, who immediately applauded Marlene.

"You have spunk, huh? That's what I like!" She gave her a tip: "When a man starts to play hard to get, when he starts playing games, that's when the woman should take the initiative. That's right! The trick is to pounce on him! Why not?"

Marlene stammered, "God forbid!"

By now her friend was all worked up, as if she had something personal at stake. She insisted, "Take my word!"

Marlene didn't know what to do. She was both attracted and repulsed by her friend's brazen attitude. Finally, she decided to call Leocadio again.

He was as cheerful as possible.

"Forgive me, darling. Something came up; you know how these things are. But I'll be there tonight with my fiancée."

Just then Marlene exhibited an unexpected boldness.

"No, not with your fiancée!" It was such a spontaneous, unexpected outburst that it surprised them both.

"Why not with my girlfriend?" Leocadio asked, not fully understanding.

She had gone too far to pull back now. Enunciating her every word, she said, "I want you. Just you. No one else. Do you understand?"

He answered softly, "I do."

She even added, "For God's sake, don't make me spell it out." Later that evening she called her girlfriend to tell her the latest.

"You're one of mine," the friend gushed. "You're one of mine! I want a full report tomorrow!"

The Wait

Marlene told the maid to take the evening off. She wanted to be alone, totally alone. She got ready with painstaking attention to detail. She insisted on wearing her ermine slippers that, for reasons unknown, she found cute and alluring. Suddenly, there was a knock on the door. She rushed to open it. It was a messenger with a cablegram from her husband. It practically made her nauseous to read, "Million kisses, miss you dearly." She tore up the message and threw the little pieces out the window.

She still held out hope till two, three in the morning. She went to bed in tears, exclaiming, "Idiot! Idiot!" That morning she called him, devastated.

"I didn't deserve what you did to me. It wasn't right!" She ended defiantly, "You seem like you're scared of me!"

"I *am* scared," he explained. "Very. Scared. Because I have feelings for you; I always have."

Marlene latched onto his words.

"Me too. Me too." Then Leocadio, calm yet afflicted, said, "I won't betray my best friend. Never. I'd rather put a bullet through my brain than betray my friend. Period."

Marlene yelled hysterically into the telephone, "Mummy! Imbecile! Clown!"

Revenge

She locked herself in and would not venture out of the house for any reason. She only broke out of her dull, frantic pain to dress down Leocadio by phone. She used the most vulgar and distasteful expressions. He listened in silence, without hanging up.

After one month went by, her husband returned in another four-engine airplane. He had missed her dearly, certain that his wife was the best wife in the whole world. In the cab on the way home, Marlene, her face still showing traces of suffering and hatred, said, "Do you want to know what that friend of yours, that dog Leocadio did? He grabbed me and kissed me. He's been chasing after me like a dog in heat!"

One hour later Rafael walked into Leocadio's office. On seeing his friend, Leocadio flashed an affectionate look of surprise. Rafael drew his gun and shot him four times, point-blank. Leocadio died instantly, unable to even shed the friendly, almost sweet smile from his face.

The Doll Cemetery

He was forty-five years old and used body-length drawers, the type you tie to your shins, two times around. He would greet everyone without regard to class, age or color. This random cordiality greatly impressed all. It was said of him enthusiastically and unanimously, "The man is a saint!"

And he, in turn, would answer, "One does what one can! One does what one can!"

He could not see a child without taking a nickel out of his pocket and caressing the kid's face. This soft spot for children went beyond simple affection; it bordered on an affliction, a mania. If by chance he witnessed a woman hitting her child, he would get on his soapbox.

"Ma'am, don't do that! That's no way to raise a child!"

The mother, an old-fashioned type, would explode.

"Children need a good beating every now and again!"

And he, in turn, would lose his composure.

"Grown-ups are the ones who need a good beating! Yes, ma'am, adults are the only ones responsible for the crime, adultery and abuse in this world. And what's more, we adults are the ones who should be learning from children…!"

Dr. Basilio

His name was Basilio, and he was a doctor. A child's mere toothache or earache tormented him more than the death of an adult. And nothing moved him more than finding out that a child was an orphan. It would lead him to ask innumerable questions.

"Who died, your father or your mother?"

"My mother."

If it were both the mother and the father, he was moved to tears. He had an ulcer in his small intestine. His compassion for the plight of children seemed to have a direct effect on his ulcer. In short, the orphans' afflictions affected him as if they were his own.

One day he awoke, bug-eyed, with trembling lips. "I had a dream…." He was visibly shaking when he tried to describe it, as if he were consumed by a fever. Someone insisted, "Tell us, tell us!"

He dreamed that a voice had called on him to go out into the world and do good deeds for the orphans of Brazil. His friends, frightened, saw in this a sign of mental illness. One, who was closer to him and who was bolder than the rest, suggested, "You need to get married! I know this widow who is really something!" But Dr. Basilio seemed to have found his destiny. At home, at work, in the trolley, his voice trembling, he would say, "Why didn't I think of this before?" He gave notice at his job at the ministry, where he was chief of his division. The minister could not believe his ears.

"What's the matter, Dr. Basilio? Is something wrong?"

The answer was sober and emphatic.

"Sir, I'm sick and tired of leading a useless and selfish life. From now on I will dedicate my life to little children."

In the hallway, alone after his conversation with the minister, Dr. Basilio opened his arms and murmured with tears rolling down his face, two at a time, "Suffer the little children to come unto me!"

Everyone, from the minister to the lowest-level employee, was certain: "The old man is off his rocker."

But Dr. Basilio was convinced that the moment had arrived for him to carry out his grand mission in life. He had money in the bank, and he made arrangements to mobilize it. Days later he was renting a huge house in Tijuca with immense living room and bedrooms, a basement that could serve as living quarters, and a spacious and cool veranda. In the front there was a garden overrun with weeds, with two cypress trees, thin and somber, one on each side of the gate; in the back there was a huge yard full of trees, including a jackfruit tree. The old man rubbed his hands together.

"Excellent! Excellent!"

In his impeccably creased striped pants he oversaw the work on the house. Occasionally the workers would find in the darkened corridors or in the bathrooms a scorpion or some poisonous insect. Two weeks later the old house was, in the words of the new owner, "a jewel." But he went further, and he took measures to create there a first-rate educational establishment for orphaned girls. Pacing back and forth with an inspired air about him, shaking both arms, he announced in his booming voice, "Sirs, I show you the orphans' new home!"

The Saint

There could be no doubt now – Dr. Basilio was not, as was mistakenly believed before, an old kook. Against all odds, he was able to melt away the world's skepticism with his overwhelming kindness. It could be said he was a saint. A pair of sandals would have been the appropriate footwear for such a man. But such a superior being could be forgiven his one vain touch – old-fashioned spats which he insisted on wearing over his shoes. But all of his gestures, his inflections, betrayed the dignity of his purpose. In no time at all the house was filled to capacity with forty orphan girls! One day a deaf and dumb boy showed up.

"We only take in girls," Dr. Basilio stated, with a mixture of tenderness and intransigence.

It was a policy of the utmost propriety. According to Dr. Basilio the coexistence of the two sexes was a "thorny" issue. The policy became clearer when he added that it would lead to "debauchery." Sex to him was vile. The deaf and dumb boy left empty-handed. Thus, in the Dr. Basilio Shelter girls who had no mothers, no fathers, could find a new home, a new family. Occasionally, reporters and photographers came knocking. They would take photographs of everyone, including Dr. Basilio and the headmistress, a certain Dona Emilia, an ex-midwife, plump and covered with varicose veins. And the old man outdid himself when suggesting ideas. He invited reporters and photographers to eat at the same table as the students. He would apologize.

"Today the food is not up to par!"

A reporter, smacking his lips, would beg to differ.

"It's great! Delicious!"

As a matter of fact, whether by coincidence or not, the days when reporters visited coincided with the most amazing selection on the menu, such as (imagine!) chicken à la king. For dessert there would be peach preserves or, in the worst case, guava paste with cream cheese. Upon leaving, the reporter would think to himself, "What a life these kids have!"

Glory!

The stories began coming out in the newspapers, abundantly illustrated with photographs. One detail would never be omitted: Dr. Basilio had turned down with Franciscan selflessness a job on the public payroll, which would have allowed him to live like a nabob, just so he could dedicate himself to his mission. The old man would not rest; imbued with the respect he commanded, he would go door to door raising funds. He would gesticulate and explain, "We accept all amounts."

And, indeed, from ten cents on up, all amounts were accepted. The donors wanted more details, which he would abundantly supply. He would insist on emphasizing that he "did not live there." Why?

"Isn't it obvious! A house full of girls. What would they say of me?"

And the interlocutor would respond, "But you're above suspicion!"

The old man would sigh, "You never know."

Every evening at seven Dr. Basilio, briefcase in hand, would ostensibly leave the establishment. He would walk down the sidewalk greeting all, including strangers. He had the habit of saying that strangers were also God's children. When he passed by, the old women at the windows would sigh, "When he dies, he's going straight to heaven!" Thanks to the newspapers, the nation was convinced that Dr. Basilio was one of those rare men, so rare that their kind no longer walked upon this earth. On one occasion, however, in the dead of night the neighbors were awakened by howls that came from the shelter. What could it be? They knocked on the door. With a kerosene lamp in hand, the headmistress appeared at the door and explained.

"One of the girls was bitten by a scorpion."

In the morning Dr. Basilio confirmed the news.

"Old houses are a real problem. It's a real shame!"

The Cemetery

Thus, this model school celebrated its tenth anniversary. By now it was receiving grants from the government, the whole kit and caboodle. The mail Dr. Basilio received on a daily basis rivaled that of popular radio crooners. And thus life went on, glorious and peaceful, until one day a reporter from some sensationalist tabloid published an article saying that "Dr. Basylum's Asylum" was a scam and that Dona Emilia was merely a sinister "abortion-mill operator," etc., etc. All of this really got to the saintly old man, and he went into a deep depression. And one evening, still smarting at humanity's ingratitude, he collapsed and died. They laid the body out in the school's main room, and the public was invited to pay their respects. At ten at night when the number of well-wishers was at its peak, a scream was heard from the end of the corridor. Dona Emilia, dressed all in black, stood and announced, "It's nothing! It's nothing!" But the screams continued, and those assembled rushed into the hallway. Suddenly, a door opened: one of the orphans appeared. She walked, then staggered, then leaned up against the wall. And then she fell to the ground. Those assembled saw a trail of blood and noticed the awful hemorrhaging. She was barely fifteen; she looked at the strangers assembled and groaned.

"He did this! He did this!"

She seemed to be pointing to the room where the body lay. The wake dispersed; no one seemed interested in the dead man anymore. A messenger who had brought a wreath of flowers froze in the hallway, astounded at the loss of blood. They took the young girl into a bedroom. They called for help. Trembling, she confirmed that Dr. Basilio was indeed the culprit. In the hallway one of the girls wearing the school's plain, blue cloth uniform yelled out, "He did this to me too! He did this!" There was an infernal din. One of the girls called to all of the others as she ran to the rear of the yard. In no time at all, the girls were digging with their bare hands. And one by one, little skeletons began to appear, so small and fragile that they seemed like dolls. And Dr. Basilio was the one, merciless father. The most recent angel had been buried that same day. Since he was only five months old, smaller than the others, Dona Emilia had buried him in a shoebox. When the top was removed, there he lay, an angel, naked and blue.

Beloved

The night they were engaged to be married Jamil took Ivone's hands in his. He spoke softly and asked the most ancient of questions.

"Do you love me?"

"Of course! Do you have any doubt?"

He insisted: "A lot?"

Her answer was categorical: "Tons!"

They remained silent for a moment. Suddenly, deeply moved, he stammered, "Me too! I love you! I love you! I love you!" He paused and then, his voice straining, finished what he had to say.

"You mean everything to me! Everything!" he said.

Just then Everardo, Jamil's older brother, approached and addressed Ivone.

"May I congratulate the fiancée?"

Ivone allowed him to kiss her forehead. Then, beaming, Jamil, with both hands in his pockets, turned to his brother.

"I'm the happiest guy in the world!"

The Surprise

The brothers left around midnight. They were so close they were like twins. On the bus ride home, Jamil sang his fiancée's praises.

"Ivone is amazing!"

Seated next to him, nearly asleep, Everardo yawned and agreed.

"She's a great gal!"

The next day Jamil was at work when the telephone rang. He picked up and was shocked to hear his Ivone sobbing, "Come home right away! Please!"

Shaken, Jamil managed to ask, "What happened? Tell me?"

"I can't over the phone! Only in person," she said.

Jamil dropped what he was doing, dropped everything, and flew by cab to his fiancée's house. On the way he wracked his brain.

"What could it be?"

Ivone was calmer by the time he arrived. She stood when she saw him.

"Let's go talk inside, come on." She took him into the study. There, behind closed doors, she began crying again.

"Baby, we can't get married. It's impossible; you hear me?"

"What do you mean impossible?" he asked. "Is this a joke? Why impossible?"

Ivone blew her nose.

"Because I love you, but I also love someone else. Oh, God! I never imagined you could be in love with two people at the same time. Now I know it's possible."

The Other Man

At first he was more shocked than hurt. He took out a cigarette and lit it. Blowing the smoke, he tried to put his thoughts and feelings in order. He stood, walked back and forth, and suddenly froze in front of his fiancée. He cleared his throat.

"Well. Try to make sense, sweetie. You love me. OK. And you love someone else. Is that what you're telling me?"

Ivone nodded yes.

He went on: "Think about it. That makes absolutely no sense. Either you're in love with me, or you're in love with him. You can't be in love with both of us."

Now it was Ivone's turn to stand.

"Yes, I can," she said. "I've come to the conclusion that a woman can be in love with two, three, four, five men at the same time. Two hundred for all I know!"

Silence. Jamil was suddenly afraid of losing her. Crushed, he asked, "So, who is he?" Ivone stepped back, terrified. Leaning against the wall, she began sobbing.

"Ask me anything but that. Not that! That I can't tell you!"

The Name

He implored for two hours.

"The name! I want the name! Who is this guy? Speak!"

Finally, exhausted, her mouth contorted, Ivone capitulated.

"Everardo."

"Who?"

She clutched her fiancé and slid down his body. Holding onto his legs, she repeated, "Yes, Everardo! Your brother!"

He snapped. In his rage he lifted Ivone off the ground and began shaking her.

"Answer me! Of all the men why did you have to choose my brother? Why didn't you cheat on me with someone else? Why?"

"I didn't cheat on you," she insisted softly, breathlessly. "Nothing happened… just one kiss. That was it! I swear!"

He let go of her and proceeded to leave.

She, however, with unexpected strength, detained him.

"Let me finish," she said. "I can't live without you; I can't live without him!"

Jamil broke free violently. Ivone fell into an armchair and buried her face in her hands and began to sob. At the door before leaving, he said, "This is a disease! It's perverted! Goodbye!"

Fortunately her family had gone out, and the maid was in the rear – no one heard anything.

Desperate

For two whole days Jamil did not show up at home or at work. He avoided friends, acquaintances and, above all, his brother. Staggering through the streets, he kept repeating, "Slut! Slut!" On the third day, unshaven, with a cruel sneer stuck on his face, he confronted his fiancée. She rushed to hug him and felt the bulge of his revolver. Jamil took a deep breath.

"I have three options: Either I kill my brother, or I kill you, or I kill myself," he said.

They were seated on a park bench. Ivone stood aghast. Barely able to speak, she muttered under her breath, "Kill...? Die...?" She sat down next to her fiancé again. She clutched his arm.

"What if we died together? The three of us?" She paused and then proceeded, nearly delirious, "Since our love is impossible, what does it matter if we live?"

Jamil got swept up in her words. He turned to her, fascinated.

"You'll die with me? Will you?" Their mouths were almost touching.

"With you and your brother, OK?" she said. "The three of us! I know... I'm sure he'll want to. He has to... we'll die together, like soul mates."

The Pact

When things died down, they planned everything. Jamil managed to find a friend who would lend them an apartment in Copacabana. He chose the poison. Ivone would be responsible for telling Everardo the time and place. At last, on the agreed-upon day, the three met at the apartment. Ivone was deeply moved; it was as if the very thought of death had made her even more beautiful. Very few words were exchanged. Jamil picked up the three glasses and went inside to fill them. He came back a few minutes later. He gave them their glasses and kept one for himself. He whispered, "Let's all drink together." First, though, Ivone kissed them both, calling each "My love." Then they drank up. This is what happened: The only one to fall to the ground, his intestines burning, was Everardo.

Ivone stood, aghast, with the empty glass in her hand.

"I don't feel a thing!"

Then, while Everardo writhed on the rug, Jamil grabbed his fiancée.

"Only he drank poison… we drank baking soda."

Ivone stepped back in horror. She wanted to scream, but Jamil was quicker and shut her mouth with a never-ending kiss. When he let go, she said, "Kiss me again! Kiss me!"

The Blackmailer

The future mother-in-law was a teacher with the most pleasant of dispositions. She was fond of saying, "Harmony is the most important thing in a marriage."

She insisted above all on what seemed to be a point of principle for her: "No arguments! No squabbles!"

Fernando heeded her every word and when alone with his friends would boast: "Dolores's mother is like a second mother!" His friends listened in amazement. A few of the more skeptical ones would ask, "Are you serious?"

Fernando would answer with overwhelming conviction: "I swear to God! May lightning strike me dead if I'm lying!"

In fact, Dona Zuleica exercised an admirable influence over the relationship. Her sway over her daughter and her son-in-law (or future son-in-law) was so great the two would do nothing without first consulting her. When alone with her daughter she would say, "You must draw lines. No tongue-kissing!" Even in her absence Dolores would argue, "Mother doesn't think that's right, etc, etc."

Amazingly, Fernando would submit without hesitation. And thus, under the auspices of the cordial, sympathetic and clairvoyant Dona Zuleica, their engagement lasted a year under the most idyllic of circumstances until finally they were married. When the two departed in a taxi for their honeymoon in the mountains, Dona Zuleica went back into the house and closed the door. She sat down and, with a certain melancholy air about her, said, "Now I can die in peace!"

The Couple

She was hopelessly deluded. In truth of fact she could not die. Her daughter was married, that much was true, but both she and her husband needed Dona Zuleica's continual and overt attention and assistance.

Between the two of them they possessed very little that was theirs, and they had no life experience to speak of. It was as if they had no feelings or ideas of their own. When Dona Zuleica, ravaged by a pulmonary edema, finally rendered her soul to her Maker, they looked at one another in a panic. It was if they were posing a reciprocal and unanswerable question: "What now?" After all, Dona Zuleica had been a walking encyclopedia, elucidating every detail of their daily existence. What would they feel, think, do now that this beloved woman had disappeared from their lives forever? Coming back from the cemetery, Fernandinho sighed.

"Honey, we're in big trouble. I don't know how we'll manage without her."

The girl for her part had a vivid and romantic imagination and thought that at that very moment her mother and father must surely be in heaven holding hands, perhaps residing on an evening star. Five years earlier Dona Zuleica had become a widow and since then had lived a life of constant longing for her dead husband. As far as she was concerned, no one was more noble, more imbued with virtue than the deceased Clementino. So much so that when she ordered the mausoleum, which cost a pretty penny to build, she wrote the epitaph herself and had it engraved in bronze letters. Now, after a five year separation, the two were united once again, their bodies on earth and their souls in heaven. On returning home, Fernandinho made the following philosophical observation to his wife: "Life is a bitch!"

The Letters

Dona Zuleica was buried on a Thursday. By Saturday morning, after overcoming many natural reservations, Fernandinho put on a brave face and told his wife, "Honey, I think I'll go over to the stadium."

Dolores nearly rebuked him. As a daughter she was extremely taken aback. She believed that great pain did not allow for distractions, including soccer. But she held back, using the following logic: The household still resonated with the advice, guidance and wisdom of the much lamented Dona Zuleica, the saintly lady who made a habit of saying, "Don't fight," "Don't argue", "Arguments only make things worse," etc., etc.

Thus Dolores refrained from making the objections that would have been in order, so much so that the husband became increasingly excited about the game, which after all was only a run-of-the-mill match between Flamengo and Madureira. Only as he was about to walk out the door did she permit herself the following comment: "Mother was buried on Thursday, and you're already going to a game!"

"But sweetie pie, soccer is the most harmless thing in the world. I promise, there's nothing wrong with going to a game!"

Dolores, still in black and, as was proper, not wearing any makeup, stood at the gate until her husband turned the corner. It was only when he disappeared that she was frightened to discover that her neighbor, an ex-suitor, was devouring her with his eyes from a window across the street. Terribly embarrassed without any real reason, she turned completely red and rushed into the house. All alone in that sad house she started thinking about Dona Zuleica, and then without really wanting to and not knowing why, she thought about the neighbor who had looked at her in such an intense, almost immoral way. His name was Alfredinho, and three years earlier, after some short-lived flirting, they'd had a falling out because he was hopelessly jealous. Dona Zuleica intervened with her benign and gentle authority.

"He's not right for you," she said.

They had stopped talking, but Alfredinho attended her wedding. When the bride walked down the aisle, Alfredinho stood in the crowd staring at her with fire in his eyes. Even now when she thought about it, she shuddered in fear. Feeling her mother's absence more than ever, she walked into Dona Zuleica's bedroom, which she had not entered since the good woman had passed away. It was for her a very sad consolation to be able to wander among the belongings of the deceased: her books, jewelry, her dresser. She opened the dresser and saw her mother's dresses and undergarments. As her eyes welled up with tears, she examined the articles one by one until at the bottom, the very bottom of a large drawer she found a small safe that she had never seen before. She opened it in amazement and found a bundle of letters tied with a blue silk ribbon. She untied the ribbon with trepidation and read the first letter. It began as follows: "Osvaldo."

Out loud she said, "Father's name was Clementino!"

For half an hour, forty minutes, she read those letters one by one. A particularly disturbing one included the following lines: "I know your husband is sick, but I can't stand to be away from you…Our son awaits you…Tomorrow, don't be late." Another one ended with: "I've finished composing the verse for your husband's tombstone. A million kisses." Stunned, she read and reread those letters and lost all notion of time and space. They were extremely clear sentences, but still she had trouble understanding them. Everything seemed jumbled in her mind; there was a moment when she thought she had actually gone mad. She might as well be reading Greek, Chinese or Eskimo. She kept repeating to herself, "It's a lie! It can't be!" Her thoughts turned to her father who had been so cruelly betrayed. She was so engrossed in her reading that she did not notice when her husband arrived. Back from the game, he stood at the bedroom door and watched her with the letters strewn on her lap. He asked, "What's going on?"

A Brilliant Idea

Caught off guard, she did not have the presence of mind or the time to hide the letters. Her husband, his curiosity aroused, took one off the bed and read it from start to finish. Stunned, he kept exclaiming, "Well, I'll be…!"

Having read one, he felt entitled to read them all. For a whole hour, with his wife crying next to him, he learned the secrets contained in those love letters. Every now and then he would exclaim, "Wow!"

When he learned that her lover had penned the verse on her husband's tombstone he said, "Now that beats everything! That really beats everything!"

One question was eating away at him. Who could the amazing Osvaldo be? He asked his wife. She had racked her brains for over half an hour trying to answer that very question. In the family circle there was no one named Osvaldo; or rather, there was one who made very rare appearances.

"good-looking?"

"More or less," she said, struggling to remember.

"It's gotta be him. I'll bet you anything."

Just then Dolores remembered his last name: Osvaldo Palhares. Fernandinho smacked his forehead when he heard the name. Pacing back and forth, he yelled, "He's a millionaire! Filthy rich! He's got buildings, avenues named after him, God knows what else! And I'll tell you what: Your mother didn't know how to play her cards right! She could have been living on easy street."

But Dolores, buried in her pain, did not hear a word her husband said. She got up slowly with her hair disheveled and had only one thing on her mind.

"Fernandinho, we need to tear up all these letters! We need to burn them!"

It made sense since they represented a shameful legacy. The husband, however, jumped up. He squatted and frantically began grabbing the scattered pages and envelopes.

"Tear them up? Are you crazy? Come on! No, ma'am! Trust me, sweetie! I know what I'm doing!"

Since his startled wife did not understand, he explained, but only partially.

"I have a great idea! It's brilliant! I'll explain later."

The Shakedown

First, he perfected his plan and only then did he reveal it in its entirety. This Osvaldo was a highly regarded man in the community, circumspect, adult daughters, etc., etc. When he learns that he, Fernandinho, has these letters, he'll be terrified.

"He'll find me a job, I just know it. Oh! Dolores, Dolores! Your mother was a fool! She didn't know how to work this to her advantage!"

His wife at first had her doubts. Was this proper? Was it right?

Cruelly, he shut her up by throwing a question back at her: What Dona Zuleica did, was that proper? Was that right? He rejoiced, "I'm going to take his money, big time! I'm going to make something of myself!"

It would be said later that this sudden onset of greed, this obsession with money had transformed him, and not just his character. His face seemed different, his eyes, even his hands. In a fit of hysteria, he went all out.

"No one's pure in this world; everyone's crooked. And a job's not enough! I want money!"

The next day he telephoned the millionaire. He introduced himself as "Dona Zuleica's son-in-law," and announced that he had "damning letters," etc, etc. They settled on a time and date when they would meet at Osvaldo's office. The millionaire was a model of decorum during the meeting. He limited himself to saying, "Her husband knew everything, and he took advantage of me. Now it's the son-in-law's turn."

They settled on an amount. As he was leaving, the millionaire said, "Beware: Your wife will cheat on you some day."

On his way home, Fernandinho could not get those words out of his mind. Suddenly, the joy of having collected the money vanished. On reaching the front gate of his house, he turned around and headed for a bar. He went from bar to bar, getting drunker and drunker. He arrived home well past midnight, tripping over himself. Bleary-eyed, he watched his wife sleep for half an hour. Then, he worked his way to the kitchen, supporting himself against the walls to keep from falling. He put the kettle on the fire. Ten minutes later the entire neighborhood woke up to screams. Fernandinho had poured boiling water on his sleeping wife.

The Bald Man

Her mother decided to get to the bottom of things.

"Come here, honey!" she yelled to her daughter.

Julinha approached, brushing her hair.

"What, Mother?"

Dona Matilde, a plump lady with an immense bust whose size defied description, didn't know where to begin. Finally, she found the words.

"Explain something to me: Do you love Aluizio or not?"

"I do."

"I mean do you love him enough to marry him?"

Julinha sighed.

"Maybe."

"Oh, no! You have got to be kidding me. What kind of an answer is that? How long have you been seeing each other? Two years now!"

"Three, Mother."

"Three," the mother corrected herself. "That's right, three. More than enough time. Make up your mind if you do or don't and put an end to this." Julinha sighed again.

"I will, Mother. This week I'll decide once and for all."

Strange Romance

Indeed, it was a strange romance that had dragged on for days, then weeks, then months, causing everyone to wonder: "Will they or won't they get married?" The girl, her family, acquaintances, all agreed: Aluizio was a great catch – a high-level government official who always wore a vest, a flower in his lapel and perfectly creased pants. He always gave the appearance of having just washed his face ten minutes ago. People actually commented on how smooth his skin was. Some joked, "Aluizio doesn't perspire. The man doesn't sweat!" In all other aspects he was delicacy personified – incapable of being coarse or angry. Julinha, who acknowledged all of his virtues, had only one objection: "He's too nice!"

You could say that his combined qualities disenchanted her. Approximately three years earlier Aluizio had asked for her hand in marriage in the following manner: "I like you a lot... I love you. But I'm in no hurry. Give it some thought, study the matter, and then give me an answer. OK?"

"OK."

Time passed and there was still no answer. They were together wherever they went, though. At parties Aluizio was her constant and inevitable companion. And although the engagement had never been formalized, Julinha always introduced him as "my fiancé." Deep down, perhaps she might have wished for a more eager and demonstrative boyfriend. Since things were going nowhere, the family started to increase the pressure.

"Hurry up and get married! Get married and get it over with!"

The mother insisted: "He's such a good boy! And we get along so well!"

That was another of Aluizio's virtues; he would butter up his mother-in-law, or future mother-in-law, in the most shameless ways imaginable. It was so patently obvious that one of Julinha's rather outspoken cousins commented, "He's a real suck-up!"

Decision

The pressure to marry was so great that Julinha finally felt she had no choice. She turned to her mother and said, "OK, I'll get married. There, I'll do it."

When Aluizio found out, he lifted the girl's hand to his lips. Julinha said nothing, but inside she thought, "Why didn't he kiss me on the lips?"

The truth of the matter is that she was unsure whether she loved him or not.

That night, alone with Dona Matilde, she sighed.

"Mother, I think what I'm feeling is love or it must be."

Dona Matilde thought for a while and then observed, "Love is an illusion, sweetie. Friendship is much more important."

Forty-eight hours later a small episode occurred whose importance would only become clear later. The couple had gone downtown and were returning home. At a major intersection on Avenida Sete de Setembro, the light turned red. While they waited at the light the girl witnessed the following: The traffic cop working the intersection removed his cap, exposing his head to the light of day. But it was no ordinary head – it was smooth, naked, devoid of even the slightest vestige of hair. A billiard ball was not as smooth as his dazzling dome. She nudged Aluízio.

"Look! Look!"

He looked, startled at his fiancée's delight.

"Daddy's head was like that!" she continued exhilarated. "He didn't have a single strand of hair on his head. Not one."

The light turned green. The car drove off, leaving the traffic cop behind. Julinha had not been lying: Dr. Venancio Almendariz, her father, a high level official of the Ministry of Justice, had suffered from a scalp condition that caused him to lose all of his hair in one week. His baldness was so striking as to appear artificial, the type you see on stage. His subordinates at the ministry had the habit of saying in whispers that Dr. Almendariz was "the baldest man in all of Brazil." He died that way. The bald corpse was enough to cause shivers in some of the well-wishers. Someone even covered his naked head with dahlias and carnations.

Lamentable

Julinha adored her father and defended his memory fanatically. When she arrived home she threw herself into her mother's arms.

"Guess what I saw! Guess!"

She described the incident at the intersection.

"It was so beautiful, my God!" she said as Dona Matilde and Aluizio looked on uncomfortably. She gushed so much that her fiancé, with his usual circumspection, intervened.

"Hold on a second!" he said. "When have you ever seen a good-looking bald man?"

She turned, shocked, "You never have?"

He was emphatic: "Of course not! I even think there's something slightly immoral in a bald man, something almost…"

Julinha interrupted him violently.

"Well, if you want to know the truth, I wish you were bald! That you didn't have a single strand of hair on your head, OK?"

"That's in bad taste," her fiancé replied.

Resentment

It was the couple's first fight. Dona Matilde tried to intervene.

"You're acting like children!" Still, when Aluizio tried to kiss her on his way out, she moved her face. She was blunt: "I'm angry." The next day it was more of the same. Dona Matilde had to intervene again. Later the diplomatic young man called his fiancée's mother to the side and voiced his concern in a polite but sincere tone. He concluded by saying, "Ma'am, I think Julinha went a little batty when she saw that bald traffic cop."

In one way or another, Julinha was never the same again. She was polite, but that was all. When she was with her fiancé, she would suddenly become silent for long spells and a faraway look would set in. Once she dreamed of a legion of bald heads all night.

The Wedding

Finally, they were married. First in a civil ceremony, of course. And later came the church wedding. Julinha looked like a bride out of a fashion magazine. When she entered the church, there was such a gasp of delight that it bordered on being inappropriate. It was twilight when a gloved attendant opened the door to the chauffeur-driven limousine. The car took off. Precisely on the corner of the aforementioned intersection on Avenida Sete de Setembro, the light turned red. The car came to a stop. By coincidence the same traffic cop stood in the intersection directing traffic.

He repeated the same gesture as before: He took off his cap to dry his head. His bald dome emerged in all of its glory. Then something happened that no one could have predicted: Julinha let go of her fiancé's arm, opened the car door and ran across the asphalt like some nuptial ghost. Dumbfounded and frozen, Aluizio watched as the deranged bride got on her tiptoes and kissed the resplendent skull that so magnetized her.

The Canary

Suddenly, she began showing an interest in the little birds in the trees, on top of fences, on telephone wires. When the two, husband and wife, would go out, arm in arm, she would freeze all of a sudden.

"Oh, how cute!"

"What?"

"A wren."

At times it wasn't a wren, it was a sparrow, or something of the kind. At other times Lucia would not see, but would hear a kiskadee. She would start searching for it. And if per chance she should find the bird, she would tug at her husband's sleeve and insist he look too.

"There, honey, over there."

"Where?"

On top of that tree there, that one, that one!"

Malvino was nearsighted and, what's more, he had a prosaic and ingrained indifference to birds, regardless of color, features, or name. To humor his wife, he would finally give in.

"Now I see it."

All aglow, she would stand there motionless, staring with great interest, as the little creature jumped from branch to branch. Suddenly, the kiskadee would beat his wings, fly off, and disappear. Lucia, still flushed with excitement, would be reluctant to leave, secretly hoping that the bird would return. One day, after dinner, as she stirred her coffee, she said, "You know something?

"What?"

"I'm going to buy a cage tomorrow."

For Malvino there was no rhyme or reason to her plan; and, as was to be expected, he reacted with surprise.

"A cage without a bird?"

For a brief moment, Lucia felt a little awkward, as if she perceived the absurdity of her own idea.

Finally, she explained, "I can always find a bird!"

The Bird

Malvino did not pay it much heed. It was right before a major soccer match, and all he could think about was the coming game. A die-hard Botafogo fan, he would rub his hands, anticipating the outcome with pleasure.

"It's going to be a walk in the park! We're going to take them to school, just you watch!"

And he would make the gesture implying that they were going to mop the floor with Flamengo. At night, he would dream of the goals Botafogo would score. Sometimes, he would have horrible nightmares that the referee had called a penalty against his team. When he woke up he would hit the headboard.

"Knock on wood!"

Well, a diehard fan does not have the ability to judge and interpret so many subtle changes in the marital household. For example, shortly after they were married, the wife had brought a cat to live with them from her parent's home. The cat's name was Bonifacia (for reasons that were not completely clear), and she was the apple of Lucia's eye. She went so far as wanting to

sleep with the animal. As the man of the house, Malvino felt obliged to put his foot down.

"No, now you've gone too far! That animal isn't going to sleep in our bed. No way. What are you thinking?!"

"What's the big deal, honey?" she said. "She's always slept with me!"

"You were single then! Now, things are different."

Well, time went by until suddenly Lucia, out of the blue and without warning, began her obsession with birds. Malvino, had he not been so absorbed in the championship, might have easily found it odd and asked, "What's this? Since when have you…" But instead he thought it a passing fad. Nor did he notice when Lucia stopped paying heed to the cat. It had been two weeks since she had given Bonifacia a saucer of milk. The cat could occasionally be heard meowing, understandably missing the affection and the coddling she'd once enjoyed.

One day Malvino arrived home from work and found his wife in the kitchen, wholly entertained by a cage. He was flabbergasted.

"What's this?" he asked.

"Can't you see?" she said, beaming. "It's a cage!"

Yes, she had bought the cage, the seeds, the works. Hammer in hand, she banged a nail into the wall. She placed the cage on top of a little stool. Malvino made the only comment he could in such a situation.

"Are you crazy? Are you? I've never seen such a thing. A cage with birdfeed and no bird. Women!"

Lucia insisted that it was easy to find a bird, and things were left at that because it was time for the sports news, and Malvino turned the radio on. The following day he found Lucia in the kitchen, her face practically inside the cage, where, already making himself perfectly at home, sat a golden-breasted canary. Malvino's astonishment knew no bounds.

"Where did you get that bird?"

She beckoned him closer.

He pulled up a stool, climbed on it and remained there, amused, whispering sweet nothings to the bird. Lucia whistled to try to get a reaction out of the little creature. The canary, however, remained stubbornly silent.

"Doesn't he sing?" Malvino asked.

"He sings. He can't stop singing."

Thus began a new phase in the couple's life. Every morning the bird would bring in the new day with veritable arias. Indeed, he sang – a lot, perhaps too much. Lucia, smitten with the canary, would wake up earlier than usual to go and check on him. She would change the water, add birdfeed and clean the cage, which was a jewel of a cage. She would get up in the dark of night just to take a peek. She lived in constant fear that the cat might knock over the cage and devour the little bird. After making sure that the bird was intact, she would return to the bedroom, more at ease. The worst was when the bird, for one reason or another, started to sulk, stopped singing or hid in a corner as if sick. Lucia's panic was so out of proportion as to be irritating.

"There's something the matter with him! I know there is!"

"What, woman! There's nothing wrong with him! Please!"

Until finally Malvino began making snide comments.

"My wife doesn't give a damn about me anymore! All she cares about is the damn bird!"

He wasn't too far off the mark; for his wife the bird was a passion, an obsession, an addiction. She could think of nothing else. She wouldn't leave the house, even to see a movie, lest, in her absence, Bonifacia were to swallow the canary. That remote possibility drove her mad.

"Oh, I could kill that cat!"

The Revelation

Until then it had never occurred to Malvino to worry about where the bird had come from. After all, what harm could there be in acquiring a little bird? There were stores throughout the city that sold all sorts of birds, not to mention the vendors that came to one's door. One day, however, a neighbor appeared at Malvino's house, a real shrew. She was generally unpopular and greatly feared because of her scandalmongering. She saw evil in everything, and she would masquerade her poison behind her overly courteous manners, which were ever so irritating. Neither Malvino nor Lucia liked her, but they showed her respect. Dona Lourdes was commenting on several cases of infidelity. Suddenly, with the most innocent air in the world, she said, "Dona Lucia, you know who has a canary just like yours? Dr. Linhares! He's also crazy about birds! He has an aviary that's a sight to behold!"

Lucia said nothing. Eventually, Dona Lourdes left, all graciousness. She even said at the gate, "Come by some time." It was getting late, and the couple was tired. In the bedroom, before turning off the lights, yawning, Malvino asked, "Do I know this Dr. Linhares? Who is he?"

He learned that he lived at the end of the street and that, in fact, he truly did love birds. The following Sunday, Botafogo lost, and Malvino, returning from the game in a nasty mood, heard a lady greet a gentleman. "How are you, Dr. Linhares?" she said. Malvino looked on and confirmed that, beyond any doubt, the doctor was an extremely good-looking man. Immediately he began associating ideas in his mind, for he remembered Dona Lourdes's allusion to Dr. Linhares' birds. Already furious that his team had lost, his resulting psychological state led him to meditate on the canary, his wife, Dona Lourdes and the striking gentleman. He walked into the house and found his wife on top of the stool whistling to the bird. He said nothing, or better said, he muttered under his breath, "Damn bird!"

The Innocent

Then, two weeks later, he received an unsigned letter in his office. "Dr. Linhares is on top of the world, and he's not crowing." He turned the paper over and over; he read it many times. After work, he changed his usual route home so as to pass by Dr. Linhares' house. He stared at the aviary, and he made up his mind. He walked in without kissing his wife. He went straight to the kitchen, stuck his hand in the cage and pulled out the live bird. The wife, aghast, did not say a word or make a gesture. In silence, he twisted the canary's beak and pulled it off. His wife lost it. She yelled as if possessed, so that all the neighbors could hear.

"It's true, you hear? Yes! I love Dr. Linhares."

Malvino exited. He wandered the streets for hours on end. Suddenly, he felt something. There, still in his hand, was the beakless bird.

The Jerk

When he learned that his fiancée had ridden the bus with Dudu and shared a seat with him, he grabbed his head.

"With Dudu!"

"Yes, with Dudu," she said.

Hands in his pockets, pacing back and forth, Lima finally stopped in front of the young woman.

"Look here, Cleonice, I'm going to ask you a great big favor. OK?"

"Sure."

He pulled out a cigarette.

"It's like this: From now on... are you listening? From now on I don't want you even to say hello to Dudu."

"Why, honey?" she asked, startled.

"Because Dudu is a pervert, a degenerate, and a jerk. Nothing is off limits to this man, not even a lamppost, not even his own sister-in-law. Saying hello to Dudu is enough to put a woman's reputation at risk. Do you understand me?"

"Yes."

Still all worked up, he dried his forehead with a handkerchief.

"Good."

And that was that. It so happened, however, that Cleonice was extremely taken aback by what she had heard. She got along well enough with Dudu – although hardly close, they were on cordial terms. She had danced with him two or three times in the past, and since Dudu was a good-looking man and always very polite, she had come away from those brief encounters with a positive impression. It was a real shocker then to discover that "not even his own sister-in-law" was off limits to him. It would have been left at that, but one day, seated on a park bench, Lima picked up where he had left off.

"Sweetheart, you know that I'm not the jealous type, right?"

"Yes."

He cleared his throat.

"I'm only jealous of one person: Dudu. And don't you forget: He is a jerk, perhaps the biggest jerk in all of Brazil. Everyone has some bad traits. But that's all Dudu has, bad traits."

Not experienced in the ways of the world and of men, she asked, startled, "Is that really true?"

"Absolutely. May God strike me down if I am lying." Then he added in a fury, "He shouldn't be allowed to set foot in a decent house!"

Obsession

Thus, without meaning to, without realizing what he was doing, Lima made Dudu a larger-than-life figure who dominated their conversations.

"You're very green and innocent," he argued. "You've never had another boyfriend besides me. Do you want an example? I'm your fiancé; we're going to get married. Very well. What has happened between the two of us so far? Kisses, little kisses, that's it. Right?"

"Of course!" she answered, startled.

Lima continued.

"Let's imagine the following scenario: That instead of me, Dudu were your boyfriend. Do you think he would respect you the way I respect you? I doubt it! I doubt it very much! Dudu doesn't respect family; he doesn't respect anything! He's a beast, a hyena, a jackal!"

Cringing, Cleonice sighed, "It doesn't seem possible such a man can exist."

"I'm going to let you in on something," Lima said. "When Dudu sees a woman he mentally undresses her!"

The Party

A few days later Cleonice was talking to her girlfriends when the subject of Dudu came up. She looked left and right and then lowered her voice, "I heard that Dudu hit on his sister-in-law!"

One of her friends, who knew Dudu and his family well, objected, "Dudu doesn't even have a sister-in-law!"

Later that evening, terribly embarrassed, Cleonice questioned Lima. He explained it away.

"I never said Dudu hit on his sister-in-law. I said he would if he had one. You weren't listening."

A couple of days later, the two were at a family gathering. They walk in, and who should be there but Dudu! They saw his silhouette outlined against the window. He cut a strong and handsome figure, smoking from a cigarette holder, looking pale and seductive, all eyes drawn to him. Lima grabbed his fiancée by the arm and said, with teeth clenched, "Let's go."

"Why?" she asked, frightened and startled.

Lima dragged her from the room.

"Dudu is here! It wouldn't be right, you understand? It wouldn't be right. Imagine if he were to ask you to dance. God no!"

The Fear

On the way hone, an irritated tone crept into Cleonice's voice.

"Stop talking about Dudu! You talk about him so much that I can't stop thinking about him. And you know what? I'm frightened!"

"Frightened of what? That's ridiculous!"

She appeared confused.

"These things leave an impression on a woman. Don't talk about him anymore," she begged him once more. "Please."

But he was stubborn, "I will, why shouldn't I? You have to see Dudu for what he is, a worm."

Cleonice sighed.

"You know best."

Hatred

Time went by. Every day Lima would come up with some reason or other to mention Dudu.

"I saw that animal with another woman!"

If there was something that hurt him deep down inside, it was the jerk's amazing luck with women. He would vent to his fiancée with a bit of hyperbole, "Tons of girlfriends! He has a girlfriend in every neighborhood!"

One day he exploded.

"It seems like you women like scoundrels! Take me, for example. I am a decent, respectful, law-abiding guy. Very well. I had trouble finding one girlfriend in this town. Till this day I can't believe that you preferred me over Dudu." He paused and lowered his voice, confiding an embarrassing secret to her.

"Because Dudu stole all of my girlfriends, one by one." This was, in effect, the root of the hatred that was poisoning Lima's soul.

The Wedding

The wedding day arrived. Minutes before they exchanged their oaths, Lima whispered in his fiancée's ear, "Dudu took all of my girlfriends except you!" Very well. They were married in city hall and then in church. At around midnight the two were finally alone, face to face in the apartment that would be their new home. Extremely nervous, Lima lowered his voice and said, "Kiss me."

She moved her face at the last second.

"No!"

Lima did not understand. Cleonice explained, "You spoke so much about

Dudu and said such horrible things about him that I fell in love with him. I won't betray the man I love, even if it's with my own husband."

Lima understood that he had lost her. Without a single word he left the marital bedroom. In his pajamas and slippers he walked down to the street, and he sat on the curb and began to cry.

The Monster

His wife cried into the telephone, "Get over here! Quickly! Hurry!"

Maneco didn't waste any time. He yelled to his business associate, "Hold the fort. I don't know how long I'll be."

He finished putting on his jacket in the elevator. On the way down, he racked his brain with infinite scenarios. "What could it be?" He hadn't wanted to ask Flavia, afraid that the news might be tragic. In the taxi he concluded, "It can't be good!" The most persuasive hypothesis was that a member of his wife's family had died. His father-in-law had a heart condition, and it wasn't at all unlikely that he had finally succumbed to the heart attack the doctors had predicted. He imagined the old man dying, and the truth is it gave him a cruel and embarrassing pleasure. He arrived in front of his house and was so anxious he handed the driver a two-hundred cruzeiro bill and forgot to ask for the change. He charged into the huge house in Tijuca where he lived with his wife, her parents, three married sisters-in-law and one single one. Right away he knew that his hypothesis of a death in the family was wrong. The lack of female commotion in a house with so many women told him as much. Puzzled, he muttered, "Well, I'll be!"

Maneco found his wife weeping in the bedroom. He sat next to her and held her hands. "What happened? Tell me."

First she blew her nose and then, sniffling, she dropped a bomb.

"We have a pervert living in this house!"

Maneco turned pale. For a brief moment he thought that he might be the "pervert" in question. He thought, "Great! She must have found about one of my escapades!" He swallowed and stammered, "Who?"

"Bezerra!" she said.

The "Pervert"

When he discovered he wasn't on the hot seat, his spirit was lifted. A sudden euphoria came over him, and he was now eager to hear the full story. Bezerra was married to Ruth, Flavia's older sister. "Why a pervert?" Maneco wanted to know.

Flavia exploded.

"The lowlife doesn't even respect the roof he lives under!" She actually pointed to the roof. "Do you know what he did? Do you have any idea?" She lowered her voice, "Inside this house, practically under his wife's nose, he made a move on his sister-in-law. Just as shameless as can be. Can you believe it?"

"Which sister-in-law?" Maneco asked, aghast. He thought it might be his wife. He only calmed down when Flavia pronounced the name, in utter horror.

"Sandra! Imagine! Sandra! He singled out my little sister, seventeen years old, who's like a daughter to us! The dog!"

"Gee whiz!" the husband shuddered in disbelief. He stood.

"You know something? I'm stunned. Bowled over."

She grilled him, "Is he or isn't he a pervert?"

With both hands buried in his pockets, Maneco paced back and forth and ventured a few thoughts.

"Look here, sweetie. I always told you, didn't I, that a sister-in-law should never get too friendly with her brother-in-law?" He went on, "Of course not!

It's obvious! What do you expect? Because, let's be honest, a sister-in-law is not a sister. After all, he's made of flesh and blood! Let's take your little sister; remember the time she bought that little yellow bathing suit, made of lycra or whatever it was? She gave a show in this house for her brothers-in-law. Am I right?"

Flavia leapt to her feet.

"Now hold on one minute. Are you excusing what this idiot did? Are you? So you're just like him, huh? A pervert like him!"

Maneco, in a panic, blurted out, "God forbid, no! I'm not defending anyone. Bezerra can go to hell for all I care!"

His wife stepped back and asked, "When you saw Sandra that day, what did you feel, huh?"

"Me?" he blurted out. "Well, nothing. Nothing! It's different with me. I'm married to you, and you're the best wife in the world. OK?" By now, his mouth was nearly in his wife's ear, "No woman is your equal. No one comes close. Give me a little kiss, come on."

He grabbed her and then kissed her for as long as he could hold his breath.

When he let go she was reeling and had lipstick smeared all over her face. She shuddered in awe. "You know how I love it when you're bad."

"Get it while it lasts!" he said playfully.

The Drama

But things were indeed critical. The entire family, including the maid, began to loathe the pervert. Even the dog, a glorified mutt, seemed infected by the mood; he walked around the house gloomily, with his ears down. As for the guilty party, consigned to staying in the garage, he was in a state of utter despair. Sulking in the corner, disheveled, a shadow of his former self, he said to Maneco, "Next thing I know they'll spit in my face."

Maneco looked to the left, then the right, then lowered his voice, "You really blew it! You really outdid yourself this time."

"I didn't do anything!" he protested. He clutched his brother-in-law. "By the light that shines on me, I swear I didn't do anything. She came on to me. She practically attacked me in the hallway. It was just my luck that the maid came. She saw everything. Now it's turned into a thirty-five act tragedy!"

175

Dying of curiosity, Maneco whispered, "So what happened, huh?"

Bezerra was modest.

"Nothing. I sucked on that cute little mouth of hers. I would have kissed her entire body if I could. I'd start at her feet. But I didn't have time to. Everybody's making a big deal about it, I don't know why!"

Maneco looked on, wide-eyed, with a mixture of admiration and jealousy. "You're really something, you know that?" He preached to him, "Your mistake was to go for broke. You should have used a little diplomacy."

Bezerra held his head in his hands.

"I'm just thinking what's going to happen when the old man finds out."

"He's going to go ballistic!"

The Father-In-Law

Indeed, Dr. Guedes was the object of great veneration and fear in the family. His wife, daughters and sons-in-law were unanimous in their praise. He was so thoroughly virtuous he was above suspicion. He exuded respectability down to the very way he dressed. Rain or shine, he'd wear a vest, an alpaca wool jacket, striped pants and button-up half boots. When alone with his brothers-in-law, Maneco would confess, "You know what really terrifies me about him? He uses drawers that go down to his feet – the kind you tie around your ankles. Can you believe it?" It so happened that Dr. Guedes arrived home late that night. By then Maneco, exhibiting a cowardliness typical of most husbands, had allied himself firmly with the rest of the family. Solemnly and cynically, he agreed that Bezerra was "a world-class pervert." Very well. Dr. Guedes arrived home carrying his usual silver-handled umbrella. He was met by terror-stricken faces wherever he looked. The oldest daughter started crying. At last, the old man asked, as he unbuttoned his vest, "Did someone die?"

Calamity

The daughter dragged him into the study and proceeded to tell him everything. She concluded by saying, "I admit, husbands can have their flaws. But with my sister? No! Never!" She repeated, "With his wife's sister? It's disgraceful!"

The old man stood, trembling.

"Where's that bastard?" He ground each syllable with his teeth.

"Filthy dog!" Outraged, he searched through his pockets for something, then threw open several drawers.

"I'll shoot him in the mouth!"

His wife, in tears, kept repeating, "He had to go after the youngest one! A girl, a child, my God!"

By then, the old man had already thrown open the door and burst into the living room. He stomped his foot, "Bring me that bastard!"

The others looked on aghast. Flavia nudged her husband, "Go on, honey. Go on!"

Maneco dashed out. He found Bezerra in the garage, in the back, squatting like an animal. He tapped him gently on the shoulder, "The old man is calling you." He warned him, "Things look black. He's talking about gunshots and God only knows what else!"

Bezerra jumped up.

"If he shoots me, he'll be doing me a favor. I hope he does!" He squeezed Maneco's arm, and confided desperately in him, "I know Sandra is a shameless liar, but if she comes on to me again, I swear I'll give her what she wants and then some."

Humiliation

In the living room, a Dantesque scene unfolded. The father-in-law held Bezerra up by the collar with both hands.

"OK, scumbag! What do you think this is, a brothel?"

Suddenly, the poor wretch fell before the old man's feet, sobbing. The women held their breath as they watched Bezerra get kicked like a soccer ball. They snarled words like *monster*, *pervert*, etc., etc. Only one sat quietly and unemotionally. It was Sandra, the youngest. She was cleaning her fingernails with a matchstick, completely absorbed in her task. Finally, she decided things had gone too far. She stood, walked to the door of the studio and announced, "Dad, come in here a minute, please." She insisted, "Dad?"

Just then Dr. Guedes was banishing Bezerra from the house. "Out! Get out!" That was when his youngest daughter, without the slightest hesitation, grabbed her father by the arm. Her energy was so unexpected and forceful that he submitted immediately. They went into the study, and Sandra closed the door. Dr. Guedes stood before her, startled.

She got right to the point.

"Daddy, I know that you're seeing this woman who lives in Grajau who happens to be..." etc, etc. "Do you understand me? You have two choices: Either fix this situation now, or I'll crush you in front of everyone!"

He stared at his daughter, who was threatening him so brazenly, as if she were a stranger.

She concluded by saying, "Bezerra is not leaving. I want him to stay!"

The old man reappeared five minutes later, having regained his composure. He cleared his throat.

"Let's put an end to this. That's the best thing we can do. It's water under the bridge. It's time to go to bed, people."

One by one, the couples marched out of the living room. The last two were Bezerra and his wife. When he put his foot on the first step, Bezerra glanced back very quickly at Sandra. The young girl winked at him. And that was that. Five minutes later, the old man was glued to the radio, listening to the announcer read the eleven o'clock news.

Forever Faithful

He turned to his girlfriend.

"You know something?"

"What?" she asked.

They were sharing a soda through a straw at an open-air café on Quinta da Boa Vista. In a half-serious tone he lowered his voice.

"I don't believe you love me."

She was taken aback.

"Are you serious?"

"I swear!"

"Why?"

He took a drag from his cigarette.

"Because I don't trust women, none of them, you understand? Look, I've had about ten girlfriends. Ten, maybe twelve, thirteen. Very well. All of them, bar none, have cheated on me. At times I think that my lot in life, my calling is to be cheated on."

Stunned, Odaleia stirred the bottom of the empty glass with the straw. She lifted her head.

"Can I say something?"

"Go ahead!"

She grabbed her boyfriend's hand above the table.

"No love in this world compares with mine. You will be my first love and my last!"

A Complex

They left Quinta da Boa Vista more in love than ever. At the trolley stop Odaleia, moved to the core of her being, asked, "So? Now do you believe me? Now do you believe I love you?"

He took a deep breath.

"Yes."

When Odaleia arrived home her mother met her at the kitchen door, drying a plate.

"Well? Is everything all right?"

The girl put her purse on the table and sighed.

"Mother, it seems like things are finally looking up."

"Did he mention marriage?"

"He did, Mother; for the first time he did. Oh, Mother, I am the happiest woman in the world!"

"God bless you, dear. God bless you!"

The next day they met again. Odilon, however, did not exhibit any traces of his previous exuberance. He sat there, taciturn, a slight sneer on his face. Suddenly, Odaleia said, "What's the matter. Is something wrong?"

They looked at one another. Odilon lowered his gaze.

"You might think I have a complex, but the truth is I don't believe you. I can't. Do you really think I can marry you knowing you'll cheat on me?"

She sat up aghast.

"If I didn't know any better, I'd be insulted!"

"You see? You're already insulted! A woman who loves, who really loves someone, doesn't get insulted. You can't have true love and get insulted!"

Odaleia grabbed her boyfriend.

"What do I have to do to prove my love? I'll do whatever you want!"

A Test of Love

They parted ways filled with sadness. Before the girl boarded the bus, he said, "Do you want some advice? Do you? Then listen to me."

He sighed and continued, "Dump me while there's still time. I don't interest you or any other woman for that matter. Right now, this very minute, I'm thinking that someday you're bound to cheat on me. I must have a disease. I'm mentally ill." All choked up he said, "Find yourself another boyfriend, someone who believes you!"

She responded in tears, "What if I can prove I love you? What if I can prove to you that I'll be faithful till the day I die?"

He shook his head.

"How? How can you swear to something that hasn't happened? Today you love me. Fine. But how about tomorrow? Will you still love me then?"

"Of course! I won't change!"

Odilon grabbed the girl by the arms.

"Run. I'm a lost cause. There's no hope for me!"

The bus was coming. Odaleia wanted to stay, but he insisted, "Go, go! We'll talk again tomorrow!" She boarded the bus. From a little window in the back she waved goodbye to him.

Sorrow

The mother, a plump lady with varicose veins, had followed the romance from the very beginning. She saw her daughter arrive in tears and was scared.

"What happened?"

For the first time Odaleia told her everything about the relationship, including the details that she had previously omitted. The old lady held her head in her hands.

"This man is crazy, sweetie!"

Odaleia blew her nose in a little handkerchief.

"I don't know if he is or not, Mother. The fact is that I love him, and that's all there is to it."

"Oh, come on!"

The girl was not through.

"Can you imagine how Odilon must be suffering? Imagine a man who is unable to trust even one woman. He must be miserable. I have to find a way, a manner of proving to him that I'll always be faithful to him, that I will never cheat on him. And I will."

The Solution

They saw each other another three or four times. They were torturous meetings; he tormented her mercilessly.

"When will you cheat on me? When?"

Odaleia, who loved him dearly, and more so with each passing day, answered, "Mark my words: I will show you one day that I'll never cheat on you!"

"I don't think so!" he said.

They stopped seeing each other. Two weeks later, Odilon, in a state of abject bitterness, sized up the situation.

"She must have found someone by now and is probably gallivanting around town with him."

Then one morning a friend arrived, gasping for air, at Odilon's house. He said, "Hurry, man, your girlfriend is dying!"

Odilon dressed hurriedly and rushed to her house. There he learned everything: Odaleia had killed herself the previous night, imbibing some poison or other. Rushing past the relatives and neighbors gathered there, Odilon reached the girl's bedroom. Through the door he saw her body. He took two steps into the room and froze. He read what Odaleia had written on the wall before dying: "The dead don't cheat."

Stunned, Odilon fell to his knees before the bed. He grabbed the hand of the girl who would forever be faithful to him and covered it with kisses and tears.

182

The Crown of Orchids

There was a great movie showing, and, in the morning before leaving, Rodolfo made the arrangements: "Tonight, the movies, eight o'clock."

In the afternoon, Jupira called and broke the news.

"Sweetie, the movie's off!"

"Why?"

She took a deep breath.

"Imagine: Maciel died!"

"Your friend's husband?"

"That one. And there's no way out; I have to attend the wake. I'm headed there right now."

Rodolfo fell back into his chair.

"I'll be damned!" He couldn't hear about the death of others without thinking about his own. Occasionally, he could be heard saying, "Death's a bum deal. Why do we have to die? Why?" If it were up to him, no one would ever die. With such thoughts weighing on him, he went to pay his respects to Alaide's husband. He entered and saw the body lying in a coffin surrounded by four large candles, and a very unpleasant thought occurred to him: One day he too would be laid out in a casket, etc., etc. He greeted the widow, who was weeping in the corner, being consoled by her girlfriends. Just then, Jupira dragged him into the hallway. She admonished him as if he were a child.

"Rodolfo! Look sad!"

The Widow

There was nothing that made this wake different from any other. Every now and then Rodolfo would glance at the widow and take note of her face, a face that pain had transformed into an ugly, unpleasant, almost grotesque mask. He thought to himself, "I can't wait to get out of here!" And, every time the opportunity arose, he would whisper to his wife, "This is a real drag!" To which Jupira would reply, "Poor so-and-so!" When they finally managed to leave, Rodolfo exclaimed, "Thank God!" It was only when they were back home that Jupira, already in bed, yawning, announced, "I invited Alaide to come spend a few days with us."

Rodolfo, who was buttoning his pajama top just then, turned to his wife. "What the hell possessed you to do that!"

Then the wife, who had a very good heart, got on her soapbox and let him have it.

"Sometimes I wonder about you, Rodolfo! What do you think? That I'm going to abandon a friend like Alaide, a childhood friend who's like a sister to me? For God's sake! What kind of person do you think I am?"

The husband lay down in bed. He'd have to take the day off tomorrow because of the wasted night. But he was going to have his say: "I'm not in favor of bringing strangers into the house. It's asking for trouble!"

The Bereaved

And, just like that, against his will, Rodolfo saw himself forced to share in a pain that wasn't his. Alone with his wife, he unloaded, "It's asking a lot, honey. I've got nothing to do with this, and when it's all said and done…"

Two days after her husband's death, Alaide moved in with the couple. Goodbye to movies, the theater, outings, freedom. Rodolfo would go from work straight home and not go out anymore. From then on, it was as if he and his wife existed solely to minister to Alaide's grief. At his wits end, Rodolfo sneered, "I've renounced this world." As the days went by, however, a certain routine was established, and before long the presence of that lady in black crying night and day for a dead man, with admirable steadfastness, no longer seemed unusual. The truth of the matter is that Alaide seemed to insist stubbornly on nurturing her suffering. She perhaps even felt a touch of pride in her lush pain that seemed to defy time. Even Rodolfo was impressed.

"Your friend really loved her husband, huh?"

It was then that Jupira explained that Alaide and Maciel's love was something out of a soap opera, a novel, the movies.

Rodolfo let a few minutes go by and then asked, "You think she'll get married again?" The following day, as if answering that question, Alaide said, "I might as well be dead!" The couple felt that their friend carried within her an immortal love.

The Kiss

A month and a half later a very distressing scene played out. After dinner, in the widow's presence, Rodolfo did something that most would consider routine among couples: He gave his wife a quick, conventional kiss on the mouth. That was enough for Alaide to get up, run out, and break out in tears. The couple, in a panic, ran after her in close pursuit. What happened? What happened? The widow, her face covered in tears, explained, "It just occurred to me... when you two kissed, it occurred to me that I'll never be kissed again... that Maciel will never kiss me again, oh God!"

Husband and wife, feeling an overwhelming sense of guilt, exchanged glances. Later that night, in the bedroom, as he put on his pajamas, Rodolfo sighed, "Who would have thought?" And Jupira: "That's right, honey. That's right!" They went to bed and Rodolfo was already asleep when his wife woke him and said, "Sweetie, do you know what the solution is? Plain and simple?"

"What?"

"We're going to find Alaide a husband!" she said. "She's young, pretty, looks a lot like Kay Francis. You remember Kay Francis, don't you?"

Love

The husband wanted to put a damper on his wife's enthusiasm.

"Don't get involved. Stay clear of this." But Jupira confessed that "when I set my mind to something, watch out." She dedicated herself to her mission with all her heart. Truth be told, she was very adept, crafty, and resourceful. She let some time go by and then went to work in the most subtle and sly way possible. One day, she suggested, "Why don't you put some makeup on?" The reaction was swift.

"God no!"

Days later, Jupira was at it again as if nothing had happened: "Let's do the following: Put on some rouge. Just a smidgen on your cheeks. That's all."

She again encountered resistance, though this time not absolute. She offered to help: "I'll put it on for you." And so she lightly colored Alaide's cheeks. Without missing a beat she invited her to see the results in the mirror. Within a minute or two Alaide was admiring her own countenance with a look of surprise and delight. At night Jupira boasted radiantly to her husband, "Everything is going according to plan!" From then on, she began to be more direct with her friend, letting her have it straight.

"Honey, stop being a fool. Anyone with a cute face like yours and a body like that has no business hiding herself." She kept plucking the same string: "Your body would drive any man crazy." Little by little, against her will, without noticing, Alaide was allowing herself to be touched by her friend's sweet and constant insistence. At times she would sigh with false modesty, "My best years are behind me." Jupira would then respond with a bit of hyperbole.

"Listen here, for a man not to be attracted to you he must be made of stone! Your body's to die for!"

A Twist Of Fate

The day she stopped wearing black, Alaide called her friend. Rather haltingly, she gave her the news: "I think I'm in love…"

Jupira, gushing, made a scene and peppered her with questions – her feminine curiosity took over and she insisted on knowing everything in painstaking detail.

Alaide was discreet.

"For the time being, it's a secret… one day I'll tell you…"

Jupira ran to her husband.

"Did you hear the latest?"

Rodolfo listened and yawned.

"You want some advice? Drop it!"

His wife, all excited, added, "And I suspect he's married." Even so, she encouraged her friend along.

"Strike while the iron is hot, honey!" She insisted on one thing: "You have to tell me everything, you have to promise!"

The following day, another call from Alaide, at night.

"Lord have mercy! It happened."

"So soon!"

Alaide confirmed, that that same evening, in such-and-such a place…

And another question from Jupira: "How was it?"

Her friend sighed, "Spectacular!"

Two weeks later, Alaide made the jarring, almost sacrilegious revelation: "He's much more interesting than my husband." It could be said that only now, for the first time, did Alaide know love. She repeated, "That's what love is. That's true love." As for marriage, there was one impediment that made it impossible: The beloved was married; he lived with his wife. Jupira would have continued with her endless questions, had not, suddenly, the unpredictable occurred: Rodolfo fell ill, gravely ill.

The Blow

They tried everything. For about two months there was a parade of doctors. Rodolfo only grew sicker and sicker. He practically lived in an oxygen tent. The family doctor had already warned the relatives of the most unpleasant of possibilities. Until one day, in the early evening, after a brief, almost imperceptible spasm, he died in his wife's arms. Hours later, in a navy blue suit and patent leather shoes, he was laid out in the living room amid four large candles. The widow preferred that the corpse leave for the cemetery from the house where they had had such happy moments and not from a chapel. Jupira's mourning attire was improvised: a sober black dress a girlfriend pulled from the armoire. At midnight the flowers began to arrive. Suddenly, a crown of orchids arrived, so colossal that a murmur of amazement could be heard from those assembled. Who could have sent it? The widow, in all of her pain, could not resist a curious glance. It was one of those wreaths that would have created a sensation in the funeral of a king or head of state. It was placed in the living room near the coffin, and the messenger untied the ribbon. What mysterious impulse led the widow to get up, startled, to read the handwritten inscription? It said, "May all my love be with you. Yours, Alaide." Humiliated to the very core of her being, Jupira suffered in silence for two hours. She might have forgiven a secret, unconfessed passion. But this sudden and vulgar display, under the candles, only fueled her despair. All turned when she suddenly headed for the stairs and ascended them, her face inscrutable as a theater mask. Someone tried to follow her but gave up. She returned forty minutes later. The makeshift mourning dress had been replaced by a stylish, light summer outfit with a floral pattern, something a teenager might wear. She wore a scandalous amount of makeup. Accompanied by a girlfriend or relative, she left the house without so much as a glance at the casket. At the break of dawn Alaide arrived.

She embraced the coffin and screamed, "Oh, my love!"

The Cleavage

She was a strong, tough, old-fashioned mother. A diabetic and an asthmatic with seventy years of living behind her. She got into a cab in Tijuca and gave her son's address in Copacabana. Her arrival came as a surprise. The daughter-in-law, who disliked her shrewd, autocratic mother-in-law, turned up her nose. The son, on the other hand, for whom his mother meant everything, rushed to welcome her, shaking with emotion.

"It's a miracle!"

He offered her his arm. It had been two years, for all intents and purposes, since Dona Margarida had set foot in that house. She had had a fight with her daughter-in-law, whose beauty irritated her, and decided to cut off all relations: "I'll never set foot here again."

Clara thanked God. Her mother-in-law and her sharp tongue exasperated her. And Aderbal, who was a good son and an even better husband, limited himself to declaring vaguely and faint-heartedly, "Women are really

189

something else!" And that was that. It was only now, two years later, that Dona Margarida set foot in that house again. It was a heroic double sacrifice, physical and emotional, on her part. She locked herself in the study with her son. And she asked, "Do you know why I'm here?"

Concerned, he asked, "Why?"

Dona Margarida sighed heavily.

"I came to ask you if you are blind or if you've lost all sense of shame."

He was not expecting this full frontal assault. He stood uneasily.

"What do you mean?"

Ignoring her habitual sickly state which made her every movement painful, Dona Margarida stood too. She continued, relentlessly.

"Your wife is making a spectacle of herself around town. Or don't you see this?" Holding back her tears she implored, "Are you a man?"

His answer was sober.

"I am a father."

The Father

Fifteen years before, the two had been married in civil and religious ceremonies and, like every newlywed couple, exhibited a tremendous and reciprocal passion. The honeymoon lasted, what, fifteen or sixteen days? But on the sixteenth or seventeenth day Aderbal met some friends at a bar and, in between whiskeys, said in so many words, "Man is polygamous by nature. One woman is not enough."

When he arrived home late and semi-drunk, he was confronted by Clara.

"Well, just look at you!"

He could have tried to be diplomatic, but the alcohol made him combative. He talked back, and she, in her naive and heartfelt disenchantment, assumed an accusatory tone: "How dare you! In the middle of your honeymoon!"

His answer was quick and brutal.

"What honeymoon? The honeymoon is over!"

For three days and three nights straight Clara did nothing but cry. She would say to herself, "If he'd done this later that would have been one thing. But to do this now..." The truth is she was never the same after that. One month later the first signs of pregnancy became apparent, a fact later confirmed by the doctor. But while she, in her resentment, grew cold towards him, Aderbal, totally unexpectedly, fell at her feet in adoration. Sentimental to the core, he could not see a pregnant woman without being moved, without feeling an absurd desire to protect. In his most inspired moments he would say, "There's nothing a pregnant woman doesn't deserve!" And Clara, by virtue of being his wife, deserved even more. At the conclusion of her pregnancy, a girl was born. Interestingly, while Clara suffered through the throes of childbirth, Aderbal was in the hallway experiencing the worst toothache in his life. But once the child was born, his intense pain miraculously disappeared. And from the very first moment he was, above all, a father. He might forget his wife or neglect his marital duties... but he would never under any circumstances cease adoring Mirna. He did all of the usual bragging that fathers engage in. He would ask, "Doesn't she look just like me?" The relatives and friends could not help but comment, "Aderbal is crazy about his daughter."

The Wife

When Mirna turned eight, he received an anonymous letter, playful in tone, which said, "Open your eyes, man!" For the first time he sat up and started paying attention. He began taking notice of his wife's behavior. She was neglectful as a mother and could always be found at parties, showing off her dresses, her cleavage, her beautiful naked shoulders. One day he had a talk with her: "You need to choose your friends more carefully..."

Clara, who was filing her nails, said, "Try not to butt in, OK? It's my life."

Taken aback, he wanted to press on. But before he could say anything, she yelled, "You've never paid attention to me. You've never given me the time of day."

Aderbal felt obliged to pull back.

"Well. I won't butt in. But I want to say just one thing: Don't you ever forget your daughter."

Her answer was curt.

"Bug off!"

That was the last time. They never argued again.

Aderbal became a silent and blind witness to the frivolous life his wife led. He had only one thing on his mind, his daughter. Time and again he would remind her, "Never forget that you are a mother." And that was that.

And now that Mirna had turned fifteen, Dona Margarida marched into his house. They argued. The old woman's logic was as follows: Clara was unfaithful, and thus they should separate and then get a divorce. Aderbal let out what sounded like a howl, "And my daughter?"

Dona Margarida exploded, "You've got to be kidding!"

Aderbal was adamant.

"Mother, I don't exist. Do you understand? Only my daughter exists. I can't put her through this. Never!"

The old woman tried every argument she could think of, but to no avail. Aderbal stubbornly came back with the same response: "She may have lovers; God only knows what she's done, but she's the mother of my child. And if my daughter loves this woman, then she is sacred as far as I'm concerned. That's all there is to it!"

At last, her patience exhausted, Dona Margarida left, leaning heavily on her cane. She stopped at the door.

"You should be ashamed of yourself!"

The Sinner

About forty minutes later Aderbal spoke to Mirna.

"Come here, honey. Do you love Mommy?"

She seemed taken aback.

"Do you doubt that I do, Daddy?"

He tried to backpedal, "I'm just kidding."

Seated on her father's lap, the young girl, who looked very much like Clara, sighed, "I love Mommy and you. Both of you."

Tormented, he let a couple of days go by. On the third day he spoke to his wife and tried to set some ground rules.

"I know that you don't love me, but at least respect your daughter."

They could have kept things civil, but Clara was so fed up with the man that she could no longer resist. Her husband's voice, his gestures, his clothes, his hands, his skin – everything disgusted her. After sixteen years of marriage she understood that for a married couple lack of love was worse than hatred. She lost it and said things she should and should not have said. Aderbal tried to remain calm.

"My daughter can't know any of this."

Then Clara maliciously began to tear into him.

"You talk about your daughter. How about you? After all, you're the husband!"

Very pale by now, Aderbal grew silent.

She continued disdainfully, "Or are you going to pretend that you don't know?"

In his seething rage, he wanted to leave. But Clara had already placed herself in front of him, blocking his exit. She had just arrived from a dance, dressed to the hilt, her cleavage amply visible, her naked brown shoulders smelling of perfume. Then she placed both hands on her hips and let him have it.

"Where do you think you're going?" she asked. "You started it, didn't you? Now you're going to have to take it!"

"Not so loud. Your daughter might hear you!" he said softly.

In spite of herself, Clara obliged. She lowered her voice, but for the first time she told him everything. Aghast at the evil that gushed forth from his wife, gratuitous and terrible, he limited himself to, "Why are you saying this? Why?" He tried to stop her, "Shut up! Shut up! I didn't ask you! I don't want to know!"

But Clara could not be held back.

"Do you know so-and-so? Your friend who you've done so much for in the past? Well, he was the first one!"

"So-and-so? It's a lie!"

"May God strike me blind if I'm lying! Do you want to know who the second one was? So-and-so! Do you want another one? Do you? So-and-so. Seventeen altogether! You understand? Seventeen!"

Disfigured by hatred, he said, "The only thing keeping me from killing you right now is the fact that my daughter loves you!"

He said this and left the bedroom.

The Daughter

Ten minutes later he was lying face down on the sofa, crying impotently. Suddenly, he felt a hand on his head. He turned in surprise. It was his daughter, who in her little fur slippers and her pink embroidered pajamas, had come downstairs silently. She kneeled at his side. Taken aback, he cleared away the tears with the back of his hand. Then, as modest as always, Mirna said, "I heard everything. I know everything." She continued in a slow and serious tone.

"I don't love Mother. I don't love her anymore."

He seemed to meditate on those words for a moment, as if he were seeking some mysterious meaning in them. Then he stood. He went to a table, opened a drawer and took out a gun. He went upstairs in no particular hurry. Clara stood before the mirror squeezing pimples. On seeing her husband, she laughed. With the others she was kind, normal, even friendly – she was only cruel with this man whom she no longer loved. Her terrible, shrieking laugh was just one more unnecessary touch. Aderbal came closer. He fired twice in the middle of her cleavage.

Ugly as Sin

When he arrived home, his sisters were anxiously waiting with the question, "Are you still going out with that girl?"

"Yes."

There were shrieks of disbelief.

"No way, no way!"

"What's the matter?"

In a savage chorus they yelled, "Because she is butt ugly! She's an ugly witch! Find someone else. Someone who's prettier! Cuter!"

The young man turned pale, resentful at their cruel comments. He took a noble and manly stance. First, he called them all "nosy bitches," and then he said, "I want you all to know that that 'ugly witch' is going to be my wife. End of story."

He turned his back on them and went off to play pool at the corner pool hall.

The Girl

The sisters and their mother looked at one another. One of the girls sighed, "It looks like he's serious."

There were general nods of agreement.

"Very serious."

The mother, who loved her son dearly, abstained from casting her vote. She merely used a metaphor.

"He can hitch his donkey to whatever tree he wants. He wants to get married, doesn't he?"

They grudgingly admitted, "It looks that way."

"So let him get married and live happily ever after."

There was, however, a general hope and desire that Herivelto would with the passage of time come to his senses and recognize the girl's hideousness. But it seemed hopeless. He was deeply in love and eager to get married at any cost and as soon as possible. One day the mother, who possessed an uncommon degree of common sense, called her son for a talk.

"Come here, son. Let's have a heart-to-heart."

Herivelto obliged, but he warned her gravely, almost threateningly, "We'll talk, Mother, as long as you don't say anything bad about so-and-so."

His mother quickly agreed, "Of course not! I'm actually quite fond of her." She cleared her throat and continued, "So you intend to get married, do you?"

"Yes."

Then she asked point-blank, "With what money, my child? You can't get married with only the shirt on your back. You barely earn enough to pay your way living here with us."

The young man rose to his feet. He paced back and forth with his hands in his pockets. Suddenly he halted and announced, "Mother, you want to know what I think? I think in life you need to have guts. Guts are all you need to get married."

That night he told the girl what had transpired.

"Will you live with me?" he asked. "We can rent a room." This was a crucial moment in their relationship.

Jacira, however, was not fazed. She rose to the occasion.

"Honey, I'll live anywhere with you as long as I'm by your side."

Ugly as Sin

The truth of the matter was that in their state of passion both the young man and the girl would have been willing to go hungry if need be. Herivelto even went so far as to craft an adage about marriage and money: "Marriage," he would say, "is a matter of love, not of comfort." They tried to warn him, "Be careful, or you'll regret it." He would answer optimistically, "So be it!"

One day, after a very pleasant courtship, they wed. According to one eyewitness account, when Jacira entered the church holding her father's arm, she looked "downright scary." Someone was even overheard saying, "She must come from money." But no, she did not. The truth of the matter was that no one could understand how a good-looking fellow like Herivelto had chosen her among all the others. The groom's family would cling to one melancholy consolation: "She's not pretty, but she has a good heart."

It was only on the seventh or eighth day of the honeymoon that Herivelto began to suspect the truth. Jacira sat in front of a mirror squeezing pimples. She did this with extraordinary delight and pleasure. In silence, interrupted by occasional whistling, the young man would spy on his wife, and he couldn't help but judge her physical appearance. She turned to him and said, "Gosh! My skin is a mess."

The Others

From then on, whenever he was home, he would constantly shoot sideways glances at his wife and take note of her ugliness. One thing left him bitter and astounded.

"How could I have been so blind!" Now when he looked at Jacira, all he could see was her lack of grace and femininity. On top of that he was constantly irritated and would on occasion get physically ill. One day, when Jacira looked particularly unappealing to him, he posed a perverse question.

"Do you think an ugly woman knows she is ugly?"

Jacira didn't take the hint. She scratched her head with a hairpin and laughed, "Of course not. Ask a dog if she's a dog. Go ahead, ask her."

For a split second Herivelto felt tempted to ask, "How about you?" He resisted, though. Any traces of any illusion he might have had had now completely vanished. He now knew that his wife, the woman to whom he was married till death do them part, was ugly, extraordinarily ugly. Intolerably ugly. He started breaking out in rashes, somewhat akin to allergies, when confronted by their tremendous physical incompatibility. He needed to vent his frustrations. He ran to his mother.

"Mother, I must have been drunk, totally drunk when I married her!"

Beside himself, holding his head between his hands, he shrieked, "She's ugly as sin! Ugly as sin!" Certain conjugal duties and customs now became intolerable to him. For example, when going off to work or coming back home, he used to kiss his wife on the lips. Now, whenever he would pretend to be distracted and graze her face with his lips, she would lovingly complain, "On the mouth, sweetie, on the mouth." He would cringe. Soon, he developed a phobia for these kisses. What's worse, he couldn't help but compare the women he saw on the streets or on the buses to Jacira. If he saw a woman who was more shapely than his wife, he would exclaim, "Now that's what I call a woman!" or "Look at that sweet little tail!" And if he was out with a friend he would nudge him and say, "Check that out!"

The Lover

What made matters worse was that Jacira had such a sweet disposition. She loved to caress and be caressed. In the evenings when Herivelto arrived home she would sit on his lap and pour out sweet nothings.

"Do you love your sweetie pie? Do you?" Exasperated, doing everything he could to restrain himself, he would mumble, "Relax. There's a time for everything. And now it's time for dinner." If they would go to the movies, Herivelto would return extremely annoyed.

"I really don't think that Lana Turner's all that. She's very plain, if you ask me," Jacira once said.

It so happened that she was extremely unforgiving when it came to other women's defects. Barbara Stanwyck seemed "so unattractive" to her. Herivelto almost fell off his chair. He stood, furious.

"Barbara Stanwyck, unattractive! Are you drunk?" He felt like asking her point blank, "If Barbara Stanwyck is unattractive, what are you?" But their marriage was beyond repair at this point. He was now obsessed with one single thought: "I have to find myself some action on the side." And so he did; he found himself a woman who worked at a boutique. She reminded one of a thoroughbred filly. The truth of the matter is that, before long, Herivelto was in love. On one occasion she saw Jacira from a distance. The first opportunity she had, she said to Herivelto, "Your wife is really ugly, you know that?"

He responded, his teeth clenched, "A real dog." His wife's ugliness humiliated him. What is interesting is that Jacira was totally oblivious; she had no idea that she disgusted her husband so much.

The Cheater

Then the inevitable occurred. One night Herivelto arrived home drunk. To make matters worse, he had lipstick stains on his neck, his handkerchief, all over. Jacira, for whom the idea of an affair was inconceivable, turned into a lioness. She went after her husband with her finger pointed at his face.

"What's going on? What's the meaning of this?"

Barely able to maintain his balance, her husband demonstrated a sincerity typical of drunks.

"I have a lover... a lover."

At first she didn't comprehend. She repeated his words, aghast: "A lover." But her husband was rolling in bed by now, face down, mumbling unintelligible things in his own drunken language. In a fit of rage, she turned him over, held him up by the lapel, shook him and yelled, "I'm going to cheat on you too, do you hear me!"

The next morning when Herivelto woke up, Jacira, who had not slept at all, repeated what she had said earlier: "I'm going to do the same thing to you. God is my witness!"

Tragedy

She was in no hurry. For forty-eight hours she was engaged in a torturous internal debate. In theory cheating was, or should have been, very easy, but one question remained: With whom? She went over the names of all of their friends and acquaintances in her mind. She excluded them one by one through a process of elimination. Finally, she decided on one of her husband's friends, a man by the name of Mascarenhas. She called him without revealing her identity. Upon hearing a woman's voice, he grew very excited. He said that he wanted an immediate rendezvous in such-and-such a place. She used all of her feminine wiles to delay the meeting. After about two weeks of phone calls Jacira yielded. Mascarenhas set a time and gave her the address of an apartment that he kept for precisely such occasions. Two hours later she was there ringing the doorbell. He opened the door, and Jacira walked in. He seemed aghast, as if not comprehending what he was seeing. Jacira noticed on his lips an expression of abject disappointment. She waited for him to say one word, to make one move. He never did; instead, he just stood there in silence. Finally she prompted him.

"So?"

"I'm sorry, I can't," the man stammered, "I'm very sorry… forgive me."

For the first time Jacira understood. She rushed home, feeling like a criminal. At home, in the bedroom, she stood before a full-length mirror. She looked at herself from top to bottom. She understood everything. She understood why she had been so cruelly rejected. As luck would have it, that night her husband arrived home drunk again and spit out the word, "Dog! Dog!" She felt hatred, an inhuman hatred, well up inside. Indiscriminate hatred for herself, for her husband, for the world. She waited for Herivelto to fall into his drunken slumber. Calm by now, she poured alcohol on him and lit a match. Engulfed by flames, he contorted his body as if he were being tickled. He fled howling, pursued by the flames. Neighbors threw buckets of water on him. But Herivelto died right there, naked and black.

The Great Widower

Back from the cemetery, he addressed his family.

"Well... I want you all to know one thing: My wife is dead, and I'm next."

Those assembled listened in alarm. His relatives exchanged silent glances. The widower's father stood.

"Take it easy, son! Take it easy"

Jair turned to him abruptly.

"Take it easy because she's my wife, not yours! I'm not taking it easy, Dad. I don't want to take it easy. Do you know the only reason why I don't kill myself right now?"

"Have faith in God!" a spinster aunt interjected.

Jair came very close to unleashing an obscenity. He restrained himself. In an intense and burning serenity, he continued where he had left off: "The only reason I don't kill myself right now is because I want to design my wife's mausoleum. Hers and mine. I want two tombstones side by side. For the record, I want to be buried with Dalila, do you understand?"

No one said a word. After all, it is very hard to argue with a man who is in a state of total despair. They followed Jair with their eyes as he walked towards the stairs, a shattered wreck; it devastated them to see him in so much pain. He trudged up the stairs and locked himself in his bedroom.

Inconsolable

In his absence the young man's uncle asked, "You think he's capable of killing himself?"

The boy's father took out a cigarette and gave his opinion.

"I don't think so. His bark is worse than his bite."

There was a silence as those assembled pondered this.

"You never know," someone said.

The father, who was skeptical of everything and everyone, continued, "All I know is: A widow or widower's pain usually lasts for only about forty-eight hours."

"Let's not exaggerate."

The father insisted.

"Yes, sir. That's right!" He referred to an example that all those present knew well: "Take the next door neighbor, OK? Her husband was buried in the morning, and that same evening there she was at the front gate sucking on a popsicle. How's that for pain!"

The episode with the popsicle left a deep impression. Sensing that his words had had the desired effect, the old man ended on an optimistic note.

"Let's give it some time. This will pass." Then he added philosophically, "Everything passes."

The Pain

Two weeks later, however, the widower was as despondent as the day his wife died. He couldn't take two steps in that house without coming across a picture, a memento of the deceased. There was more: Through the indiscretion of the cleaning woman, it was known that every night Jair slept with his wife's dresses, her nightgowns, her pajamas next to him. Once, a curious thing happened: He placed his hand in his pocket and pulled out the dead woman's panties. Even the father no longer knew what to say or think. He growled that his son was cuckoo, bonkers. His ruthless pragmatism even led him to consider having his son committed.

"Committed because he misses his wife? Committed for being a widower? Hold your horses!"

"But damn it, any day now he'll put a bullet through his brain!"

Someone remembered something Jair had said, namely that he would kill himself once work on the mausoleum was completed. Faced with a son who filled his pockets with his ex-wife's undergarments, the old man shuddered.

"Why is it that every great pain always seems so pathetic?" It anguished him that Jair would spend his days in the cemetery hugging the dead wife's tombstone, crying like a baby. What was worse was that his son the widower was not shy about expressing his grief. Back from the cemetery, Jair ranted and raved.

"You can't just forget the greatest woman in the world. I dare you to find a woman who is half the woman she was!"

In fact, Dalila was much more loved in death than in life. Jair even began to feel a certain pride that his pain would not subside. He continued, faithful to the thought of suicide. He kept plucking the same string: He did not believe a surviving spouse should remain alive. Once, when the father tried to argue against this dated notion of suicide, his son cut him off.

"Dad, don't bother. You already lost your son. I'm practically dead as it is."

Curiously, perhaps through the power of suggestion or perhaps due to his health, Jair's skin began to acquire the greenish tinge typical of cadavers.

The Other

The family began desperately seeking a way to save him. One of Jair's distant cousins had an idea. He called the young man's father.

"It's like this: There's only one way to save Jair."

"How?"

The cousin lowered his voice.

"Destroying what ties him to the deceased: his love for her."

The old man's eyes widened.

"But how! How? It's impossible!"

Supremely confident, the cousin rested his cigarette on the ashtray.

"Nothing is impossible!" He cleared his throat and continued. "Let's just suppose the deceased had a lover."

The old man leapt up.

"But Dalila was the picture of virtue. Beyond reproach!"

The cousin laughed.

"I should know. But so what? There's not a woman dead or alive who can't be slandered if you really put your mind to it. We could invent, could we not, a two-bit lover? And who's to say he didn't exist?"

The father, pale, stammered, "Go on."

"Well, once he finds out that Dalila was a tramp, Jair will automatically fall out of love with her. Do you understand the move now?"

It took a while for the father to answer.

"I do."

The Revelation

The idea of slandering the wife was so persuasive that after some half-hearted objections on moral grounds, the family gave their approval. "The ends justify the means," someone said by way of rationalization.

One morning, while the workers at the cemetery were busy with the mausoleum, a family meeting was called. The father, extremely nervous, opened by asking his son, "Are you certain your wife was deserving of all your suffering?"

Jair immediately sensed something in the air. He cornered his father, who had no option but to proceed with the ruse.

"Although it's very unpleasant to talk about a woman who is dead, the truth is Dalila had a lover!"

The widower stepped back.

"A lover? What do you mean a lover?" It was as if he couldn't comprehend what he was hearing. Then everyone in the room, possessed by the lie, confirmed that they too knew about the lover, that they were well aware of his wife's infidelity. Bewildered, he asked, "Who is he? I want a name! I need to know his name!" The truth of the matter is that this important detail had escaped everyone's notice.

Beside himself, Jair grabbed his father by the shoulders and shook him.

"I'm willing to believe she had a lover. But I want a name. Who is he? Tell me! For God's sake tell me!"

The father hid behind a proverb: "You can name the miracle but not the saint!"

The son made outlandish promises.

"You think I'm going to kill him, don't you? That he's as good as dead? I swear I won't. I won't lay a finger on him!" He was screaming by now. "If you tell me his name I won't kill myself! I need this man alive. He'll be my friend. My one and only friend. My friend forever! Tell me!"

Silence. He waited. Since no one spoke up, he jumped back and pulled out the pistol that he had carried with him since his wife's death. He lifted the gun to his head.

"Either tell me his name, or I'll kill myself. Now!"

Suddenly, his father turned to the cousin and pointed at him.

"It's him!"

Terror-stricken, the cousin didn't know where to hide. Jair put the revolver on the piano. He approached the cousin slowly. Suddenly, he froze and raised his arms.

"Thank you!" he said. "You've found the one man I can talk to about Dalila. As an equal!"

He grabbed the startled cousin.

"Tell these asses, will you? Was she or wasn't she the greatest woman in the world!" He broke out in tears on the poor devil's shoulder, as if he were his true brother, his comrade, his fellow widower.

The Ulcer

The family meeting was a solemn, almost funereal event. Even the in-laws attended. Once they were all packed into the living room, including the family doctor, the question was posed: "To operate or not to operate?"

Silence. The family doctor looked from one face to the next and then spoke. With both hands planted firmly on his knees, he began, "I think the operation is the best bet."

Mayhem. All spoke at once. The more optimistic and eager ones were emphatic.

"Yes, operate!"

The more cautious ones scratched their heads.

"Wouldn't it be better to wait? Don't you think a change of diet might do the trick?"

They turned to Oliveira, the husband.

"How about you? Where do you stand: for or against?"

The husband stood, buried both hands in his pockets, walked to the window amid general anticipation; then he sat down again and proceeded to disappoint everybody.

"I'm not getting involved," he said. "I don't have an opinion."

General "Oh's!" of indignation were heard. But he was steadfast. He was by nature an enemy of anything that smelled of blood and gore. Surgery to him was akin to butchery, and a surgeon was a sort of licensed Jack the Ripper. Letting his feelings get the better of him, he exaggerated: "I'm against anything that has to do with knives! You can count me out!" Exclamations were heard all around: "That's silly!" "Come on!" He stood and walked towards the door, making an exit that bordered on being impolite. In the husband's absence they turned their attention to the main interested party, who was in the corner with a faraway look in her eyes and an air of exhaustion, distant from everything and everyone. Stretched out on a couch, very pale, her wrists delicate and transparent – Dagmar seemed to ignore that it was her they were all talking about, that it was her operation. When she felt the attention turn to her, she opened her eyes and, battling fatigue of body and soul, sighed: "Let's put an end to this... I'll go ahead and get the operation..."

First Night

Dagmar and Oliveira had been married for five years. While they were still dating, she had revealed, "I have severe stomach ailments." Indeed, she suffered from horrible bouts of heartburn, painful and fiery, the kind that burned the throat. She would squeeze her abdomen with her two hands and complain, "You know what it feels like? Like there's an open wound inside!" She would underscore the point: "Right here!" Their first night as a married couple was a disaster. While still in church in front of the altar, she had been tormented by heartburn. That night at the apartment, Oliveira, all hot and heavy, kissed her on the mouth. She threw her veil off and broke free of his clutch.

"Wait, sweetie," she said. "I'm sorry, but I feel awful! God, I can't stand it!"

She made her husband place his hand on her stomach.

"Right here. Do you feel it throbbing?"

"Lie down for awhile till it goes away," he said.

She did, trembling, except it didn't go away. In the wee hours, unable to fall asleep, Oliveira said to himself, "Just my luck!" Days and months went by. As soon as Dagmar improved a little, things would look up; then she would invariably get worse. Suspicions of an ulcer surfaced, but Dagmar avoided x-rays at all cost, fearing she would need an operation. Her sister, Verinha, seventeen, cute and vivacious, would constantly advise her, "If I were you, I'd go under the knife as soon as possible and get it over with!"

"Stop it!" Dagmar would say, knocking on a nearby table for good measure.

Dagmar held out hope that it was the liver or something of the sort. She just didn't want it to be an ulcer; the very word terrified her.

When her sister kept insisting on an operation, she exploded, "The way you talk, it's like you want to see me six feet under!"

The Martyr

They ended up taking x-rays and confirming that it was an ulcer. The aforementioned family meeting occurred, and Dagmar herself, tired of suffering, put an end to all speculation: "I'll go ahead with the operation..."

The family doctor, gleefully rubbing his hands, was optimistic.

"Young lady, the operation is as easy as can be! A piece of cake!"

That night as husband and wife prepared for bed, Oliveira, unbuttoning his shirt, made the following comment: "It's all for the best. Do the operation and get it over with."

"What if I die?" asked Dagmar, sitting in front of the mirror taking off her earrings.

Oliveira could barely conceal his annoyance.

"Oh God, there you go again! Come on!"

But Dagmar insisted sweetly and firmly, "It can happen. Why not? I might even die on the operating table. But it's neither here nor there." Then she lowered her voice, leaned on her husband's shoulder and said softly, "If I die, will you marry again? Will you?"

"Stop it!"

"You will; I know you will. I know men. It's only natural. But I just want you to promise me one thing: Marry any woman you want except one, Verinha. Not my sister, you hear? Never!"

"Oh, Dag!" he said, pale, his lips trembling.

"It always seemed indecent to me for a widower to marry his wife's sister," she said in tears. "And if you do after I asked you not to, I swear..."

Oliveira, who was genuinely moved by what he heard, hugged his wife, who by now was sobbing uncontrollably.

"Don't be silly! You're being childish!"

The Operation

Finally, the day of the operation arrived. Oliveira, his nerves on edge, announced to anyone who would listen, "I'm not going to the hospital because when I see a surgeon I feel like punching him in the face. I swear I do!"

When the time came to say goodbye, she hugged him and whispered in his ear, "I'm sure Verinha wants to see me dead. But I have faith in God!" Oliveira stayed at home, chain smoking, Verinha at his side. He couldn't get his wife's strange and morbid request off his mind. What made the request even stranger was that the two sisters adored each other. Still waiting for any news, tired, he sunk into his armchair and closed his eyes. Suddenly, he felt a hand on his. He opened his eyes; it was Verinha; it couldn't have been otherwise. He didn't move and even stopped breathing. They looked at one another like two people seeing each other for the first time. Just then the phone rang. They both rushed to answer: It was the first news they were hearing.

"You mean to tell me everything went well?" Oliveira asked, terribly relieved. "Everything's OK?"

They left for the hospital by car. There they ran into the doctor, who offered Oliveira his arm and led the young man to a quiet corner. He told him that the operation had gone very well, but when they opened her stomach they discovered that it wasn't an ulcer.

"What was it then?" Oliveira asked, stunned.

The doctor stared at him firmly and broke the news.

"Cancer."

Agony

For three or four days Oliveira railed against medicine in general and surgery in particular. Grabbing his head with both hands, he shouted, "What a stupid operation, my God!" He looked up at the heavens. "So they had to open my wife's stomach for this?" Dagmar, lying in bed, her gaze fixed like a condemned woman, short of breath, her arms increasingly thin, believed herself to be convalescing, to be out of harm's way. She wanted to know: "You mean to tell me I can eat anything I want now?"

The doctor, who possessed his profession's requisite ability to lie brazenly, answered, "Soon, soon." A procession of family and friends entered the hospital room as if attending a wake. They already knew that she would only have three or four months at most to live.

One night, while Oliveira and Verinha were sitting with the dying woman, she took a turn for the worse. Feverish, unaware of the presence of the two witnesses to her delirium, Dagmar called her sister "indecent" and "filthy." Engaging in a conversation with herself, she yelled, "Marry any woman you want except one... that tramp!" Oliveira listened, aghast, wishing to God she would shut up. As for Verinha, she simply stood there, expressionless. She seemed to be soaking up her sister's hatred. When Dagmar finally grew silent, perhaps forever, Verinha, who was on the other side of the bed, came around with slow, steady steps. Standing in front of her brother-in-law, she bent down quickly, held his face in her hands and gave him a long kiss on the mouth. Then she went back to her place, sat down and began to pray. Her sister died at the break of dawn.

The Faithful Husband

The two women were arguing about men and cheating. Rosinha was categorical.

"I trust my husband more than I trust myself!"

Ceci flashed a sardonic half smile.

"You mean to tell me you think your husband is faithful?"

"I don't think. He is!" she replied. "Very faithful."

The friend found this funny.

"Do you want a bit of advice?" she asked. "Advice you can take to the bank?"

"I'm listening."

"Don't vouch for any husband. Not one. The only faithful husband is a dead husband. I'm an expert on the subject: I'm married. I have no illusions. I know my husband will cheat with a lamppost if he gets the chance!"

Rosinha lost her temper.

"I don't know about your husband; I really don't care. I can only tell you about mine. And I can vouch for mine one hundred percent. I pity the day he cheats on me! I pity the day! I'm very nice and all. But no one makes a fool of me. I'd like to see him try!"

Featherbrain

Ceci, who was a friend and neighbor, left a short while later. Alone now, Rosinha thought, "Who ever heard of such a thing!" From the time she was single she had always had very firm opinions about fidelity and marriage. As far as she was concerned, the worst thing that could happen to a wife was to be cheated on. Food, clothing, a roof over her head were of very little importance. So much so that she had given Romario a warning before she married him.

"I'll go hungry with you. I don't care. There's only one thing I won't put up with: cheating!"

It should be noted that Romario's conduct as a boyfriend, fiancé and husband seemed exemplary. They had been married for three years. Until it could be proven otherwise, his life consisted of going from home to work and from work to home. In matters of love no one was more delicate and affectionate. Even after they married, he would make small gestures typical of a boyfriend. Sprawled out on the chaise lounge, Rosinha told herself, "I'm more likely to cheat on him than he is on me!" This was the sweet and firm conviction on which their marital happiness was based. That evening when her husband arrived home from work, she jumped into his arms and kissed him with the voraciousness of a newlywed. Then she asked him point-blank, "Would you be capable of cheating on me?"

"Don't even say that. It's bad luck!"

"Would you?" she insisted.

"Whoa, take it easy!"

Rosinha told him of the conversation she'd had with Ceci. The husband broke out in exclamations.

"Oh, come on! Get off it! Gee whiz! Are you going to listen to that featherbrain? Ceci is a snake, a vulture, a scorpion! Besides, she's got a complex because she's been cheated on at least two hundred times. Spite, that's what this is all about!"

Ceci

Be that as it may, the conversation with Ceci left a deep impression. As Rosinha brushed her teeth before going to bed, she surprised herself with the following conjecture: "Does he cheat? Is he cheating?" The following day she went next door to Ceci's house.

"Don't tell me I'm naive, OK? If I tell you my husband doesn't cheat it's because I have good reason."

Ceci, who was squeezing pimples in front of a mirror, looked up, startled. "And what would that be?"

"Because," she explained, all worked up, "I always know what my husband is up to. Day in, day out, his schedule never changes. He gets up, he goes to work; at noon he comes home for lunch; then work again and finally back home. There hasn't been one time when I've called him at work and he hasn't been there, as steady as Sugarloaf Mountain. Even if Romario wanted to cheat on me he couldn't; he'd have no time!"

Ceci sighed.

"Rosinha, Rosinha! You know who is blindest? The one who refuses to see. What can you do!"

Rosinha exploded.

"I beg your pardon! Blind? OK, explain to me then how my husband can cheat if he's either at work or at home with me? Do you really think it's possible?"

Her answer: "Yes. I'm sorry, but it is possible."

Maracanã Stadium

They left it at that. That Sunday after lunch Ceci showed up to catch up on the latest gossip. Nosey as always, she noticed Romario wasn't in.

"Where's your husband?" she asked.

"He went to the game," Rosinha answered curtly.

"At Maracanã?"

"Yes, at Maracanã!"

Ceci slapped her own forehead.

"Now I've seen it all!" Beaming, she grilled her neighbor, "Didn't you say your husband was either with you or at work? Very well. How about Sundays?

He goes to a soccer match while you stay at home! He spends the whole afternoon, the entire time, away from you. Am I right?"

"Oh, please!" Rosinha shouted. "What could be more innocent than a soccer match? It's completely innocent!"

Really getting into it now, pacing back and forth, Ceci insisted, "All right! What if it's not a game he's going to? He tells you he goes. But it might be just an excuse, a pretext, am I right? Of course I am!"

Rosinha, pale by now, stammered, "Stop playing."

Her neighbor lowered her voice and made a diabolical suggestion.

"Shall we see if I'm right? Huh?"

Rosinha would have none of it.

"It's not worth it. It's silly!"

Ceci flashed a cruel smile.

"Are you scared?"

Rosinha, almost unable to speak, denied it.

"Why would I be afraid?" But she was. She felt the onset of one of those panic attacks one never forgets.

"It's no big deal, silly. We'll have fun. We'll go there, and we'll ask them to call your husband over the PA system. If he shows up, fine. If he doesn't, you'll know: He's in the arms of some blond. OK?"

Rosinha struggled before answering.

"OK."

The Public Address

Under relentless pressure from her neighbor, Rosinha put on a nicer dress, patted a little rouge on her cheeks and skipped the lipstick. At the front door she grabbed Ceci by the arm. Solemnly, she warned her, "What you're doing to me is sick. It's evil! What if he's not there? Have you thought about how that will make me feel? What do you think? That I can go back to living with my husband knowing he cheated on me?" Then she made a wrenching confession, "I'm scared! I'm scared!" During the whole trip to the stadium Ceci justified her actions: "I'm doing this for your own good, OK?" Rosinha took a deep breath, "If Romario's not there I'm moving out!"

"Why move out?" Ceci asked. "You want to know something? The only thing that justifies a separation is when there's no love in a marriage. There's no love; both go their own way, and that's the end of that. But cheating, no. A real woman knows how to be cheated on."

When they arrived at the stadium, Ceci moved right into action. She made acquaintances with several Maracanã employees, including the public address announcer. Rosinha stood to the side, mesmerized, merely taking everything in. Finally, the announcement came over the PA system, "May I have your attention please! Mr. Romario Pereira, please report to the stadium office urgently."

The Appeal

The announcement was repeated once, twice, five times, ten times, twenty times. The two waited at the stadium offices. Romario was nowhere to be found. Pale, her lower lip trembling, Rosinha asked the announcer, "Could you please try one last time? If you don't mind." There came a time when the repetition of the futile announcement bordered on the comical. Rosinha pulled Ceci to the corner; she poured her heart out.

"I always prayed that I would never be cheated on! I never wanted to be cheated on!" She squeezed her friend's arm, "I would have lived out the rest of my life never suspecting anything. Why did you have to open my eyes? Why?"

Oblivious to her neighbor's pain, Ceci seemed ecstatic.

"Didn't I tell you? Didn't I! It's our cross to bear, honey. Women were born to be cheated on!"

Rosinha did not utter a word, but instead just sat there anguished. It could be said that the stadium had suddenly been transformed into a giant tomb. It was useless to wait any longer. Then, forever convinced she was being cheated on, Rosinha lowered her voice.

"Let's get out of here. I can't stand it anymore."

The announcer, in an exemplary show of cordiality, bowed.

"At your service, ma'am…"

As they exited the stadium, Rosinha repeated, "I didn't need to know! I shouldn't have to know!"

To which her neighbor replied triumphantly, "The trick is for the cheated wife to know how to tough it out!" Just then, they were waiting to cross the street. Rosinha grabbed her friend's hand, and they went across. When they got to the middle they froze: A bus was coming towards them at full speed. Panic. At the very last second Rosinha let go of Ceci's hand and ran. Not so fortunate, Ceci was hit head-on and was hurled into the air; her body did an improbable somersault before striking the asphalt. Rosinha arrived before anyone else. She rested her neighbor's bloody head on her lap. When she realized that Ceci was dead, had just died, she burst into laughter. Softly at first and then louder and louder, in a crescendo, until she appeared to be possessed, as if she were being tickled to death.

"It serves you right! It serves you right!" she screamed.

Threesome

The father-in-law was a saint and an all-around jovial fellow. On seeing Filadelfo, he rushed to him with open arms.

"How is my man doing?"

Filadelfo hugged him and let himself be hugged. Then he growled gloomily, "Your man is not doing so well."

This caught his father-in-law by surprise.

"Geez. Not doing so well? What's the matter?"

As he walked along the sidewalk next to the affable man with a big belly, Filadelfo enumerated his trials one by one, and they were worthy of Job.

"It's your daughter's temper. She disrespects me at every turn. Pretty soon she'll start hitting me!"

Dr. Magarão nodded, grave and bothered.

"I know, I know." He sighed and admitted, "Just like her mother. Same temper. The mother is the same way!"

Filadelfo stopped in his tracks. He put his hand on his father-in-law's shoulder and asked, "Sir, I want you to answer me one thing. Is this right? Is it fair?"

The old man hesitated.

"Well. Whether it's fair or not, I don't know."

He meditated on the issue and then asked, "Do you want my honest opinion? No cock and bull story. Do you?"

"Yes."

"Then let's sit down and have a drink over here. I am going to tell you some things every married man should know."

The Theory

They entered a small bar and sat at a discreet table. Dr. Magarão spoke as the waiter placed two glasses on the table and served them their beers.

"You, of course, know that I am married. Very well. I am not only speaking from personal experience, but also from what I've observed in others. I have learned that all virtuous wives are like that."

Filadelfo was taken aback.

"What do you mean?"

The fat man continued.

"Like my daughter. I'm giving it to you straight. My friend, you should distrust the nice, the cordial, the pleasant wife. Virtue is a sad, bitter and ornery thing."

Filadelfo recoiled in his chair.

"Give me a break! You can't be serious!" And he repeated, bug-eyed, licking the beer foam off his lips, "You can't be serious."

But his father-in-law insisted. He asked, "Do you know who the nicest wife I ever met in my life was? Do you? A woman who cheated on her husband with half of Rio de Janeiro. I should know because I was one." He slapped his chest, relishing the memory. "I was one. And she treated her husband like a king!"

One hour later the two left the small bar. Dr. Magarão with his opera buffa belly, drunk by now, thundered, "Consider yourself lucky! You should be counting your blessings! You should thank God!"

The son-in-law, wobbly-kneed and red-eyed, grumbled, "We'll see about that."

The Disgraced

He wasn't lying. His married life was indeed in a sad state. Excluding his honeymoon, which he counted at eight days, his wife had never treated him well. He had endured the most humiliating indignities, at times even in front of guests. Once, at a well-attended dinner party she humiliated him with the following remark: "Stop chewing on your dentures, will you."

There was a tremendous awkwardness in the room. The poor husband felt like jumping out the nearest window. Three years of married life had taught him to expect nothing but indignities from his wife. What he couldn't understand, though, was why Jupira, who was so kind to everyone else, made an exception of him, her own husband. After leaving his father-in-law, he returned home desperate. He opened the front door, climbed the stairs, entered the bedroom and was met with a warning: "Don't turn the lights on!"

He obeyed. He undressed in the dark and then, like a blind man, fished around for his pajamas. When he finally managed to lie down in bed he had a melancholy thought: It had been ten months, perhaps a year since they'd kissed on the mouth. Intimidated, the most he would allow himself would be to graze her face with his lips. If he wanted to be more tender, she would quickly dissuade him: "Not on the mouth! Stop!" Another thing that made him bitter was his wife's total disregard for her appearance around the house. She wouldn't fix her hair or wear perfume. Lying in bed next to her, he remembered his father-in-law's theory. Could it be that virtuous women had to smell bad too?

The Change

One month later he arrived home from work and something happened that had never happened before. His wife threw herself at him, all dolled up and drenched in perfume. It was such a big surprise that Filadelfo almost fell over backwards. Next she squeezed his face and kissed him on the mouth, going all out just like a girlfriend, a fiancé or a newlywed. He picked up the newspaper that he'd let fall. Dumbstruck, he asked, "What's this? What happened?"

Jupira answered with a question of her own.

"What's the matter? Don't you like it?"

He sat down confused.

"I like it, I like it, but…" He laughed. "It's different that's all, you never kiss me."

Jupira added a gesture he loved: She sat on his lap and touched her face to his. She stroked him. He asked her, "Explain the mystery to me. Something happened. Right?"

She sighed.

"I changed, that's all!"

Suffering

At first Filadelfo said to himself, "It's just today." The next day, however, it was more of the same. He scratched his head. "There's something fishy here." It just so happened that around this time his in-laws came for dinner. While his wife spoke to her daughter, Dr. Magarão took his son-in-law over to the window.

"So? How are things?"

"I'm stunned!" Filadelfo answered. "I'm completely bowled over!"

The old man jutted out his opera buffa belly.

"What happened?"

"We had that conversation, right? Well, Jupira's changed. She's a lamb now, and you have to see the way she treats me!"

The old man nodded as he chewed on his unlit cigar.

"Great!"

"So great I'm starting to get suspicious!"

The old man put his hands on Filadelfo's shoulders.

"Do you want some advice? Man to man? Don't be suspicious, all right. Would it hurt you so much to turn a blind eye? Look! Husbands shouldn't be the last to know, you understand? Husbands should never know!"

The Honeymoon

Following his father-in-law's advice, Filadelfo decided not to investigate the reasons for his wife's sudden change in temperament. He tried to take maximum advantage of the situation to the point where he felt as if he were living a second honeymoon. Days later, however, he received a very detailed anonymous letter, seemingly very authentic, with names, dates and addresses. The unknown writer of the missive began as follows: "Your wife and Cunha…" Cunha was his best friend, and he would eat dinner two or three times a week with the couple. The letter even gave the address and the floor of the building in Copacabana where the two lovers would meet. Filadelfo read and reread it and then tore the sordid letter into thousands of little pieces. He thought about Cunha: single, amiable, almost good-looking, good teeth. An inescapable conclusion dawned on him: At the end of the day, he owed his newfound conjugal bliss to Cunha. Filadelfo decided to go on with his life as if nothing had happened, especially now that Jupira was reliving the golden moments of their honeymoon. One night the three were eating dinner when Filadelfo's napkin fell. He leaned over to pick it up, and he saw, unmistakably, under the table, his wife's feet and those of Cunha's, in an amorous entwine. A few days later Filadelfo heard the news: Cunha was getting married! He came home extremely anxious. He found his wife face down on the bed sobbing. In a blind rage, she repeated over and over again, "I want to die! I want to die!"

Filadelfo simply stared without saying a word. He walked to a table, pulled out a revolver and went looking for Cunha. When he found him he laid out the crux of the problem.

"Listen here, you dog, either you call off your wedding, or I'll shoot you in the mouth!"

The following day, Cunha, terrified, called the man who was to be his father-in-law and called the wedding off. That night he showed up, sullen, for supper with the couple. At the dinner table, Filadelfo turned to his friend.

"From now on you'll eat dinner here every night!" he said.

When Cunha left, shortly after midnight, Jupira threw herself in her husband's arms.

"Baby, you're a darling!"

The Abyss

His friend pulled up a chair and sat next to him. They engaged in light chatter, and then the friend lit a cigarette.

"I met your future son-in-law yesterday," he said.

By now Eurilo was standing next to a file cabinet reviewing some documents. He turned, shocked.

"My future what?"

The friend repeated what he had said.

"Your future son-in-law. Your daughter's boyfriend. Your youngest one's boyfriend."

Stunned, Eurilo closed the drawer. He approached and said, "I don't understand. My girl's boyfriend? The little one? It can't be! It's impossible! None of my daughters have boyfriends, much less the youngest one!" He insisted, "It must be a mistake."

The friend was emphatic.

"I spoke to the young man. I spoke to the boy's mother! I'm not making this up!"

Eurilo laughed bitterly.

"Well, now I've seen it all," he said. "It's the same old story: The father is always the last to know. I bet you it's nothing serious, God willing."

The Beast

On their street he was cordial with everyone, perhaps overly cordial. Once on the bus, something interesting happened: He had a run-in with the driver, and the driver hurled an epithet at him. Eurilo simply did not react. Instead, he hid in a corner seat, pale, while the driver ranted and raved. Very well. He was affable and even cowardly when it came to others, but he was a beast at home. Widowed for sixteen years, he had five daughters on whom he meted out the most barbaric punishments. The daughters walked around the house on eggshells, terrified of their father. They were so browbeaten that they lived in constant fear. Eurilo would go from raising his voice straight to corporal punishment. Of the five, only the youngest, Terezinha, sixteen, would allow herself certain liberties behind his back. For example, when old man Eurilo was absent, she would go to the movies with her girlfriends. Or she would flirt with the boys from the neighborhood in front of their houses. But, as for the others, they submitted to their father's authority with utter docility; and they complied with his edicts even in his absence. Eurilo had already warned, "The first one I catch in any hanky-panky I'll beat to a pulp. Consider yourself warned!"

The Rebel

That evening he arrived home beside himself. He locked himself in his office with the oldest one. He asked, "Is it true that Terezinha has a boyfriend?"

His daughter cowered before him.

"I don't know, I don't know."

The father held both her arms.

"Answer me: Does she or doesn't she?"

Since the girl continued to equivocate, Eurilo ripped his belt off. Immediately, the poor girl fell to her knees, sobbing.

"Yes, it's true! She's dating someone!"

In a voice choking with anger, the old man said, "I knew it! I knew it!"

As his terrified daughter walked by him to leave the room, her head down, the old man lashed at her with his belt. Alone now, he collapsed in his chair, exhausted. He closed his eyes and thought, "They're all the same! All the same!" Five minutes later he appeared at the door and called Terezinha, the youngest one. Of the five sisters, four barely showed any vestiges of femininity. They were sad spinsters with no grace or spark. Only the little one displayed any charm. With a cute body and face, eyes to die for, beautiful and tender lips, she turned heads wherever she went. The father turned to her, seething.

"So, you have a boyfriend, do you?" he asked.

"Me?"

"I know you do," the old man continued. "All right. Bring the boy tomorrow to talk to me. Let's do the following: Invite him for dinner. I want to meet my future son-in-law."

The Dinner

His name was Armando. The following day he appeared at the girl's house with an air of panic. Eurilo, who arrived a little earlier than usual, welcomed him relatively cordially. First they had a sad, funereal, and silent dinner. Once the dessert and coffee had been served, Eurilo stood. He leaned on the table with both hands and addressed the visitor.

"Are your intentions honorable? Do you really want to marry my daughter Terezinha who is present here?"

The young man cleared his throat.

"Certainly."

Eurilo raised his voice.

"Very well. If that's the case, you'll need to know certain peculiarities about your girlfriend's family. First of all, my daughter told you, of course, that her mother died giving birth? Right?"

"Yes."

The old man slammed his fist to the table and let out an ear-piercing scream: "It's a lie!" He put his hand over his collar and loosened his tie, as if he were having trouble breathing. He continued.

"The death of my wife was a myth I invented for my daughters' sake. Until this day, until this moment, they don't know the truth, which I am going to reveal right now. My wife, twenty years ago, after giving birth to Terezinha, ran away with another man. Do you understand? Did you hear what I just said? She ran away!"

"I understand."

Eurilo burst out in derisive laughter.

"Are you interested in the daughter of a tramp? Are you interested in the daughter of a remorseless woman who destroyed two households? Are you? Answer! Do you want to know something? Of all of my daughters, the one who most resembles my wife, who is a dead ringer for her, is Terezinha!"

Armando, his face white, his lower lip trembling, shrank before such violence. Eurilo made his way around the table to where Armando sat. Terrified, the young man stood. The two were now face to face: the possessed old man and the cowering teenager. Eurilo grabbed him by both arms and shook him.

"Do you want to be cheated on?" he screamed. "Cheated on like I was? Do you? Speak! Do you?"

The young man looked as if he was about to cry.

"No!"

Eurilo grabbed him by the arm. He dragged him to the door and pointed. "Out! Out!"

The Tragedy

He came back into the apartment breathing heavily, his mouth disfigured by a cruel scowl. He took in his daughters' frightened faces. The youngest stepped forward, breaking ranks with her terrified sisters. She approached her father, sobbing.

"I'll kill myself, Dad! I'll kill myself!" she said.

He stepped back as if astonished.

"You'll kill yourself? You would have the courage to kill yourself?" He laughed louder and louder in a crescendo. Suddenly, he stopped. Staggering, he walked to the window and opened it wide; it looked out onto an abyss. He started laughing again.

"Fortunately, we are on the twelfth floor. It's so simple, so easy to jump from here. It's the easiest thing in the world. Do really you want to or not? Come on, come on!"

He climbed onto the sill while his stunned daughters looked on. Standing before the abyss, he urged his daughter on, screaming.

"If you die, you'll never cheat! You'll never cheat like your mother! Go ahead!"

The youngest approached the window as if drawn by a magnet. Her sisters stood at a distance in a tight cluster, united in terror.

Suddenly a scream was heard in the night, but it was the scream of a man and not a woman. A mighty masculine howl. He had lost his balance and fallen to his death from the twelfth floor. All thought it a suicide or, at best, an accident. The police came in a patrol car. Then, without a single tear, her face an expressionless, inscrutable mask, the dead man's youngest daughter stepped forward.

"It wasn't a suicide," she said. "It wasn't an accident. I pushed my father! I did it…!"

Cheapskate

Zuleika had come down with a bad case of the flu. The coughing was so severe she writhed in pain. She called her husband in.

"Come here, Belmiro. Come here."

He put his newspaper down and obliged.

"Listen," she said.

Indeed, Zuleika's bronchial tubes practically whistled. After a particularly violent bout of coughing, she shuddered, "I think it must have been that gust of wind."

"I'm taking you to see the doctor," Belmiro said.

"Why a doctor? Slow down!"

Doctors terrified Zuleika; she thought they were all a big rip-off. "They're not taking my money!" she'd say to one and all. She'd recite the couple's financial woes: Belmiro earned very little, a pittance; and the money she made from sewing barely helped make ends meet. In arguing with her husband, she was unbending.

"Imagine if we had to spend money on doctors and medicine."

She couldn't shake the flu, though. It was several days now since she'd been consumed by fever, shortness of breath and cold night-sweats. Worst of all, however, was the coughing that ravaged her lungs and nearly choked her – it was as if she had contracted whooping cough. She tried the cough syrup someone recommended. It did nothing. She would wake up in the middle of the night and sit up in bed coughing for long spells.

"I'm going to die. My God, I'm going to die!" she'd cry in despair.

The Lung

"Get an x-ray," someone suggested.

"With what money?"

"Hit up so-and-so!"

Zuleika was stubborn; she always had been. She'd rather die than give in. But one night after a particularly violent coughing fit, she tasted blood in her mouth. Sensing something was not right, she turned on the light, touched her tongue to the sheet and saw pink-colored saliva on the white fabric. Zuleika, who ridiculed the thought that she might be sick (she insisted it was only a "silly cold"), was suddenly overcome by a harrowing fear. She remembered an aunt, one of her mother's sisters, who had died of consumption at a sanitarium in Campos do Jordão. She shook her husband, who was sleeping next to her, and yelled, "Blood! Blood!"

Convinced she had tuberculosis, she could not go back to sleep. And the taste of blood wouldn't go away. She kept a handkerchief by the bed. Any little thing and she would turn the lights on and touch her tongue to the handkerchief only to see a pink stain again. The next morning she made up her mind: "Let's go to Dr. Borborema, right away."

The husband objected.

"Dr. Borborema? That old ninny? He's a fool!"

"No! I don't want anyone else! It has to be Dr. Borborema!"

"Suit yourself!" said Belmiro, slipping his suspenders over his shoulders.

Indeed, Dr. Borborema was tiny, old, nearly senile, and of very dubious effectiveness. The poor devil was incapable of curing anyone; his greatest and perhaps only virtue was that he charged his low-income clients reduced rates and waived his fee if they couldn't pay. He saw his patients in an office where the filth had long ago settled in unchecked; it was even rumored that they had found scorpions or some such creatures there. On the way Belmiro griped.

"He's a moron, this Dr. Borborema."

"Who cares? It doesn't matter!" she shot back, annoyed.

Inside the dilapidated consultation room, the old man put a towel over Zuleika's back and listened. Like a doctor from the horse-and-buggy days, he placed his ear on the patient's back and instructed her to, "Say thirty-three."

"Thirty-three."

"Cough."

She coughed several times. The coughing soon turned involuntary and uncontrollable; she writhed and came close to suffocating. A plaque on the wall read: "As long as the sick are alive, there is still hope."

"So, doctor?" Belmiro asked anxiously.

The old man was already scribbling the prescription with his fountain pen. Without looking up, he pronounced, "It'll go away! It'll go away!"

Belmiro, dying to know more, insisted, "So, there's nothing the matter with her lungs?"

"Nothing."

"Doctor, you don't know how relieved that makes me feel," he said.

The doctor even escorted them to the door. Not only did he not charge, or charge very much, he was also extremely polite, a real gentleman. By force of habit, or perhaps as a distraction, he clicked his dentures (which he had both on his upper and lower jaws) in and out of place as he walked them to the door.

The Tragedy

By the time they arrived home, Zuleika had already taken a turn for the worse. Now, in a complete reversal, it was she who railed against Dr. Borborema.

"Fool! What does he know!"

"Didn't you choose him? Damn it!"

"I'm going to die, Belmiro!" she cried, sinking her nails into his arm. "I'm going to die!"

"Oh, stop being silly! You're not going to die! You're being childish!"

She became obsessed, body and soul, by the thought. It wasn't merely a hunch, though; it was a conviction, an utter certainty. She sat in the rocking chair in the living room for hours in deep meditation. When the husband spoke of filling the prescription, she was resolute.

"No!"

"Why not? You're really something, you know that!"

"We'd just be throwing money away," she said in a steely whisper. "I know I'm dying..."

Belmiro turned on their favorite soap opera. In her haunted state, it occurred to her that she would never know the endings of the several radio soaps she was in the habit of listening to throughout the day. That night she could not fall asleep. First because of the damn cough; then because she got to thinking deeply about the world she would soon be leaving. Her thoughts turned to many things, including her own funeral. She wanted it to be beautiful, so beautiful as to impress everyone on their street, but above all her next-door neighbor with whom she'd had a serious falling out. What a shame that modern burials were not like the ones in the old days when funeral coaches were pulled by plumed white horses. Suddenly, the thought occurred to her: Where would the money come from? Where, when and how would Belmiro get enough money for a luxury burial? She thought of nothing else until sunrise except how he could get the necessary money for the funeral arrangements. And it had to be magnificent enough to humiliate the said neighbor. She thought so hard about it that when she finally came across a solution, she felt the need to awaken Belmiro. He turned over, sluggish and grumpy, but when he heard her speaking of death, he reined in his anger. Softly, persuasively, Zuleika explained to him how she wanted a beautiful burial. Since she knew he had no money, she suggested that he approach Humberto. Her husband jumped up.

"I don't even know the guy! Besides, he's a jerk. He thinks he's some hotshot just because he has money!"

"When he finds out it's for me, that it's for my burial, he'll give you the money, Belmiro. He'll pay for everything. I swear!"

Belmiro looked at her suspiciously.

"Hold on," he said. "Why would he pay for it? Huh? Why? What's this clown to you, anyway?"

It's unclear whether Zuleika would have told him, but just as she was about to open her mouth, she began violently spitting up blood. Seeing the vast amounts of blood coming out of his wife's mouth, Belmiro's jealousy vanished. He screamed; the neighbors rushed in. They tried injections, calcium, ice bags, but nothing could stem the bleeding. During her bouts of spewing, Zuleika could think of nothing but the unpleasant neighbor, and wanted more than ever to dazzle her with a grand burial. She looked over at her husband as if saying, "I want a luxury burial!" If she could have spoken, she would have added that she wanted a seventh-day mass with violins, a choir and untold altar boys. Finally, no longer able to resist, she made a superhuman effort and whispered, "Beautiful... burial... and mass... a mass..."

Her nails were blue by now, and her effort to speak only hastened her death. Realizing his wife had passed away, Belmiro had a violent breakdown and had to be forcibly removed from the bedroom. Half an hour later in the living room while they dressed the body, his thoughts turned to Humberto. It was obvious that... a neighbor interrupted his reflections, offering to take care of the burial arrangements.

"Thank you!" he said. "That won't be necessary, I'll take care of everything."

The Arrangements

What followed was very odd. Humberto, whom Belmiro barely knew by sight, welcomed him with astonishment and, from what Belmiro could sense, a certain degree of alarm. On hearing the news of Zuleika's death, however, right then and there, in front of the bewildered husband, he had a near breakdown.

"Poor thing! Poor thing!" he repeated amid sobs.

Humberto was still crying when he heard her dying wish: an expensive burial and a mass.

Humberto insisted on paying for everything. With maximum discretion, Belmiro said, "I'll figure out how much it costs. I'll be back soon with the numbers."

At his request the Santa Casa Funeral Home gave him estimates for two burials: the most expensive and the cheapest one. The former amounted to fifty thousand cruzeiros. Belmiro ordered the cheapest one, to the amazement of the funeral home director. Then he went back to Humberto's office where he received fifty thousand cruzeiros plus some money thrown in for a monumental wreath.

The following day, in the early morning hours, a funeral coach barely worthy of a pauper departed from Belmiro's home. As the procession passed, the neighbor Zuleika didn't get along with watched from a window. On returning from the cemetery, the widower was already thinking about the arrangements for the mass. Fortunately, due to scruples that were to be expected under the circumstances, Humberto never attended. Thus, Belmiro was able to seek him out several days later at his office. He took home enough money for a mass with three priests, ten altar boys, a choir, violins, etc., etc.

The Daughter

The father jumped a foot and a half off the ground.

"I won't allow it, you hear? I won't allow it!"

His name was Rosas, and he was not the only one who wouldn't allow it. Besides Rosas, all of the relatives, friends, acquaintances, and neighbors denounced Livinha and Alexandre's relationship. They wanted to know, "Who is this Alexandre guy, anyway?" He didn't have a penny to his name. On top of that he was a born and confirmed loafer. He lived by his wits, bumming money off friends, acquaintances — sometimes as little as ten cruzeiros at a time. They grilled Livinha.

"You want to die of hunger?"

"I do!" she insisted.

Livinha was in love. It should be pointed out that she was a very warm person. She liked everyone and everything. Even alley cats were the object of her affection. She knew Alexandre was not squeaky clean; it was for precisely this reason that she was attracted to him. She thought she could change him. For his part the young man was in love too. In the beginning the family tried to explain to her, to lecture her. But Livinha was a strong-willed girl. She stood up to the family's fierce opposition.

"I'll marry him. End of story!"

It was then that Rosas warned his wife and the neighbors, "I'm going to take the gloves off!" Dona Adelaide even gave her blessing: "You can hit her, but just don't hurt her!"

The Whipping

He had never laid a finger on his daughter before. That evening he rolled up his sleeves and, belt in hand, called the young girl in. "So? Are you going to dump him or not?"

"No!" she answered, lips trembling.

The old man lifted the belt in the air. The neighbors, previously informed of the beating, pricked up their collective ears. And indeed they could hear every lash. But the girl did not let out a single peep. While he hit away, the neighbors whispered, "He's really letting her have it!" At last, exhausted, huffing and puffing, Rosas asked, "How about it? Do you give in?"

She raised her head and stared at him with a steely gaze.

"No!"

He was going to pick up where he left off, but his wife, the maid and a neighbor subdued him.

"Stop! That's enough!"

Livinha, who had cuts on her arms and legs, clenched her teeth in anger.

The Boyfriend

Rosas was at a loss. He had only one meager consolation: Livinha, although she had a woman's body, had just turned sixteen. As a minor she could not marry without the family's consent. Rosas was already contemplating a second beating when someone whispered in his ear, "Instead of giving your daughter a beating, why don't you give her boyfriend a beating?"

Rosas rubbed his hands gleefully.

"Of course! She won't give in, but he just might!"

The neighbor wasn't done.

"Let him have it, Rosas! Let him have it!"

The old man had a museum piece of a gun that couldn't kill a sparrow. Still, it was probably enough to get the job done.

The next day he went looking for the young man. He found him in a bar and called him out to a dark alley. There he laid it all out. He began by asking, "Look here, boy! What do you want from my daughter? Don't you see she's too good for you? Speak!"

The young man stammered, "I love your daughter!"

The old man exploded.

"The hell you do! You don't love anyone! You're a degenerate! Watch yourself, you bum!"

When the young man saw the almost one-hundred-year-old pistol in Rosas' hand he panicked. He cried like a little boy. He begged for the love of God, "Don't kill me! Don't kill me!"

Ecstatic at his own ruthlessness, Rosas began laying out conditions.

"This time I'll let you go. But if I find out you were with my daughter, I'll shoot you in the mouth!"

He shoved the boy a couple of times for good measure.

The Girl

The next time Livinha called him, Alexandre trod gingerly.

"I've been giving it some thought, and it's not going to work out. Your father's right. It's best we separate. And do me a favor: Don't call me any more. Goodbye!"

Livinha screamed at the telephone, "Alexandre! Hello! Hello!" He had hung up. She left the sewing supply shop from where she had placed the call and walked home livid. She arrived sobbing.

"What did Daddy tell Alexandre? What!"

Livinha felt like banging her head against a wall. Suddenly, she turned to her mother and sisters.

"I wanted to get married with a veil and a wedding dress, and you didn't want me to. Don't complain later!"

She stayed locked in her bedroom, face down, crying for two full days until she had no more tears to cry. On the third day she got up. She even made light of the situation: "All good things come to an end." She turned the radio on as if any vestige of love had vanished from her soul.

Revenge

Time went by. Occasionally she could be heard around the house saying, "You didn't want me to get married. I won't get married, period." One afternoon Livinha appeared at her father's office just as they were about to lock up. He immediately knew something was wrong. Her gait was a little shaky, and her gaze showed the telltale signs of alcohol.

"I just sold myself to a stranger," she said. "We went to his place for drinks; we had a real party. He gave me a hundred bucks."

Livid, the father stood in slow motion. He tried to mentally register what he had just heard.

Livinha continued, "He's not the first. You drove me to this, Dad. You! You deserve half the money. Here!"

She crumpled a bunch of bills and threw them in her father's face: the money she had made from selling her body.

Twist of Fate

She was sitting in front of the mirror applying lip gloss when her daughter entered.

"Are you going out?"

"Yes."

"Where?"

"None of your business," she answered curtly.

"I'm going too," the daughter said.

Irritated, Julieta threw the lip applicator down. She turned to Maria Lucia.

"Are you spying on me? Is that it?" She asked her daughter: "And where do you think you're going?"

"Wherever you're going."

Julieta, who was in her slip, her beautiful naked shoulders exposed, stood.

"So now I have to tow you around, is that it? I don't think so!"

The girl picked out a dress from the closet without uttering a word, while the mother, seething, looked on. Julieta blew her top.

"I'm not going out anymore! There, are you happy? Listen carefully: You've been on my case for a long time now, but your father's going to hear about this. So back off!"

Julieta put her robe on over her slip and stormed out, muttering under her breath, "What did I do to deserve this?"

Two Women

Julieta was the young, still beautiful, mother of an only daughter, fifteen. For about a year now she'd been saying, facetiously at first, "My daughter is on my case." And it was true. None of Julieta's gestures, words, or acts seemed to escape her daughter's scrutiny. If she were to laugh out loud, Maria Lucia would nudge her, "Don't laugh like that, Mother!" The truth of the matter is that as time went by the feeling of being watched, being spied on, became more and more intense. Whenever she was about to go out, her daughter would appear as if by magic: "I'm going too." What at first seemed like an occasional occurrence, now seemed to happen always. And Julieta, who at first found it amusing, began to get annoyed: "Oh, please!" She would confront her husband: "Do I have to ask her permission everywhere I go now?" Trying to strike a conciliatory note, the husband genially advised her to "Let it be! Let it be!" He added, "She loves you." There came a point, however, when her daughter's meddling became too intrusive and disturbing. One night at a party, the mother danced several songs with the same partner. On the car ride back she didn't hear the end of it from her daughter.

"You made a spectacle of yourself!"

"Me?"

"You! You danced five hundred times with the same guy. I've never been so embarrassed in my life!"

Julieta lost it.

"Look here, Maria Lucia, try not to butt in, OK? You're an obnoxious brat!"

But the girl got in the last word.

"It was so embarrassing!"

Incidents of this nature occurred more and more frequently. Julieta had the torturous feeling of never being alone, of always being watched over by her own daughter no matter where she went. That evening, as her daughter read in the study, Julieta rushed to get dressed for a night out. As we saw, Maria Lucia appeared at the last moment. Livid, Julieta waited for her husband to arrive. When he finally walked through the door, a little after seven, his wife gave him an earful.

"Our daughter's intolerable, Heitor! I can't take it anymore!"

Father and Husband

He was not one to talk much but was a man of principle. His sober demeanor was at odds with Julieta's young, outgoing nature. She loved parties, trips, the theater, dropping in on friends. He would much rather call it an early night and would tell her, "Find someone to go with you. I'll stay home." As a father he was also very discreet, which meant he was his daughter's great confidant. That night he seemed very troubled by what he'd heard from his wife. He patted Julieta's cheek reassuringly.

"I'll take care of it. I'll have a talk with her."

A short while later he was scolding his daughter.

"What's this I'm hearing? You're giving orders to your mother? Who do you think you are? No, sir!"

Maria Lucia, who had been seated until then, stood, her face pale.

"You mean to say you're against me?" she said.

"Of course!"

Then, that young girl who loved her father so very much, became enraged.

"Don't you understand that I'm doing this for you?" She latched onto him. "Mother is very young and pretty and…" What she wanted to tell him, in short, was that a beautiful woman could be dangerous and that the only thing preventing untold things from happening was her presence.

Heitor tried to cut her off.

"That's enough!"

Maria Lucia, though, was stubborn and vehement.

"My mother does things she shouldn't! She dances with everyone!"

Heitor yelled at her for the first time.

"Not one more word out of you!"

A supersensitive girl, Maria Lucia broke into tears. Heitor gave her a real tongue-lashing.

"Don't you ever talk about your mother like that! A child can never pass judgment on her own mother! I don't care if she's the worst mother in the world! You have to show her respect at all times!"

Maria Lucia raised her head high.

"You mean to tell me my mother can do whatever she wants?"

"That's your mother's business, not yours. What I don't want to see, what I won't stand for, is for you to criticize your mother. Why? I'll tell you why: Because I'm the husband, and I have total, and I repeat, total confidence in my wife!"

The girl stood. She spoke with tears streaming down her face.

"I was looking after Mom. But since you don't want me to and neither does she, fine. But I want you to know one thing." She paused and then continued, "If one day I find out something happened, I… I swear, I swear I'll kill myself!"

Sad Girl

Maria Lucia had been tormenting Julieta for one year now. Then, suddenly, things changed. Heitor himself, in his discreet but inflexible manner, took the initiative.

"I don't want you to go out with Maria Lucia anymore," he told his wife. "She needs to learn."

Julieta took a deep breath. She was free at last. From then on, Julieta was constantly at parties, plays, get-togethers accompanied by girlfriends all as extroverted as she. Her girlfriends would say, "You've come a long way, baby!" She would answer, "More or less." Never had freedom tasted so sweet. If at a party they should ask about her husband, she would answer, "He likes to go to bed early."

She had one last argument with her daughter. Maria Lucia came to her and said, "You're free now. Daddy couldn't care less, and I won't be with you anymore when you go out…"

Julieta, who was taking her earrings off, sighed.

"You're so silly, for God's sake!"

240

Paying no heed to her mother, Maria Lucia continued, "Don't you ever do what a wife shouldn't do... and if you do, I'm warning you, you're going to cry tears of blood..."

It was the first time she had used the expression "tears of blood," which she took to mean a supreme horror. Truth be told, it wasn't so much her words, as the adult, stony look on her face, that shook Julieta. In no time at all, however, she was again immersed in her splendid and frivolous life, and she soon forgot her daughter's inscrutable expression.

Illness

The girl had changed completely. One night after dinner, she asked to speak to her father.

"She doesn't love you..." she whispered. "I know she doesn't..."

Heitor's first instinct was to be forceful, but he sensed such an overwhelming sadness in Maria Lucia, such a heart-wrenching sweetness in her beautiful and desperate eyes that he didn't say anything. A little while later, he said to his wife, "Maybe the best thing is to take Maria Lucia to a psychoanalyst."

Julieta, who was busy filing her nails, seemed amused at the suggestion. "Why?"

He lit a cigarette.

"There's something different about her. She's going around saying strange things, having strange thoughts!"

Julieta clicked her tongue dismissively.

"She just wants attention! To be the life of the party!"

Sin

The following morning Julieta was on the telephone whispering for what seemed like forever. Pure feminine intuition led Maria Lucia to conclude, "It's a man." She kept her eyes glued on her mother the rest of the day. In the evening, Julieta began intricately and delightedly preparing herself to go out. When she finished and left the bathroom, even her daughter had to admit, "She looks beautiful!" Maria Lucia had been waiting for her mother in the hallway and tried to block her way.

"Don't go… I won't let you to do this to Daddy…"

Julieta pushed her out of the way. Her daughter ran ahead of her. With desperate agility she lifted a glass off the sideboard. Julieta froze aghast.

Her daughter said frantically, "This is poison! Poison!" On the brink of life and death, she screamed, "You can't cheat on my father. No! I don't want you to! Never!"

The mother charged. But she only managed to knock over the already empty glass. Maria Lucia had drunk everything in one gulp and lay writhing on the floor. The mother was suddenly consumed with guilt over her daughter's suicide. When her husband arrived, Julieta was screaming, "She tried to prevent something that already happened last night! Poor thing!"

Rest In Peace

Norberto approached while she typed away.

"May I have a word with you?" he asked.

"When?"

"When you get off work."

"OK. Where?"

He hesitated.

"I'll wait for you at the corner bar."

Julinha, her heart racing, stammered, "I'll be there. For sure." From that moment she couldn't keep her mind on her work. When 5 p.m. finally came round, she ran to the lady's room and checked herself in the mirror. She touched up her lips and powdered her nose. When she arrived, Norberto was seated in the corner with a bottle in front of him. He helped her sit and called for the waiter.

"What are you having?" he asked.

Julinha had an upset stomach.

"Tonic water."

While the waiter went about his business, Norberto cut to the heart of the matter.

"You know I'm married, right?"

She sighed.

"Yes."

"Very well. You also know I have feelings for you, right?"

She answered that she wasn't sure but suspected as much.

"Well I do. Very much so. More than you can imagine." Suddenly, he asked her a question that left her speechless.

"Will you marry me?"

The Wife

For a moment she didn't know what to say or think.

"You mean to tell me... but how? What about your wife?"

Norberto was prepared for the question.

"It's like this, angel: My wife is in a very bad way." And he wasn't lying. Norberto's wife was a wisp of a woman: asthmatic, sunken chest, chronically ill. Come wintertime, she'd pay for all her sins – any stupid little cold, and she couldn't breathe and would be left gasping for air. She was bed-ridden and getting worse by the day. About eight months before, she'd had an x-ray taken of her stomach. The results confirmed that it was an ulcer. Another one, this time of her lungs, revealed tuberculosis. Julinha was horrified by the combination of diseases, the number of trials his wife faced.

"How horrible!" she exclaimed.

Norberto wasn't through.

"You want to hear something? Today when I left she was spitting blood. We weren't sure if it was her stomach or her lungs hemorrhaging."

"Poor thing!"

"The doctors already warned us she won't last much longer. Three or four months at the most. She might very well take a turn for the worse and go before then. It's one calamity after another. But what I wanted to say was this: You have feelings for me, and I have feelings for you. I give you my word that as soon as I can I'll marry you. Will you wait for me?"

Julinha lifted her head and said, with utter sweetness, "Yes."

The Other Man

From then on her life was an interminable wait – days, hours, minutes. It so happened that at the office there was another coworker hell-bent on winning her affections. His name was Queiroz. He had fallen hard for her and wouldn't leave her alone. If it hadn't been for Norberto, whom she fancied more, and his unexpected declaration of love, she might very well have given Queiroz a chance and gone out with him. But Norberto, seeing that Queiroz was on the prowl, had made the first move. The next day when Queiroz invited her to "catch a flick," she put her cards on the table.

"I'm very sorry, but there's no way. I'm in love with someone else."

"I don't believe you!"

"I swear!" she said.

Since Queiroz refused to believe her, she made the following extreme vow: "I swear on my mother's life."

Astounded, he stammered, "Who is he?"

"It's a secret."

"Oh, come on!"

Julinha lost her cool.

"It's none of your business. I don't owe you any explanations."

The young man left in a bitter mood. "It smells fishy," he sneered. "Like you're seeing a married man." And from that moment on, he jealously kept an eye on her. He found out that Norberto and Julinha had been seen after hours at the corner bar.

"Bastard!" he cursed.

The Martyr

Every time she'd arrive at work, Julinha would look at Norberto's desk. If he happened not to be there she would ask herself, "Could it be he didn't come because his wife died?" One time she ran to the office boy.

"Where is Norberto?"

"He went out for a cup of coffee."

Thus, she knew that his wife was still alive. They tried as best they could to hide their relationship. "After all, you're married, and I come from a respectable family," Julinha reasoned. On the other hand, there was something slightly mysterious, fascinating, and exhilarating about the secrecy they were obliged to maintain. Thus, day after day, Julinha followed the wife's suffering from afar. There were times when Norberto would go out to the street to call her. He would spare no details.

"She's all skin and bones. I don't know how she's still alive."

At first, Julinha was uneasy about waiting and wishing for the poor woman to die. But, as time went by, the more she talked about it, the more sensitive she became. Until one day she surprised herself.

"I want you to come clean. How much time does she have left? More or less." Norberto thought about it.

"About two weeks."

At home in her bedroom, Julinha got to thinking.

"Two weeks, plus about six months... I might be married in one year's time." But two weeks came and went and nothing. Trying to conceal her irritation she asked over the telephone, "So how about it? You said two weeks and then two weeks later..."

"Yeah. Isn't that something!" he said on the other end. "I can't believe how strong she is. Just today the doctor said he's never seen anything like it."

Julinha sighed. "What can you do? What can you do?" For the first time, though, she admitted to herself that the woman's condition was perhaps not as bad as was thought. Finally, she asked Norberto point-blank, "You're not taking me for a fool are you?" He swore and gave his word of honor. Dejected, Julinha made the following revelation: "You better not be because I've already spent money on the trousseau. I bought a lot of stuff! I hope you're being straight with me?"

Exhibiting confidence in himself and their future, he was adamant: "Great, great. Go ahead, buy everything. I'm glad. What's more, I insist on buying the wedding dress. I want something really special."

Agony

Two more weeks went by, and Norberto's wife, in spite of the ulcer, the tuberculosis and the asthma, fought on. Desperate by now and sensing Julinha was starting to doubt him, he proposed the following: "Let's do this:

I'll make up some excuse at work, and I'll take you home with me to see for yourself. Would you like that?"

Julinha, who was beginning to feel like the victim of a big hoax, said, "As a matter of fact, I would."

The next day she was at her rival's home. Her stomach shrank when she saw the woman sunk in her bed. She was indeed a skeleton. A skeleton covered by a thin, a very thin layer of skin. It seemed incredible that that creature was still breathing, was still alive. At the first opportunity that presented itself, Norberto whispered. "What did I tell you? You see, angel. She's a medical miracle. She's going to die any day now."

By coincidence the doctor showed up just then. When he spoke to Norberto and Julinha he was unequivocal.

"I've never seen anything like it, your wife should be dead."

Julinha was impressed.

"What a struggle it must be for her. She's a martyr."

"That's right," said the doctor in a monotone.

And the wait continued. Little by little Julinha grew desperate. The thought that the woman would never die and that she was a living mummy crept into her thoughts. Meanwhile, Queiroz continued to insist and wouldn't let up in his pursuit. Without her even noticing, her behavior towards him changed; she became more affectionate.

He was definite: "I'll marry you in two months time."

Julinha's attitude gave him some hope. She said, "Let's wait and see." Days later she went even further.

"I'll give you an answer in one month's time."

Death

She believed that by then Norberto's wife would surely be dead. Very well. One month went by and nothing. She lost her patience.

"That's it. He's playing me for a clown."

Queiroz, who was counting the days on the calendar on his desk, would not let up.

"So, how about it? Did you make up your mind?"

Julinha sighed deeply.

"Yes"

"So?"

"All right."

They agreed on everything right then and there, amid whispers. He argued for maximum speed and kept insisting, "Two months tops." He rubbed his hands in glee when he discovered that Julinha had already picked out many of the items in her trousseau.

"Come with me," he whispered in her ear.

He took her out to the corridor and kissed her on the mouth. When he returned to the office, he went from desk to desk and announced, "We're engaged." The coworkers all made a big to-do about it. Suddenly, the phone rang. Julinha answered, and... she was shocked to hear Norberto's voice. He spoke softly, his mouth touching the receiver.

"My wife is in her death throes," he announced. "Now it's certain. It's just a matter of minutes. Big kiss," he said, and he hung up.

For a moment she didn't know what to do. She was overcome by joy, her eyes welled up in tears, and she forgot her commitment to Queiroz. When he walked up to her, she didn't show the least bit of tact. She told him point-blank, "Look, we can't go through with this. I'm sorry," etc, etc.

He turned white and even tried to insist.

"You can't do this to me. I'm not some bum." As soon as he realized that he had lost her, he did not hesitate. He was from the backcountry; he sank a switchblade into one of her breasts. Julinha died right then and there before help could arrive.

Minutes later the telephone rang. It was Norberto again, announcing that at last his wife had died. No one at the office was in any mood to answer. Norberto gave up trying. With all of the composure expected of a widower, he went back to where his wife's body lay. And he said to those assembled, "May she rest in peace."

Hell

When she told him she had a child, a twelve-year-old boy, Romualdo was stunned.

"A son!"

"Didn't you know?"

"I didn't have a clue," he said.

"Well, I do," she said. "He just turned twelve, and he's in school."

"Strange!"

"Why?"

Romualdo proceeded as gingerly as possible. He told her she didn't look like anyone's mother, much less the mother of a boy approaching manhood. As a matter of fact, the boy's age startled him. Lucilia was so fragile, so petite, so young; her eyes, her smile, her mannerisms all made her seem so carefree and single. Surprise wasn't his only reaction. He felt a certain alarm. Her son, her man-child, unexpected and growing, frightened him. He was, however, exceedingly tactful and skilfull in concealing his discomfort and exceedingly presumptuous in making the following statement: "I'll be a second father to him!"

"God no!"

"What do you mean?"

Lucilia sighed.

"Let me explain," she said. "Let's go in here for a moment."

The Son

They entered an ice cream parlor. After sitting down and being served, she began explaining between spoonfuls of ice cream.

"Odesio can't know; he can't even suspect."

It was a condition imposed in no uncertain terms. Either Romualdo accepted, or else he could forget about their relationship. He tried to object.

"You're exaggerating!"

"Come on Romualdo! Please! Are you forgetting that you're married, that you live with another woman, that you have children? Are you?"

"You have a point."

"That's right, I do, don't I!"

It was 6 p.m. when Romualdo put Lucilia on a packed bus. She had to stand the whole way home. The depravity on that bus was palpable: Crammed, pressed, crushed in that mass of bodies, she felt violated, degraded, debased. A man who was getting off at the next stop shoved his way through the throng; when he got to her he nearly knocked her over.

"Animal!" she muttered.

Her problems weighed heavily on her, though, and she stopped paying heed to the unwelcome and brutish contact typical of such situations. Lucilia's dilemma was as follows: She was afraid, terrified that her son should find out... his opinion was what mattered most to her in the world. She feared it more than Judgment Day. At the same time she was crazy about Romualdo, and the thought of a life without him was intolerable. Hanging from her strap, she shuddered, "Oh, God!"

Love Story

Thus began one of the most bittersweet and painful of love stories. She would return home from her encounters with Romualdo filled with dread. Her son would invariably be on the street playing soccer or some rowdy game with his friends. One day the boy kicked the ball awkwardly, and his big toenail went flying. The toe became inflamed; and when Lucilia returned home from a rendezvous with Romualdo, she was filled with shame and remorse. As she washed her son's bruised foot, she thought to herself: While she was out cavorting with a man, a very married man, her son was alone and in need of her. What if it had been more serious than an injured toe? How would she feel then? The boy put on a brave face and barely complained. She had to insist, "Does it hurt?"

"A little."

"If it hurts, let me know."

The next day Lucilia showed up looking dejected.

"What a life!" she sighed.

"What do you mean 'what a life'?" Romualdo asked, annoyed.

She put her cards on the table.

"I know I'm to blame because you, being married and all... I shouldn't... No, Romualdo, it's just not right." She paused, then continued: "If I at least didn't have to share you!"

"Look here, Lucilia!" he fired back angrily. "Next you're going to ask me to leave my wife! I'll bet that's what this is all about!"

They said goodbye, stiffly. Resentful, he barely let her kiss him. He merely said, "Get home safe. Go on!"

That night he vented his frustrations to a friend, who, when he found out there was a twelve-year-old boy in the picture, was emphatic: "You're in a pretty pickle; that's for sure!"

"Don't you think it's outrageous?" Romualdo asked. "That she wants me to leave my wife? Think about it!"

"Of course it is!"

The next time they met, Romualdo did not mince words.

"You have two choices," he said. "Either you take that frown off your

251

face and start smiling, or else we're going to put an end to this thing right now, sweetheart. I really, really don't like the direction this is going."

The word "thing" seemed to her abominably vulgar, so prosaic as to make her feel humiliated. Then there was the tone in which it was uttered, as if she were someone he'd just met on the street! She too lost her cool.

"Stop yelling! Who do you think I am?"

"I'll yell if I damn well please! I don't play games. Try it on someone else!"

She didn't say a word. She picked up her purse; by force of habit she looked at herself in the little mirror on the flap, and then, slowly and resolutely, she walked to the door. She paused for a second, a fraction of a second. She was hoping maybe Romualdo would yell her name out. She would have turned around, and they would have made up passionately. But instead he shouted angrily, "There's plenty of women out there! Not to mention my own wife!"

Could there have been a more clear, undeniable snub? She left, never to come back.

Abandoned

The memory of her late husband and their marriage weighed heavily on her. He had been a noble soul who lived for her and their son. But everything he did that was good, heroic and pure hit up against her lack of love for him. And this absence of love was worse than hatred. She had cringed when the poor devil tried to show any affection. One time she couldn't take it anymore and exploded.

"Don't kiss me!" she lashed out. "I don't want to be kissed. What a pain!"

By then he had already been very ill. It is likely that the episode only hastened his death. Six months later, not mourning him in the least, she had had her first affair in the form of the married Romualdo. It was then that she learned that her late husband had interested her about as much as the anonymous man from the sanitation department who came by to spray the drains with insecticide. It was a passionate love affair that ended, as we saw, in the stupidest way possible. For days on end Lucilia, buried in a dull sadness, awaited a call, a note, a message. Nothing. Absolutely nothing. Then she learned, through third parties, that Romualdo was going about town with a part-time typist who worked at a government agency. The two had been seen strolling along a busy boulevard where they stopped to have their pictures taken by a street photographer. Lucilia locked herself in her bedroom and spent hours on end face down on her bed, crying. She no longer cared what her son thought. On hearing his mother sobbing, the boy asked, "What's the matter, Mom?"

"Leave me alone! Bug off! Scram!"

She would call her lover's office in front of her son. They wanted to know her name. Lucilia would identify herself. The inevitable answer was, "He's not in." Once, however, it so happened that Romualdo picked up. When he figured out it was her, he exploded.

"Leave me alone, will you? I want to live in peace! Stop bothering me!"

Her son listened in silence. He was a mute witness to everything. He did, however, memorize the name and would repeat it to himself: "Romualdo, Romualdo." He knew him by sight. He would think about him night and day with an obstinacy usually reserved for people one loves or hates. He holed himself up in the house and stopped playing ball; he would spend hours on end next to Lucilia, his eyes wide open, as if her despair, in spite of everything, fascinated him. He heard his mother, during a particularly vehement outburst, curse the man who had abandoned her.

"God, I hope he dies! I hope he gets run over by a car. God, I hope he does!"

Until one day she stopped caring altogether. She wanted nothing from life; or better said, she wanted to die. She stopped eating, and the way she neglected herself, her clothing, her hygiene was frightening. She went days on end wearing the same slip. In one of her darkest moments she admitted, "I haven't brushed my teeth in three days." Her son clutched her in his arms and cried, "It's all right, Mother. Please don't cry!"

One day the boy overheard someone on his street say that a dying man's wish could never be denied. Someone's "last wish" was terrifying, sacred and had to be obeyed at all costs lest the one it was told to be subjected to some terrible curse. Later he said to his mother, "He'll be back, Mother! He will! I swear to God he will!"

The Return

Romualdo was standing at the bus stop waiting for his bus when a boy he'd never seen approached and said he was Lucilia's son.

"Go back to my mother," the boy said. "It's my last wish."

Romualdo didn't understand. Or, better said, he only understood when the boy threw himself under a speeding bus. He died on the spot. In the dead of night one more person appeared at the boy's wake to pay his respects: It was Romualdo, haunted and haggard. He had come back after all. And he kept coming back, a slave to the boy's last wish. When at last she grew tired of him and wanted to leave him, Romualdo simply reminded her of the boy's wish. It was then that Lucilia understood that they were united, forever, in hell.

The Silver Wedding Anniversary

His friend paid him a visit at the office.

"Let's get a drink."

"Some other day," he said. "Not today"

But the friend, who was a close friend on familiar terms with him, wouldn't take no for an answer.

"Screw some other day. Now! Come on, get your jacket, hurry up!"

Dr. Hildegardo put on his suit jacket, then took off his glasses and slid them into his shirt pocket.

"I'm going to get home late! You're going to get me in hot water!"

"Why? Who cares?"

"My wife doesn't like it when I get home late! It drives her nuts!"

They headed for the corner bar and sat down. While they waited to be served, Dr. Hildegardo's thoughts turned to his wife, their daughter and their cook. When the drinks finally arrived, he sighed with relief. After knocking back a few, he smacked his lips and, with a touch of bravado, made the following revelation: "I've been married for twenty-five years. I've never cheated on my wife."

"Never?"

Tipsy from his third drink, he repeated: "Never."

The Faithful Husband

The friend didn't believe him. The very idea upset him.

"There's no such thing as a faithful man! It's never happened!"

"Well, you're looking at him. As faithful as can be. I swear; cross my heart. And there's more: At the end of the month I'll be celebrating my silver wedding anniversary, and you're invited!"

"A faithful man is an ass! They might as well put a bridle on him and trot him around town."

Half an hour later a panicked look crossed Dr. Hildegardo's face. Already drunk by now, he took out his pocket watch and read the hands: "Eight o'clock!" He moaned, "My wife must be going berserk!" He paid the bill and dragged his friend by the arm.

"You're coming with me. You have to! My wife will kill me!" The friend went along, grumbling. They hopped in a cab, and for the entire ride the subject rarely changed. In a panic, Dr. Hildegardo exhorted the driver, "Step on it! Like you mean it!" Suddenly, he slapped his forehead.

"You have to do me a favor, a huge favor."

"What?"

"You're going to tell my wife that you already ate."

"Huh?"

Leaning against his friend's shoulder, his breath reeking of alcohol, Dr. Hildegardo explained.

"It's like this: My wife doesn't like it when I bring anyone home for dinner. She can't stand it. She and the maid will have a fit."

The friend rolled his eyes.

"I'm beginning to understand everything!"

The Dinner

They rushed into the house, two nervous wrecks. By now the friend had become infected by Dr. Hildegardo's feelings of fear and guilt. When Dona Odete saw her husband, she didn't even acknowledge the friend. It was obvious just by looking at her that she was a lady who commanded respect. Dr. Hildegardo froze; his wife placed her hands on her hips, looked him up and down, and shook her head.

"Well, well!" she said.

The husband, after recovering from the initial shock, rushed to his wife's side and planted a loud smooch on each cheek. He then went into a convoluted explanation about some mysterious and unforeseen business matter. Still smarting, she grilled him, "Is this any time to come home?"

"Daddy is a piece of work!" the daughter whispered to her boyfriend.

Dr. Hildegardo hung from his wife's shoulder.

"I brought a friend, sweetheart, but he already ate!"

The wife, pleased with the dressing down she had given her husband, allowed him to introduce his friend who had already eaten. From the kitchen came the sound of slamming pot lids. Dona Odete looked to the guest for support.

"Just imagine the nerve! Look at the time! My cook is fuming, and she has every right! Every right!"

The friend, whose name was Bezerra and whose eyelids were growing heavy from the drinking, mumbled, "Absolutely... absolutely!"

During dinner Dr. Hildegardo flattered his wife in the most servile and shameless ways imaginable. He boasted openly, "I'm a lucky fellow, Bezerra! My wife is a saint!"

He repeated his earlier invitation.

"You're invited to our silver wedding anniversary!"

The Serpent

The following day Bezerra showed up at Dr. Hildegardo's office. He lowered his voice.

"Are you serious about what you told me? Scout's honor?"

Dr. Hildegardo was vehement.

"Of course! Why would I ever cheat on my wife? What would I get out of it?"

"I see. I see," said Bezerra.

Dr. Hildegardo stood. He paced back and forth in his office, invigorated by the joy that his marriage brought him.

"Twenty-five years aren't twenty-five days. The best move I ever made was to get married. A real coup! She's not just a wife. She's a friend, a mother, the whole package!"

By now Bezerra was sinking into his chair. He hesitated for a moment before making the following proposition: "Look here. Today I'm meeting up with these two girls. One is with me, of course. But the other one needs someone to keep her company. What do you think?"

He edged closer and added the following bit of information, "First-rate material!"

Dr. Hildegardo recoiled as if he couldn't believe his eyes and ears.

"You have the nerve? You, who met my wife and know that I never, do you hear me, never...! Did you forget that we celebrate our silver wedding anniversary at the end of the month? Really!"

Bezerra had heard enough.

"Come on, get with it, Hildegardo. Stop being a sucker! What's the big deal? Everyone does it! When it comes to love, all men are scum!"

"Not me! No way! Come on! And there's more; when it comes to sex, in my book there's only one position. The classical one, the traditional one: missionary!"

His friend insisted, his stubbornness bordering on the indecent. His arguments were of the following kind: "Just this one time, OK? Don't be a fool! She's a cute little minx!"

Dr. Hildegardo, who was sweating by now, was having none of it.

"No! Never!"

A new salvo of arguments came his way, and then at last Bezerra lost it. He grabbed Dr. Hildegardo by the collar and shook him while his friend listened on helplessly.

"Now you're going to listen to me! A man who's never been with another woman is a loser! You should be ashamed of yourself!"

Forty minutes later a defeated Dr. Hildegardo called home. "Honey pie, you'll never guess. I'm up to here in work! Something's come up that I have to take care of, and I won't be home for dinner…" When he was finished, he turned to his friend, who stood there rubbing his hands with disgusting smugness. Dr. Hildegardo addressed him with the air of a martyr.

"You want to drive me to ruin. You really do!"

Standing in the elevator with his friend, on his way to cheating on his wife for the first time, he had the unmistakable look of a prisoner on his way to the gallows. He shuddered, "There goes twenty-five years of happiness down the drain."

The Other

The following day it was Dr. Hildegardo who came looking for Bezerra. As soon as he saw him, he asked him eagerly, "So, when are we going to do that again?" Bezerra wanted a full report: whether he liked it, whether she was first-rate material or not, if she really was a cute little minx. Dr. Hildegardo, reminiscing in awe, gave his sworn statement: "She's a whole lot of woman! She's the real deal!"

Bezerra nudged him.

"Didn't I tell you? Stick with me, and you'll do all right. Live it up a little!"

They went out that time and many others. Every now and then Dr. Hildegardo would suffer a moral crisis.

"It's just not right! I love my wife!"

One day the two were out drinking. Bezerra, after knocking back several beers, was overcome by a raging bout of sincerity typical of drunks.

"Your wife is a dog! A real bitch!"

When he heard this, Dr. Hildegardo broke down in tears. The two then had it out. Right then and there at their table they engaged in a drunken row, with Dr. Hildegardo insisting that his wife was a saint of a woman, a real angel.

The Silver Wedding Anniversary

Finally, the day of the silver wedding anniversary arrived. Bezerra was present, steady and grave. Relatives came from as far as up north. Their only daughter's boyfriend was also there, dressed in navy blue. After everyone had arrived, Dr. Hildegardo stood in the middle of the living room and gestured for the guests to gather around.

"Silence! Silence!" he asked. All obliged, expecting a speech. Dr. Hildegardo addressed them in a very loud and clear voice.

"I wanted to let you know that I am leaving this household. From this day on I no longer live here!"

There was total silence as the relatives tried to absorb what they had just heard. The first one to react was Dona Odete: She passed out cold. Then a clamor spread through the room. Hypotheses flew fast and furious: Madness? Drunkenness? A practical joke? By then Dr. Hildegardo was headed straight for the door, followed by a triumphant Bezerra. The two cut through the crowd, nearly running over the big-hatted ladies by the door. The daughter fainted, and the future son-in-law left her to chase after Dr. Hildegardo. The young man caught up to him at the sidewalk.

"What happened?" he stammered. "Don't do this!"

Dr. Hildegardo came clean.

"I'll tell you what happened: For twenty-five years now my wife has been making a clown out of me. And I've had it! She's a pain in the neck!"

"What about your daughter?"

Dr. Hildegardo, who had already advanced several feet, froze.

"Oh yes! My daughter!" He returned to where the boy stood. "Do you want a piece of advice, young man? Tell my daughter to go jump in the lake. She takes after her mother. Learn from me: Stop being a sucker! Dump her!"

The Faithful Man

Simão was an exemplary boyfriend for five dates. He treated her like a queen, even better: Every day he'd take her a bag of popcorn, nice and warm, which he'd buy at the corner store. Enraptured, Malvina would tell her mother, her sisters, the neighbors, anyone who cared to listen, "He's the greatest! The greatest!" But on the sixth date she asked him a question.

"Do you believe in God?"

"It depends," he answered.

"What do you mean, it depends?"

Simão was brutally honest.

"I believe in God when I get asthma."

Malvina stepped back, alarmed. At first all she could do was stammer, "Oh, Simão!" But now that he had unleashed the truth, he went on, "When I have an asthma attack, I even believe in Santa Claus!"

Then Malvina, who was fond of all forms of mysticism, broke out in sobs. Amid tears, she exclaimed, "It's a sin! It's a sin!" She managed to utter, "God punishes, Simão! He punishes!"

Asthmatic

Malvina's weeping had not been in Simão's plans. At heart he was a softy, and it was a wonder he didn't fall to his knees.

"Forgive me, angel. Forgive me," he said.

She took a little hankerchief from her purse, blew her nose and proceeded to accuse him: "You're evil, Simão!"

Deeply in love, he did his best to win her back.

"Listen, sweetie…" He went on to explain how this was not some cruel and sacrilegious joke on his part, but rather that all of his weaknesses and virtues, including his faith, could be traced back to his asthma. He gave an example.

"When I get married, I'll have no choice but to be faithful. One thing is for certain; like everything else in my life, my faithfulness will be because of my asthma."

Malvina was stunned. She forgot his irreverence, which had seemed so wicked to her only moments before. Now that they were talking about fidelity, she also set aside his duplicitous on-again, off-again atheism. For Malvina everything in the world could be summed up in the phrase, "to be or not to be cheated on." She held him.

"Answer me: Will you cheat on me?"

He joked, "With my asthma I can barely be with one woman, let alone two!"

"Listen," she said. "I can put up with going hungry, getting hit, anything. I just won't accept being cheated on. Never!"

Simão grabbed her. He kissed her face, her mouth, her neck. He ran his hands down her back to her hips. Malvina felt mortally torn as he grabbed her buttocks. Already wheezing from the asthma, he said, "Asthmatics are the only ones who don't cheat!"

Until their engagement, this had been the only run-in they'd had. In fact, a more compatible couple when it came to education, temperament, taste, and intelligence could not be found. Simão's time was divided between the two: the woman of his dreams and his asthma, which would come out of nowhere to assail him. The first time she saw him suffering an attack, she

LIFE AS IT IS

suddenly understood everything. At his parents' house, his face on the table, the poor man begged, "Take off your shoes! Walk in your socks!"

Even noise aggravated his tremendous difficulty breathing, so the family would walk on tiptoe or bare feet and would speak in whispers or simply not speak at all. Malvina returned home terrified. She told her mother and sisters, "Now I understand why an asthmatic can't have lovers!"

They scheduled the wedding in six months time. Malvina now had her own ideas about what made for a happy couple. She would preach to her friends: "I discovered that there can be great advantages to a sick husband. At least he won't be cavorting around town like other men."

They protested, "It's not so black and white!"

Malvina, worked up by now, gave a personal example to buttress her point.

"Why did I fight with Quincas? He was an iron man, but what good did that do me? He cheated on me every chance he got. Even my sisters weren't off limits!"

It was true; Simão's predecessor was athletic, possessed an impressive physique, and sported a tan like a Hawaiian in a Hollywood movie. Malvina, who had loved him dearly and been proud to have a boyfriend with such a body, broke up with him because of his constant and shameless cheating.

The Wedding

With Simão, thank God, there were never any issues with fidelity. Even with his fiancée he was the picture of moderation. If she were to get caught up in the moment and want to go further, he would stop her: "Let's not get carried away, sweetie." She, who prided herself on her self-control, obeyed immediately. Until the night before the wedding. At two in the morning Simão was saying goodnight. Malvina, in a very amorous mood, accompanied him to the front gate. She sighed, "We're almost married, you know?" As her fiancé was walking away, Malvina stopped him.

"Kiss me. Like you mean it!" She was already offering him her semi-opened mouth and anxiously awaiting a kiss.

He stepped back.

"No, baby, no!"

Not understanding, she asked, "Why?"

"Well. I went to this new doctor today, and he told me I shouldn't get too excited."

"That's strange!"

He insisted though.

"That's right. He told me to be careful with the honeymoon. All this love stuff can really take its toll and can trigger an attack."

Malvina was at a loss. She settled for the peck Simão gave her on the cheek and turned around. The wedding took place at city hall at two-thirty in the afternoon and at the church at five. It looked like rain, and Simão came back from church very distressed. In the car already short of breath, he said, wheezing, "Imagine the tragedy if I got sick... I'm beginning to feel something weird!"

Malvina, very sweet and beautiful in her wedding gown, stammered, "Stop! It's bad luck!"

The First Night

They stopped briefly at her parents' house. The receiving line had been at the church as per the invitation. Malvina changed out of her wedding dress; they said goodbye to relatives on both sides and left by cab to their new residence, an apartment nearby. It was windy, and Simão, terrified of an attack, began to panic.

"I knew it! I knew it!"

Holding her husband's arm in the cab, Malvina tried to stay positive.

"I'm sure it's nothing."

Well, they arrived at the apartment. Malvina, who had dreamed of this moment for so long, threw herself into her new husband's arms.

"Kiss me! Kiss me!" They had their first married kiss, and Malvina, enraptured, did not want it to end. Suddenly, Simão broke free. She tried to hold on, but he pushed her away. Wheezing, looking at her with the eyes of a man being choked, he said, "My asthma! My asthma!"

He collapsed into the armchair, totally useless.

Shocked, she protested, "Why now!"

He looked at her, defeated.

"It's the kissing!"

Malvina was desperate by now. She sat beside Simão, but he pushed her away.

"For God's sake, don't speak to me. Go to bed…"

She even tried gently passing her fingers through his hair, but he rebuffed her: "Women only think about sex!"

This was more than she could stand. Without uttering a word, she went into the bedroom, while in the living room her husband fell to pieces, wheezing in agony. This was how they spent their first night… and all fifteen subsequent nights. It was only on the sixteenth day that Simão started to improve. That was the day Malvina went to visit her family. There, in front of her elderly mother, she broke down in tears.

"I'm a wife who has never been kissed, Mother."

Her mother tried to console her, to no avail. Malvina left more desperate than when she arrived. Simão welcomed her home with the following thought: "Sweetie, I'm certain it's the kisses that are triggering the asthma. Let's hold off on the kissing."

Her answer: "You know best."

Three days later Malvina called Quincas.

"You're a no-good, filthy wretch, but at least you know how to make a woman feel like a woman."

They talked for about half an hour. Quincas gave her a street address and an apartment number in Copacabana. The following day Malvina was there, knocking on the door.

Sordid

"You want to have a little fun tonight?" he asked.

Camarinha, seated across from him, yawned.

"Today I can't. Some other day."

Nonato would have none of it.

"Listen here, you moron. It's got to be today. I just finished reading Corção's[1] column. And let me tell you: When I read Corção I cry out for an orgy, an orgy of Cecil B. DeMille proportions!"

Camarinha yawned again.

"Stop joking!"

"Who's joking! I'm serious!" said Nonato, with ferocious abandon. His theory was that Corção compromised the very values he defended in his columns. He went on, playfully belligerent.

---

[1] *Gustavo Corção (1896-1978), Conservative Catholic author and columnist.*

"Because of Corção I've given up on eternal life. I don't want to be eternal anymore, OK? When I think about Corção's wholesomeness, I prefer – scouts honor – I prefer being an abject scumbag!"

Camarinha smiled. Finally, he gave in.

"All right. We'll have our little fun. I'll bring those two girls."

"Do that. And listen: We'll split the cost."

The Disciple

Nonato hung up and announced to his coworkers, "Tonight I'm going to be in an orgy of Cecil B. DeMille proportions!"

A typist who wore glasses and had bad teeth smiled.

"You sure like your partying, don't you, Sir!"

In a theatrical burst, Nonato took out a clipping of Corção's column and rubbed it in his coworkers' faces.

"You see how Corção's column smells!"

The typist (who had a tremendous overbite) shuddered, ecstatic.

"You're really something, Sir! A real blast!"

The young man, feigning a solemn look, handed her the article.

"In all seriousness: Read it, ma'am! Please be so kind. Then tell me whether I'm right or not. Sometimes virtue gives off an unpleasant odor. Corção is a case in point!"

Just then from way back in the office came Zé Geraldo, nearly tripping over the chairs in his eagerness. He was a confirmed disciple of Corção.

"Hold on!" he said. "Just a minute! Corção is above you. Way above you. You're not even qualified to read Corção!"

Nonato answered him in a playfully argumentative tone: "After I read Corção, I feel like stealing chicken! I feel like dragging women back to my cave. If tonight I engage in sordid behavior, you only have Corção to blame!"

The typist sat to the side and listened, aghast. Instinctively, she placed the article under her nose, and through the power of persuasion or for some other unknown reason, she thought that the article did indeed emit a strange odor. Corção's disciple flailed his arms wildly.

"You're filthy!" he yelled.

To which Nonato, seemingly possessed, replied, "My filth stinks less than Corção's virtue!"

Bacchanalia

The fight never materialized. Come 6 p.m. Nonato left hastily and met up with Camarinha at the corner of Mexico and Araújo Porto Alegre. His friend looked gloomy.

"It's off," he muttered.

"What?"

"The party."

"Don't say that! I'm raring to go!" Nonato told him how he'd read Corção and how it vaguely reminded him of excrement.

His friend explained, rather jokingly, "I'm sordid enough without reading Corção. Anyway, one of the girls, the little one, ate a meat patty and got sick."

Nonato grabbed his head.

"Oh, no! Damn it!" The two walked toward *Pardelas* while Nonato worked his friend over.

"Find another girl! Girls! You know everyone!"

"I'll figure something out," Camarinha promised.

They went inside *Pardelas* and sat down. A short time later they began drinking. Fifteen or twenty minutes later the beer started to work on both of them. Nonato continued with his obsession.

"Because of Corção I've already said goodbye to eternal life. I prefer to rot with dignity."

They were semi-drunk by now. Suddenly, Camarinha raised his head.

"I know! I know a woman for you. Sexy as hell."

"Who is she?" Nonato asked with a glazed look.

Camarinha passed the back of his hand over his mouth.

"Surprise," he said, laughing coarsely.

Camarinha paid the bill. They staggered out, barely able to keep from falling. Nonato asked, "Where are you taking me? Do I know this woman?"

The answer was the same.

"Surprise."

They took a taxi. Nonato insisted, "Hurry up and tell me! Don't be a jerk!"

Camarinha seemed offended.

"Do you trust me, or don't you?"

Nonato said he did. Camarinha, however, was a stubborn drunk.

"If you don't trust me, we'll get out right here!"

"I do. I trust you. I swear."

When the taxi came to a stop, Nonato was fast asleep on Camarinha's shoulder. Camarinha nudged him. They paid and got out. Nonato looked around. He recognized Saenz Peña Square. His vision blurred and his legs shaky, Nonato had to be dragged along by his friend. Camarinha was the more sober of the two. They turned a corner. Nonato, who rarely came to this neighborhood, was completely lost. Suddenly, Camarinha stopped.

"We're here." He grabbed his friend's arm and lowered his voice.

"I want to get back at her. I'll introduce you, but listen: Before you leave, give her five cruzeiros. If you don't have any change, here you go. There. Five cruzeiros. Take it. Don't lose it."

Nonato pocketed the bill. He pushed the gate open, and they walked in. They knocked. A woman, a real looker, opened the door. Camarinha entered and pushed her out of the way with a curse. Nonato froze.

"But… It's your wife!"

She stood erect and motionless. Camarinha laughed crassly.

"Yes, my wife. She cheated on me. I found out, so now every day I bring her a new man. You hear me? The guy gives her five cruzeiros. Tonight it's your turn. Over there. Through that door. Right there."

Without a word, Camarinha's wife led the way. Nonato grimaced in horror.

"But it's your wife!"

Camarinha shook him.

"Either you go, or I'll beat you to a pulp!" He shoved him along. Nonato stumbled into the room. The wife locked the door. They stared at one another. She waited. Nonato spoke first.

"I won't lay a finger on you, ma'am. I won't touch you."

Suddenly, he fell at her feet. On his knees, clutching her legs, he repeated, "Oh, God! Oh, God!" She passed her fingers gently through his hair with a melancholy, almost sweet look in her eyes.

The Shoebox

Two days before the wedding she felt something strange. She brought it to Dona Flor's attention.

"Look, Mother, my arm!"

The old lady came to take a look.

"What?"

"I have goose bumps all over!" Olivinha said.

She was right. Every now and then, in spite of the warm weather, for brief and intense spells, she would feel cold all over. She would even shiver for a few seconds. Dona Flor scratched her head with the crochet needle.

"The flu?" she said, with a touch of concern.

Olivinha rejected the possibility.

"No, no. Nerves," she said.

It was a natural and almost necessary emotion for a bride on the eve of her wedding. Then the mother, in a sudden moment of nostalgia for her own antediluvian wedding, sighed.

"Oh, the same thing happened to me," she said. "The exact same thing.

Do you know that in the church, on the way to the altar, I was so nervous I nearly threw up?"

"Oh, gosh!" Olivinha said.

Fear

Olivinha was in love and was in turn loved. That night her fiancé showed up. Gilberto was his name (last name Peçanha), and he was an Apollo of the beaches, all the rage at seaside volleyball games. Proud of being the fiancée of such a handsome and athletic man, Olivinha had only one regret: that he couldn't walk around all day in a bathing suit, nothing but a bathing suit so he could show off his chiseled chest. Gilberto came in exhibiting the euphoria typical of a groom two days before his wedding. He kissed the girl on the cheek and said mischievously, "I can't wait to get my hands on you."

He rubbed his hands with a scandalous, suggestive glee. He lowered his voice.

"We're going to go all out on our honeymoon, if you know what I mean!"

Olivinha stared at him and feigned disapproval.

"Today you're unfit for minors!"

They both laughed in a perfect moment of mutual joy. Suddenly, she froze. It was the same shiver again. She instinctively crossed her arms and bit her lip. Gilberto leaned forward, concerned.

"What's the matter?" he said.

She closed her eyes and lifted her head. She stammered as if having a revelation, "I'm afraid!"

"Why in the world are you afraid? Afraid of what?"

She lowered her eyes. "I'm too happy. I am so very happy."

Gilberto, however, with the optimism one would expect of a volleyball idol, put both hands in his pockets. "Wonderful! If you're happy, that's wonderful."

She insisted: "But I'm afraid something might happen before the wedding, something that…"

Before she could finish, Gilberto squatted. He knocked lightly three times on the floorboard. He was optimistic but superstitious too.

"Knock on wood!"

The Omen

It was around midnight when he said goodbye, but before leaving he gently chided his girlfriend.

"You're being childish. You have to stop with these negative thoughts!"

Be that as it may, Olivinha did not fall asleep till dawn, overcome by an overwhelming sadness. This feeling of impending doom had infiltrated her very being; it had poisoned her life. She imagined the most mysterious and catastrophic scenarios. One such chain of events she obsessed over was that either she or her husband-to-be would die before reaching the altar. She began crying in the darkness of her bedroom, afraid of her own happiness that to her seemed almost a sin. But when she woke up the next day, she was a different person altogether. Normally, she would go from her bed straight to the bathroom, barefoot. This time, though, she was more prudent. Afraid of catching a cold, the flu or even a serious case of pneumonia, she slipped her naked feet into little ermine slippers. Later, downstairs, she flashed a half-smile, which only increased her beauty.

"Another twenty-four hours before the wedding!" she sighed.

All of the fear in her heart subsided. She no longer cowered at the thought of her own happiness. At the breakfast table she boasted, as if challenging every woman in the world, past, present and future: "No one is happier than I am right now!"

The Present

Olivinha was at the breakfast table biting into a saltine cracker when someone knocked on the door. The maid went to see who it was and did not come back for the longest time. When she reappeared, she seemed frightened.

"There's someone at the door with a package for you, ma'am."

"Well, take it then," she said to the maid curtly.

"She says she'll only deliver it to you, ma'am. Or else she won't deliver it at all."

Assuming it was a gift, Dona Flor nudged Olivinha.

"Go on, child, go on."

The girl obeyed. She went to the door and there encountered a woman she'd never seen before. Tiny, scrawny, overly polite, the woman had the face of a possum.

"Are you Dona Olivinha?" she asked.

"Yes, how can I help you?"

Satisfied that there was no possibility of mistaken identity, the woman handed over the package. In a soft voice, without taking her eyes off the recipient, she said, "Ma'am, this is for you."

"Very well."

It occurred to Olivinha to ask the identity of the sender. By then, however, the stranger had walked off hastily, hugging the wall, as if running away. Olivinha went back inside. She thought to herself, "It feels like a shoebox." She sat in a chair in the hallway, rather perplexed, and unwrapped what was in fact a shoebox. She innocently opened the lid and then screamed in utter horror.

The Angel

Everyone in the house rushed in. The neighbors, alarmed by what they heard, followed suit. Sobbing uncontrollably, Olivinha pointed to the ground. There lay the open shoebox, and inside was a little baby only days old, naked and dead. They had to drag her away she was so hysterical. In her bedroom, surrounded by her mother and women from the neighborhood, she sobbed, "They send me this the day before my wedding!"

The father, who rushed home from work, could not make sense of the gruesome gift. Pacing back and forth chewing an unlit cigar, he blurted out, "This is some kind of black magic!"

The Suspect

The police came to the scene. Reporters and photographers even showed up. And then something unforeseeable occurred. Olivinha, who was crying softly just then, screamed out, "I know!" She faced her mother and the neighbors with the fiery eyes of a prophetess and announced, "It's his! The baby is Gilberto's!" She insisted with unshakeable certainty, "I know it is!" And that was that. Granted, it was an unfounded and abominable theory, but tremendously persuasive nonetheless. All assembled looked at one another other, touched by a feeling of near certainty. Gilberto was called in by the family and showed up looking terrified. The father brought him into the study and locked the door. He asked Gilberto point-blank, "Is it your child? Yes or no?"

At first he wanted to deny it, but he confessed, "It must be."

Then his fiancée's father held him firmly.

"Whatever you do, don't confess! Not even at gunpoint! In love, always lie! Your best bet is to lie!"

Devastated, Gilberto agreed: "OK."

The Drama

A short time later he was being grilled by his fiancée. He lied. She gave him two choices: "Either you confess or I won't marry you!" Her relatives held their heads in despair. The father was afraid of even the hint of scandal and wanted the marriage to go forward at all costs. Standing, with her arms crossed, her eyes cold and cruel, Olivinha insisted, "Either you confess or…"

Gilberto was weak, cowardly and what's more, deeply in love. He caved in.

"Yes, it's true. He's my son."

With unflinching inquisitiveness, Olivinha extracted the rest from him. Gilberto, crying, reduced to a shadow of his former self, told of his affair with a poor girl who used to stalk him and kept insisting, "I want to have your child." The girl knew he was involved with another woman, his entire situation from a to z. It didn't matter to her. When she had his child, though, she changed completely and was overcome by sudden and frightening bouts of jealousy. It was she who most likely killed the baby.

When Gilberto finished, Olivinha leaned up against the wall pressing both hands to her stomach. She bit her lip, overcome by nausea. She screamed, "Get this man out of here! For God's sake, get him out of here. He's disgusting!"

The wedding never took place. Gilberto, who was madly in love, tried to win her back. But every time she saw him, Olivinha doubled over. The mere sight of her ex-groom was enough to summon up the image of the dead angel in a shoebox. First it was only Gilberto. Later, all men became loathsome to her and induced nausea. Finally, she saw in every woman a possible killer of angels.

The Road to Perdition

She arrived home and poured her heart out.

"Mother, have you heard the latest?"

"No!"

Ismenia put her purse down, sat on the nearest chair and sighed.

"There's this boy who works in the building in front of our office…"

"I think I know where this is leading…."

Ismenia, with a mixture of joy and sadness, confirmed her mother's suspicions.

"That's right, you guessed it, Mother. I think I have feelings for this boy and…"

Dona Crisalida, who had the habit of listening to five radio soaps a day and was sentimental to the core, put down the dish and drying cloth and moved closer to listen to her daughter.

"What's he like?" she asked.

"I don't know," Ismenia confessed.

"Oh, please! What do you mean you don't know? Isn't he your boyfriend?"

Ismenia scratched her head with a hairpin and explained.

"No, he's not my boyfriend! He's never even spoken to me, and I've never spoken to him. So far there's nothing between us, Mother. He stares at me, and I stare at him. That's it."

Disappointed, Dona Crisalida returned to the dishes in the sink.

"You mean to tell me you like some 'guy' you've never met," she muttered. "For all you know he could be married. Probably is!"

"He doesn't look married, Mother," Ismenia replied optimistically. "I bet you he's single!"

The Boyfriend

The following morning, as Ismenia exited the bathroom, Dona Crisalida, who was walking by, stopped suddenly and had one of those inexplicable flashes mothers sometimes have. She warned her daughter, "Open your eyes, sweetie!"

Ismenia, who was now seated in front of the mirror in her slip, applying talcum powder under her arms, turned to her mother.

"Open my eyes why?" She had already forgotten the previous day's talk.

"Do you know what you see more and more of nowadays?" Dona Crisalida asked. "Single women going out with married men. It's a disgrace!"

Slipping into her dress, Ismenia found this amusing.

"Don't be silly, Mother!"

Dona Crisalida walked away, murmuring, "It's an outrage!"

A short time later, riding on the bus, Ismenia's thoughts turned to the first man she'd ever had feelings for. Seventeen and cute, she had dated a few boys but never really cared for any of them. The stranger who worked in front of her office was the first man who had really made an impression on her. They had been exchanging glances through the window for two weeks now, but there was still nothing between them. They had never even spoken. Not even by telephone. How absolutely delicious, though, this love affair without words, this romance without phrases, made up strictly of stolen glances. Her girlfriends would nudge her: "Call him, silly!" Others suggested a prank call.

She resisted, though.

"No. Why should I? He's the man. He should call me, not the other way around." When she arrived at work that morning they gave her a message.

"You received a phone call."

"Man or woman?" she asked.

"Man."

She turned pale as she put her things away in her desk drawer. She allowed herself to think the unthinkable: that it might have been he who had called. But the clock ticked away; the minutes turned into hours, and whoever it was never called back. Like every other day, he was there in his office, stealing glances at her, with charming stubbornness. And that was that. She left work utterly disappointed. "He's an idiot!" she thought to herself. She froze, though, at the door: There he was, waiting for her in the middle of the sidewalk. And he was walking towards her. He introduced himself.

"My name is Osmar Braga."

"Ismenia" she said, trembling.

The Drama

She was overcome by a sort of giddiness. Passersby stopped on the street upon seeing them together. Indeed, the physical contrast was glaring: He was big and took big, massive steps like a catch-as-catch-can wrestler; she was tiny, frail and graceful. Shortly afterwards they were sitting at a café in Cinelândia. She was crushed to learn the truth. The young man had just placed his hand on the table. There it was as clear as day, undeniable, for all to see: his wedding ring. Her anguish knew no bounds, and she couldn't help but blurt out, "What a shame!"

At first, he didn't understand.

"What?" he asked. She pointed to the ring. His first instinct was futile: He tried to hide his hand. They sat in silence for a while. Finally, he spoke.

"Yes, it's true; I'm married." He said, "Neither one of us should be here."

Almost in tears, she picked up her purse.

"I'm leaving."

But the young man, who had dreamed long and passionately about this moment, said, "Can I ask you a question?"

"What?"

He hesitated, as if choosing his words carefully.

"I'm married, and you come from a good family. So there can't be anything between the two of us."

"Obviously."

"This is our first and last date." He paused and then went on. "How about if we go to the movies for the first and last time? It would be a sort of farewell, OK?"

For a few moments Ismenia struggled inside.

Osmar insisted softly but avidly, "Just this one time. That's all." Squeezing her arm, he asked, "Shall we?"

She sighed.

"OK."

They walked into the movie theater without the slightest idea of what was showing or when.

Inside, Ismenia felt the delicious and scintillating sensation of sin. Those two hours spent in the dark in front of a screen they barely looked at, whispering all sorts of nonsense, were almost Dantesque in their sweetness. They had the impression that they had always had an affinity for one another, even in previous lives. At last they left the theater. He addressed her soberly and categorically.

"I'll never go out with you again. Ever. This is the last time."

Just then the girl, who was as tender as can be, displayed a desperate courage: "And what if I want to keep seeing you?"

They looked at one another with a mixture of surprise, fear and sorrow. He was firm.

"Even if you want to, I don't want to."

She stammered, "Why?"

He was almost brutally frank: "Because it would be your ruin." Finally, he said, "This will be our last kiss." She let herself be kissed and kissed him in return. It was as if she'd died in his arms, a delicious annihilation. The girl looked on aghast as she realized he was leaving.

"Goodbye!" he said.

Obsession

The next morning as she left the house, she was cryptic with Dona Crisalida.

"Mother, say a prayer for me." She'd spent the entire night awake, thinking. She made up her mind, "I love him, and that's that." When she arrived at the office, she grabbed the telephone.

Osmar was coldly polite.

"For your own good, I shouldn't talk to you anymore." He repeated what he'd said earlier: "You come from a good family, and I'm married."

"I don't care," she replied. "I want to be with you. Nothing else matters."

Finally, Osmar resorted to a sentimental reason why he couldn't see her that he thought would put matters to rest: "I have a sister your age. I don't want to do to you what I wouldn't want done to her."

Ismenia, who was not expecting this much resistance, exploded.

"Are you a man or aren't you! Oh, God!"

Osmar kept his composure and proceeded to hang up.

"Excuse me, but I have things to do."

Ismenia buried her face in her hands. One of her girlfriends asked, "What's the matter?" She answered, "That idiot!" She looked devastated. During her lunch break in the bathroom with that same girlfriend, she had a near breakdown.

"My God! I can't live without him," she said, sobbing. For about three days she resisted the urge. But on the fourth day there she was waiting for him, meekly.

Once again, he left no room for doubt.

"It can't be. If you were any other woman, any other woman, I would say, OK. But, no. You're a child. You remind me of my sister…"

She humiliated herself in front of him by crying and repeating, "I *am* a woman! I am!"

Osmar, sad, filled with pity for her, explained, "God forbid you should lose your way because of me."

Dry-eyed by now, she whispered, "You don't want me to lose my way?"

Thinking back to his sister, he answered with total sincerity, "Never!"

Ismenia again lost it.

"Look: Whatever happens to me is going to be your fault and your fault only. Loser!"

Guilty As Charged

Time went by. She never sought him out ever again. Occasionally, in the middle of the workday, he would engage in ardent meditation. He felt a pain in the flesh of his soul, a sudden and sharp longing for that girl with angel eyes. He opened up to several friends. He would hear no end of it: "You blew it; what a fool! You should have jumped on that!" He answered, "No way! I did the right thing. How would you like to have that on your conscience?" He could never shake, however, the sadness surrounding that frustrated love affair. Until one year later some friends invited him to take part in a nighttime escapade. He accompanied them to one of those houses where one pays women for their company. He was in a group, drinking with a blond on his lap, when he saw coming down the stairs, arm in arm with a client, a woman... it was her – a little less of a girl and perhaps even more beautiful than before. She was dressed like all the others in a skin-tight purple satin dress that revealed plenty of cleavage. She caught sight of him and, after the initial surprise, approached. Osmar pushed the blond away. He stood and, face-to-face with Ismenia, said: "You? Here?"

The girl crossed her arms as if feeling cold. She stared at him and spoke.

"It's your fault. Because of you, I am what I am now." Through clenched teeth she said, "I wasn't yours so now I belong to everybody! It serves you right!"

Not understanding her spite, he stared at her for a long time, his eyes welling. Suddenly, standing before her naked shoulders, her skin-tight dress, he felt a fatal desire to make love to her. He tried to kiss her... but Ismenia managed to break free.

"Any man but you!" she screamed as if possessed. And she repeated, "You, never!"

Osmar knew then that he had lost her once again, this time forever. Then, right there in front of everyone, he fell to his knees, buried his face in his hands and cried like a baby.

Motherhood

They were only recently engaged, and they were already arguing about children. Very assertive, Olavo didn't mince words: "No, no and no."

The girl and her family, as was to be expected, were shocked.

"What? How can you say that!"

He held his ground.

"If I were a woman, I swear I wouldn't want children. Not if you paid me!"

They found this amusing.

"Gosh! Why? It's the most natural thing in the world!"

"Why? You want to know why?" he asked. "Because there's no such thing as a beautiful pregnant woman."

"Oh come on! Don't say that! Motherhood is sublime!"

So they cited the example of packed buses: Some selfless fellow always gave up his seat to a pregnant woman. The more they insisted that childbirth was natural the more upset he grew.

"You keep talking about it being natural. Damn it! Nature makes all sorts of mistakes!"

"What do you mean?"

With his hands shoved in his pockets, he ranted.

"It's obvious, of course!" Then he jabbed his finger in the faces of his opponents. "I don't answer to nature, OK? I don't give a damn about nature. She wants to have children, right? Well, I don't want to, OK? I've made up my mind. That's the end of that!"

Hearing these things alarmed Guida. Her father, though, who was cordial and enlightened, laughed heartily.

"Don't you see what's going on? It's fiction!"

"Fiction?" Guida asked.

"Of course! Sheer drivel!"

The Allergy

One day the two entered into a sort of pact. Taking advantage of a moment when he was in a particularly good mood, she said, "Sweetie, let's make a deal."

He was still in high spirits from a raise he'd just received and gave her a quick kiss. Snuggling up to him, she said, "Just one, OK?"

Olavo didn't understand. "What do you mean just one?"

She tickled his earlobe.

"One child, sweetie. Just one and that's it. We won't ever mention it again."

"God, you're stubborn! Children are a big headache! Besides, I'm allergic to pregnant women."

With great tact and with the soft touch of a woman who knows she's loved, Guida kept working on him.

Finally, smiling widely, he capitulated.

"All right! All right!" But he had one caveat: "Hold on! Only after we've been married for a year. Not right after we're married."

When he left, she ran straight to her family.

"Olavo agreed. He said he agreed."

"Didn't I tell you?" said the father, brimming. "Drivel."

The next day, though, her fiancé changed his tune.

"Why do we need a child? Schools are a big rip-off nowadays. Take my word for it. No kids is the way to go for married couples. It's much better that way!"

When he saw the look of utter disappointment on her face, he resorted to aesthetics.

"Sweetie. You're a peach. A real peach. Imagine yourself as one of those poor fatsos you see wobbling around. Imagine!"

Marriage

They got married. Deep down Guida was certain that Olavo's resistance was silly and that he would eventually come around to seeing things her way. The father, who knew a thing or two about life, insisted, "He'll make a great father!"

"I hope you're right, Dad! I hope you're right!"

On day fifteen of their honeymoon, Guida called home.

"Mother! Mother!"

The poor woman's heart skipped a beat.

"What's the matter?"

"I'm feeling something, Mother," she said.

"It's still very early, dear. It's probably a false alarm."

Glued to the phone, she said, "Oh! I really, really want to be a mother!"

"Let's see."

Indeed, she had dreamed of being a mother since she was a little girl. She couldn't see a baby without wanting to pick it up, kiss it, bite it lovingly. When they returned from the mountains, she told one and all about her symptoms. Someone said, "It's a sure bet!"

She begged those present, "For God's sake, please don't tell my husband! I want to be the one to break the news, OK?"

She went to the doctor, and he hesitated.

"I can't be one hundred percent certain. It's too early to tell. Let's do an exam just in case," the doctor said.

Guida had the test done. She called the hospital, extremely nervous.

"I had such-and-such an exam done. Can you tell me the result?"

The nurse left to check and then came back.

"Positive."

The Shock

It was the happiest moment of her life. She called everyone.

"It's finally happened!"

"Are you serious?"

She was so elated she replied with a mere, "Thank God!"

She went to meet her husband at the front gate that evening and gave him the news point-blank.

"Honey, I'm going to have a baby!"

He turned pale.

"You're lying!"

"I swear!" she said, hanging onto his arm. She was overjoyed, beautiful, and moved to the core.

Olavo just stood there on the sidewalk, numb. He looked at her from head to toe as if she already were suffering the deformity of pregnancy.

"I don't care if it's a girl or a boy," she said dreamily. "Either one is fine with me."

It was only inside the house, before even taking off his jacket, that he started in on her.

"You're going to get rid of it. Right away!"

"I don't understand? Get rid of what?"

For fifteen minutes, without saying a word, she listened and watched as her husband raged. "Pretty soon he'll start hitting me," she thought. Olavo's words terrified her.

"You think I'm kidding? I'm serious! I can't stand pregnant women, OK? I would fall out of love with you! May God strike me blind if I'm lying. We're going to the doctor tomorrow, and we'll settle this once and for all!"

Guida did not recognize her husband. In front of her was a cruel and vindictive man whom she was meeting for the first time. But she showed courage and stood up to him.

"Never! You hear me? Never! Not you, not ten of you will ever lay a finger on my child! You hear me!" Instinctively, she retreated behind the coffee table as if protecting the incipient life inside her.

"You mean you're not going to get rid of it?" he screamed.

"No! Never!"

For three full days they barely spoke. Under the same roof husband and wife were like two strangers or, worse, like two enemies. There was one thought she couldn't get out of her mind: "He hates my child!"

Finally, on the fourth day, returning home from work, Olavo made an unexpected gesture that moved her deeply: He grabbed her in his arms and kissed her – a long kiss on the mouth. It was truly heartwarming how they made up. He asked her forgiveness.

"You'll have your child. I want you to. I swear I'll be a great father."

Amid the reciprocal show of affection, Guida made an admission.

"Do you realize I prayed you'd change?"

Just then they were the happiest couple on earth. As they were getting ready to go to bed, he yawned and said, "Tomorrow I'm going to take you to a doctor we can trust. He can even deliver the baby."

The Doctor

There was nothing inviting about the clinic; on the contrary, it conveyed an impression of a total lack of hygiene. Olavo made light of the situation.

"You can't judge a book by its cover."

Guida spent about forty minutes there and at times had to clench her teeth to keep from crying. Her husband on one side and the nurse on the other tried to console her.

"It's normal."

The doctor even made a quip: "You're a real crybaby, you know that?"

She left sad and tormented. As she walked through the waiting room, she saw the other patients: poor people of color. They looked like maids and had startled, frightened looks on their faces. At home hours later, the hemorrhaging began. She held her head in her hands.

"My God, why am I bleeding!" Her husband had already gone back to work; she almost called him. At the last minute she decided instead to call the family doctor.

"Hurry, doctor! I'm losing a lot of blood."

The old man appeared, examined her and looked at her aghast.

"What on earth did you do, honey? Huh?"

She looked at him, confused.

"I didn't do anything, I..." Suddenly, she understood everything. She heard the doctor out: "On top of everything, the curettage was very poorly done."

When her husband arrived, she got out of bed in her bare feet. She walked to him, leaving behind a trail of blood. With the little strength she had left, she yelled, "You lied to me... you killed my son!" Then she fainted.

The Drama

Guida was at death's door. Finally, she began to improve because she was very healthy and had a strong desire to live. While convalescing, she told her husband, "Do me a favor: Don't ever kiss me again." They looked at each other in silence. He felt in his wife's fixed gaze a mortal hatred. Terrified, he ran to Guida's family.

His father-in-law comforted him.

"She'll get over it. It's just a phase, she'll get over it."

Now that she was cold and indomitable, he loved her more than ever. One day he came home early. The radio was playing a waltz or something of the kind. In the living room his wife was humming and whirling in time to the music. She froze and turned pale when she saw him. The next day the family doctor sought him out.

"Your wife is in such-and-such a state. But this time you'll keep the baby, right?"

His answer was simple: "Yes."

He went home; he found his wife and stammered, "I forgive you..."

She lifted her head high and looked at him with a steely gaze, as if challenging him.

"I don't want your forgiveness."

The Future Mother-In-Law

The old man was a high-level Treasury official.

When his son broke the news that he wanted to get married, the old man stood, rubbed his hands in glee and made several observations, including the following: "You do well, Son." Then he added solemnly, "It's a law of nature none of us can escape."

Then, out of the blue, he asked, "How about your girlfriend's mother?"

The son was taken aback.

"Why, Dad?"

"It's like this, Son: I've learned that a good mother means a good daughter. Let's say your future mother-in-law is a wonderful wife. Your girlfriend will be too. Do you understand? It's a sure bet. A sure bet."

Edgar was at a loss.

"Well, Dad, as far as I know, her mother is an extremely upright woman. I never saw or heard anything that would lead me to think otherwise."

The father, whose name was Daniel, put a hand on his son's shoulder.

"If that's the case, then great! But look into it first. And don't forget: In a marriage the most important thing is not the wife. It's the mother-in-law. A wife just perpetuates the virtues and the vices of her own mother."

The Father-In-Law

Edgar left the meeting with his father deeply disturbed. On a packed bus, hanging from a strap, he thought, "Damn! What kind of theory is that? What kind of mentality is that?" His father never failed to come up with the most unexpected and extravagant opinions. In their family the old man was dismissed as being unorthodox or, better said, crazy. When he got off the bus and walked towards his girlfriend's house, Edgar thought to himself, "Dad's a piece of work! A real character!" Still, when he shook his future mother-in-law's hand a few minutes later, he couldn't help but look at her in a new way. Dona Mercedes was a forty-year-old woman of Spanish descent, very well-preserved with a tight body and a very sweet and enticing look in her eyes. The whole time he was there, Edgar kept asking himself obsessively, "Did she ever cheat on her husband?" He glanced at his future father-in-law whom he found to be a "standup guy." His name was Wilson, and he was an old, potbellied, fun-loving man brimming with life. It so happened that the subject in the house that night turned to male infidelity. A peevish young woman from the neighborhood suggested, "The only faithful man you'll find is in the grave. I don't believe there is such a thing!" Just then Wilson yelled, "I protest!" All eyes turned to him. He stood and, filled with emotion, said "I swear, you hear? I swear on my dead son's grave that I've never cheated on my wife!"

His eyes welled up with tears as he spoke.

Theory

The son Wilson referred to had died some time ago, run over by a car when he was nine. It was a brutal blow to the old man. So when he swore on his dead son's grave, everyone believed him unequivocally. The following day Edgar passed by his father's house to tell him what had transpired. His father listened attentively. When his son was finished, he muttered, "I knew it! I knew it!"

Edgar was taken aback.

"What!"

Then the old man explained: "I said 'I knew it' because in every couple there is always a cheater. It's either the husband or the wife. A victim is unavoidable, OK?"

The son put his hands on his head.

"Give me a break, Dad! Give me a break! For God's sake! What are you insinuating: That you have to cheat so you don't get cheated on?"

"Exactly," the old man said. "There might be no logic to it, but unfortunately it's the truth. And if your fiancée's dad is so faithful then I wouldn't vouch for his wife. The bigger the cheater the more they're loved."

This was more than his son could take.

"Come on, Dad! Come on! You're disgusting! What kind of thing is that to say!"

His father sighed.

"If you don't believe me, so be it. I wash my hands!"

The Engagement

Things died down. Days later, Daniel, under pressure from his son, accompanied him to Eduardina's house for Edgar to request her hand. They became officially engaged. Later that day Edgar, still on cloud nine, asked his father, "Don't you think I have good taste, Dad? Isn't Eduardina a catch? Isn't she?"

The old man scratched his head.

"I have my doubts, OK? I have my doubts. To be honest, I don't know who's better: your fiancée or her mother. I swear I don't! It's a dead heat!"

Startled and disturbed, Edgar wanted to know, "You honestly think there's a comparison?"

Daniel rubbed his hands in glee.

"I do. I'm going to give you some unwanted advice, Son. Some advice you're not going to want to hear. It's like this: Don't get too close to your fiancée's mother. Stay far away. She's dangerous, a real menace!"

Edgar looked at his father wide-eyed.

"Who do you take me for, Dad? Do you think I have no sense of family? Of honor? Of dignity?"

Daniel interrupted him coldly.

"Son, what I think is that you're a man. And any man can be driven to ruin when faced with such a woman!"

The Anonymous Letter

Daniel's words had a curious effect on his son, a mixture of fascination and disgust. Edgar even had trouble sleeping; and for the first time he feared his father's insinuations might contaminate him. He did his best to avoid him, especially because every time his father saw him he would wink and nudge him and say, "How's your future mother-in-law?" Edgar refused to answer, fearing he might explode in a fit of rage. He admitted something to himself that was repugnant to his sensitive nature: "I'll end up hating my own dad!"

One day he received an anonymous letter, the first in his life. He read and re-read the vile little note. It went right to the point: "Man, call off your wedding and go after your fiancée's mom. She's two hundred times better than your fiancée." The offensive tone, the utter sordidness, everything about the note fascinated him. From the very first moment, though, he was absolutely certain as to the identity of the sender. Beside himself, he rushed to the Treasury.

Frothing at the mouth, he showed his father the offending letter. He asked him in a tortured voice, "Did you write this? Answer me, Dad! Was it you?" He mouthed the words so others wouldn't hear them.

Daniel, pale, did not say a word.

His son insisted, "Be a man, Dad! Was it you?"

Daniel finally answered, "Yes."

The son moaned, "Why?"

The old man picked up a cigarette.

"I did it for your own good. It's my opinion, you hear? Your fiancée's mother only offers advantages. Your fiancée, on the other hand, does not. She will be the death of you. It's one or the other: Either she'll cheat on you, or she's already cheating."

Edgar stood up, nearly crying.

"Father, listen carefully to what I'm going to tell you: You're an abomination, Father!"

The End

Edgar left home and went to live in a hotel. He made no secret of his falling out with his father. He notified his fiancée, her mother, her father, the whole world: "As far as I'm concerned, my father is dead and buried. He can't even come to the wedding!"

Very well. One afternoon he was at work when they told him he had a call. It was his future mother-in-law, hysterical.

"Come right away; something horrible just happened."

Ten minutes later he arrived at their house. As soon as his girlfriend's mother saw him, she broke the news, sobbing.

"Eduardina ran away! With your father! She ran away with your father!"

His fiancée's entire family was present. Edgar's first reaction was a sort of vertigo. His legs buckled; his vision blurred. Suddenly, he regained his bearings. He felt a ferocious and crude desire for revenge, for retribution. Like a tiger, a vulture, a wild boar, he pounced on his fiancée's mother. He grabbed her. And he tried to kiss her on the mouth.

Her husband had to beat him away with his cane.

Diabolical

The night they became officially engaged, Dagmar went to the window arm in arm with her fiancé and looked out into the yard. Seized by a sudden sadness, a sort of premonition, she sighed and made a vague comment: "Oh, gosh! Oh, gosh!"

"What?" Geraldo asked, softly and sweetly.

Dagmar hesitated. Finally working up the courage, she pointed with her eyes.

"Do you see my sister?"

"Yes."

They looked on in silence as little Alice, thirteen, picked a flower from a vase to give to who knows whom. "Pretty, isn't she?" Dagmar asked.

Geraldo agreed, "Beautiful."

Placing her hand on her fiancé's arm, the young woman went on.

"Just a child. But in one or two years she will be quite a woman."

"Gorgeous!"

Dagmar smiled sadly.

"Yes, gorgeous!" She paused and then demonstrated a valiant sincerity, "She'll be more beautiful than I am."

"I doubt that very much!" Geraldo said.

Her response bordered on being rude.

"Don't lie! I have a mirror! Now that we're engaged I want you to know something."

"What?"

"You're a man, and I know this fairy tale about men being faithful is just that. But you're on notice: If you ever cheat on me, it better not be with a neighbor, a friend, or a relative. Do you understand?"

Startled and somewhat amused, Geraldo exclaimed, "You're really something else, you know that!"

The Sisters

The two were four years apart: Dagmar, seventeen, Alice, thirteen. Until then, Geraldo considered his girlfriend's sister an utter child. Deep down he perhaps felt she would always be a child. Dagmar's remarks caught him off guard, though. He began to look at Alice with a new and secretive curiosity. The woman inside the girl was beginning to blossom. This realization bothered him and in fact made him slightly woozy. When it came time to leave, he said his goodbyes. His fiancée accompanied him to the gate. After he kissed her on the cheek, she said, "Don't forget: Alice is off limits!"

This was more than he could bear. He was hurt and protested, "What kind of thing is that to say? Who do you think I am? If I didn't know any better, I'd be insulted, you know that!"

She crossed her arms and held her ground.

"Why should you be insulted? Aren't all men liars?"

"I'm not!"

"You're just like the others. You're all the same," she said.

Family

When Dagmar revealed to her parents the warning she had given her boyfriend, all hell broke loose. Her mother held her head in her hands.

"Are you crazy?"

The father really tore into her: "It was a bad move on your part! Very bad!"

"Well, I don't think so."

The old man tried to drive the point home.

"Now you've planted a seed in his head!"

She answered, confidently, "Daddy, I know very well what I'm doing."

The father paced back and forth nervously. He came to a full halt.

"How can your fiancé look your sister in the eye now? Women! I tell you! You should start from the following principle: A sister should be above all suspicion! Family is family, come on!"

Dagmar did not flinch.

"Father, I love Alice very much. She's a very nice girl. She's wonderful and all that; but a pretty sister cannot be on intimate terms with her brother-in-law. No! Never!"

Morbidly Jealous

There was an immediate uproar within the family. They were unanimous. Everyone agreed that this was not normal, could not be normal. One of the strongest arguments had to do with little Alice's age: "How could you? How could you?"

The father, as he chewed his cigar, argued, "You can be jealous of anyone and everything, even a lamppost, for God's sake! I think a woman should defend her man tooth and nail! But a sister, that's different!"

With a melancholy air about her, she replied, "I'm not stupid!"

And her father: "Neither your sister nor your fiancé deserve this!"

They began to talk openly about her case. The girl's cousin, who was a pediatrician, suggested, "Why don't you take her to a psychiatrist?"

Bending to her own tired will, she ended up going. The psychiatrist, after a frightful consultation, arrived at the following conclusion: "The solution is to extract her teeth!" The girl's father was stunned and cried bitterly upon receiving the bill.

"What an animal! What a clown! Is he a dentist or a psychiatrist?" he asked.

The truth is that little by little the family's pressure prevailed over Dagmar. The fiancé very skillfully played his part.

"You don't have to fear any woman. As far as I'm concerned, no woman is more beautiful than you. You have my word!"

The Bathing Suit

The only one who seemed oblivious to all the hullabaloo was little Alice herself. She treated her sister and future brother-in-law the same as always. She was so guileless and innocent that she once walked into the living room wearing an extremely risqué bathing suit she had just bought and wanted to show off to Dagmar and Geraldo. It was enough to cause a panic. For a moment the gaping Geraldo did not know what to say, what to think. He turned pale, and...

Alice spun around like a professional model and asked, "So, what do you think?"

For a split second Dagmar thought she would explode in anger; but she had convinced herself that she needed to rethink her ways. She fought back her first impulse. As if absolutely nothing were the matter, she said, "Pretty!"

Stunned and dazzled, Geraldo quivered, "It's a hell of a bathing suit!" When he left his fiancée's house that day he seemed profoundly affected by what he had seen. Later that night at the pool hall with his friends, he coined the following saying: "No woman is more beautiful than a beautiful sister-in-law."

Crafty

Next day, Alice walked by him and winked.

"I'm not a child anymore! I'm not a kid anymore!"

That could mean a whole lot or a whole little. Flustered, he began to sweat.

Two or three days later Alice went looking for him at his work. She sat next to him and said, "Are you afraid of me?"

The poor devil stammered, "Why would I be afraid of you?"

She stared intensely at him with the gaze not of a child but a woman.

"You are; yes, you are!" She seemed amused by it all. Suddenly, she turned serious, stood and came closer. They were in Geraldo's office. Alice leaned forward.

"Kiss me," she said.

Pale, he obeyed. He grazed the girl's cheek lightly.

"That's not a kiss. I want a real kiss," she insisted.

Geraldo stood. He stepped back terrified, as if the girl represented a mortal danger. In what resembled a sob, he screamed, "I love Dagmar! I love your sister!"

She stood there facing him. "Just one!"

Petrified, he let himself be kissed once, then several times. He couldn't understand how a thirteen-year-old girl could be so ruthless.

Before she left, she said, "Now you're mine too!" And, perfectly confident in her wicked ways, she threatened him: "I'm warning you; if you start anything, I'll tell the entire world that we went all the way!"

Geraldo fell back in his chair; he howled, "Devil! Devil!"

The Kiss

From then on he was her slave. It was interesting that while he felt attracted to her, he also hated her. He saw in her an abhorrent precociousness. But he was weak, defenseless, defeated. Until one afternoon he entered a police station sobbing and announced, "I just killed my girlfriend's sister, Alice so-and-so at such-and-such address." He was giving his sworn statement when Dagmar burst in. She had gone to the scene of the crime and had seen her sister's body face down with a dagger sticking out of her back. Beside herself, she had run straight to the precinct. There something happened that no one could have predicted. Dagmar approached her fiancé, grabbed his face between her hands and started kissing him on the mouth, madly. They grabbed her and dragged her away. She tried to break loose from the detectives who struggled to restrain her.

"Oh, thank God! Thank God...!" she screamed.

The Wretch

In a circle of his friends he complained bitterly. He ranted to one and all.

"My life is a tragedy!" His eyes gleaming, he repeated, "A tragedy!"

One of the friends slapped him on the back playfully.

"You? Complain? Tragedy my foot! A guy like you, surrounded by women. Listen here, Peixoto: You have more women than you know what to do with!"

"Pimentel, look... that's just it," said Peixoto. He opened his arms wide. "That's precisely my tragedy. You understand? Too many women. Let me finish! I was born with a dangerous proclivity. I can't see a woman without wanting to chase after her. I even chase after the butt-ugly ones!"

His friends made good fun of all this.

"Give one the boot then! Send one my way. I need a girlfriend."

Feeling needled from all sides, Peixoto began kicking the air in frustration. He appeared both ridiculous and frightening.

"I'll give them the boot! Sure! I'll have a fire sale! I'll have a going-out-of-business sale on Avenida Passos!"

The Disease

Minutes later he got up and left. Pimentel, who had an appointment to keep, walked out with him. Peixoto was truly dejected; the confessions he made to Pimentel as the two walked down the street were even more dramatic in nature.

"Imagine. Today at home... under my own roof!"

His friend's thoughts immediately turned to the maid. But Peixoto was emphatic.

"If only it had been the maid! If only! My sister-in-law, Pimentel! Do you understand? My own sister-in-law!"

"Which one?"

They stopped at the corner and waited for the light to change.

"The widow!" said Peixoto, beside himself. "She lost her husband two months ago – not even! – and today I nearly pounced on the poor woman. Imagine if my wife hadn't shown up. It was pure coincidence. I would have jumped on my own sister-in-law! Imagine the pickle that would have put me in!"

Pimentel cleared his throat.

"Well... but... your sister-in-law is worth it. Besides, a woman in black does something to a man. It's a turn-on."

Peixoto took a deep breath.

"You have no idea what you're talking about! It's a disease! I'm going to see a doctor! I'm telling you, it's a disease! See you later, goodbye."

The Doctor

The next day he consulted his friends at work.

"What do you call a doctor who treats guys who can't stop thinking of women?"

"Is that a disease?" asked Carvalhinho, the junior accountant, astounded.

"This isn't a joke, OK! In my case it is a disease!" Peixoto snarled.

Faced with his friends' amused curiosity, he explained that he was infected by an indiscriminate and all-consuming urge. It didn't matter the woman's color, age, marital status, etc.

"This is not normal! It can't be normal!" He paused for a moment and then resumed, "There must be some drug. There's got to be a drug!"

Then Carvalhinho had an idea.

"Go see Ribas. He's a psychiatrist. Top-notch."

"Is he expensive?" Peixoto asked.

"Steep but worth it."

After lunch Peixoto went off to see Ribas. He paid the receptionist one thousand cruzeiros and thought, "These doctors are a bunch of gangsters."

Finally, his turn came. He found himself facing a lanky, pale man in a white coat. Dr. Ribas, seated in his swivel chair, asked his first question, and Peixoto anxiously started explaining.

"Doctor, my problem is as follows: I think I suffer from excess vigor."

Tapping his pen on the table, the doctor wanted to know, "What do you mean, excess vigor?"

Rather embarrassed, Peixoto went on.

"I can't look at a woman without desiring her, Doctor. I don't care what she looks like. Even the ugly ones, the god-awful ugly ones. I don't select. I'm unable to select."

The doctor stood. He paced back and forth and spoke: "In love, selection is a fallacy or, better said, a deficiency. Only the weak are overly choosey. My friend, nature does not command us to prefer Ava Gardner or Gina Lollobrigida. As far as nature is concerned all women are equal. The butt-ugly ones are also God's children, and what's wrong with that?"

Confused, Peixoto stammered, "But doctor, my problem…"

The doctor cut him off.

"My friend, don't call this a problem. This has never been a problem, not here, not in China."

Peixoto was at a loss for words.

"You mean to tell me…"

"My friend," Dr. Ribas continued, "if all husbands were like you, female mental illness would be at an all-time low. Lack of love is almost always what puts women in the insane asylum. You can take that to the bank."

Peixoto didn't know what to think or say. Deep inside he was all torn up about the thousand cruzeiros he had just paid for the visit.

"You mean to tell me I'm not sick, Doctor?"

Dr. Ribas laid his hand on Peixoto's shoulder.

"Sick? My friend, relax! You should count your lucky stars. You hit the jackpot. I only wish I had your disease. I wish it were contagious. I really do!"

He escorted him to the door. He lowered his voice and addressed him soberly.

"Congratulations!"

The Poor Devil

When he exited the psychiatrist's office, Peixoto did not know whether to jump for joy or cry. He shared the elevator with an overweight woman all decked out in jewelry, wearing a skin-tight dress that displayed a spectacular cleavage. For Peixoto just one look was enough. The fat lady got out first with Peixoto in tow. A little further down the block, his lips trembling, a glimmer in his eyes, he asked over her shoulder: "Do you mind if I walk with you?"

The woman turned. She looked him up and down.

"Do you want me to call the cops?!"

"Forgive me!" he said. "You misunderstood."

He snapped. In the opposite direction came another woman. Beautiful? Ugly? Peixoto couldn't say, nor did he care. Then he turned and followed another one. With huge eyes and the stare of a Svengali, he stammered, "Ma'am, please listen. I feel a strong attraction to you."

The woman picked up her pace. Then his gaze focused on another one. And then another one. Finally, beside himself, he approached an older gentleman.

"Sir, hold me back, please. Please do me a favor and hold me back. Either you hold me back, or I'll assault every woman on this block. All of them!"

The man didn't understand.

"I want to be tied up!" he sobbed. "I need to be tied up!"

About ten men were needed to hold him back.

The Faithful Wife

She was extremely virtuous and what's more, proud of her virtue, so
much so that it bordered on vanity. She had been married to Valverde –
Marcio Valverde – for six months, and she loved her radio soaps. Should the
heroine be unfaithful, Luci could not contain her anger. She could often be
heard saying, "All of this talk about cheating on your husband, you can count
me out." Then she would take a spiteful pause and add, "If you ask me, it's
unconscionable!"

She kept a vigilant eye on her girlfriends and her female neighbors –
especially the married ones. If she should catch a suspect look or a
questionable smile, she would arrive home in a huff. On one occasion she
completely lost her composure.

"So-and-so should be ashamed of herself! What kind of a way is that to
act! A married woman, with children! It's disgusting!"

She wouldn't drop the subject. She got so worked up that she and her husband ended up arguing. Valverde, in his striped pajamas, trembled when faced with her aggressive and in-your-face virtue. He took refuge behind his newspaper as if it were a shield. He whispered, "Keep it down, Luci! Keep it down!"

"Why should I? That's a good one! After all, am I in my own home or not?"

"The neighbors will hear you."

"I couldn't care less about the neighbors! Just look at you!"

Valverde was an asthmatic. Whenever the weather would get a little cooler, the dampness was like poison to him. When he wasn't feeling well, his bronchial tubes all wheezed in unison, and he would be overcome by a fear of choking. His timidity was probably the result of this woeful condition. Skinny as a rail, with a chest like a boy's and long, thin arms like Olive Oyl's, poor Valverde did not have the physical makeup of a man of courage. At times he tried to imagine how a physical altercation between him and his wife would play out. Although a woman, Luci was much more robust. There was no doubt that the odds would be overwhelmingly in her favor. Her superiority, however, was not just physical. No. What made her indomitable and overpowering was precisely the mantle of virtue that she wore like a suit of armor. She considered herself a wife of the utmost moral standing, completely above suspicion, and would constantly rub her fidelity in her husband's face. Not one single day went by when she wouldn't remind him, "You won't find a wife like me anytime soon. You won't find a wife more faithful than me. I doubt it!"

"Did I say anything?"

"No, you didn't, but you insinuated!"

"Come on, Luci!"

She jabbed her finger at her husband's scrawny chest and exploded in a fit.

"Men are idiots! They don't know how to appreciate an honest wife. You should thank God you have a wife like me!"

There were no two ways about it; she treated him deplorably and even disrespected him in front of guests. She rationalized it as follows: "I don't go for all of that hugging and kissing; it's a bunch of rubbish if you ask me. But I never cheated on you, do you understand?"

The Prank Call

Since her husband earned so little, she found a job as a civil servant. She left for work at the break of dawn. So as not to attract any unwanted advances, she walked around with a scowl on her face. Walking around with a scowl on one's face is one of the hallmarks of the virtuous woman. Whether because of the ferocity of her expression or for other reasons unknown, no one bothered her as she walked down the street. It's not that she was ugly. She might not be what you would call pretty, but she was buxom. And it is a fact, a well-known fact, that there are Casanovas who specialize in buxom women. A mere glance her way, however, was enough for her to fly into a rage. Once while she was riding in a bus, a middle-aged gentleman seated in the front looked back two or three times during a forty-minute ride. In a very loud voice, so that the whole bus could hear, Luci yelled out, "Never seen a woman before?"

The man, duly chastened, melted into his seat. Some rowdy youngsters laughed out loud. When she arrived at her stop, she yelled, "Men nowadays are shameless. They only learn if you smack them in the face with your purse!"

She didn't know how to live without her profound virtue. One day her neighbor knocked.

"Dona Luci! Dona Luci!"

Luci appeared at the door wearing a robe. It was a telephone call. She was surprised.

"For me?"

Nonetheless, she answered the call. It was a man who said bluntly: "Ma'am, I am a great admirer of yours."

Luci was so shocked she didn't have time to become indignant.

"What did you say?"

"I have very deep feelings for you, ma'am."

This was more than she could bear. Although she was in her neighbor's apartment, or precisely for this reason, she raised hell.

"Listen here you dog, you filthy pervert. You have the wrong woman, you hear? And you should know that my husband is man enough to break your face!"

The anonymous voice on the other end did not lose its cool. He abandoned the use of 'ma'am' and simply stated the following, using the most unpleasant and vulgar expressions: "Don't be an idiot, I can see right through you…" etc., etc.

The Explorer

The neighbor's family marveled at so much virtue. Luci returned to her apartment perspiring, but euphoric at her show of fidelity. Never in her life had she felt so chaste as during that phone call. That night when her husband got home, she told him everything. Valverde had a head cold and was deadly afraid of getting an asthma attack. He listened in silence. Then Luci dropped a bomb.

"I think I know who it is."

"Who?"

"First of all I want to make sure. But if it is who I think it is, I'm going to ask you a favor."

"What?"

"You're going to shoot this man!"

"Me? Are you serious? Have a heart!"

"Because if you don't shoot him, I swear I will."

Yes, she suspected someone. For the last six months whenever she left home for work early or came back in the evening, a neighbor would be at the window watching. Well, for someone so sure of her own righteousness, a mere look was enough to tarnish a reputation. She herself held to the belief that nothing was so immoral in a man as a look. And the neighbor in question, without saying a single word, without flashing a smile, would look lustful daggers at her. His actions were so persistent, obstinate and impudent, that Luci finally inquired about the young man. She discovered incredible things and one that actually sent shivers up her spine: Although he was young (around thirty-something), he was supported by a rich old woman. He suffered humiliations from the old woman, who cried poverty with every penny she gave him. But the young man, with amazing stoicism and shamelessness, tolerated all of these indignities to keep from going hungry. Luci, in spite of finding abominable this business of being supported by an older woman, felt somewhat sorry for the slights that this scoundrel had to endure.

However, she fought off this sentimental lapse because, after all, the young man was nurturing disreputable, though unexpressed, thoughts towards her. Later, she learned the Casanova's name: Adriano. It was, as can be seen, the name of wine and of fireworks. At night, before going to bed, already wearing her thick nightgown, she made enigmatic comments whose significance Valverde did not fully comprehend: "Men nowadays don't even respect married women."

She said this in front of the mirror as she tried a new acne medication a friend had recommended. Her husband lay still in bed, pale and weak, looking at his wife through the corner of his eyes, fearing an asthma attack. In silence he reflected: He had a coworker whose wife cheated on her husband shamelessly. In spite of this, or perhaps precisely because of this, she treated her husband like a prince. Whenever she would return from a rendezvous with her boyfriend, she would bring her husband a gift. Valverde almost envied his friend. Sitting before the mirror, Luci continued obliquely and enigmatically.

"But they are mistaken if they think I'm one of those women. They have another thing coming!"

She went silent then because evidently she could not share her tribulations with her husband.

The next day, when she was walking to the bus stop, there he was, the seducer of older women. Was she imagining things or did he flash a telltale half-smile at her? She was indignant. She said between clenched teeth, "I never!"

She was terribly worried as she rode the bus. Obviously, the rogue was no longer content to simply admire her from afar, semi-respectfully. No. He was beginning to close in on her. That whole day at work she felt cornered. Worst of all, when she returned home, there the man was: standing on the sidewalk wearing a light green short-sleeve shirt. Luci was able to ascertain for the first time that he had strong, beautiful arms, which should have come as no surprise since every Sunday the wretch played volleyball on the beach. This brazen exhibition of arms made his intentions of conquest more patently clear than ever. The way things were going it was evident that the young man would pretty soon dare to speak to her. If he were to try, Luci would be woman enough to break his face with her umbrella. Till one day she fell ill and stayed home from work.

Orchids

The husband left in high spirits, saying that he was going to play the lottery. He had dreamed about some number the previous night and had decided to play his hunch. Possessed with a fertile imagination, Luci began to imagine the worst case scenario, above all one that was particularly electrifying: that the neighbor would take advantage of Valverde's absence to break into the house. She could have bolted the front door, but she didn't dare. At four in the afternoon the unbelievable occurred: A delivery person brought a box of orchids. There was no indication as to who the sender was. Luci shivered. For the first time in her life she understood all of the emotional frailty, all of the tremendous vulnerability of her sex. Would she tell her husband? No, never. Valverde, in spite of his asthma, of his scrawny chest, might just shoot the Casanova. On the other hand, it was now clear to her that the neighbor nurtured more than a merely physical attraction for her. Who knew, he might even be in love with her – a great, indomitable and fatal attraction. That evening Valverde came home euphoric. On seeing him, Luci was taken aback, as if seeing him for the first time: What a pathetic little man! She couldn't help but compare her husband's skinny little arms with "his" arms. Valverde tried to kiss her but she dodged his attempt with a look of disgust.

"Back off."

The poor man rubbed his hands in glee.

"I won. I played the lottery and I won!"

She paid him absolutely no mind. She turned the radio on, but all she could think of was the orchids. Valverde went into the bedroom and suddenly reappeared wearing pajama bottoms and the sleeveless black and red jersey of his favorite soccer team, which he always wore around the house. Then he asked a question: "Did you get the flowers?"

"Flowers?"

"The ones I sent you?"

She turned pale.

"You sent them?"

"Of course! I won the lottery, and you know how I get when I win!"

Beside herself, she refused to believe what she was hearing.

"You mean to say it was you? I don't believe it! Since when does a husband send flowers to his own wife?"

With his twig-like Olive Oyl arms, he insisted that it really had been him, and he explained that he had sent the flowers anonymously as a joke. When Luci finally convinced herself that what she was hearing was true, her rage took over. In a crescendo of anger she went after her husband, who was already cowering, and unleashed the full brunt of her wrath.

"Idiot! Moron! You mouse of a man!"

By the time she was finished, she was weeping uncontrollably. Baffled, Valverde thought back to his coworker's wife who was unfaithful yet treated her husband so very nicely.

The Lady on the Bus

Carlinhos knocked on his father's door on a rainy night at ten o'clock. The old man, who suffered from low blood pressure and all sorts of other ailments, looked at his son, frightened.

"You, here? At this hour?"

His son sank into an armchair and sighed heavily, "That's right, Father, that's right."

"How is Solange?" the old man asked.

Carlinhos sat up, walked to the window and looked out furtively. Then he sat down again and dropped a bomb: "Dad, I think my wife is cheating on me."

The old man looked at him aghast.

"Solange? Have you lost your mind? Is this some kind of a joke?"

Carlinhos laughed bitterly.

"I wish it were, Dad; I wish it were. But the thing is, I learned some things about my wife… and she's not the same; she's changed a lot."

Then the old man, who adored his daughter-in-law and put her on a pedestal beyond all suspicion, exploded, "I won't stand for this! I'll break off all relations! I won't give you another penny!"

Filled with emotion, arms raised to the heavens, he thundered, "Imagine! Doubting Solange!"

By now his son was at the door ready to leave. But before doing so he said, "If what I suspect is true, Dad, I'm going to kill my wife! Mark my words; I'll kill her, Dad!"

A Suspicion

They had been married for two years and were the picture of marital bliss. Both came from excellent families. His father, a widower and a general on the verge of retirement, had the dignity of a Roman statue. Solange's side of the family was a virtual 'who's who' of doctors, attorneys, bankers, and even ministers. Just about everyone who knew her said that she was as "lovely as can be." A few were more unequivocal and would say that she was "as sweet as pie." Her mannerisms and her delicate, fine features gave her an otherworldly aura. The diabetic old general would have been willing to walk on fire to defend her honor. And anyone who knew her would do the same. And yet… The night of the storm, it so happened that a childhood friend of the family's, Assunção, had had dinner with the couple. He was one of those close friends who could walk in through the kitchen door and have the run of the house, bedrooms and all. In the middle of dinner a simple twist of fate occurred: Carlinhos dropped his napkin. He bent over to pick it up and observed Solange's feet on top of Assunção's or the other way around. Carlinhos picked up the napkin and continued to participate in the three-way conversation. But things were no longer the same. He said to himself, "Huh! That's strange!" His fears got the better of him. The damage was done even before he could put words to his suspicion. What he had seen admittedly was not a lot. Still, the entwined feet and shoes appeared to him as damning as any contact imaginable. After his friend departed, he had run to his father's house and given voice to his fears for the first time. First thing next day, the old man sought out his son.

"Tell me what happened, from the start."

And he did. And the general blew his top.

"Just look at you! You should be ashamed of yourself! A grown man worried about these idiocies!"

It bordered on a sermon. To try to free his son from the grips of jealousy, the old soldier even went so far as to confide the following: "Jealousy is a disease! It hurts me to say this, but I was once jealous of your mother! There was a time when I would have gone to my grave insisting that she was cheating on me. Can you believe it?"

Certainty

However, Carlinhos' certainty no longer had anything to do with objective facts. The seed had been planted. What had he seen? Perhaps very little or, better said, a mutual touching of feet underneath the table. No one cheats with their feet obviously. Still, he was "sure." Three days later there was a surprise encounter downtown with Assunção, who announced cheerfully, "I ran into your wife on the bus the other day."

Carlinhos lied for no apparent reason.

"She told me."

Back home, after kissing his wife, he asked, "Have you seen Assunção lately?"

While painting her nails she answered, "Not since we had dinner."

"Not even yesterday?"

"Not even yesterday. Why yesterday?"

"Nothing."

Carlinhos did not say another word.

Livid, he went into the study, grabbed the revolver and put it in his pocket. Solange had lied! He saw in this one more sign of her infidelity. An adulterer lies even when it is not necessary to do so. He went back into the living room and called out to his wife, who was about to enter the study.

"Come here a minute, Solange."

"Just a minute, honey."

"Now!"

Frightened, she obliged. As soon as she entered, Carlinhos locked the door. Then he placed the revolver on the table. With arms crossed and his wife looking on aghast, he began to tell her everything. But he never raised his voice or made any sudden moves.

"It's no use denying it! I know everything!"

Her back to the wall, she asked, "You know what, honey? Is something the matter? Tell me!"

He yelled three times in her face the word "Bitch!"

He lied and told her that he had hired a private detective to shadow her, that every step she took had been scrupulously followed. Until then he had not pronounced the name of her lover, as if he knew everything but the identity of the son of a bitch.

"I'm going to kill that dog Assunção! I am going to kill him and his entire family!"

Solange, who until then had looked on expressionless and only slightly frightened, clutched her husband's arm, yelling, "No, not him!"

He savagely tried to escape from his wife's grasp. But she stopped him dead in his tracks by what she yelled out next: "He wasn't the only one! There were others!"

The Lady on the Bus

In complete control over her emotions, exhibiting an eerie calm, she began talking. One month after they were married, she had begun to leave the house each night and get on the first bus that passed by. She would sit down next to a gentleman. It didn't matter whether he was old or young, ugly or handsome. Once it just so happened that her fellow passenger was a mechanic, a blue-collar type who was getting off at the next stop.

The husband sunk in his chair, head in his hands, and cried out, "A mechanic?"

Solange, in her measured and polite manner, confirmed, "Yes."

An unknown mechanic. Two corners later she nudged the young man.

"I'm getting off with you."

The poor devil was frightened by this beautiful and elegant stranger. They got off the bus together. This unlikely adventure was the first, and it was the starting point for many others. After a while drivers were squinting into the distance for signs of her. One even pretended his bus had broken down to try to be alone with her. But anonymous encounters that didn't leave a trace were not the hardest pill to swallow. What drove Carlinhos mad as he sat there were the ones he knew. Who was there besides Assunção?

She began naming names: So-and-so, and so-and-so and so-and-so...

"That's enough! Stop!" Despondent, he engaged in the following bit of hyperbole: "Half the city. You've been with half of Rio de Janeiro!" Carlinhos yelled out.

Then, suddenly, the fight drained out of him. If it had been only one, if it had been only Assunção. But there were so many! After all, he couldn't go around town hunting down all of her lovers. She explained that every day, as if she had an appointment to keep, she would escape and get on the first bus she saw. Her husband looked on in horror, amazed that she seemed so beautiful, composed, and immaculate as she spoke to him. How could it be that certain vile acts and sentiments did not emit a foul odor?

Solange grabbed him and yelled, "It's not my fault! It's not my fault!" And, indeed, there seemed to be in the deepest reaches of her soul an almost infinite innocence. You could say that it was someone else who gave up her body to others and not her. Suddenly, her husband passed his hands over her hips.

"No panties! You're walking around with no panties! Slut!"

Cursing, he pushed her out of the way and headed for the bedroom. Before walking out he said, "I'm dead. I've died to the world."

The Corpse

He entered the bedroom and lay down on the bed fully dressed in his suit, shoes and tie. He joined his feet tightly at the heels, clasped his fingers at chest level and just lay there. A short time later his wife appeared at the door. She stood there for some time, still and silent, contemplating him. Finally she muttered under her breath, "Dinner's served."

Perfectly still, he answered, "For the last time, I died, I'm dead."

She didn't insist. She left and told the maid to clear the table and that her services would no longer be needed. Then she went back to the bedroom and stayed there. She picked up a rosary and sat by the bed. She accepted her husband's death as a given. It was as a widow that she prayed. After what she had done on the buses, nothing frightened her. She maintained a bedside vigil through the night. The following day the scene repeated itself. She only went out in the evening for her delirious escapades on the buses. She returned hours later, picked up the rosary again and continued the wake for her living husband.